SAMANTHA SANK DEEPER INTO THE FRAGRANT BATH

"What's this all about?" she asked, as Boston handed her a glass of champagne, his eyes gleaming wickedly in the candlelight.

She watched as he slowly untied his robe and shrugged it off. The sight of him standing before her, his virility displayed, caused her hand to tremble, and the icy champagne spilled on her naked breast.

He smiled. "Careful, sweetheart. That's to drink, not bathe in." He stepped over the high sides and settled down at the opposite end of the large tub.

Flesh caressed flesh as his legs slid along hers. Lifting one foam-covered foot, she planted it in the center of his chest.

"This is a nice surprise." Samantha kept her voice innocent. "Just what did you have in mind?"

Boston chuckled. "Why, the very same thing you've had on yours all day. . . ."

WELCOME TO...

HARLEQUIN SUPERROMANCES

A sensational series of modern love stories.

Written by masters of the genre, these long, sensual
and dramatic novels are truly in keeping with today's
changing life-styles. Full of intriguing conflicts
and the heartaches and delights of true love,
HARLEQUIN SUPERROMANCES are absorbing
stories—satisfying and sophisticated reading
that lovers of romance fiction have long been
waiting for.

HARLEQUIN SUPERROMANCES
Contemporary love stories for the woman of today!

Evelyn A. Crowe
SUMMER BALLAD

Harlequin Books

TORONTO • NEW YORK • LONDON
AMSTERDAM • PARIS • SYDNEY • HAMBURG
STOCKHOLM • ATHENS • TOKYO • MILAN

To my mother,
who always believed in me.
To Carla, who endured
the late-night phone calls.
To Star,
who made a dream come true.

———————————

Published April 1984

First printing February 1984

ISBN 0-373-70112-8

Grateful acknowledgment is extended to the following:
BLACKWOOD MUSIC INC., New York, for use of the lyrics
from "Show and Tell" by Jerry Fuller. Copyright © 1973 & 1981
by BLACKWOOD MUSIC INC. & FULLNESS MUSIC. All rights
administered by BLACKWOOD MUSIC INC. Used by
permission. All rights reserved.

CHAPTER ONE

THE CUSTOMARILY INDOLENT ATMOSPHERE of the opulent and dignified Warwick Hotel lobby was shattered by hordes of moving bodies. Voices rumbled across marble floors, slipped around corners and bounced off silk-covered walls. Signs of wealth abounded, from the rustle of haute couture and the winking of precious jewels to the mingled scents of expensive perfumes and masculine colognes wafting across the room on the cool circulating air. Bellboys and other hotel staff rushed around half-dazed, apologizing frequently with only curt nods as they sped about performing their duties.

An elegantly shod foot tapped in a rapid impatient tempo on the marble floor while slender fingers beat an identical rhythm on the walnut countertop. "What do you mean you can't find my room reservation?"

The raspy jaw-clenched whisper brought the desk clerk's head up for a second time. Harassed and overworked, he barely stifled a groan. It was quitting time and he didn't need any additional problems; this day had been filled with too many already.

"I'm sorry, Miss Griffin." His red-rimmed eyes focused on the woman before him. He sighed, opened his mouth to repeat his statement, then stopped as for the first time his weary eyes really looked at her. Intense, brilliant aquamarine eyes met his awestruck gaze levelly. She was tall, at least five foot eight, slim and stylish. Swallowing hard, he watched as pearly teeth bit down on a pale sensuous lip. When he thought of redheads and freckles, visions of petite, pug-nosed little urchins crossed his mind. But not this lady! Her face was fine boned with a wide intelligent forehead, high prominent cheekbones and a small straight nose. The only flaw in the smooth satiny skin was freckles, which appeared to darken as her pallor increased. And that hair! There was something magnetic and fascinating about it. Not just any insignificant shade of red, but a shocking poppy red.

The wide mouth trembled slightly at one corner and he watched her bite down again, harder this time, to control the tremor. His pity suddenly surfaced. She looked tired, sick and ready to burst into tears. Sighing silently, he resigned himself to the overtime task of finding a room—though heaven only knew how or where!—to fulfill the supposedly confirmed reservation.

"Ma'am. Are you all right?"

Samantha took a shallow breath, exhaled slowly, then nodded. The dull headache that had started on the plane from New York was getting progressively worse. "I'm fine, thank you. Look, if you can't find my reservation, just give me any room and we can straighten it out tomorrow." She rubbed absently at one pounding temple and mentally cursed the inefficient Alice, her boss's secretary. This was just another blunder in a long list of mishaps since she'd left New York that afternoon.

"I'm afraid it's not that simple. We're all booked up. So is every hotel in Houston." At her bewildered expression he explained. "It's OTC time." He forced a smile, but her face remained a blank and he tried again. "The Offshore Technology Conference," he said sharply. "This is the time of year Houston holds the annual oil show. Businessmen come from all over the world to attend."

Samantha acknowledged his explanation with a nod, remembering when she'd lived here and the problems the show had caused a still-growing Houston. "What am I going to do?" Her voice faltered. She hated showing weakness, but her head was now pounding violently, her vision was beginning to blur and she could barely think straight.

The desk clerk shrugged and looked at her sympathetically, then snapped his fingers, causing her to wince at the loud crack. "Could it be under another name, a company name?"

"I don't think so...maybe...yes, try Duncan, Stark Ad Agency in New York." She gave a silent prayer, hoping beyond hope that Alice would come through.

"Miss Griffin, there's a suite registered under Duncan, Stark, but I don't think—"

"What's the number?" She reached down for her makeup case and looked around for a bellboy.

"Number 216. But, Miss Griffin—" Just at that moment he was interrupted by his relief shift. The woman was already signaling for the boy to pick up her things. With a speculative look the clerk handed over the key and departed before another problem could detain him from his late dinner.

Samantha stepped into the elevator and smiled stiffly at the young man juggling her luggage. She watched him as he looked at the key in his hand then leered at her, running his eyes insultingly over her from head to toe. Puzzled, she glanced down to check if she was unbuttoned, unzipped, or if her slip was showing.

Nervously she twisted the leather strap of her shoulder bag, her mind dazed. The way he was smiling made the color rise in her pale cheeks and she turned forward, determined to ignore the insult. The elevator doors slid open silently and she followed him out and down the plush royal-blue carpeted hall, keeping a good distance between them. She didn't want to be caught in the room alone with him.

Reaching the open door, she watched him deposit the bags on the luggage rack. As he turned and walked toward her with the same smirk on his silly face, her heart began to match the pounding rhythm in her head. When he stopped before her and held out his hand for a tip, she returned his sneering look. "I'd advise you to leave at once and thank your lucky stars I don't call the front desk and report your behavior."

His young face flushed beet red and his Adam's apple bobbed spasmodically as he rushed out, closing the door softly behind him.

Samantha slid the lock home and sagged against

the door, pressing her hot forehead to the cool hard surface for a few seconds before turning. Still using the door for support, her fingers trembling, she slipped off her cream linen jacket and began to unbutton the jade-green silk blouse. She straightened, kicked off her shoes, stepped out of the matching linen skirt and wiggled out of her panty hose. Bed—it was the only thought her throbbing head was capable of. Throwing her clothes over her arm, she bent to scoop up her shoes and had to grab a nearby chair for support. The bile rose in her throat and she swallowed hard, fighting the dizziness that threatened to leave her a sprawling heap on the floor. She hadn't had a migraine like this in years. Unsteady legs carried her to the bedroom, where she dropped her clothes on a long blue chaise longue and headed directly for the bed, clad only in a lacy camisole top and brief bikini pants.

"Well, well. . . what have we here?"

Samantha whirled around at the sound of a deep growling male voice. Her pain-glazed eyes widened at the sight of the famous singer Boston Grey, standing across the room wearing nothing but a towel around his neck.

Boston Grey? Blinking rapidly, she tried to clear her vision. What was he doing here? He should have been in his own room patiently waiting for her call. She opened her mouth to demand an explanation, but her throat refused to cooperate. Why was he in her room? And naked! She tried to move, but her feet felt as though they'd taken root in the carpeted floor.

"Cat got your tongue?" he challenged.

The hot band of pain in her head slipped a notch tighter and she squeezed her simmering eyes shut, sure she was hallucinating. But the voice continued.

"I'll have to hand it to Ken. When he said he had a surprise for me, he wasn't joking. He really outdid himself this time."

Samantha's eyes flew open when she realized this man was not a figment of her imagination. The pounding in her head turned to a steady excruciating pain and she wasn't sure she was hearing correctly.

"What's the matter? Surely you're used to seeing men without their clothes? Kinda goes with the job, doesn't it?" He walked toward her, a frown grooving the strong brow. His heavy lidded black eyes narrowed as he leisurely appraised the long slim shapely legs, the narrow waist his hands could span and the small rounded breasts that trembled invitingly beneath their satin-and-lace covering.

Samantha opened her mouth to answer, and when nothing came out she panicked and backed away from his advancing form. His intent was clear, and even in her befogged state she knew he was not a man to play games. His slow easy stride moved him closer as she took another step back.

"Come, come," he cajoled. "Let's not play coy. Aren't you even going to sing 'Happy Birthday' or tell me your name? Or is your style not to talk at all to your clients?" He paused a moment. "That's a rather novel idea, a silent woman. I might enjoy it any other time, but I think I'd prefer to hear you vocal in my bed." He smiled his famous lopsided grin.

Her befuddled brain finally straightened out the jumble of his words. Horrified, she quickly retreated another step, then another, till she backed into the low footboard, lost her balance and fell, sprawling across the king-size bed. Boston followed her down in one smooth movement. He braced himself above her, arms extended, supporting his weight so he lightly touched her length with his. A warm breath fanned her cheek as he began to nuzzle the sensitive curve of her back.

"I usually don't go in for redheads, sweetheart, but you're about the most tempting firecracker I've ever laid eyes on—freckles and all." His lips found the wildly beating pulse in her neck and he nibbled a second before moving on to the velvet skin of her earlobe.

"Please," she barely whispered, "there's been a terrible mistake." She forced the words out and felt him stiffen. He cocked his head to one side, listening. The sound of voices from the living room reached her. Quickly he moved away from her, picked up the towel from the floor and wrapped it around his waist.

Before Samantha knew what was happening the room was filled with men, laughing and joking— until they took in the scene. A flash went off and there was a roar from Boston. Samantha grabbed the bedspread and wrapped herself in a protective cocoon, trying to hide her face. Boston stepped in her line of vision, shielding her from the curious leering eyes.

"Get out of here," he yelled, his professionally

trained voice vibrating off the walls and her head. "What's going on?"

Samantha uncovered her head, straining to hear what was being said.

Boston raised his voice again. "Someone catch the fool who took that picture. The rest of you get out." He shot them a hard look as they left and motioned to the blond man beside him to stay.

"I appreciate the birthday present, Ken, but did you have to ruin...?"

"What present?" the man asked.

"Her." Boston pointed to Samantha huddled under the covers.

"Who is she?" Ken surveyed the tousled red hair and dilated eyes.

"Don't you know?" Boston demanded.

"No."

"Hell, you mean you didn't send her up here as a joke?"

"Not me." Two pair of eyes bored into her, one as blue as the morning sky, the other as black and sullen as the night. The pitch-black eyes narrowed and the strong mouth tightened.

"Then who is she? Some fan who found out I was here?" He turned angrily on Ken. "You're my manager. I thought you said my stay here was being kept a secret until the press conference. I'd like you to explain what those reporters were doing in my room."

"Calm down, Boston. Let's take one thing at a time. The reporters out there were *my* surprise." At his friend and client's raised eyebrows, Ken went on hurriedly. "I rounded up a few of your old buddies."

Samantha closed her eyes and ignored the conversation until she heard another reference to her.

"We'll have to find out who she is and get her out of here. Ken, I think she's either drunk or on something. She hasn't said two words since she came in." Boston began to pace the floor, his towel slipping farther down his narrow hips.

"I'm not drunk and I don't take drugs." Samantha spoke through gritted teeth as large tears filled her eyes. Both men swung around at her words. "My name is Samantha Griffin." She ground the name out, her eyes going from one face to the other. Picking the kinder of the two, she asked the blond named Ken, "Would you hand me that small brown case? Thank you." She opened it and rummaged through it till she found the bottle she was looking for. "I'm production director for Duncan, Stark." She kept her head turned away and sniffed, the now-steady stream of tears hampering her vision as she tried to uncap the medicine. For a second she thought her aching head was playing tricks on her; one moment she had the bottle, the next it was gone, leaving her to stare dumbly at her empty hand.

"What's this?" Boston sneered. "Looks like drugs to me." He shook the bottle at her. "I've got news for you, sweetheart. Nobody takes this junk around me." He spun around and walked toward the bathroom.

"No—*please*," she shouted, her hands flying to her throbbing head. "Please," she whispered, "they're for my head. I have migraines." She saw his uncertainty. "Look at what it says on the bottle."

Boston brought her a glass of water and handed her the prescribed amount, watching her closely. "Are you really with the agency?" At her slow nod he sighed with relief.

Samantha flopped backward, closed her eyes and listened as Boston began to give orders to the other man.

"Ken, get rid of the crowd in the living room. Set up another meeting for tomorrow. Oh, and Ken—" he stopped his manager at the door "—find that weasel of a reporter who slipped in here and get that roll of film. If you can't make a deal with his paper, call around and see if Kane Stone's in town. If we don't have enough pull to retrieve the film, I know damn well Kane does." Boston raked an impatient hand through his hair and studied the glassy-eyed redhead nestled comfortably on his bed. "I'd hate to see Miss Griffin's and my picture across the morning papers."

Ken turned away and yanked open the door. His face a thunderous mask, he called over his shoulder, "Lana wouldn't appreciate it either, would she?"

In a drowsy haze Samantha tried to follow the threads of conversation, catching only bits and pieces of what the two men were saying. The urgency in their voices made her shake her head to clear away some of the fog, and strain harder to concentrate on their words. Blinking heavy lids, she stared up into the deep black pools watching her intently. "Who's Lana?" she whispered hoarsely. The silent eye contact lengthened and she wondered if she'd spoken the words out loud.

"My fiancée, Miss Griffin."

"Oh." She blinked rapidly again, trying to make some sense of what he'd just said, but the medicine she'd swallowed had taken hold and everything seemed fuzzy and unreal. "What are you doing in my room?" Her words came out a little slurred.

"Your room?" he questioned. "This is my room."

"No's...not...mine."

"You're in no shape to argue. Go to sleep. We'll straighten it out tomorrow." He tucked her in and began to dress, throwing sharp looks at her all the while. Before he left he lingered at the door a moment and smiled at the bright red hair flaming across the stark white pillowcase.

THE FINGERS OF DEEP SLEEP loosened their hold, and as the hazy mist began to clear Samantha moved restlessly beneath the unfamiliar leaden weight pressing her ribs. She pulled the covers higher, her hand snaking its way out to push at the irritating pressure. Her fingers froze as they touched the warm hard arm carelessly flung across her body. Slowly her sensitized fingers skimmed the long surface till they came in contact with an unmistakably masculine hand. Sleepily one unbelieving eye opened, and she stared at the object her questing hand had found. *Don't panic!* she told herself sternly.

Opening the other eye, she turned her head. Her mind staggered at the sight of a male head resting close to hers, a thick black head of hair tucked into a downy pillow that obscured his face. Her body twitched with the effort it took to lie perfectly still. She didn't want this man—whoever he was—to awaken and ask questions she had no answers for. What was she doing in bed with him anyway? Who was he? Taking a shallow breath, she shifted her eyes to the ceiling and tried to put all the pieces together. *Calm down and think!* There had to be a logical explanation as to why she was in a strange room, half-clothed and in bed with a naked man. But she couldn't think of one.

Looking down, she watched warily as the man's hand began to move, his thumb making small circular motions on the exposed skin above her panties. She swallowed her rising panic and tried to pull away a fraction of an inch, only to stop when the hand clamped around her waist and the man mumbled something unintelligible. She settled back and frowned in concentration, desperately trying to remember the events of the past few days. Retrace your steps, she thought, and surely it will lead you to what has happened.

She concentrated hard and Los Angeles popped into her mind. She'd left there bone tired after finally wrapping up the set of commercials for Captain Puff cereal and had taken a late flight to New York. Working with child actors and their stage mothers didn't make for an easy atmosphere. The stops and delays were so nerve-racking that at times she had felt like pulling hair—and not necessarily her own. But she'd coped, and the final product was one she was proud of. It was the first time her boss had let her have complete control, and she had used all her creative abilities to produce the commercials. Everyone on the set was ecstatic and the compliments and congratulations came freely and honestly. Some of her co-workers even went so far as to place bets that at least one would be up for the prestigious *Clios*, the Academy Award of the advertising world. She smiled to herself, wiggling her toes at the imagined thrill of having her name engraved on the coveted award for all to see.

Her movements caused the man beside her to shift and groan. His hand curved around her hip, giving it a faint squeeze as if to encourage her fantasies. She tried to put him out of her mind, and continued her search.

SHE HAD ARRIVED at her New York apartment travel weary and had checked in with her message service, frowning at the steady stream of frantic calls from her boss. Ben Johnson and his wife, Barbara, were expecting their first child, and Ben was a bundle of nervous energy. As the weeks and days grew closer to fatherhood, he took his anxieties out on his staff, working them almost to the breaking point. If he weren't such a generous man and a sweetheart at other times, they would all have quit.

Samantha checked the clock and shrugged. It was one o'clock in the morning. His messages had said to call him the moment she arrived. Dialing, she propped the phone on her shoulder and flipped through her mail.

"Ben, Samantha here. What's the problem?"

"Thank heavens. I had visions of you flying off to

Texas instead of coming home first." His voice sounded tired and worried.

"Texas is my home, Ben, and you know I had to come back here to pack for my vacation." She had three weeks due her and nothing was going to delay her this time. Twice she'd had to put her vacation off because of one of Ben's harebrained schemes.

"How would you like four weeks, pet?"

"Okay, Ben, what do I have to do?" she demanded, her chin jutting ominously. She knew that persuasive tone.

"You're a suspicious wench," he laughed.

"Come on, Ben, what are you up to?" She paused for a moment. "I'm going home tomorrow, Ben. My family is expecting me." Her tone was firm and she heard him sigh.

"This will only take two days out of your schedule, and just think, you'll get an extra week's vacation for your troubles."

"This is blackmail, Ben." But she was smiling at his wheedling tone. He knew when he'd won.

"You remember the Texas beer account we were working on? Well, get this. We got approval from the client last week. While you've been in sunny California playing nursemaid to a bunch of rug rats we've put together the commercials—"

"That's wonderful, Ben," she interrupted, "but what does this have to do with me? You and Larry were handling it."

"Samantha, Larry's father died yesterday, and the doctor wants Barbara in the hospital tomorrow. They're going to induce labor. So you see the fix we're in?"

"Oh, Ben. I'm sorry about Larry's father, but what about Barbara? Is there something wrong?" Barbara Johnson had become a close friend and Samantha was suddenly worried. Ben and his wife had taken her in and treated her like a daughter when she'd first gone to work for Duncan, Stark.

"Don't fret, pet, everything's fine. Larry and I talked about the deal before he left and we decided you could take over. The script is ready and the arrangements are made. All you have to do is show up and give it your magic touch."

Samantha preened at his vote of confidence. All her hard work and late hours were beginning to pay off.

"And guess where we're shooting?" Ben's voice intruded on her thoughts.

"Where?"

"Houston."

"You're joking?" she shrieked, then smiled at his indignant snort at having his eardrum practically ruptured. "Ben, Houston's only a few hours from my home."

"I know. Now listen, Alice has changed your plane reservations and taken care of a hotel room. All you have to do is pick up the script, your tickets and the information folder at the office tomorrow, then head for the airport."

"I can't believe this." Her smile wavered a moment. "Ben, today's not April the first, is it?" She relaxed at his choked denial that he was not pulling another of his famous jokes.

"No, pet. Oh, I forgot to tell you who's doing the commercial." He was quiet for a long moment, dragging out the suspense, but she refused to bite.

"Don't you want to know?"

"Yes."

"Are you ready?"

"Ben!"

"Okay, okay," he laughed. "Boston Grey."

"What!" she yelled.

"Boston Grey." He chuckled at the stunned silence that followed.

SAMANTHA SLOWLY TWISTED HER HEAD SIDEWAYS and surveyed the ruffled black hair next to her. Everything began to roll back, the exhaustion, her migraine and the trouble over the room. She shut her eyes and moaned out loud. The whole sordid scene fell into place and was forever printed in her mind's eye. The sight of Boston standing naked across the room was something she'd never be able to forget. Her eyes opened and roamed over his sleeping form.

As if her thoughts reached him, Boston stretched out on his back, the sheet slipping away and giving her a full view of his male form in all its natural glory. He was long and lean, not an ounce of excess fat. His feet nearly touched the foot of the king-size bed, attesting to his height, and rock-hard muscles gave the impression of great strength.

Samantha swallowed and let her eyes continue their inspection, her pulse beating faster. One arm lay across his smooth tan chest; no mat of curling hair, but velvety brown skin stretched across hard planes. Shifting her gaze to his face, she remembered the heavy-lidded coal-black eyes and saw the reason for their sleepy look—thick lashes that shadowed the high slanting cheekbones. She looked at him squarely and her brow furrowed. Hollows and sharp angles made up a face most women dreamed about—not dreams of love and tenderness, but of lust and desire. Her hand itched to reach out and trace the perfect arched line of his eyebrows. She watched in fascination as his sensuous mouth suddenly curved up at one corner. She wondered if in some mysterious way her thoughts were communicating themselves to him.

She knew she should get out of bed before he awoke, but she was too fascinated to move. Her gaze fixed on the long white scar that ran from his hip bone to midthigh, and she reflected on the clippings and profile Alice had assembled for her to study on the plane. An internationally famous romantic balladeer, Boston Grey was always mentioned in the same breath as Johnny Mathis and Barbra Streisand. It was a great shock to the world when three years ago one of his concerts had been bombed. After all, no one expected that sort of nasty incident to happen to a singer of love songs.

One person had been killed in the blast and Boston Grey had been carried away broken and bleeding from a stampeding audience. His injuries were numerous but not critical. What had rocked the world was the news from his tearful manager that Boston's voice had been damaged by a flying object that had struck his throat. Whether or not the damage would be permanent, only time would tell. Fans waited patiently outside a hospital room guarded by police. Their idol had fallen, and they were devastated.

Then the man who had sung love songs to lovers across the continent for five astoundingly successful years disappeared.

After his release from the hospital he simply dropped from sight. Exposés on his career and love affairs with famous beauties had appeared in the press. For months every aspect of his past was examined under the fine and sometimes cruel microscope of the news media, but there was no sign of the man himself. Then recently his name started to resurface in the music field. Songs performed by other artists carried Boston Grey's name as writer and composer. A musical score for a romantic movie gave credits at its end to Boston Grey. But still no one could find his retreat.

Samantha took a deep breath and flipped the sheet over his exposed body, embarrassed at her close scrutiny.

"Thank you."

She whipped her head up and met twinkling black eyes. Her face flooded with color. "I. . . ."

"Do I get the same privilege you've enjoyed for the last few minutes?" His husky voice slid down her spine, and her toes tingled at the thought. "But I don't think I'd get the same thrill since you're still partly clothed."

"I'm. . .sorry," she stammered. "You could have at least let me know you were awake." Her eyes flashed, showering him with their brilliance.

"And deprive you of your private peep show?"

She quickly decided it prudent to change the subject. Sitting up, she pulled the covers to her chin and glared at him. "What are you doing in my bed?"

His laughter rang out and she squirmed at the look he gave her. He rearranged the pillows and made himself comfortable. "I think you're a little mixed up. This is my room and my bed. You waltzed in here yesterday uninvited, did your striptease act, then passed out." He grinned at her shocked expression and leaned forward, bringing his face inches from hers. "Do you know those fantastic eyes are shooting blue sparks at me?"

"Now, look here. . . ."

"Believe me, I am," he murmured. His lips touched hers lightly and her palms pushed hard against his chest. Their eyes locked, his narrowed with desire, hers wide and angry.

"Stop that." The words came out in an unconvincing whisper, not the forceful demand she'd hoped for. His nearness and the warmth of his body were doing strange things to her. Then, surprisingly, he backed off and relaxed against the pillows, folding his arms across his chest.

Samantha cleared her throat and retrieved the fallen covers, tucking them under her arms. "We need to decide whose room this is. And by the way, why couldn't you have had the common decency to sleep on the couch?" She looked into his laughing eyes and bristled. "I don't think this is the least bit funny." She glared at him.

"Calm down, Sparky."

"Sparky!" She sputtered at the name and felt herself blush as his eyes wandered over her body.

"The room's mine. Your company made the arrangements, and as to sleeping on the couch, why should I? I didn't invite you to spend the night with me, remember. Besides, I like having a warm body next to mine."

Samantha opened her mouth, then closed it. From what she'd read and heard he was very seldom without one. "Then why didn't you put me on the couch?"

"I'm a strong man, Sparky, but you're not exactly little."

"Don't call me Sparky. I don't like nicknames."

"That's too bad." He reached over and picked up the phone.

She made a lunge across his chest and grabbed the receiver. "Who are you calling?"

Boston dropped the instrument and wound his arms around her, pulling her close. "I didn't know you cared."

He brought his mouth down on hers, and something shattered with his searching kiss. His tongue forced its way between her closed lips, and her hard mouth became soft and sweet. Her body went limp, bones melting into his as his hands moved up and down her back. He broke their embrace and stared at her a long moment. "I *was* going to order some coffee." He couldn't disguise the husky tremor in his voice and she knew he was just as affected by that kiss as she was.

The fire her of anger was extinguished and replaced by a different flame, one she'd never dealt with before. Frightened, she moved away. He was watching her closely and she tried to compose her face into some semblance of a smile, but it came off weak and strained.

"You're going to be big trouble, Sparky. I feel it in my bones."

Samantha sat quietly while Boston called room service. Never had she reacted to a man's kiss in such a way and it was frightening. Desire with love she could handle, but pure lust for a man was something she was not prepared for. If she could stay out of his way, she could avoid the situation. The problem was that she was going to be in very close contact with him for two days, and if she couldn't get another room the contact would be very close indeed.

"Do you want the bathroom first? I think we need to dress before we continue this discussion." His question brought her wandering thoughts back to reality.

"You go ahead," she told him absently. When he started to throw back the sheet she pulled the covers over her eyes. She heard his deep chuckle and cringed.

"How can you hide your face now after the lengthy inspection you gave me earlier?" At his words she felt her face turning bright red behind its shield. "Sparky, I bet you know every hair, nick and scar by heart."

The bathroom door shut firmly behind him. Lowering the sheet, Samantha let out a gusty sigh of relief. The man was an infuriating tease. She jumped as the door suddenly jerked open and Boston's head reappeared.

"Want to join me?" He retreated quickly as a pillow sailed through the air, bouncing off the spot where his head had been. She could hear his muffled unintelligible curse and smiled, the tension melting away.

She waited for the steady drumming of the shower before scrambling out of bed and attacking her suitcase. She yanked out a pair of designer jeans and a pale gray silk shirt. After pulling them on hurriedly she crammed her clean undergarments into her make-up bag. She knew it was silly to dress only to undress again to take a quick bath, but she didn't want to give Boston any ideas—never mind her own. She'd have to deal with them later.

CHAPTER TWO

"ARE YOU GOING TO EAT those eggs or play with them?"

Samantha pushed the plate aside in disgust. Picking up her cup of coffee, she eyed Boston over the rim. His attitude, which had changed drastically, was puzzling. Silent to the point of rudeness, he would stare at her for endless seconds, then return to the script he was studying.

"Do you think you've memorized your lines by now?" She raised her eyebrows questioningly at him, then flushed as his stony gaze met hers. She was being nasty and knew it, but she couldn't seem to help herself. For half a million dollars he only had to say three or four words. The amount of money seemed outrageous, but it was the only figure that would bring him before the camera again. Their client hadn't blinked an eyelash when presented with the proposal. They were so overjoyed at getting Boston to do their commercial that Samantha figured his manager could have stuck them for twice that amount.

Boston leaned forward, propping his chin on folded hands. "You couldn't be from New York, not with that soft southern drawl."

"No, I'm not." She hesitated and then went on.

"Actually, I'm from a small town not far from here. Tomball, Texas." Before he could probe further into her life she asked, "What about you? I've read your press releases, but they only talk about your career. Where are you from, and do you have any family?"

"Not the kind of family you're talking about. I'm an orphan, raised on a boys' ranch in West Texas."

Because of his coloring, she wondered if his heritage was Latin or Spanish, but she saw on closer inspection that his high, prominent cheekbones and the slight feline slant to his jet eyes bespoke an American Indian heritage. "Do you know anything about your parents—who they were?" Realizing how snobbish her question sounded, Samantha immediately apologized.

"That's all right—and no, I don't know anything about my birth or who my parents were. I was literally found on the orphanage doorstep one night. They named me Boston because Father Brian, the new director, had just arrived from that city. I don't know where they found Grey for a last name. Maybe it was the color of the blanket I was wrapped in." He shrugged, dismissing the issue.

She marveled at his lack of bitterness and thought of all the fun—and heartache—a loving family could give. "Have you ever tried to find out who your parents were?"

He shook his head. "No, I figured if they ever wanted me to know they would have found me by now." He watched the different emotions play across her face. "Don't pity me, Sparky. It may sound a gloomy existence to you, but let me assure you it wasn't that bad. I was amply fed and clothed, and given an excellent education, and when they found out I was musically talented and had a good voice, they did everything in their power to see to it I had the best training available.''

Musically talented! He had a masters degree in music. After college he had won a scholarship to the Juilliard School of Music in New York, where he had studied classical piano and played the guitar with such feeling and love his music could bring tears, and often did, to the most hardened critic.

"You remember my manager?" He flashed her a wicked grin as the color flooded her cheeks. "Ken is another example of orphanage life. We were raised together and he hasn't turned out so bad. A lawyer, manager and financial wizard. So you see I did have a fairly normal childhood, more than most."

It was time to change the subject. She didn't want to think about the previous night and they were getting dangerously close to the subject. There were still too many things she couldn't put together.

"Boston, we need to settle this business over the room. Do you call the manager or do I?"

He stood up to his full height and grinned down at her. "Why not stay here? Who's to know? Besides, you make a nice bed warmer."

"You must be out of your mind. I can't stay here. What would people think?" She shook her head. "I can just hear the uproar when my boss calls for my reports on how the taping went—to say nothing of the chaos it will cause with my family. They're sure to phone the minute they find out I'm in Houston."

While Boston made the call, Samantha poured another cup of coffee and picked up a cold piece of toast. As she nibbled at one corner, a thought rushed up at her like a locomotive. No! She refused to believe what was running rampant through her mind. She would know—wouldn't she?

"The manager said he'd be up in a few minutes. By the way, he asked if you were still here. It seems they've found your reservation, but there's a problem he needs to discuss with you." Boston sat down and reached for the coffee pot.

Samantha remained stone still, not taking her eyes from the half-eaten piece of toast, and said in a strangled voice, "Boston. . .?" His name was drawn out and lay quietly between them.

"What?" Looking up, he watched the play of emotions slip like a silken scarf across her face. Then he leaned back, studying her with gleaming eyes.

"Were there pictures taken of us last night?"

"Don't you remember?"

She bristled at his amused question and couldn't quite meet his searching look. "No, not really. I have a vague memory of flashing lights and your voice yelling to stop someone and something about film—I think." She glanced up. Her eyes met his, then bounced away in embarrassment. Her mind raced through the muddled events of the past evening, but there seemed to be long periods of time that kept coming up blank. No matter how hard she tried, she couldn't recall anything in minute detail, just fragments that she wasn't sure if she had dreamed.

Boston pulled a roll of film from his jeans pocket and placed it on the edge of her plate.

"Thank you. Did...uh...I mean...." She stopped and smiled at him uncertainly. "Did anything else happen...important...between us?" They stared at each other. The silence stretched, and Samantha shifted uneasily in her chair. She didn't like the way he was smiling. "Well?"

Boston shot her an injured look, his voice sad. "You really don't remember?" He shoved back his chair and walked away from the table.

Samantha jumped up, grabbed his arm and swung him around. In response he threw back his head and laughed, a mellow sound that grated on her already-frayed nerves. She glared at him, her eyes bright jewels. "This is not funny."

"You may not think so, but I do. Women don't usually forget me so quickly."

The way he was smiling now made her want to slap his face. She tightened her grip on his arm. "Are you telling me we made love last night?"

"I didn't say *we*, now did I?"

She stared at him, stunned. "While I was out like a light—" her voice choked over the next words "—you made love to me!"

"I didn't say that, either."

"Then just what *are* you saying."

He pried her fingers loose and held her away from him. "What do you want me to say? If I told you I didn't, you're not going to believe me. Now, which one do you want to hear?"

She stood very still, confused and bewildered by

his evasions. "The *truth*. That's what I want to hear!" Realizing she was shouting in an undignified manner, she clamped her lips shut and ran a distraught hand through her hair. Her temper was simmering. "Tell me," she growled.

Boston cupped her face and dropped a light kiss on her clenched lips. "I never kiss and tell."

Her gaze scorched him from head to toe. "You're a sorry excuse for a man if you had to make love to a lifeless body." She took a deep breath. "I never would have thought it of you." Her challenging words did not have the effect she hoped for. They only caused his smile to deepen and a chuckle to rise to his lips.

"Sparky, I'm sorry." He tried unsuccessfully to straighten his features. "I didn't think this would upset you so much. After all, you're a grown woman—of what, twenty-five?" She nodded. "It's not as if you're an unfledged virgin, but a businesswoman of the world. These things happen."

"What things! For heaven's sake, did you or didn't you seduce me last night?"

"Seduce?" He sounded vastly amused and she felt the blood rush to her face. "How can you say that? You were such a tempting morsel, cuddling up to me all night. So lovingly and openly inviting."

"Ooh, you...you...insufferable boor. You conceited...."

"Now, now. There's no cause to get nasty." He grinned and took hold of her elbow, guiding her to the table. "Sit down and we'll discuss this like two grown-ups."

"Hateful, obstinate, overbearing," she mumbled under her breath.

"What?"

"Nothing," she snapped.

Boston reached across the table and ran his finger down a flushed freckled cheek. Jerking away from his touch, Samantha wondered if a few age-old tricks would help. Large tears floated to the surface of her eyes and she blinked rapidly to aid their course down her cheeks. "Are you going to tell me?" she whispered, her lips trembling just enough to be noticeable.

"Dear Sparky." His deep baritone voice caressed each syllable. "How unforgivable of me. Of course I'll tell you."

She waited, only half concentrating on his words as she forced more tears over the brim.

"When little snowballs fall on Texas in July."

She sat stunned, watching him try to control his hilarity. Then they stared at each other until she squirmed in her chair. He had seen right through her little act. The wicked sparkle in his black eyes belied his innocent expression, and she realized he wasn't going to tell her the truth. Not yet.

"Why won't you tell me? It's not as if I led you on, then passed out drunk in the middle of a passionate embrace. I was sick!" she wailed. "And in pain." He just kept smiling. "I didn't think you would stoop that low. You're the type of man who wants a willing and eager partner."

"Sweetheart, your quick study leaves a lot to be desired. You know absolutely nothing about me, my likes or dislikes.'' The doorbell buzzed and he hurried to the door, giving her an exaggerated wink before opening it. She watched, furious, as he shook hands with the hotel manager.

''Miss Griffin—'' the manager turned to Samantha ''—I'm Harold Windthrope. I can't tell you how sorry I am about this mix-up. We found our confirmation this morning.''

''Good. I'll just go get my things together.''

The manager cleared his throat and looked helplessly at Boston. ''It's like I told Mr. Grey when I called. It's not possible to move you, Miss Griffin.''

''Why?''

''We don't have any vacant rooms.'' He rushed on. ''There's not one room available in this town. Believe me, I've checked.''

''And just what do you suggest I do, Mr. Windthrope?'' Her voice was low and dangerous.

''You could stay here,'' he offered, his face turning red at the silence that met his words. ''It's only for one more night.''

Boston shifted his gaze from the hotel manager's flustered expression to Samantha's hostile one. ''Mr. Windthrope, have you thought of what happens when the press get hold of this?''

''I promise, Mr. Grey, they won't.''

''What about our calls and sleeping arrangements?''

''Now wait just a minute—'' Samantha tried to interrupt.

''I'll set up separate phone lines and have a rollaway bed brought in.''

"Well, Sparky, what do you think?"

Samantha studied her hands for a moment, then looked at both men. "I don't have much of a choice, do I?"

"Of course, your stay with us will be compliments of the hotel, Miss Griffin."

"NO!" Boston and Samantha shouted in unison.

Boston shook his head. "Oh, no, Mr. Windthrope. That would be a dead giveaway. When Miss Griffin's company doesn't receive a bill there will be questions asked—embarrassing questions."

"Of course."

Boston took a strong grip on the manager's shoulder and urged him toward the door. His features were hard and unyielding. "There'd better not be any mix-up, Mr. Windthrope. I hope you have a discreet staff and an alert switchboard operator. If any of this ends up in the press, Miss Griffin and I will hold you personally responsible."

"Yes, yes. I fully understand, Mr. Grey."

When the door finally closed on the manager's reassuring words, Boston turned and leered at her. "Looks like you're stuck with me—sweetheart."

She couldn't contain her laughter at his bad imitation of Bogart. "That's terrible." She smiled, then glanced at the clock. "Good grief, look at the time. We're going to be late for the shooting." She jumped up and began to gather her scattered items of clothing and cosmetics, dropping them as fast as she picked them up.

"Are you always so messy?" He trailed behind her, retrieving the articles as they fell.

"Yes," she hissed.

"Listen, there's no need to be nervous about spending the night with me again."

"I'm not."

"Yes, you are. I solemnly promise—" he held up three fingers in his best Boy Scout salute "—there won't be a repeat of last night unless you instigate it."

"Damn you." She yanked up her purse and stormed out, followed by his muffled chuckles.

SAMANTHA HELD HER BREATH with excitement. Looking around Durango's Saloon was like taking a step back a hundred years in history. It was the perfect western setting for shooting the commercial, and her mind began to work furiously, setting the scenes, as her professional eye scanned the large room.

Old plank tables sat haphazardly arranged on scuffed hardwood floors. Chairs of different types and designs surrounded each table, adding to the illusion of disarray and the sense of a bygone era. A monster of a player piano crouched in a far corner, its snaggletoothed, yellowing keys grinning evilly at the occupants of the room. She shifted her gaze to the focal point for the commercial. A twenty-foot-long antique mahogany bar spread its length across the back of the room, its worn brass fittings gleaming softly in the artificial light.

"Where is everyone?" Boston's voice cut through her musings.

"They're probably in the restaurant." Samantha pointed to a set of shuttered swing doors. "The steak house takes up the other half of this building." She gave the room another glance. Somehow the rugged setting made her uneasy. It reflected a strong aura of hard men, whiskey, and fast guns slung low on slim hips. It seemed a place where no woman of virtue and morals was ever allowed. She turned her back on Boston and the room, but was stopped by a firm hand on her shoulder.

"Are you going to continue to pout the rest of the day?" Boston smiled indulgently at her frown.

"I don't pout."

"Yes you do. You sat hugging the corner of the limousine all the way here. Do you know what's wrong with you?" he asked, a smile twisting the corners of his lips. "You've been spoiled rotten."

Before she could retaliate, a delicate cough from behind caused them both to turn and face a short, gray-haired man, whose sharp brown eyes watched them with interest.

"You must be Samantha Griffin. We were beginning to wonder what happened to you. I'm John Byrd, director for your film crew." Turning to Boston, he held out his hand. "There's no need to ask who you are. I'd recognize that face and voice anywhere."

Samantha moved away from the two men and began introducing herself to the rest of the crew. To save the expense of having their own film company flown in, she had urged her boss to hire a local group. Now she wanted to meet and talk with the various crews to make sure they could handle the job professionally. With a client spending such a large amount of money on just two commercials she didn't want to send a low-quality product back to New York. Looking at the equipment, she gave a silent sigh of relief. Everything was as first-rate as she had hoped for. She grinned when she remembered the way her boss had balked at the idea of using a local crew. Firmly imbedded in his mind was the notion that if the shoot wasn't done in New York or by a New York crew it wasn't going to meet his high standards.

Samantha walked over to the group of men and women circling Boston. As he signed autographs, she caught his eye and raised an inquiring eyebrow. She jammed her hands into the rear pockets of her jeans, wondering whether it was always like this for him and how he'd learned to cope with the fame. She watched the makeup and wardrobe woman, Janel, place her hand on Boston's arm, her fingers caressing the fine brown silk shirt. Her lips tightened and she deemed it time to start work.

"Mr. Byrd." She raised her voice authoritatively and the room went silent. All eyes turned in her direction.

"John, please." The director walked toward her, followed by Boston.

"Would you have the crew start setting up." Her eyes searched for the makeup woman. "Janel, will you take Boston and get him ready."

"You bet. Come along, sweetie," she purred. Laughing at the groans of the others in the room, she took Boston's hand and led him away.

Samantha eyed Boston's wide inviting smile with disgust. The man was a menace to any woman.

Thirty minutes were spent checking lighting and camera angles. Two crews were needed to shoot both on film and videotape. They scurried around taking her directions, never for a second doubting her abilities. Finally she sat down before the video prompter and waited. Everything was ready. When Boston walked out, her eyes narrowed in concentration, then swung around the room. The effect was all wrong! His bright and shining cowboy clothes were completely out of character; his outfit didn't fit the setting or the man. Everything he wore was new and the newness showed, from his sharply creased hat to the spit shine on his boots. Their eyes met and she could feel his silent protest. He felt an incongruity, too.

"That's the best looking hunk of man I ever laid eyes on," Janel gushed to the room at large.

Swearing under her breath, Samantha walked around Boston, eyeing him up and down. His eyes followed her, an appeal in their depths. He didn't say anything to undermine her authority, but his disapproval was evident in his rigid stance.

She grinned and answered Janel. "He's positively beautiful, but it's not right." There was a collective sigh from several people and a hardy one from Boston.

"What do you mean it's not right?" Janel squealed. "I read the script and this is what it called for."

"I'm well aware of how the script reads. But I don't like it. This is not Boston Grey." Samantha pivoted, her voice low and angry. "I want him in some worn boots, faded jeans and shirt. Find a poncho for him to wear." She rapidly fired orders and stood back, forgetting everything but what she was seeing in her mind. "Take that hat, roll it in the dirt for a while and then dust it off lightly. Get some of your makeup and add a couple of days' shadow to his face." She could feel the excitement in the room at her directions.

"I think you're wrong, Miss Griffin," Janel retorted and began to walk away.

"Janel!" Samantha gritted her teeth. She'd had enough of being questioned. Then suddenly she realized her reaction to the makeup woman's stubbornness was only an extension of her reaction to Boston's harassing. She inhaled deeply and forced a smile to her stiff lips. "Janel, you're right as far as the script reads, and I know you're the best in your profession or John wouldn't have hired you for this shoot. But I think if you'll just stand back a second and try to visualize Boston as I've described you'll see what I'm talking about."

She watched Janel's skeptical expression change to a thoughtful intensity. Then it lighted up as her artistic imagination was stirred. "See what I mean?" Samantha urged gently. "Now can you imagine the viewers' reactions—especially the women's—to this deadly, gorgeous man? Can you feel their chills as they gaze into those dark brooding eyes?"

"Hmmm," Janel purred, then grinned sheepishly. "Oh my, yes! Follow me, darlin'," she called over her shoulder as she hurried out of the tension-filled room.

"That's a girl." Boston leaned down and kissed

Samantha's freckled cheek. "Did you know your eyes turn the most incredible shade of turquoise when you're in a temper? Almost the same shade they were last night, and you weren't angry then." He chuckled and walked away, leaving her to wonder for the hundredth time that morning if he had made love to her the night before.

CHAPTER THREE

SALOON DOORS RATTLED on their hinges as a tall gun-slinger stood silhouetted against the bright, burning sun that spilled across the barroom. His eyes shifted, taking in every detail, every gun strapped to a hip, every face. The half-smoked, half-chewed thin cigarillo rolled from one corner of his hard mouth to the other. With feline grace he walked to the long bar, his spurs tinkling like tiny bells in the deadly silence. Propping a worn dusty boot on the brass railing, he surveyed the room from the mirror-lined wall behind the bar.

A pale portly bartender wiped his way down to the stranger. "What'll it be, mister?"

"Beer." He bit the words out around clenched teeth.

"What brand, fella?"

Flat black eyes narrowed menacingly, one corner of his mouth twisted into a sneer. He was a coiled rattlesnake ready to strike, and the room waited. The bartender's forehead reflected a fine sheen of fear.

"Texas Light, what else?" He arched an arrogant eyebrow at the frightened man.

"*Cut!* That's a print."

"Beer's on me," someone yelled above the applause.

Samantha leaned back from the viewer and closed her eyes, seeing again the raw sensuality of Boston's face. The black eyes touched something deep within her; the lips she vaguely remembered as being warm and firm. She knew that he above all men had the power to send her to heaven and plunge her to hell in the same instant. His long lean body could turn her mindless in a second. Oh, yes, Boston was a dangerous man on the screen or off. His affairs with women were legend, and she didn't plan to join the endless line. Just thinking about him was unnerving. Opening her eyes, she absently watched the crew and extras laugh and congratulate one another. A smile touched her lips. They had worked five hours' overtime, but the results were incredible. Lost in her thoughts, she jumped when John spoke to her.

"You're a first-rate producer and director, Samantha. If you ever decide to move to Houston and need a job, please call me." He handed her his business card and she thanked him.

"He's right, you know. You are good." Boston placed a beer down beside her. "Give me a few minutes and we'll go have dinner." He narrowed his eyes and sneered the same way he'd done for the camera. "I might even tell you what happened last night."

"I know exactly what happened last night," she told him sweetly. "Nothing!"

"Is that right?"

"Yes."

"You're sure?"

"Absolutely."

"If you say so." He walked away chuckling and she burned with impotent rage.

Would she ever get him to tell the truth? The problem was she wasn't sure herself. She seemed to remember those burning black eyes close to hers, his breath warm on her face, the touch of his hands. It was so frustrating. She'd have to find a way to make him tell—before it drove her crazy.

Only a few members of the crew remained, coiling up the miles of cords and wires, when Boston returned. "You ready?" He grasped her elbow and they turned toward the restaurant door. Samantha jerked to a stop and gasped, her mouth dropping open in surprise.

Boston followed the direction of her eyes and started visibly. Lined before the entrance were six of the biggest men he'd ever seen. Maybe individually they weren't so big, but together they were a sight to make any football coach drool with visions of a winning team. There wasn't any doubt in his mind who they were related to; their red hair was a waving flag of kinship.

Samantha launched herself at her oldest brother. "Adam," she squealed. She was bear-hugged by him, then passed like a rag doll from one brother to the next. "What are all of you doing here? Never mind." She whirled around. "Boston, come meet my brothers." Turning back, she noticed something was very wrong. Her brothers, always good natured, were staring at Boston in the most murderous way. She'd seen that look before, when she was seventeen and had come home late from a date. She remembered standing on the front porch silently fighting the young man's busy hands, repulsed by his not-too-gentle persuasion. She was just about to slap his face when her brothers came home from a basketball game. They'd seen her struggles and jumped her date, sending him on his way with the beginnings of a black eye and numerous bruises.

"Boston, I'd like you to meet Adam, Luke, Matthew, John, Abel and Mark." No welcoming hands were extended and she shifted uncomfortably from one foot to the other. "What's the matter?"

"Here." Adam shoved a newspaper into her hand. "Take a look at that." An angry finger punched the headline splashed across a local scandal sheet—Famous singer makes more than a Comeback. Her brothers began to circle around her and Boston while they stood side by side studying in horror the picture of last night's bedroom scene.

"I thought you said you got that film away from that reporter!" Her angry eyes caught Boston's. As she watched him grimace she realized what she'd said and how incriminating it sounded. Looking up, she was just in time to shout a warning to Boston as her youngest brother drew back his fist.

Boston ducked and Mark's hand whizzed past her ear, connecting with Luke's midsection. There was a grunt of pain and Samantha ducked as Luke took a swing at Mark.

"Stop it," she yelled, crouched down between her

arguing brothers. Looking at Boston, squeezed down beside her, she shrugged helplessly.

"Well, this is *another* fine mess you've gotten me into."

His shoulders shook with restrained laughter.

"Don't you realize this could be dangerous?" she demanded. "You don't know my brothers. When they get like this they're not rational."

Boston looked around at the mass of tree-trunk legs. "Shall we crawl through and head for safety?"

Grabbing hold of Boston's arm for support, Samantha tried hard to control the bubbling lightness in her chest, but it erupted into a full-blown case of the giggles. The two of them tottered precariously on their heels until Samantha pulled them down into a sitting position, clinging to each other. A sudden silence brought both their heads up to meet six pairs of varying shades of angry blue eyes.

"It's not what you think, Adam," she gasped. "Really it's not."

"Let me hit him, just once," Mark pleaded.

"Get up, Sammy." Abel, the shy one, helped her up and extended his hand to Boston.

"There really is a logical explanation for this," Boston said, looking at each man, smiling his famous smile.

Samantha groaned. That was the last thing to impress her brothers.

"Let me hit him!"

"Shut up, Mark," Adam shouted. "Samantha, how could you do this to dad—he's brokenhearted. You'd better get your things together. We're taking you home." He turned toward Boston and placed a big, beefy hand on his shoulder. "You, too, mister. Dad wants to talk to both of you."

"Oh, but, Adam, Boston's not needed. I can explain everything."

Boston draped an arm around her waist. "That's okay, Sparky. I don't mind answering a few questions." He was smiling again and Samantha realized he thought this was all a fabulous joke. She could feel her brothers bristle at his casual treatment of the situation.

Mark piped up angrily, "Maybe you think this is all very funny, Mr. Big Shot. But let me tell you, this could ruin our father's chances for reelection. His opponent is running on a strong moral platform, and Federal Court Judges' lives are always open for inspection. Just think what the opposition is going to make of this little bit of news. Why, they're probably throwing a victory party this very moment." He stomped off, his alligator boots thumping loudly in the stillness that followed.

Samantha closed her eyes in despair. How selfish she'd been. Not once since seeing that disgusting picture had she considered anyone but herself.

"Come on, Sammy." Abel's quiet voice urged her out the door.

"Is dad really upset?"

"Yes, honey."

THE HOUR AND A HALF DRIVE to the Griffin farm was made in nerve-racking silence, except for Mark. His hotheaded nature wouldn't allow him to let go and he turned around repeatedly, threatening to rearrange Boston's smiling face. Adam drove the big custom Cadillac station wagon at a furious pace, weaving in and out of Houston's rush-hour traffic, honking his horn as if he owned the road.

Seated in the back, Samantha unconsciously clenched her hand around Boston's thigh. "I'm sorry about this." She felt too embarrassed by her brothers' rough treatment even to look at him. "I hope you understand their concern?"

He covered her hand and began to play with her fingers, but stopped when a sharp elbow gave him a hard nudge. He turned and met John's gentle blue-gray gaze and pulled his hand back; crossing his arms over his chest, he smiled apologetically. He considered his chances of getting out at the first stoplight, then shook his head. If these three didn't get him, the other three following on their bumper would.

"I understand, Sparky." His deep voice whispered the words close to her ear, and she looked at him and smiled. "If I had a baby sister as beautiful as you, I don't think I'd react any differently."

They turned off the main highway and began the long drive over back country roads. Samantha felt Boston tense, and followed his eyes as he surveyed the landscape. She chuckled at his expression. "They're not looking for a place to dump your body. This is a short cut to our farm."

He brought his attention back to Samantha. "I'm glad to hear that." His body relaxed. "What does your family raise besides children?"

"Horses." She had his full attention now. "Quarter horses."

The car turned sharply and rattled over a cattle guard, throwing Boston against her. His hand grazed her breast as he tried to pull her away from colliding with the door frame. She quivered at the tingling sensation, and turned to meet Boston's eyes, surprised to see a fire in their jet depths. He was as affected as she was. What was wrong with her? Every time he touched her she could feel the most peculiar warmth in her middle. She stared straight ahead, afraid he might be able to read her expression.

The car made another turn onto a gravel drive lined with wide spreading oaks and her home came into view—a sprawling brick monstrosity with the proportions of an old-fashioned hotel. They circled the front drive and headed down the side toward the rear of the house. The back driveway looked like a parking lot for a modern shopping center and Samantha groaned aloud. Her whole family was there. Nieces and nephews of various ages were playing in the yard and around the huge swimming pool.

She turned angrily to John. "What's this, a summit meeting? I just don't believe this. Is *everyone* here?" At his nod she slumped back in her seat. Her eyes flashed at Boston. "You can take that stupid smile off your face, because if you think this is going to be fun, you're in for a rude awakening."

"You mean this is not the annual family reunion?"

She opened the door and stepped out. "Very funny, but you just wait."

The rest of her brothers arrived, and amid the slamming of car doors and the kids' greetings she lost sight of Boston. She searched the crowd and spotted him surrounded by the younger members of her family. He was signing autographs. Swearing under her breath, she marched through the kitchen. Matthew's wife, Sara, stared after her in openmouthed surprise at the language she was hearing.

Shocked at the mass of people that met her eyes, Samantha stopped sharply inside the living-room doorway. She felt she'd walked into another dimension. One by one, each chattering voice died away till complete silence prevailed and all eyes were turned toward her in hostility. Then a blistering blast of accusations poured out.

"How could you...?"

"Don't you ever think of anyone but...?"

"...to ruin your dad's...."

"...been heartsick ever since he saw that terrible article." Karen, Adam's wife, shouted over the babble of voices, only to be outvolumed by Alice, Luke's wife.

The voices continued their abuse, hitting her from all directions, berating her from all sides.

"...to think of all he's...."

"How in the world did you get mixed up with a singer?"

"It comes from all that wild living in New York. That's what! I told Adam when she left it was a mistake to let her go. But does anyone listen to me where their darling Samantha is concerned?"

"We never thought we'd see you do...."

" . . . I was never so embarrassed in all my life when I saw. . . ."

"What will people think?"

They were no longer talking to her but to each other, going over her faults with a vicious enjoyment that not only appalled her but hurt deeply. She sagged against the door, tears welling up in her eyes.

Boston slipped in from the kitchen munching a large wedge of apple pie. "I don't believe I've seen so many redheads in all my life." He saw the tears streaming down her cheeks and surveyed the room, picking up bits and pieces of conversation. His lips tightened and he stepped in front of Samantha, shielding her from further pain and insults. "Please don't cry, Sparky. They don't mean what they're saying. It's just in the heat of anger." He flicked her tears away with a gentle finger.

"He's right, my dear." They turned toward a quiet voice at their side. Boston accepted the clean handkerchief offered by another brilliant redhead, this one wearing clerical clothes and a white collar. He lifted Samantha's chin and tenderly began to mop the tears away.

"Did they draw you into this, too, Uncle George?" She gave him a wan smile and introduced Boston.

"What's going on in here?" Still dressed in his riding clothes, her father came and stood behind her uncle.

"Another one of your family councils, daddy?" she asked, the bitterness and emotion making her voice husky.

"Hello, baby." He leaned down and kissed her cheek, then straightened, his blue-gray eyes looking around with interest. "Looks that way, doesn't it?" Without another word he walked toward an over-stuffed leather chair by the huge fireplace. Boston urged Samantha to follow and seated her in a chair opposite her father while he leaned back nonchalantly against the mantel.

For as long as she could remember, important family decisions were discussed by them all. Each person, no matter how young, was always included and had a vote. Her father would stand, call them to order, then meticulously lay out the problem for open debate. Tonight he sat quietly and listened.

"Well, I think she's disgraced us all with her behavior," charged her sister-in-law Karen. "With her usual lack of consideration she's more than likely ruined Papa Griffin's chances for reelection. Something has to be done to salvage the situation."

"What would you suggest I do, Karen? Allow you to burn me at the stake or brand me for all to see what you think I am?"

There were a few titters around the room from some of the younger nieces.

"You see! Always a glib comeback. Well, this time you've gone too far, and believe me, everyone in this room thinks the same way I do."

"And I'm sure you encouraged them every chance you got." Samantha glared at her sister-in-law. "Didn't you?"

"Karen! You've said enough," Adam admonished his wife.

"Oh, no, I haven't. All of you have spoiled her, worshiped her to the point you can't see her faults. It's time you opened your eyes to what she's done and the trouble she's caused."

Samantha could feel her temper rising and had to bite her tongue to keep quiet. Her hands tightened on the arms of the chair till her knuckles whitened. She felt a cold hand cover and pat hers gently. Glancing sideways, she gave Abel's timid wife a strained smile.

Dawn returned her smile with one of apology, and her round brown eyes filled with tears. "I'm so sorry, Sammy," she whispered, so softly Samantha had to lean forward to catch her words.

"It's all right, Dawn. I'm used to Karen's vindictiveness and jealousy." A movement caught in her peripheral vision, and she looked up at Boston. Her lips began to curve when she saw his concerned expression change to a blank mask at Karen's next words.

"They'll have to marry, of course, as soon as possible. The press can be told they've been engaged—secretly—for some time. Later on they can divorce."

Samantha sat motionless in the explosive stillness, staring fixated at Karen's smug face as the room roared to life with loud voices. She felt revolted at her sister-in-law's maliciousness and jealousy. Suddenly the rage she'd forced down earlier washed over her with such violence she began to tremble, then shake.

"How dare you," she whispered. Then she shouted, "How could you!" Her blazing eyes touched each member in turn, accusing them. "How dare you

plan my life for me? Who gave you the right to play
God? Secure in your sanctimonious self-
righteousness, you've judged and condemned me
without giving me a hearing—or even asking for an
explanation. And my sentence is to be marriage—
marriage that I don't need or want. You have the
nerve to blame *my* behavior for this trouble on my
moving to New York, but do you really want to know
the reason I left?'' She slowly surveyed the room.
''Because of you—all of you. Your smothering over-
protectiveness nearly drove me crazy.''

Taking a deep breath, she went on. ''I moved to
Houston, found myself a job in my field and a nice
apartment, and what happened? Every weekend I
had family there. Karen needs to do some shopping
for the boys. The kids want to go to Astroworld.
Luke has a business meeting on a Friday and decides
to spend the weekend and take little sister out. Matthew and Sara want to get away from the kids. Do
you take me for a complete idiot? Do you think I was
totally unaware of your intentions?'' She turned to
her father. ''Did you have so little faith in me that
you considered my judgments untrustworthy?''

He looked appalled, then glared at his family.
''I'm sorry, baby. I never knew. It seems a conspiracy was contrived without my knowledge.''

''It doesn't matter anymore,'' she said wearily.
''You've all showed me what you think of me and I
may never forgive you. Karen, you talk so glibly of
marrying and divorcing. If I remember correctly,
four years ago you were whistling a different tune.
You and Adam were having serious problems and

you came crying to me, begging me to talk to my brother. What was it you said so tearfully and gallantly? 'Marriage is a contract between two people and God. It's for a lifetime, and any problems can be worked out if you love someone strongly enough.' And I agreed. Yet you're asking—no, demanding—I marry. Not for love or dad's sake, but to save your hypocritical face before your local women's club.''

Unsympathetically, she watched her sister-in-law's composure crumble before the censuring eyes of the family as they became fully aware of Karen's jealousy and pettiness. ''I feel like a pawn in a chess game,'' Samantha continued, ''helplessly moved in one direction, then the other, all for the benefit of my *loving* family. So, let me repeat what I said earlier so there's no mistake. I will *not* marry Boston Grey or anyone else just to please your sanctimonious morality. Is that perfectly clear?''

''Yes, you will!'' Boston's deep voice rumbled over the quiet room with determination. Samantha's eyes flashed blue fire at him. ''Because, my sweet Sparky, through all of this no one—*no one*—has considered my feelings or the adverse publicity I may receive. If you envision marriage as a lifetime bargain, then so be it.'' His face turned hard and granite cold. ''I never had a family, and from what I've witnessed here tonight, maybe I was the lucky one. But whatever it takes, this discussion will stop here and now. I've watched you tear each other apart in anger, bitterness and resentment. A family should support one another in times of trouble, not rip one another apart. You've all said things tonight that will never be completely forgotten or forgiven.''

He turned to her father, and something passed between them she couldn't fathom. She seemed to remember a lengthy whispered conversation between them and Uncle George while she was having her say.

''I won't do it!'' she announced. ''I will not marry you.'' Stubbornly she crossed her arms over her chest and dared him to contradict her final decision.

Ignoring her outburst, Boston addressed her father. ''I need to make a private call, sir. Would you show me where I might make it undisturbed?'' He turned back to Samantha and smiled. ''Then we'll find a quiet place to talk.''

''Of all the. . . .''

''Follow me, my boy.'' Her father stood and took hold of Boston's arm. Together they strolled out, trailed by Uncle George.

Samantha sat back defiantly and wondered how Boston thought he could convince her to give in to his demands. What if he told her father there was a possibility she could be pregnant? That would work. Then the whole family really would have something to talk about. No! He wouldn't do that, because he hadn't made love to her. At least she didn't think so. Mentally she cursed. If only she could remember. Lingering memories flitted through her mind: smooth warm flesh under her hands, the thrill of strong teeth nibbling on her neck, the brush of fingers over swollen breast. Did she? Did he?

''Sammy—Samantha.'' Her father stood in the

open doorway. "Boston would like to see you now. He's in the library."

"Daddy, I won't marry him, no matter what."

"It's all right, baby. Go talk with him and don't worry." She passed him and he leaned down and whispered cryptically, "Whatever happens, just remember I love you and believe in you."

She heard the battle of voices behind her as she walked out with leaden steps. At the sound of her father's roaring commands, she smiled.

"Sit down, Mark."

"But, dad. That man should be watched. There's no telling what he'll do. Why, I wouldn't trust him alone with Aunt Sally."

"That's enough! Sit!"

The lion voice faded as she shut the library door. Boston had his back to her, gazing out the window. "Well," she demanded, "whatever you have to say, let's get it over with. But you'd better realize here and now that nothing you can say or do will change my mind."

He turned, a smile spreading across his features. "You've hurt me to the quick."

"Boston, this is no laughing matter."

"You're right."

"Then what do you find so amusing?"

"Come over here and I'll tell you."

She took a few tentative steps, then stopped. "Tell me what?"

"Come on," he urged, still smiling.

He held out his hand and she placed hers in his. Strong fingers tightened around her wrist and he drew her toward the window, shoved it open, then kicked out the screen.

"What do you think you're doing?" she demanded. He was out the window, pulling her through, before she realized what was happening. "Ouch, let go. You're hurting me."

"Hurry up, we haven't got all day."

Breathlessly, she stood beside him and looked around. "All day for what? Just what do you hope to gain by this?"

"Escape." He shot her an evil grin.

"You must be out of your mind. We'll never get away from here...."

"Watch and see."

She dug her heels into the soft pine-covered ground, only to be jerked off balance by a hard yank. "Dad will turn my brothers loose on you, you fool."

"He knows."

"What! Knows what?"

Boston dangled a set of car keys before her disbelieving eyes. "How do you think I got these?"

"But...but...."

"Quit asking questions, Sparky," he growled, "and just do as I say."

Suddenly the whole situation struck her as absurd, and she began to laugh.

"Hush, do you want them to hear?"

"I though you said dad knew?"

"He does—your brothers don't."

"Oh, no!" she wailed. "We'll never get away. The minute they hear a car engine start they'll be in hot pursuit."

"No, they won't. Take a look."

Her eyes followed his pointing finger. For a moment nothing looked unusual; then she noticed most of the parked cars were leaning at a strange angle. When the back of a red head popped up, she couldn't believe it. The head turned with a guilty start of surprise and hurried toward them, brandishing a handful of stick matches.

"Uncle George!"

"You were right, Boston. I did just what you said," he explained breathlessly. "Wedged these little numbers in the air valves and hiss—out comes the air—and a nice flat tire."

"Uncle George!"

"Well, someone had to do something. We decided this was best." His angelic face split from ear to ear in a beaming grin. "I don't remember when I've had so much fun. Oh, to see those interfering boys' faces when they try to drive off. You two had better get going before you're missed." Chuckling, he ducked down, and on tiptoe ran to another car, calling over his shoulder, "I still have one more to do."

Boston grabbed her arm and pulled her along. "Come on. Our getaway car is over here."

"Where are we going?"

"Uh...Houston."

The Cadillac engine purred to life and Boston gunned it to a low growl, letting it warm up before putting it into gear.

Samantha twisted around in the seat to get a better view. "Better hurry," she urged. "Here they come."

Boston reversed at a fast speed then spun the

wheels and headed for the open drive. She watched with bright eyes as her brothers piled out of the back door, bumping and pushing each other in an effort to reach a car first. Hanging over the back of the seat, she reached across and shook his shoulder. ''Look, Boston.''

He turned in time to see her brothers staring first in shocked surprise, then anger, before he accelerated down the gravel driveway.

Turning back around, Samantha wiped her wet cheeks with shaking fingers, then fell victim to a new fit of giggles. ''Did you see Mark raise his fist at you? I hate to tell you this, Boston, but if he ever gets hold of you he'll probably tear you apart.''

''He's got to catch me first.'' They both were laughing as he turned the big car onto the farm road.

''When we get to Houston, you'd better check out of the hotel. I'll get my things and take the car home.'' She sighed.

''What's the matter?''

''I'd better go to Aunt Sally's for a few days and let things cool off. Where are you going? Home?'' He didn't answer and she turned her eyes to the road ahead. What a stupid thing to ask, she silently chided herself. He's probably going to meet some gorgeous woman. And just why should you care? But the question stayed with her, unanswered. Her attention was drawn back to the road when Boston stopped sharply at the sign to the main highway.

''Hey, you're going the wrong way. Houston's that way.''

''No, I'm not.''

"Yes, you are. I ought to know. I've driven this road all my life. Houston's in the opposite direction." She watched the wolfish grin spread across his face.

"We're not going to Houston, Sparky."

CHAPTER FOUR

SAMANTHA STARED at the man behind the wheel, speechless and bewildered. "What!" Her voice came out high and squeaky.

"We're not...."

"I heard what you said, Boston. I want to know why."

His grin stretched into a flashing smile. "You'll see."

"This is kidnapping."

Boston shifted his eyes off the road ahead and examined her slowly from head to toe, lingering on her full shapely mouth and the small swell of her breast. His voice dropped to a sensuous growl. "You're no kid, Sparky."

She faltered a second, then shook herself back to reality. "Would you please stop calling me that absurd name and tell me where we're going."

"On a little trip." He was openly amused and she simmered with anger.

"You're insane! I have to get back to my job."

"No, you don't. Your father told me you were on a four-week vacation. He said you've been overworking and needed a good long rest."

"But . . . but he'll think I'm in Houston."

"Plans change according to the circumstances." He grinned. "I decided if you stayed in Houston your brothers would find you, and the whole mess would start all over again. Only I wouldn't be there to defend your honor."

"Defend my honor!" She yelled at him, her freckled face flushed with resentment. "We didn't do anything."

"Didn't we? Still don't remember, do you?"

"I hate you," she hissed in his ear.

"No, you don't. You're just upset because I have the upper hand. You know, one thing your sister-in-law said was true. Your family has spoiled you."

"Why. . . you—" She raised her hand, but before she could make contact, his fingers were wrapped around her wrist in an iron grip.

"I wouldn't do that if I were you. I hit back."

Samantha drew in a deep calming breath. She couldn't remember ever being so angry with anyone in her life, not even her brothers. Boston Grey could elevate her temperature at least ten degrees every time he opened his mouth. She leaned back in stony silence, her eyes on the open road ahead. "Where are we going?" she asked again for what seemed the hundredth time.

Black eyes twinkled at her and she gritted her teeth. "I think I'll let it be a surprise. Trust me, Sparky—I know what's best, and you'll have a wonderful vacation."

"You don't know me at all. We met last night for the first time."

"How can you say that—" he clucked his tongue at her "—after all we've been to each other?"

"Nothing happened last night," she wailed.

"If you say so."

". . . and I don't want to hear any more about it."

"That's fine with me, but I must tell you, you have the most adorable strawberry birthmark on your left breast." Chuckling, he flipped on the radio and whistled along with Kenny Rogers.

It was a plot, a conspiracy between Boston and her father to drive her crazy for past misdeeds. She began to plan her escape. They would have to stop sometime and she'd find a way to get help. She'd call home, tell her father what Boston intended to do and fabricate a few grisly tales of her own. Call home! With what! Looking around, she realized she had nothing with her: no purse, no money, not even a comb. Suddenly she relaxed against the car seat and smiled. The idea of getting away from the intolerable situation at the ranch was certainly appealing. And the fantasy of being kidnapped only added to the excitement and tickled her fancy. She knew he'd have to stop his little game sometime and they'd have a good laugh before he drove her back to Houston. But till then, she chuckled to herself, she'd play along.

As the big car ate up the miles, she began to wonder just how far he intended to go before turning around. Sneaking a peek at the gas gauge, she groaned. The tank was three-fourths full. She placed her hand lightly on Boston's thigh. "I'm hungry."

"We'll get something later."

"I haven't eaten since breakfast and I'm starving.

Couldn't we stop?'' She pouted up at him and prayed she sounded convincing.

Boston drove the car onto the shoulder of the road, switched off the engine and turned on the emergency flashers. His eyes gleamed at her in the diffused light. "Do you take me for a idiot?" She gave a guilty start. "The minute we get among people you'll make a run for it."

Samantha felt her cheeks flush brighter than her hair. She looked away. Was the man a mind reader? It was totally disconcerting to think she couldn't have any private thoughts at all.

"That's the plan, isn't it?" His hand cupped her chin and forced her head around. "Isn't it?"

"Yes," she replied tersely. She met his hostile eyes and glared back at him, furious with herself for being so obvious.

"I thought so. Let me give you a little warning." His voice purred. "When, and if, we do get around people, you'd better use that beautiful mouth only for smiles."

"If I don't?"

"Then there really will be a scandal to ruin your father's career—and anyone else's close enough to feel the heat."

Samantha's eyes widened and her mouth dropped open in astonishment. He was serious! Her laughing, teasing devil had suddenly sprouted horns and a forked tail. This was no longer a joke. But why?

Boston reached out and with a gentle finger closed her mouth.

"You wouldn't."

"Try me!" He covered the hand lying placid on his thigh and gave a bone-crushing squeeze. "Let me give you another piece of advice—don't ever again use your coquettish tricks on me." Boston leaned closer, his face within inches of hers, and his words fell like tinkling ice cubes in a glass container. "You're dallying with the wrong man, my sweet."

Samantha saw it coming, but before she could move, Boston caught her shoulder and pulled her against the hard wall of his chest. His mouth covered hers in a searing kiss. She pushed ineffectually at his solid form, trying in vain to get away from him, thinking she'd suffocate if he didn't stop. It wasn't supposed to happen this way. She hadn't realized the pouting tricks that had worked successfully over the years on her father and brothers would be useless against this man. She struggled helplessly, and as pulsing seconds stretched out she went limp in the circle of his arms.

Sensing her total surrender and appalled at his cruelty, Boston murmured her name in a tender apology, stroking her hair as if she were a hurt child. He nibbled gently at the trembling mouth, his warm persuasive tongue channeling a path between her parted lips, exploring the honey sweetness there.

Mindlessly Samantha slipped her arms around his neck. His mouth was so invitingly familiar. Her hands threaded their way through the springy waves of his hair, slipping to the soft curls at the nape of his neck, savoring their thickness. Didn't she already know that silky feel? Her body swayed against his in abandonment, urging his mouth closer, returning his passionate kiss with her own. She followed the suggestive and erotic motion of his tongue as the kiss changed character. They clung together, forgetting everything in the intensity of the wild flame of fever that boiled in their veins and threatened to consume them both. The world faded around them, the only sounds in the confined space of the car their heavy breathing and murmurs of pleasure.

Boston's hand tangled in the thick lustrous red hair. His fingers tightened and he pulled her head back, resting his forehead against hers. "This is madness." He choked the words out. "You picked a fine place to seduce me."

Samantha smiled shakily and closed her eyes, her husky voice velvet with emotion. "You started it. I thought I'd finish." Her flippant remark lay quietly between them, lightening the tension.

Laughing, Boston pushed her gently aside, started the car and eased it back onto the highway. "I'll have to remember that and make sure we have better accommodations next time. You've left me in one hell of a state." Uncomfortably, he shifted his weight on the seat and accelerated the car.

A smile of sympathy curved at the corners of her mouth, and erotic thoughts tumbled over each other in confusion as she tried to sort out her feelings. Never in her adult years had a man's kiss had quite that effect. A purely sexual response, she told herself fiercely. It probably happened at one time or another in every woman's life. The thing to do was to get as far away as possible from its source. Only heartache and pain could come from being involved with a man like Boston Grey. He was too used to having women fall in love with him.

"Boston, you do see now why we can't spend any more time together?"

"No."

"Oh, come on. How can you say that after what just happened between us?" Her eyes flashed. "And don't you dare say it was nothing."

"I wouldn't think of saying such a thing," he murmured. "I knew you were going to be trouble the minute I laid eyes on you. There's something there, some chemistry between us. It would be better to face it than run away and wonder the rest of our days what might have been. Do you understand what I'm trying to say?"

"I don't want to find out."

"Why not?"

How could she tell him without sounding silly and immature that she was afraid of him. She'd never been in love before, but she had a sinking feeling in the pit of her stomach that she was falling in love with him and a relationship would never work.

Boston turned off the main highway onto a paved private road that wound through tall pines and thick shrubs. Between the breaks in vegetation she could see a string of lights in the distance.

"Where are we?" she questioned. Deep in thought, she'd missed the sign and was now totally lost.

"I have a friend who maintains a private airport. He's going to fly us out as soon as we get there."

"Fly!" She almost choked on the word. "Boston—'' she grabbed his arm ''—your little joke has gone far enough. Now turn around and take me back to Houston.'' Her hand squeezed harder on the taut muscles of his arm in an effort to regain his full attention. ''Stop this car right now. Have you lost your mind? I'm not flying anywhere with you.''

''Don't start that again.'' He grinned and pried her fingers from his arm. ''I made a promise to your father and I intend to keep it.'' Slowing down, he made another turn as the lights of a long, lighted runway came into view. ''Remember what I told you earlier—not one word.''

''Boston,'' she wailed, ''you can't do this to me.'' She watched with a sinking heart as he stopped the car, got out and hurried over to shake hands with a tiny plump woman. They exchanged a few words and he returned, opened the car door and pulled Samantha out.

A high whining sound pierced the still night, then an engine roared into life and a sleek white ghost taxied out of the darkness. Boston guided her lagging steps along the side of the runway as the small Lear jet rolled to a stop. Samantha backed away when the steel stairs slid down.

''Don't even think it,'' his voice warned beside her.

''But . . . .''

''I told you, not one word.''

He helped her up and into the plush aircraft, then fastened her safety belt. The pilot glanced at them briefly, then the plane began to move forward. As it gained momentum Samantha watched the blurred lights and shadows speed past.

Once they were airborne, Boston placed a wicker picnic basket on the table between them and began to dig around in its contents. Samantha glared at his bent head and promised herself she'd get even. Somehow, someday, he'd pay for this.

He poured the white wine and began to unwrap the sandwiches, handing her one with a napkin. Mutely she accepted his offering, gulped the wine down and held her glass out for more. He arched an eyebrow in amusement and filled her glass.

Samantha's eyes dared him to make any further comments. She nibbled the sandwich thoughtfully, her mind racing through a lifetime of pranks, whims, temper tantrums and finaglings used to get her way with her family. Boston's persuasiveness had the touch of a heavy hand and he needed to be taught a lesson. If you didn't succeed the first time. ... After all, what could he possibly do now? She'd failed once and he'd seen through her plotting, but with a carefully laid plan she'd have him eating out of her hand in no time. She leaned back and closed her eyes, the wine warming her body, her ears attuned to sound of movement, as Boston slid into the seat beside her.

"Boston." She let a faint degree of sadness creep into her voice. "I don't believe you realize just what you've done or the hurt and trouble you've caused my family." She sighed and peeked at him through long lashes, noting the somber alertness of his expression. "My father will be expecting me to return to the farm. What kind of anguish do you think he'll go through when I don't show up and he can't find me anywhere? Can you imagine what it's like for a father to worry about the whereabouts of one of his children, especially a daughter?''

Samantha squeezed a tear from the corner of her eye and let it trickle down her cheek, inwardly smiling. She had his full attention now. The calm, heartbreaking tone never failed to work, and she felt him move uncomfortably. "Daddy's an old man." Mentally she begged her father's forgiveness. He was as healthy as a young horse. "He hasn't been well lately." Turning her head sideways, she used her most seductive smile and raised innocent eyes to his. Biting hands clamped around her arms and Boston hauled her onto his lap.

Samantha gasped as his fingers knotted in her hair and pulled her head back. He stared directly into her startled face. "You just won't give up, will you? I would have thought you were smart enough to heed my first warning." He chuckled but there was no trace of amusement in the rich long sound. She tried unsuccessfully to squirm out of his hold. "Lady, I've been without a woman too long for my liking and I don't take your kind of provocation lightly."

His lips swooped down on hers and she braced herself for their hard contact, but he only nibbled at the corner of her mouth. She quickly realized it wasn't his lips she had to control but his hands. They were everywhere. Breathlessly, she pushed and shoved but to no avail. "Stop it, Boston!" she pleaded. Those experienced hands were too wise. They knew just where to touch, seeking places to make her tingle. "Please stop."

He set her aside, his breathing as erratic as hers,

but his face was a stoic mask while Samantha's flushed with anger and excitement. "You're a spoiled, self-centered and selfish woman." With those words he got up and moved down the aisle to another section of padded seats.

Dumbfounded, she wondered what had happened. *Your ploy has backfired, that's what,* a tiny voice in her mind sneered. *He's not like your father or brothers—or for that matter any other man you've met. He can see right through you and your games.* Samantha moved restlessly, arguing with herself till she finally realized the voice was right. Boston Grey would always know what she was up to. There was an electric chemistry between them, more than sexual awareness. She'd heard stories of women who met men like this. Sometimes a relationship worked out, sometimes it didn't. The encounter could happen anywhere: on the street; in an elevator; at a party, where two pairs of eyes collided across a crowded room. They'd cling and caress with that special something. Her eyelids slipped shut as the day began to take its toll, but before she slid into sleep she wondered if she was strong and wise enough to make the fire between them burn longer and brighter. . . .

"Wake up, Sparky, we're here."

She shook off the persistent hand and opened sleep-swollen eyes, then shut them again. "Go away." A deep voice chuckled in her ear as she was rudely pinched on the bottom. Her eyes flew open and she tried to swing her hand, only to find it tangled in the folds of a soft wooly blanket.

"Come on, sleepyhead. There's a car waiting for

us." He helped her down the plane's short steps into the chilly night air. His hand guided her stumbling movements across the runway to a truck parked in the semidarkness. Once in the warm space, she leaned her head on his shoulder, struggling to wake up and listen to the murmuring of voices; but warmth, wine and exhaustion won out.

SAMANTHA STRETCHED out a cold foot, seeking warmth, and gathered the covers tighter around her bare shoulders. Her foot made contact with long warm legs and she burrowed under them, wiggling her toes.

"Your feet are like icicles woman." Her eyes popped open at the deep voice and she gazed into twinkling black ones. "Come here and I'll get you warm."

Boston pulled her into the circle of his arms, and his hands began to rub vigorously up and down her back. Hot flesh pressed into cold flesh, restoring its heat and doing something more. Her sleep-fogged brain savored the lazy movements of his hands. Fingertips made enticing circles down her spine, then slipped around to cup her rounded buttocks, pressing her close against lean muscular hips. The shock of their nudity brought her fully awake and she pushed away from him, dragging part of the sheet to cover herself.

"Don't you ever sleep in anything?" She glowered at him. "And what am I doing in bed with you *again*? Where are we and what happened to my clothes?" Breathless, she opened her mouth for another spate of questions, but he laid a finger across her lips.

"Please, one question at a time. It's too damn early for one of your tantrums." He lay back smiling, a wicked gleam in his eyes. "First of all—I always sleep in the buff. And, my dear Sparky, take a good look at yourself. Ever since I've known you, you've either been partially undressed or totally naked."

Boston watched the color run up her cheeks and grinned, enjoying the situation. "As to your other questions—" he gave a shrug "—you're in bed with me because it's where you should be. You were so tired last night I undressed you and tucked you in." He turned on his side, facing her, and ran a finger lightly down her arm, lingering on the sensitive area on the inside of her wrist. "After all, it's not as if I've never seen your body before, or held you in my arms while you slept. Is it?"

Samantha snatched her arm away from his touch and glared at him. "We never made love!" she snapped.

"If you say so, my love," he chuckled.

"Stop calling me your love. I'm not your anything." The final words were spoken precisely. "Is this your house?" Her eyes traveled over the neat but sparsely furnished room. "And where are we?"

He turned on his back and smiled up at the ceiling. "Questions, questions. Are you always so talkative this early in the morning? I'll have to remember it for further use."

"Boston."

He heaved a lengthy sigh. "We're in New Mexico.

This cottage belongs to friends of mine, Cable and Sara Ford. Your clothes are being laundered." His head swiveled around and their eyes clashed. "Does that answer all your questions?"

"Some," she admitted grudgingly. "Where in New Mexico are we, and what happens now?"

Boston closed his eyes wearily. "Can't you wait till Sara brings us some coffee?"

"No."

"I can think of much more pleasant things to occupy your mouth than questions."

"I bet you can." She moved to the edge of the bed, wanting to put as much distance as possible between her fading willpower and tempting suggestions. "Just answer me."

"Hmm," he responded sleepily.

She leaned over and shook him awake, then returned to her side of the bed. "Don't you dare go back to sleep."

"It would be wiser to have me asleep than awake with these thoughts that keep running around in my head. Why, my baser appetites are liable to take over and I might not be able to control them," he teased.

Samantha gave an unladylike snort of disgust. "I wouldn't put anything past you, Mr. Grey."

"Mr. Grey, is it? How formal."

She visibly bristled. "Believe me, I'm just as sick of asking questions as you are of answering them, but you could at least have the common decency to answer me now that we're out of Texas and the reach of my family."

"Sparky, you're riding a dead horse into the ground. Let it be."

She clamped her mouth shut at his harsh words. Furiously, she began to tug and pull at the sheet, wrapping it around her body as fast as her shaking hands would allow.

"What the hell do you think you're doing?" he rasped, grabbing for the trailing sheet as it slithered across his half-exposed body.

She stood beside the bed and gave the sheet a final yank, leaving him sprawled and completely uncovered. "Freeze! I'm going to find somewhere else to sleep."

"Damn it, Sparky, you come back here." He jumped up and started toward her, but they both froze at the unexpected knock on the door.

"Boston, are you awake?" a whispered female voice inquired from the other side of the door.

"Just a minute, Sara." He grabbed the end of Samantha's sheet and pivoted, wrapping his lower half as he went.

"Come in."

Samantha watched, embarrassed, as Sara Ford stuck her head inside the open doorway and burst out laughing.

"Now that's what I call togetherness." She winked at them, then walked farther into the room, carrying Samantha's clean clothes, a new toothbrush, toothpaste and a hairbrush. "I'll leave these here and let you two dress. Coffee's made and breakfast is ready." She turned to leave then stopped. "Boston, everything you ordered from Cable is packed and ready to go." Chuckling, she shut the door gently.

"Get dressed." Boston stepped out of his cocoon and unselfconsciously walked to where his clothes lay.

Samantha watched, fascinated by his body, the enticingly curved behind, narrowed hips and endless legs. Lean muscles rippled with each step and his smooth tan skin stretched taut as he stooped and began to pull on his jeans.

"I'm glad you find my body so pleasing, but we don't have time for a closer inspection." He turned, buttoning a freshly starched white western shirt, and smiled at her bemused face. Walking toward her, he patted a flushed cheek and gave her a quick hard kiss. "You'll get used to it."

I hope not, she thought, and rushed to the bathroom. She didn't want to give Boston and Sara time to talk without her being there. She was sick of not knowing what was being planned for her.

SAMANTHA FOLLOWED THE LAUGHING VOICES and the smell of food. Barefoot, she stepped into the small kitchen, stopping conversation with her presence. Boston introduced her to Sara and handed her a hot mug of strong coffee. She didn't know how to act. He had put them in an awkward position and she could only cringe inwardly at what Sara and her husband must think. Sitting at the table, she inspected the other woman closely. Sara Ford was an attractive woman about thirty-eight or forty. Samantha guessed they were about the same height and size.

Sara caught her assessing look and smiled, her brown eyes crinkling at the corners as their twinkling depths relayed friendship and amusement. Samantha relaxed, picked up her knife and fork and began to eat, her ears alert to the conversation.

"Boston," she interrupted their reminiscing, "I can't find my shoes."

"I have them," Sara informed her, and at Samantha's puzzled look she went on. "I needed them for your size." She picked up a large box and handed it to her. The Tony Lama box proclaimed their maker and Samantha pulled out a beautiful pair of pecan leather hand-tooled cowboy boots.

"They're very nice. . . ."

"Oh, I had a ball spending Boston's money," Sara said. "I've bought you jeans, shirts, underwear, socks, a sheepskin coat and personal items." She ticked them off on her fingers and smiled hugely at Boston and Samantha, pleased with herself. "They're all on the pack mule."

Samantha choked on her coffee, coughing and sputtering as Boston pounded her back. "Pack mule!" She squeezed her eyes tightly shut, afraid to ask again but determined to find out what was going on. She cocked her head sideways and caught Boston's blank expression and knew she was in for trouble. "What pack mule?"

"Why, my love, the one that's going to carry all our provisions." His saccharine-sweet voice immobilized all movement and thought. A firm hand pulled her up and guided her lagging steps to the back door.

"I don't understand and I don't think I want to."
Her voice was scarcely audible as she took in the two
saddled horses: one a big buckskin gelding with the
build of a fine quarter horse, the other equally large
but daintier.

"The black mare's name is Sam," he laughed.
"You two should suit each other just fine."

Her eyes shifted to the stocky mule, his back load-
ed and covered with a canvas tarp. "And just where
do you think you're taking me?"

"Keep your voice down," he warned. "I told you,
to my ranch."

"On horseback? Why can't we drive?"

"Because we can't."

"I won't do it."

"You have no choice in the matter." They stood
toe to toe. Her head thrown back, she glared up into
his serious face.

"How long will it take to get there?" She frowned,
taking in his shifting eyes and evasive manner. "How
long?" she ground out between stiff lips.

"Oh. . . a couple of days."

"How many?" she demanded.

"Four or five."

"Days!" she squeaked.

"That's right." He smiled.

"Do you mean to stand there and tell me we're going to have to camp out at night, sleep on the hard
ground?" She gulped for breath.

"Yes."

"No!" She grabbed the front of his shirt, twisting
the material under her fingers. "Are you trying to

kill me?'' she hissed at him. ''I haven't been on a horse in two years and I've never, *never*, camped out. I don't want to,'' she wailed.

''You'll love it.''

''No, I won't.'' Her flaming eyes raked his face, praying this was all a hideous joke.

''Trust me, Sparky, you'll have a great time.'' He pried her fingers loose, one by one, from his mangled shirtfront.

''You don't understand.'' She raised her voice. ''I like to be clean, brush my teeth twice a day. . . .''

''You can still do that,'' he said, trying to quiet and reassure her at the same time.

''How?''

''Sara's provided everything you'll need. Believe me, this will be a luxury trip compared to some I've taken.''

The air crackled with her suppressed violence. ''I won't go.'' Each word was delivered icily. ''I will not sleep on the hard cold ground and be dinner for all those bugs—'' she shuddered ''—and crawly things.'' She turned appealingly to an onlooking Sara. ''He's kidnapping me.'' Sara frowned, and Samantha started to go on when a hand clamped over her mouth, cutting off her next plea.

''Now, now. We don't want to burden Sara with our little problems, not after all the trouble she's gone to.'' He gave her a meaningful look. ''Do we?''

CHAPTER FIVE

"DAMN, DUMB JACKASS," Samantha mumbled under her breath, glowering at the animal's broad shaggy gray rump. Transferring her dagger gaze to Boston's back, she mumbled the same words at him. They'd ridden for six hours with only one short break for a quick sandwich and a drink of tepid water for lunch. Ever since setting out she'd refused to speak to him, stubbornly declining his offer to ride at his side. Instead she trailed behind the pack mule Boston led. It seemed as if the mule had a sadistic streak like his leader. She'd rein in her horse and change sides, trying in vain to get out from behind the animal as he kicked up his hind hooves and showered her in a cloud of dust and grit and other unmentionables. She'd no sooner wipe her face and cough up the dust from her lungs than the rotten beast would move in front of her and pull the same trick again. There were times she could have sworn the animal was laughing at her as she watched his long ears twitch back and forth.

The summer heat shimmered in waves off the dry packed earth, forcing Samantha to pull the wide brim of her cowboy hat further down on her sweaty brow to shield her eyes from the glaring rays. Still, in the arid countryside there was pleasure to the eye. Wild flowers of every color sprouted between rocks and blanketed open areas with their beauty. This was a land of contrast—truly a land of enchantment with its giant mesas, canyons, high cliff dwellings and snowcapped mountains. Looking toward the horizon she sighed wistfully at the line of green in the distance and remembered Boston's telling her they'd soon reach the cool pine forest.

She shifted her weight once more on the hard seat and groaned. After long unaccustomed hours in the saddle, her body screamed in pain. Every muscle ached and she prayed for a fast death rather than the slow torture Boston was subjecting her to. She slumped further in the saddle, no longer able to hold her back straight. Her long legs hung from the stirrups, too weak to grip her horse's sides for control. Miles back she had tied the reins into a knot and looped them over the saddle horn. She just clung on for dear life and allowed her horse to play follow the leader. She thought disjointedly that if they ever stopped and she had enough strength, she was going to kill Boston Grey with her bare hands.

"I think we'll stop here and make camp for the night," Boston called back to her, reining in his horse.

With glazed eyes Samantha watched his shaking shoulders as he took in her dirty exhausted figure. Grabbing the saddle horn, she eased her leg over the cantle and let her body slip slowly down till her feet touched the ground. Please, horse, she begged silently, don't move. She rested her hot forehead against the side of the saddle and let go of her support. For a suspended second she thought her trembling legs would hold her weight, but her knees suddenly gave way and she landed with a thud on the hard rocky ground.

"Are you all right?"

"What do you care, you sadist," she snarled, too exhausted to lift her bowed head.

"Here, let me help you." He was openly laughing at her as his hands closed around her arms.

"Leave me alone." She slapped at his persistent helping hands. "Haven't you done enough to me without dragging me over the ground? *Go away*."

"Be sensible, Sparky. You can't sit there the rest of the night."

"Watch me," Samantha told him coldly, a fine film of perspiration beading her forehead. Pulling off her hat, she began to fan her hot face. She didn't want to give him the satisfaction of seeing she couldn't move or that her body felt like one gigantic bruise.

"We have to set up camp."

"Fine. You do it," she murmured tiredly, then smiled chillingly at him. "This little jaunt was *your* bright idea, so *you* do all the work." Unfeeling brute. What did he expect of her? Did he think she was made of stone like him?

"Have it your way, but you're going to get mighty cold and hungry sitting there all night."

As he walked away, Samantha followed him with her eyes, thinking bitterly that he didn't even seem tired. She watched him bend over and unbuckle the straps on one of the packs. His backside was too tempting to resist. She searched quickly for something to fill her hand. Her fingers wrapped around a pecan-size rock, and after testing its weight, she took precise aim and threw it.

"What the—" he yelped and spun around, rubbing briskly at his injured bottom.

"Sit on that for a while and see how it feels."

"You've got a mean arm, lady." His lips twisted in a half smile, then he asked with indignant interest, "Where did you learn to throw with such deadly aim?"

"I have six older brothers—remember? You learn at a very early age to use every dirty trick in the book to survive among the masses."

"I'll keep that in mind."

"You do that," she told him sarcastically, and slumped back on the hard ground, pulling her hat down over her eyes to shut out the bright glare of the setting sun. She wondered if her body would ever recover, and groaned out loud pitifully when she thought of four more days of this torture.

Samantha dozed fitfully, listening to Boston's whistling as he set up camp for the night. Loath to admit the truth of his warning, she shivered as the fierce golden sun dipped behind towering snow-covered peaks. She was cold and hungry but determined to stand by her words. Her body tensed at the approach of heavy footsteps.

"Get up." There was a commanding tone to his voice she'd never heard before and she lifted her tired dull eyes.

"I can't get up."

"Samantha," he warned. Then he really looked at her for the first time since they'd stopped. Her exhaustion was plain for him to see; her lackluster eyes focused somewhere over his shoulder and her dirt-streaked face showed him all too clearly the pain she was in. Cursing softly under his breath, he scooped her up and cradled her gently against his chest. "You should have told me. I thought you were being obstinate."

"I tried." She sniffed into his shirtfront.

Boston lowered her feet to the ground and winced at her moan of pain. "Are those real tears, or are you playacting again?"

"They're real," she sniffed.

"Can you stand?" His hands held her shoulders firmly and when he eased the pressure to allow her to stand on her own, she swayed precariously. "Lock your knees."

She didn't argue this time, but did as she was told. "Where are you going?" she asked as he turned and walked away. She tilted to the left, then corrected her stance by shifting her weight, only to tilt to the right. Her eyes widened as she heard an all-too-familiar muffled sound. "What's so funny?"

"You!" He was walking back toward her with one of his T-shirts draped across his arm. "You look like a woman who's been aboard a ship for months and can't get her ground legs back."

"Very funny," she snarled. "What's that for?" She nodded toward the shirt he was holding up to her. She watched him squint one eye as if to size up her measurements and compare them with his T-shirt.

"Well," he drawled, "as efficient as Sara is, she neglected to pack you anything to sleep in, so I guess we'll just have to improvise."

Samantha eyed the thin cotton shirt balefully. "I'm not sleeping in that. I'll sleep in my clothes."

"No, you won't. You can't get a good night's rest dressed like that. Now strip."

She closed her eyes and swayed. "Please, Boston, leave me alone and just let me die in peace." But her plea was ignored, and Boston was down on his knees lifting one of her feet, working the boot off before she could complain again. She snapped her mouth shut, too tired to continue the fight. Her forehead furrowed into a frown as she grabbed at his shoulder for support. *He's broken my spirit completely,* she thought dejectedly, and sniffed out loud.

"What's the matter now?"

"Nothing."

He looked up at her, struggling to hide his amusement as he worked the zipper down on her jeans. "If nothing's wrong, then what's all that sniveling about?" Pulling the jeans down, he lifted one foot then the other and flung the jeans aside.

"I hate you, do you know that?" she said softly.

He stood and began to unbutton her shirt. "You've told me that a few times." The shirt was stripped from her shoulders and sent flying to join the rest of her clothes.

When his fingers began to undo the front clasp of her lacy white bra, she stayed his hands with her own. "I'm not taking this off."

Boston stepped back and surveyed her stubborn face. "Yes, you are. Either you take it off or I will. Which is it to be?"

She looked into his night-black eyes, glinting in the firelight, and gave up. Snatching the T-shirt from his hands, she hurriedly slipped it over her head, groaning at her protesting muscles. Neglecting to put her arms through the arms of the shirt, she began to unclasp her bra. She watched Boston's puzzled expression at her unusual body contortions.

"Come, on." He snapped his fingers. "You're not going to sleep bound up and uncomfortable."

Samantha let the bra drop to the ground, grinning triumphantly at his surprise. She worked her arms back out through their rightful place and let them hang limply at her sides.

He shook his head and picked up the small wisp of lace. "I don't know why you even bother. You haven't enough to be so modest about."

She looked down with a grimace of disgust. "I guess your tastes run to big-chested women?" Somehow the thought made her feel worse.

Boston didn't reply but merely grinned. He picked up her bra and pitched it on the stack of her discarded clothes, then turned back one corner of the sleeping bag. "Crawl in."

She moaned in pure ecstasy as her sore bottom came in contact with the soft warm bedding, and for the first time she began to look around the campsite with interest. A small fire glowed warmly in a circle of rocks. A pan sat to one side, its contents bubbling invitingly, and the aroma of dinner assailed her senses. Her mouth began to water and her stomach growled in protest. Dragging her eyes from the tantalizing sight, she began to look around for Boston's sleeping bag. Finding nothing that resembled the one she was in, she looked down, suddenly taking note of the size of hers—theirs?

Boston squatted down beside her with a pan of warm water. He handed her a thin bar of soap and a washcloth. "I thought you'd like to wash before dinner."

"Thank you," she mumbled. He moved back to the fire and began to dish out the stew into tin plates. Glaring at his back, she couldn't help her next question, even though she knew the answer. "Where are you going to sleep?"

He turned his head and looked at her as if she'd just uttered the most asinine words in the world. "Do you see another sleeping bag other than the one you're in?" She shook her head. "Then that answers your question."

They ate in silence, Boston on the opposite side of the fire, frowning, while she was neatly tucked into their double sleeping bag. After dinner he brought her a fresh cup of water, a toothbrush and toothpaste. She thanked him and received a grunt in return. Was he angry that things weren't going according to his plan? What did he expect, a night of sexual delights under the stars? Well, she had news for him. She turned on her side and listened to him undress, then slide into the sleeping bag and zip them in.

"Would you like a massage? It might help relax some of those abused muscles."

His voice reached her in the dark, a velvet sound that slipped down her spine and ended tingling in her toes. *Here it comes*, she told herself, *the big seduction scene*. And if he wanted to force the issue, she knew she'd be lost. Not only did she lack the strength to fight him, she lacked the willpower. "No, thank you." Holding her breath, she waited and listened for his next move. None came, just the sound of his settling down for a night's sleep. She quietly let her pent-up breath out and wondered why she suddenly felt so alone.

THE SECOND AND THIRD DAY were almost identical with the first, with a few exceptions. Samantha's aching muscles had now become accustomed to the long hours in the saddle and she was riding beside Boston instead of trailing behind like a truant child. But the biggest change was in Boston. He now rode in silence, fierce scowls alternating with thoughtful frowns on his face. Samantha glanced sideways and wondered what weighty problem he was struggling to work out.

She shrugged her shoulders and looked around for the first time in a long while, taking an interest in the surrounding land. They were trudging along on a dirt road that led through piñon and juniper, sparse grama grass and the occasional clump of prickly pear with its chartreuse bloom. The scent of pine was all around. Then, climbing the high ditch on the roadside, they entered the ponderosa forest. She reined in her horse and sat in the shelter of the cool shade listening to the almost cathedral hush. It was like entering another world where every living thing moved in a quiet, easy motion so as not to disturb the serenity.

"What's the matter?"

Boston's deep voice jolted her out of her thoughts, and she shifted her wondering eyes to his frowning face. "Nothing. I was just enjoying the beauty. I don't believe I've ever seen such a place before."

He muttered something beneath his breath and started to move on. Samantha touched her heels to the horse's sides and trotted up beside him. Reaching over, she grabbed his reins and gave them a hard pull. "Listen, Boston! I'm tired of your grouchy attitude and glaring looks. I didn't force *you* on this ride—remember? So don't take your sour disposition out on me." She flung the reins loose and watched his startled horse prance away. "All you have to do to be rid of me, *mister*, is point me in the direction of the nearest town." She kicked her horse and set out ahead of him, her back ramrod straight and her chin high.

"You're going the wrong way, Sparky." His voice echoed through the big trees and she wheeled around, flashing him a look of pure loathing.

"Okay, okay," he said. "So I've been a bear. I'm sorry, but this whole thing has become more complicated than I envisioned."

"What do you mean?" She looked around, a chill suddenly slithering down her spine. "Are we lost? Is that what you've been trying to work out?" She nudged her horse to his side and reached out, her fingers biting into his forearm. "Tell me, Boston. I . . . I can take it."

Sparkling midnight eyes looked into hers. "I'm sure you could, little firecracker, but no, we're not lost."

"Just what do you find so amusing!" she demanded, bristling at being the butt of his laughter.

"You." He patted her hand, then pried her fingers loose and raised them to his lips.

She snatched her hand away. "I don't like you at all today," she said.

"Yes you do," he chuckled. "Come on, we need to find a place to camp tonight."

They rode in a peaceful silence, the tension finally broken. Bright warm sunlight filtered through heavy branches, and overhead Samantha glimpsed patches of limitless blue sky. A steller's jay scolded her from a nearby tree and a mountain chickadee swung upside down from a small branch, chattering at them for disturbing his sleep.

Suddenly she felt lighthearted and carefree, all tiredness washed away. Ahead, as far as she could see, mountains rose in a tumbled mass, their snow-capped peaks reaching almost to the sky. She took in a deep cleansing breath and let it out in a long contented sigh. "Boston, why did you agree to do the commercials?"

He turned in the saddle, watching and waiting for her to move up beside him, his face thoughtful. "Money."

"Oh, but...."

"That's all there was to it, Sparky. I needed some quick cash." He kicked his horse forward. "Most of my money is invested. I required more than the paying interest and didn't want to touch the principal."

Immediately the question came to mind and was on her lips before she could reconsider. "Will you ever sing again, Boston?" His eyebrows drew together in a scowl and she went on quickly. "I mean, it's been three years since the accident and you must realize everyone will be curious to know if you'll sing again." She drew in a short breath and gave him a twisted smile of embarrassment. "What I'm so clumsily trying to ask...."

"I know." He kicked his horse forward, moving ahead of her. "And the answer is no. I will never sing before a live audience again." He shifted around, his black eyes snapping with hostility. "I'll discuss anything with you, but not that. Do you understand?" His voice was flat and devoid of emotion. "The subject of my voice is off limits."

Samantha nodded her head and followed, sick at heart at the loss of his beautiful voice. A deep sadness engulfed her as she realized what a devastating blow it must have been for him to finally admit his career was at an end. She wondered briefly if he missed the notoriety and excitement. Of course he did, she scolded herself. Why else would he refuse to talk about his loss? And why would he need quick cash? Had he squandered his wealth as so many performers in the industry did? The thought of expensive presents lavished on beautiful women made her cringe. She remembered the last gossip item before his accident. He was escorting a gorgeous actress to her latest movie premiere. The columnist had hinted the diamond necklace she wore was a gift from a close admirer. Was it Boston? No, Samantha chuckled silently. Boston was the type of man on whom women lavished gifts. There wasn't any reason for him to pay for favors. Still, the thought of all the women he'd been associated with rankled. How could she possibly compete with their beauty and sophistication even if she wanted to?

They came to a wide stream lined with great cottonwoods; high overhead the uppermost branches rustled in the breeze. Sharp sunlight dappled the stream with sparkling colors that bounded off rocks and water. Where the heavily leaved branches hung, the bright rays had lost their sharp definition, throwing off soft cool shades of dark green. Samantha crossed her arms over the saddle horn and gazed at the clear water bubbling and swirling over slick polished rocks. How she'd love to jump in and be clean for the first time in days.

"How long before we reach your ranch?"

"You see that shallow area about a mile down?" She followed his pointing finger and nodded. "That's where we cross. My land starts on the opposite side of the stream, and it's over half a day's ride to the ranch house from there."

"We're that close? I thought you said we'd be out at least five days."

"We've made better time than I anticipated." He turned his horse from the water's edge. "We'll make camp a little farther back."

Samantha looked over her shoulder and gave a deep sigh. "Why can't we camp beside the river?"

Boston shot her a hard look and gave a snort of disgust. "You should know better than that." He studied her blank face, then went on in a tone he might have used on a simpleminded child. "After dark, animals come down to the stream to drink and wash. Believe me, it's safer not to be in their path."

She thrust her chin out, her eyes glinting. "You needn't talk down to me, Boston Grey. How do you expect me to know? Just because I lived most of my life on a horse ranch does not make me an expert on the great outdoors. I'm a city girl." She threw her leg over the back of the saddle and hopped down. Unbuckling the cinch, she pulled the saddle from the horse's back and carried it over to where Boston had dropped his. She stood still, her eyes following the line of trees, picking out the perfect place to undress and bathe privately. Spinning around, her voice excited, she asked, "Boston, do you think there are any snakes in the river?"

"Probably. Why?" He smiled at her shiver of repugnance.

She reached up and helped him untie the stiff rope holding the canvas tarp over the pack mule's load. "I want to take a bath."

"You would—city girl. If you splash around enough, any snakes in the vicinity will leave." He watched her shudder. "They're just as afraid of you as you are of them."

"You're sure?"

"Yes."

She jumped up and started to walk off, but he grabbed her arm and hauled her back. "Not so fast.

We set up camp first, eat an early dinner, then you can have your bath.''

Samantha crinkled her sunburned nose at him. ''Do you have any idea how sick I am of beef stew and beans?''

''We can change the menu tonight.'' He laughed at her brightening smile. ''Beans and beef stew.''

''Ugh.'' She gave him a dreamy look. ''Do you know what I'd give for some fresh vegetables, or a thick juicy steak—cooked rare—and some soft hot bread, dripping in butter.'' Sighing, she shook her head and picked up one of the packs. ''I bet my family is just now sitting down to dinner. Thinking of all that home cooking is driving me crazy! I can see dad at the head of the table, carving knife in hand, ready to slice the roast beef.'' She closed her eyes and could smell the tantalizing aroma. ''Poor dad,'' she murmured, ''I bet he's worried sick about me.'' A hand touched her arm and she opened misty eyes, meeting Boston's compassionate gaze.

''Your father knows exactly where you are.''

''How can that be? You told him you were taking me to Houston.''

Boston cupped her elbow and led her over to a large rock. ''Sit down.'' He sat beside her and took one of her hands in his. ''Your father was appalled at what was happening. The things your brothers had done and your sisters-in-law were saying to you made him sick at heart. Do you remember when he showed me the library to use the phone?'' She nodded her head. ''He told me then how upset he was at what they were doing to you—supposedly all for his sake, but it was really old resentments finally coming to the surface. Your father and Uncle George were planning a way to get you out when I made my offer to take you back to Houston. They were agreeable at first; then they remembered you were on four weeks' vacation and knew you wouldn't want to spend them there. We all agreed it was too close. Your brothers would find you too easily. So I made another offer to take you with me.'' He grinned at her openmouthed surprise. ''Oh, they weren't sold on the idea at first, not until I told them the setup at the ranch and assured them you'd be well chaperoned.''

''You mean they were willing to let me come away with you—alone!'' she interrupted him, her voice high with shock.

Boston straightened from his lounging position. ''Yes, of course. No matter what *you* may think, I'm a man of my word, and I gave my word to your father and Uncle George I'd watch over you.''

''Well, I'll be damned!'' She shook her head. ''You mean they believed you?''

He grabbed her arm and gave it an angry shake, then let go when he heard her soft chuckles. ''You women are so suspicious. We men understand and recognize a man of honor,'' he said with great dignity.

''Oh! What a con artist you must be,'' she laughed, leaning against his shoulder for support. ''I can see your story working on Uncle George. He's rather naive and sees only the good in people. But daddy! How I wish I'd been there. It must have been quite a scene—one old rake and one young rake conning each other.''

"What the hell are you babbling about?"

Samantha started to giggle at the picture her mind conjured up of her father's innocent face. She'd seen that expression many times over the years and knew he was at his most conniving when he wore it. Never would she tell Boston of the past couple of years when her father had tried to play matchmaker. He thought it was time she married and settled down to a home, husband and children. So far she'd managed to weasel out of his maneuverings. Now he'd thrown her into close proximity with a man he must have realized she was very attracted to. Samantha could almost hear the wheels turning with his thoughts—*keep them together and they'll fall in love*. What a devil he was.

"Would you please explain to me what you find so funny?" He gave her shoulder another shake. "And I resent your calling me a rake. Sure, I've sown a few wild oats in my time."

"A few!" she exclaimed. "From what I've read, you'd qualify for a government farm loan."

He grinned. "That's unfair.

"Samantha, do you enjoy living in New York, cut off from your friends and family?"

The lightning change of subject caught her off guard. "I have friends in New York, very close friends," she said, her voice defiant.

"Yes, but they're not like the people you grew up with. Don't you miss them?"

"Yes."

"I understand why you thought you had to move away, but so far?"

She smiled a little sadly. "When I finally got fed up with what my brothers were doing I mailed at least twenty résumés to various companies, all outside of Texas. Duncan, Stark was the first company to respond and I snapped the job up. I flew to New York for the interview on a Wednesday, returned home on Friday, packed everything I owned and moved out and was on my way back to New York on Tuesday."

Boston chuckled. "You didn't give your family time to protest or try to talk you out of moving, did you?"

"No."

"What happened to your painting? Did the bright lights of the big city seduce you to give up your talents?"

"How did you know I painted?"

"You forget, Sparky, I was in your dad's library for a considerable length of time. The painting above the fireplace is breathtaking. I don't understand why you gave it up. It's criminal. A person with your talents...." He shook his head and was silent.

"I didn't give up painting." She knew the work he was referring to. A huge canvas depicting everyday life in a Crow Indian village. She laughed a little self-consciously. "As a matter of fact, I have about two dozen finished canvases in my apartment. At first it was hard for me to adjust to New York's rushed lifestyle and I was reserved about making friends and going out. So I stayed home and painted."

"Have you ever thought of holding a one-man— excuse me—one-woman showing?"

"Oh, no. I couldn't. I'm not *that* good."

"I think you are, Sparky."

Samantha shifted uncomfortably under his warm gaze. She didn't want to continue this conversation. It brought back memories of her family and she was already a little homesick. She tried to blank it out of her mind but her thoughts set their own course, and a secret smile lifted the corners of her mouth.

For years her family had teased her about her "dabbling," everyone except her father. One year when she'd inquired what he wanted for his birthday, he led her to the library and pointed to the empty space above the fireplace.

"One of your paintings."

Thrilled, yet at the same time scared she wasn't good enough, she'd straightened her shoulders and agreed to tackle the project. She'd researched Indian life, clothing and customs for authenticity, then plunged into the assignment, nearly making herself sick with the long hours it took to complete the painting in time. It was worth every agonizing second she'd spent just to see the awed faces of her usually taunting brothers.

Samantha reached out and picked up a can of beef stew. "Let's get this gourmet meal over with. I want to take a nice long bath." She caught the gleam in his eyes and shot him a warning look. "Alone, Boston."

"What?"

"Alone. . . . I want privacy for my bath."

"Of course, Sparky. I wouldn't dream of interfering." He gave her his famous lopsided grin and walked away.

She stood stone still, uneasy with unresisting capitulation. A tingling chill ran across her skin as she remembered how she'd caught him staring at her all morning, his eyes dark and fathomless. It now seemed that whatever problems had been troubling him he'd managed to solve.

Boston ladled stew and beans onto two tin plates and handed one to her. She wrinkled her nose and pushed the globs of food around, watching him eat with gusto. She grimaced with distaste and wondered if he could truly like the evil stuff. Picking up her coffee, she took a sip, her eyes meeting his over the rim of the cup.

"Better eat while it's hot."

"No, thank you." She looked down, breaking his steady gaze. "I've lost my appetite." Taking another sip of coffee, she folded her legs, then set the cup down. "Boston, who lives at the ranch with you?" She caught the fleeting, startled expression and wondered if it was her imagination that his face paled.

Boston gulped his coffee, then cleared his throat. "Let's see. . . . There's the six ranch hands and a couple of young boys from the orphanage I hire every summer." He ticked each person off on his fingers without lifting his eyes to hers. "Then there's Pearl."

Samantha raised a questioning eyebrow at his sudden reluctance and the long pause.

"Pearl's my housekeeper and cook." He shifted his weight uncomfortably and Samantha could have sworn he was nervous. "Most weekends I have some guests," he mumbled, then continued hurriedly, "and of course there's Elijah." He gazed pensively into his coffee as the silence lengthened between them. Then, as if making up his mind, he shrugged and went on. "Elijah Lightfoot is half-breed Jicarilla Apache Indian." He looked up and smiled a warm smile of remembrance.

Samantha sat motionless, afraid if she so much as blinked an eye it would break his concentration. This was the first time she felt he was going to open up and tell her something about his life.

"I first met Elijah when I was about eleven years old. He turned up at the orphanage one morning, dirty and hungry. A pitiful sight really, but proud, and demanding a job. Father Paul was about to call the police when Father Brian walked outside. He invited Elijah in, and when they returned Elijah had a job as a handyman and the use of one of the employee's cottages. We never could figure out how he did it, and to this day he's never told me how he managed it."

Boston stared off into space and chuckled. "That old man taught us about the land and how to read it. He was quite a tracker and nothing missed his sharp eyes. We gave him a bad time about his braids at first. Later, we all tried to grow our hair long until Father Paul made us get it cut off. I don't know why Elijah took to me, I was the worst of the lot." Boston laughed again and went on. "One night some of the other boys and I broke into his cottage and I had my first taste of hundred-proof whiskey. After a while of telling tales of what the old Apache would do if he caught us nipping his firewater, the others left. I was the instigator, so I stayed to prove what a brave man I was. Well, you can guess what happened. I got sick as a dog about the time Elijah came home."

His face softened in the firelight and she asked, "What did he do?"

"Laughed—said, 'Serves you good and right, boy. Just remember this the next time you get too damn big for your britches and find yourself tempted to steal my liquor.' He couldn't shake me from his side from then on. Elijah took care of me, loved me like a father and taught me about life—his way. When I left the orphanage for college, Elijah went with me. It wasn't until later years I learned that he provided most of my clothes and pocket money. Now we've come full circle and I take care of him. He's getting cantankerous and doesn't move as fast as he used to, but don't let his age and slowness fool you. His mind is still as sharp as a razor."

Samantha looked up and studied Boston's face. Bathed in the glow of the dying fire, his features were shadowed and softened by happier memories of the past. How could one man be so complex? A tease most of the time, yet he could be warm and tender or harsh and cruel in the blinking of an eyelid. She loved his ability to laugh at himself, but what surprised her most was to find he had a great capacity for love and a strong sense of loyalty to those he gave his love to. Loath to disturb him, she rose quietly and began to gather a towel, soap and change of clothes.

CHAPTER SIX

SAMANTHA STEPPED into the clear stream and sucked in a hard breath, shocked as the icy water reached her thighs. Slowly she inched her way forward until the water covered her breasts. She took a deep breath, plunged down and came up sputtering. It was freezing. She moved to a shallow spot, pulled off the bar of soap she'd tied around her neck and began to lather her body and hair. After three days of dirt and sweat she thought she'd never get clean and she scrubbed harder at her grimy hair. She was heading into deeper water when a noise from behind caught her attention. Spinning around she glimpsed a moving shadow between the tall trees, then caught the flash of tan flesh and a long male body as Boston hit the water in a beautifully executed dive.

"Damn him," she muttered. "He promised to let me have some privacy." She stepped gingerly over the slippery rocks to get out of his way and aimed for the middle of the stream. A slick black head popped up in front of her. Bright eyes opened and the quick grin widened into a full-fledged smile. "You promised," she challenged.

"I'm just as dirty as you and couldn't wait." He moved closer, never taking his eyes from her, purpose and determination in their inky depths.

She spun around, presenting him her back, and slipped down further into the water. "Go away, Boston!"

"No."

At the unusual note in his voice she looked over her shoulder. His black eyes were fastened on hers with an intent she'd never seen there before. "Oh, no!" She dived under, leaving Boston staring at a circle of soapy bubbles. She hadn't gone far before fingers of iron clasped her arms and hauled her to the surface and against the warm wall of his chest. Her back still to his, she hurriedly pushed the wet mass of hair from her eyes. One hand slipped from her arm to a breast and pulled her closer still.

"Boston." She didn't want to want him, didn't want to feel this aching need for him, didn't want to fall in love with him. Heaven help her if she did. He was everything she should loath: a quick-talking devil, a womanizer and, most dangerous of all, a man with time on his hands and a woman too close. "No. I don't want this."

"Then why is your heart fluttering like an excited bird? You want me, you know you do. Don't pull away from me, Sparky." The last words were whispered in her ear and his hands began to move slowly down her stomach. At his touch she trembled. "See, you do want me. Did you think you could hide from me? I know you, Sparky. It might be just days since we've met, but I've known you all my life."

His hands were playing havoc with her reasoning. "Boston, please. This can't happen. It won't work.

We don't know each other, and...we live different lives in different parts of the country."

"It'll last, honey, just as long as we make it last. Nothing worth having comes easy. You have to work and fight for it."

Samantha leaned back to rest against him and twisted her head around to meet his cool lips and warm moist tongue, all coherent arguments drowning in the hunger of his mouth and his velvet voice. Why? Why was it every time he touched her she lost all willpower to fight back? Was she so lost in his special brand of seduction that resolve drifted away like a fallen leaf in the swirling river current?

There was no time to search for answers, only time to feel. Driven by need, she turned in the circle of his embrace, wrapped her arms around his neck and held him close. His hands moved slowly down her back and cupped her buttocks, pulling her to him, letting her feel his desire and need. She arched against him, her body responding to his movements as though it had a mind of its own.

"That's it, show me how much you don't want me. Touch me, Sparky."

Her hands threaded through his wet hair, forcing his lips back to hers for a long fervent kiss.

"It's been hell sleeping with you these past four days and not touching you. Waking up in the morning to find you curled up in my arms so trusting, but no more. I'm not made of steel."

"Neither am I," she whispered against his lips. "Love me, Boston."

He carried her from the river, both of them

streaming rivulets of water. As she swayed in the cradle of his arms, her lips followed the strong cord of his neck to his ear, where she nipped at its velvety lobe.

"If you don't stop that, I'm going to drop you."

She bit harder, then giggled, clutching his neck as his arms faked the drop. "Don't you dare."

He eased her down on their sleeping bag and walked toward the fire, leaving her to study him as he tossed more sticks on the smoldering embers. Firefly sparks rose and illuminated the campsite, showering him in a red-gold light, catching the glistening water on his body and turning the tiny droplets into sparkling diamonds.

He must have felt her burning gaze. He turned his head and saw her kneeling there, proud and unashamed of her natural beauty. His eyes roamed hungrily over the soft contours of her body. They lingered on the small rounded breasts, then moved downward to the tiny waist and curved hips, then farther still to the molten red triangle and long shapely thighs. He made the return journey just as leisurely until their desire-filled eyes met and fused in the mellow flickering firelight.

Boston rose, turned full view and walked slowly toward her, never breaking their locked gaze. She took in his full magnificence and her eyes widened unconsciously.

She reached out a hand exploratively and closed it around him. He was rock hard, pulsing hot and smooth as silk. She closed her eyes, wanting him suddenly with an intensity that shattered her breath and set her hands trembling. He knelt before her and she rose up on her knees, meeting his embrace with surprising strength.

His lips captured hers in a wild kiss that set the blood pumping hot through her body, her heart and mind racing with new sensations. Mouths melted into each other and harmonized, their tongues slipping back and forth. His mouth pulled away from hers and traveled to the arched column of her neck as his hands covered her desire-swollen breasts, teasing the already pert nipples. Her breath hissed between clenched teeth and she leaned farther back, allowing his mouth easy access. She ran her hands up and down the smooth ridges of his ribs, then leaned back further, pulling him with her to lie full-length on their bedding. She felt wicked and wanton and deliciously warm, all thoughts of reality blocked by his shadow above her.

Samantha rolled her head back and moaned at the fiery trail his lips were blazing. She moved her hand downward, exploring, stroking, while his hand reached to separate her thighs. And like the brilliant musician he was, his fingers strummed her sensitive body, finding the right chords and lingering over the melody of her moaning pleasure. It was heaven, and she cried out at the sheer ecstasy of his touch. He lifted his head from her breast and they devoured each other with their heavy-lidded gaze.

"You taste so good." He whispered the words against her lips. "Sweet and salty—honey and spice."

She ran the tips of her nails up and down his back,

smiling into his eyes as the muscles rippled under her touch. "Your body's so cool and I'm burning." A slim hand slipped from his back, around his ribs, then to the flat of his stomach. "Warm and smooth as velvet," she murmured. "I want you."

He smiled and covered her body with his. "Not as much as I want you, my love."

Under the jewel-studded canopy of darkness she listened to the lullaby of his sweet murmurings. Picking up the tune she turned his seductive words into a duet, rising to the increasing tempo of his movements and heavy beating of his heart against her.

"Oh, God," he groaned, "you feel so good...so hot."

"Love me, Boston, love me...love..." she chanted, and arched against him as the still night split with her cry. Boston muffled the next sound that came from her lips, turning it into a soft moan that died echoing in his own mouth.

He stirred and she caught him close. "Don't move, don't leave me."

"Open your eyes and look at me." She obeyed the command and stared at him. "You're fantastic." He growled a sound of pure pleasure and delight and before she could reply his mouth smothered hers and he began to move again.

The music of their joining grew higher and louder, like the rhythmic beating of a bass drum. Samantha clung to his body, awash with the vibrations of his soul, drowning in the perfection of his song. She feared the final clashing of cymbals would never come again, and when it did, she arched, her toes curling into the soft blanket. Her eyes flew open and she watched him this time. His features contorted in a grimace of pain-pleasure before he collapsed against her, their bodies glistening with perspiration.

She lay quiescent in his arms, listening to the slow, even cadence of his breathing. She felt serene and a little awed that she had been able to match his passion with a fierceness she had never experienced before.

"Boston."

"Hmm."

"It was beautiful, wasn't it?"

"What a damnable question to ask." His arm tightened around her. "Why is it women always want to talk afterward? You should be silent in the sweet afterglow." The teasing tone belied his words.

"I want to know, was it anything like the first time?"

"What do you mean? This was the first time—" He broke off, suddenly alert to her trap and his blunder.

"Why, you bastard." Her voice cracked and her hands balled into tight fists, pounding him anywhere she could find firm flesh.

Boston gripped her flying hands and forced them between their bodies, pulling her closer. The deep rumble of his laughter erupted. "Tut, tut—such language."

She struggled to free herself from his hold; then, realizing the futility of her efforts, she kicked him hard, inflicting more pain on her bare toes than on his body.

"Careful," he shouted, trying to capture her legs with his own. "Watch those knees, Sparky. You could ruin me for life."

"I hope I do," she snarled. Pinned down by his superior strength, she lay panting. "What a dirty rotten trick to pull."

"I'm sorry!"

The muffled apology reached her from the curve of her neck and grated on her ears. "Do you realize what I went through? Racking my brains to remember that night! The humiliation and shame of not knowing."

"Sparky, Sparky. It was too tempting to pass up." His body shook with laughter. "You looked so serious and appalled. Then you kept trying to convince yourself it never happened by putting me down." He chuckled. "I couldn't resist the chance to get in a few digs of my own."

"You're a beast!" she charged him, but there was amusement in her voice as she remembered all she'd said and accused him of. Her laughter joined his and he pulled her close, his hand moving over her back, kneading the warm silky flesh.

"Go to sleep. We have a long ride tomorrow."

"I'd love to, but if you don't move your hands," she warned, "we'll both be awake the rest of the night."

His hand stilled. "That's not a bad idea," he said, nibbling at the corner of her mouth, "but I'm just too tired to meet your wild demands."

"Boston, what's going to happen tomorrow?"

"I hope the same as today."

"Be serious." She felt his body tense.

"Go to sleep, Sparky."

Haunted by the tumble of thoughts spinning around in her head, she lay watching Boston fall deeper into sleep, and though his mind was drifting farther away, his hand had a firm, possessive hold around her waist. A wavy blue-black lock of hair had fallen across his brow, making him younger looking, almost boyish. She was tempted to brush it back but stopped herself from reaching out. What if he woke and wanted to know why she was awake? What could she say? That she wished tomorrow would never come. That she was afraid of her feeling for him and his for her—afraid she was just another available female. He'd had so many. Rich, beautiful, sophisticated women she couldn't compete with—didn't want to compete with. But how did you keep a man who had so much?

MIDDAY THEY TOPPED a high ridge and reined in. Samantha's delighted eyes traveled over the upland valley, green, lush and peaceful. A large sprawling natural-stone two-story house nestled in the center, surrounded by ancient trees, which spread their welcome shade over the sunbaked land. About a mile or more from the house she could just glimpse a bright blue stream wandering and twisting through thick vegetation.

"Oh, Boston! Is this it?" She turned in the saddle to face him and met his amused yet pleased look. He leaned over and kissed her parted lips and she thought she would drown in the mixture of desire and tenderness flaring in the depths of his eyes. "This *is* it, isn't it?" She suddenly remembered how he had awakened her in the early hours of the morning, his hands and lips teasing her into total awareness. They had laughed and romped like a pair of teenagers, telling each other little things about their lives they'd never told anyone before.

Boston turned around in his saddle and untied the mule he was leading. His eyes twinkled. "I'll race you down," he challenged. In a cloud of flying dust and small rocks they plunged down the side of the ridge until they hit the flat grass of the valley, where they kicked their horses into a headlong run.

Samantha leaned forward over the horse's mane, moving with the pounding, rocking rhythm, urging her horse on, determined to win or at least to keep abreast of the big horse beside her. She glanced over once, smiled, then laughed as she caught Boston's disbelieving glance.

Realizing she just could possibly beat him, Boston took the same forward position, surveyed the familiar terrain and set his horse over an easier route. He rounded the long curved drive with Samantha breathing down his neck, and headed toward the front of the house, pulling up short when he glimpsed their welcoming committee.

Samantha reined her horse to a stop behind his. "You cheated, Boston."

He threw back his head and laughed.

She vaulted to the ground, standing before him, hands on hips. "You did. You know the lay of the land and you took a short cut."

"Now don't be a poor loser, Sparky. A man has to use his superior knowledge sometimes to outwit you females."

"Superior knowledge, my foot!" she snorted. "You. . . ."

"Behave, honey, we have company."

Samantha spun around in time to see the running figure of a beautiful blonde throw herself into Boston's arms and kiss him thoroughly on the mouth. He wasn't pushing her away either! Who was she? His secretary? Friend? Girlfriend? Her eyes narrowed and became two sharp flames of jealousy as she watched them. A cough drew her attention and she turned to meet the disapproving look of Ken Lawson, Boston's manager.

"Hello, Miss Griffin." He extended his hand and she clasped it, her cheeks red as she remembered their first meeting. "I collected all your luggage from the hotel and brought it with me."

"Thank you." What else could she say?

He handed her a folded sheet of newspaper. "I think you'd better have a look at this." He left her to read the small announcement circled in red ink. Judge Adam M. Griffin of Tomball, Texas, announces the engagement of his daughter, Samantha Fay Griffin, to Boston Grey of Los Angeles, California. The wedding to take place. . . . She closed her eyes in an agony of embarrassment. How could he do this to her, her own father? Boston obviously misunderstood the degree of her father's tolerance of the situation. Opening her eyes, she studied the announcement once again, then slowly crumpled the paper in a tight fist.

"Hello."

The breathless greeting interrupted her turbulent thoughts and she looked down from her greater height at a petite honey blonde and the biggest, brownest eyes she'd ever encountered. Doe eyes! She forced a smile of acknowledgement across her stiff features. The woman before her was so slim, tiny and delicate—except for a bust measurement that would make any red-blooded man drool with lust. Samantha glanced down at her own inadequacies in disgust.

"I don't know what's happened to everyone's manners around here, but I'm Lana Castle, Boston's fiancée." She twitched the balled piece of newspaper from Samantha's slack fingers and began straightening it, unaware of the pained white face above her own.

Like a cannon shot exploding in her head, the name Lana triggered a memory, and before the word fiancée ever left the woman's lips, she remembered other words, this time Boston's—'My fiancée, Miss Griffin.' How could something so monstrously important have slipped her mind? Or had her subconscious, even then, deliberately rejected the thought that he belonged to someone else? And after, when they'd made love, had she still refused to admit Lana's existence, then blanked it out completely to salve her own conscience for falling in love with a man who wasn't free to return her love? Boston must love Lana. How could any man resist someone so adorable? In her own mind, Lana was everything she'd dreamed of being: petite, cuddly, with a helpless appeal men were instinctively drawn to. A pocket Venus to stand under the protective shelter of a man's arm. And Boston! The more Samantha thought, the angrier she became. Why—why with numerous opportunities had he never mentioned the engagement again? When she thought of the long days and nights they'd spent together, she ground her teeth and the fury began to bubble in her veins. How could he do this to her?

Samantha's bright, hard eyes blazed at him and he must have felt their heat because he looked up, breaking off his conversation with Ken. *You're a dead man, Boston Grey*, she thought, and watched that beautiful, lying mouth turn up as he raked a nervous hand through his hair and around the back of his neck. He jammed his hands into his pockets and with hunched shoulders walked toward her.

"Ah...I can explain."

"I just bet you can!" she retorted, her voice low and dangerous. "Let's...."

"Boston," Lana laughingly interrupted, "what in the world are you going to do with two fiancées?"

"Yes, Boston, I'd like to hear that myself," Samantha said sweetly. "Maybe you're thinking of starting a harem? Or should Lana and I plan to meet at dawn beneath the spreading old oak?"

"Cottonwood."

"What?"

"It's a cottonwood," Lana interjected, and catching the hilarity of the situation she went on. "Twenty paces, a duel till the death. Winner takes the prize. What about weapons? Cream pies?"

"Make mine lemon," Samantha said dryly.

"Wooden spoons?" Lana suggested, taking the stance of a swordsman.

"Electric mixers. We can eject the beaters at one another." Despite her burning anger, Samantha smiled at the lively woman. She was forced to acknowledge that Lana was just the sort of woman-child men fell hopelessly in love with for the rest of their lives. Never before had she felt inadequate in the presence of another woman. She hated Boston even more for his deception, and her eyes reflected her feelings.

"Hell!" Boston muttered in disgust and stomped off with Ken at his heels.

"Now what's wrong with him?" Lana asked.

"I have no idea," Samantha replied with feigned innocence.

"Oh, well, he'll get over it," she shrugged. "Come on, Samantha, I'll show you to your room. I had all your things unpacked." She eyed Samantha critically from head to toe as they walked up the stone steps. "Actually, I hope you're not offended, but I unpacked them myself. You have beautiful clothes and I couldn't stand the thought of them wrinkled and mussed."

Samantha caught Lana's appraisal and cringed at the way she must look now. "Thank you, that was thoughtful."

"Yes, you see I didn't have much to do around here while Boston was off getting himself engaged." She averted hurt brown eyes from the other woman's searching glance.

For an instant Samantha doubted the cutting

quality of the remark, but Lana's words had a definite bite to them. She must listen carefully. There was an edge to the sweet voice.

"Lana...."

"Here I am talking my head off. I bet you're tired after your long days and nights on the trail, and want nothing more than a hot bath and a rest."

In a trance Samantha followed Lana up the curving stairs, momentarily too exhausted to notice her surroundings. Disoriented, she stood in the center of her bedroom and Lana pointed out the bathroom.

"Lana...."

"Samantha...."

They started in unison, then broke off, the silence becoming awkward and embarrassing for both.

"I'd better go," Lana said, turning quickly and leaving the room.

When the door closed Samantha shrugged, abandoning the situation for the moment. She moved like a robot, collecting clean underwear and her cosmetic case. Then she headed for a hot bath and some privacy to analyze this new set of problems.

Later, dressed and standing at the window in a lemon-yellow sundress with a fitted bodice, slender shoulder straps and a slightly flared skirt reaching just below the knee, she felt whole again, ready to meet Boston on his own ground. Absently she fingered the cool crisp material as she scanned the sloped backyard. It was speckled with trees and flowering shrubs that rolled down to a kidney-shaped pool. She lifted her eyes and surveyed the landscape further, hunting, searching for the sight of a familiar black head among the barn and outbuildings. "How could you, Boston?" she whispered aloud, pain forming a lump in her throat.

She swallowed hard and forced herself to become calm. As she did, she realized there was something very wrong. Lana had kissed Boston, but Boston hadn't wrapped his arms around her in a loving embrace. He'd acted more like a brother than a lover. And Lana! She hadn't seemed that upset at first. It was only when they were alone that the frost set in.

Boston wasn't a man she could dismiss with a simple flip of her red head. Besides, to walk away from him would be impossible. She was virtually his prisoner. She leaned forward and rested her hands on the window frame, her knuckles paling at the unconscious pressure she applied. She'd allowed him to make love to her with no words of love or hint of commitment. But what was so shattering was the fact she'd returned his caresses openly, lovingly, and not once had she thought about the future—only the moment.

For the first time in her life she'd held nothing back. Under his gentle then fierce demands, the wall she'd built around herself crumbled to dust. She felt different. Altered in subtle ways. Free! There were no lingering feelings of guilt in the aftermath of their union.

She wondered what her family would think of their fallen princess now? Because no matter how hard she tried to brush aside her protected, and in many ways strict upbringing, it always intruded, leaving a faint taste of bitterness, whenever she tried to break out of

her self-imposed rules. But not this time. There was
something soft and radiant between her and Boston.
He was dangerously unlike any other man she'd
known, and if she didn't do something, anything,
he'd slip away. She had to figure out a way to keep
him. She sighed again. He should have told her about
Lana on the trek instead of letting her arrive unpre-
pared. She glowered at the scenery, her eyes focusing
on the tall figure of Boston striding toward the barn.
Samantha whipped around and raced to the door,
skidding to an abrupt halt. She turned and shoved
her feet into her white canvas espadrilles. Her face set
in grim lines, she set off down the stairs at a running
lope, mumbling under her breath, "If you think
you're going to get off easy, mister, you're in for a
rude awakening."

She flew across the backyard, and cut to a path in
the direction of the barn. Panting for breath, she
stopped in the open doorway and let her eyes adjust
to the gloomy interior. When she spotted him, his
back was toward her. She picked up a currycomb,
took aim and pitched it. It soared by his right shoulder and clattered noisily to the floor.

"What the hell!" He twisted and paled at her
angry face, her eyes blazing fury. "Sparky?"

"You deceitful, lying. . .Casanova," she shouted,
and grabbing an iron stirrup she took aim again.
"What's the matter, one woman not good enough
for you?" she sneered and released her weapon.

He dodged to the left. "Listen to me, Sparky. It's
not exactly the way it appears."

"No? Why didn't you mention Lana's name while

we were riding here?'' She grabbed a broken bridle from its peg.

''Damn it, Sparky, you never brought her name up, either.''

''Rat,'' she hissed, hurling the cracked leather bridle. ''You dragged me all over this state for days when we could have driven here.''

He laughed, then realized his mistake and backed up. ''I can explain.''

''Glib-tongued devil.'' Her foot knocked against a half-empty grain bucket, and yanking it up she flung it at him with both hands. ''Laugh at me, will you!''

Boston dived to the right, but he wasn't fast enough. The bucket glanced off his leg, showering him from head to toe in oats and grain dust. ''Stop this craziness,'' he roared.

''. . .and I thought I was in love with you,'' she said, half to herself. ''How entertaining the last few days must have been.''

''No, no. . .listen, sweetheart.'' He rubbed ineffectually at his white dust-covered face and sneezed three times.

Standing with her hands on her hips, she glared at him. ''Don't you dare call me sweetheart! Save your honeyed words for your fiancée. Heaven knows, she'll need them to put up with your infidelities.'' She whirled around and marched off, then stopped and turned back to him. ''I wish my brothers *had* beaten the hell out of you.''

''Dammit, Sparky. You come back here—now!'' he roared, then started to sneeze again.

Samantha sprinted out the barn door, passing an

openmouthed old man in her flight. It flashed through her mind that he must be Elijah.

"Well, boy! What have you gotten into now?"

Elijah's words followed her across the lawn as she fought down the sobs that threatened to escape her tight throat. "I won't cry." She gritted her teeth. "I will not cry for that man." Through the crystal blur of her tears she savagely twisted the knob of the back door and walked into the house, slowing her pace and wiping the wetness from her cheeks. She checked her steps on hearing the murmur of voices. As she headed for the stairs the hushed voices grew louder, and passing the library door she quickly glanced in. She stopped dead still, her eyes widening at the sight of Ken and Lana in a crushing embrace.

What in the world was going on? Was everyone in this household stark raving mad? Shaking her head in confusion, she hurriedly stepped away from the doorway and sped to her room, where she threw herself across the bed and closed her eyes tightly in frustration. Well, she had really done it now. All her good intentions of having a calm, rational discussion with Boston had died the minute she laid eyes on him. She groaned out loud in self-disgust and cursed her hot temper.

Nothing made sense anymore. Boston in love with and engaged to Lana; Ken was his friend and manager yet...there they were, Lana and Ken kissing. Was he consoling Lana's hurt over her own unexpected presence? It didn't look like any brotherly comfort she'd ever experienced. Samantha picked the pins from her tousled hair and dropped them on the floor beside the bed. Maybe she'd imagined the whole scene. Heaven knew she hadn't been in her right mind when she passed that door. Her heavy lids blinked sleepily and she shook her head. "Too many things to think about to sleep," she murmured out loud as a huge yawn popped open her jaw. A sharp knock jerked her out of her doze and before she could answer Lana's call, the door opened.

"Dinner's about ready. I thought you'd want to freshen up and meet us in the library for drinks."

"Thank you. Lana. . . ."

". . . Samantha."

They spoke in unison, then laughed at each other, genuinely amused.

"You go first," Samantha said, and smiled encouragingly as Lana's expression turned serious.

"Listen, Samantha. May I call you Sammy? Samantha's such a mouthful."

"Sure."

Lana sat down on the foot of the bed, her hands clenched together in her lap. "I'd like to apologize for this afternoon. I made some unkind and catty remarks that were totally uncalled for. You see, I was jealous and hurt."

With each word Samantha felt more and more like a heel. She could only marvel at Lana's control. If the position were reversed, she wouldn't have been so calm.

"I've been the center of attention in Boston's life for so long I'm afraid I have a tendency to be overly protective and possessive." She looked up from her lap and smiled at Samantha. "It's going to take some time to learn to let go."

This was crazy, Samantha thought. Lana's jealousy stemmed from lack of attention, not from the fact that Samantha had spent days and nights with Boston alone. "Lana, how long have you and Boston been engaged?"

"Well...." Lana hedged, her hands twisting together. "I wouldn't exactly call us engaged. I mean...well, you see...." She jumped up. "I have to go and see about dinner."

Samantha could sense Lana's reluctance, and though she was puzzled, she decided not to try to detain her any longer. She was a coward herself and wasn't ready to discuss the situation. Wasn't there a saying somewhere about the truth making you free? Maybe it was better to wait; she wasn't ready to be free. She swung her long legs over the side of the bed. "Do you need any help with dinner?"

"No, everything's under control." Lana gave Samantha a weak smile and laughed a little self-consciously. "I hope."

CHAPTER SEVEN

SAMANTHA STOOD in the library entrance drinking in the warmth and charm of the large room, which was paneled in straight-grain ponderosa pine. The mellow, aged wood gleamed softly. At one end of the room was a fireplace large enough to hold the huge pine logs that seemed to grow only in this part of the country. On the wall opposite the fireplace, bookshelves ran from floor to ceiling and were stocked with novels old and new. An ornately carved gun cabinet filled with shotguns, rifles and handguns nestled against the far wall next to an equally ornate bar.

Her eyes ran the length of the polished counter, then lifted to the man leaning lazily against it at one end. Dressed in casual black slacks and a close knit, V-neck shirt of charcoal gray, Boston was devastatingly sexy and knew it. He lounged against the bar, his hips thrust out. His eyes gleamed mischievously and the sensuous mouth lifted at one corner as he watched her watch him.

Samantha regarded him with what she hoped was a serene remoteness as their eyes collided, and all the while her insides trembled with a mixture of anger, pain and desire.

"Would you like a drink?" Boston held up his own glass and motioned to an array of bottles lining the back of the bar.

"Vodka and tonic. Light on the vodka, please." She turned her back on him, listening to the tinkle of ice as he prepared her drink. A light tap on the shoulder caused her to swing around; then she stepped back. He was too close. She reached out for the offered glass, but he pulled it back.

"Are you over your tantrum?" He offered her the drink again, and as before when she reached for it, he moved it out of her grasp.

She shrugged in defeat. "I'm not going to play games with you, nor am I going to beg you for my drink." She walked over to the bookshelves and pretended to study the titles. Did the man have no conscience at all about what he'd done? His teasing attitude infuriated her even further. He didn't seem to care whom he hurt. Lost in her thoughts, she jumped when his strong hands captured her shoulders and pulled her rigid body back against his.

"I know you're angry and hurt. You have every right to your thoughts about me, but, Sparky, give me a chance to explain. Believe me, there is a logical, reasonable explanation for this mess."

Warm lips nipped at her rounded bare shoulder. She drew away from his hold and turned to face him with eyes flashing. "Is there?" Her voice dripped sarcasm. "And just what excuse can you give to make me understand? That while you made love to me—hah!—that was the wrong choice of words, wasn't it? I should have said...."

"Sparky," he interrupted warningly.

"How could you do it, Boston, when all the time you were engaged to a woman you obviously love? You could at least have had the courtesy to tell me about Lana and allow me to make the decision as to whether I wanted to have a quick roll in the hay."

"Don't say things like that!" he exploded. His hands captured her face and turned it up to his. "You're the only one I want."

"Ah . . . for how long, Boston?"

A discreet cough broke them apart like two naughty children. Boston greeted the old man and with care and tenderness guided his slow shuffling steps to where she stood.

"Elijah, I'd like you to meet Samantha Griffin."

He was shorter than Boston and a little stooped with age. A fierce, noble figure with a sunbaked leathery face and salt-and-pepper hair, which hung in two shinning braids over his shoulders. She extended a shaky hand, suddenly remembering that he'd witnessed the scene in the barn and knew entirely too much about her personal affairs. The hooded eyelids lifted, and she saw coal-black eyes through which a tranquil soul shone. A genuine smile of pleasure softened her strained face as dry, callused hands patted hers.

"I've heard a great deal about you, girlie," he said, his face unsmiling and serious. Then he turned and walked away, leaving her a little shaken at his rudeness.

"Don't pay any attention to his abruptness, Sparky. He's old and doesn't like changes. He'll come around."

"Around to what?"

Boston flung a careless arm across her shoulders and she stepped away from his touch. "Listen...." He didn't get any further. Ken entered, groaning loudly that dinner wasn't near ready yet, then demanded a bartender before he returned to the chaos in the kitchen.

For the next half hour Boston stalked her from one end of the room to the other. With the agility of a cornered animal she slipped out of his reach and swiftly removed herself from his encroaching presence by stepping around tables and wing-back chairs, finally edging her way down the length of the bar, passing Elijah as he refreshened his drink.

"You'll have to do better than that, girlie. I taught him how to follow the scent of any animal—four legged or two."

She threw him a sizzling glance, then turned her attention to the open doorway. Ken stood there flushed, his hair ruffled.

"Miss Griffin, by any chance can you cook?" He pulled disgustedly at the frilly yellow apron around his waist, balled it between his hands, then stuck it behind his back.

"Yes, why?"

"Lana needs your help." He marched to the bar, dropped the offending piece of fabric, picked up a glass and a half-empty bottle of bourbon, then flopped in a nearby chair with a long-suffering sigh.

"Oh, dear. I wonder what Lana's culinary skills will produce for tonight's feast?" Boston murmured.

Amused, Samantha headed for the door. Strong

fingers clamped around her arm and a deep voice rumbled a warning near her ear. "You can't avoid me forever. Sooner or later you're going to hear me out."

Her eyes clashed with his, and she gave him a cold withering look, yanked her arm free and sped up her steps.

Mumbling under her breath about what she'd like to do to Boston, she pushed open the swinging doors and stopped. The big kitchen was strewn with dirty dishes. Several large pots were on the verge of boiling over and the air carried a distinctive smell of scorched food.

Large brown eyes met hers, pleading for help. Samantha couldn't prevent the laughter that rose to her lips; then she tried to mask her error with a cough. Lana stood before her covered with splotches of what appeared to be potatoes.

"I didn't have the beaters in properly," she whispered. "Ken called me a complete idiot." She twisted the ragged dish towel between fingers adorned with Band-Aids. "The green peas cooked to mush." Her voice began to climb. "And the roast is burned on the outside and raw in the middle." Lana gulped. "Ken said if I touched it it would *moo* at me. I tried, Sammy, really I did," she stated valiantly.

"What do men know?" Samantha patted Lana's shoulder. "If you'll show me where everything is, I'll see what I can do. But first I think we'd better clean this mess up." She started to work, telling stories about her own disasters and how she'd dealt with six teasing brothers, till she had Lana happily chuckling.

"I wish I was from a big family." Lana sighed wistfully. "Being the only child was lonely. You were lucky your mother taught you how to cook. My mom would never let me near the kitchen."

Samantha scraped the rest of the ruined peas down the disposal before speaking. "My mother died a few hours after I was born."

"I'm sorry. But how...."

"How did I survive being raised by a father, an uncle and six brothers?" Samantha grinned. "I don't know. Sheer determination, I guess." They were both occupied for a few minutes, then Samantha asked, "Where's Pearl?"

"Oh, she had a family emergency in town. She should have been back by now. That's why I put off cooking as long as possible. Then I had to rush."

Samantha bit her lip, hating herself for the sneaky way she was going about getting to the question that had been preying on her mind. "Do you know Sara and Cable Ford?" Lana nodded. "Tell me something. If you were to drive from where they live to here, how long would it take?" She avoided the other woman's eyes, added more flour to the gravy, then handed Lana the wooden spoon. "Stir."

Lana frowned at the utensil in her hand as if it were a foreign object. "From Sara's to here?" she mumbled thoughtfully. "A couple of hours."

Samantha ground her teeth together. Hours. And Boston had made her ride for days. She was definitely going to kill him. All that suffering for what? The scent of pines drifted around her, and a vision of Boston's naked body gleaming in the firelight flashed in her mind. If they'd come by car, they'd never have made love. Or would they?

"Sammy, do you think this gravy's thick enough now? My arm's tired."

"Quit complaining," a masculine voice called out, and both women jumped.

Boston, Elijah and Ken were seated at the kitchen table, relaxed, drinks in hand, and definitely worse off for the lengthy wait. Samantha wondered how long they'd been there watching and listening. She was about to ask, when the back door flew open and on a chilly gust of wind a scarecrow draped all in black stomped in.

A grin tickled the corners of Samantha's lips. This couldn't be anyone but Pearl. Six feet tall in her stocking feet, and rake thin, she towered over everyone in the household except Boston. Her age was indeterminable; Samantha guessed her to be between sixty and sixty-five. Pearl scowled at the world through owlish, wire-rimmed glasses, and her silver hair was slicked back so tightly in a bun at the back of her head it gave her faded green eyes a slightly oriental appearance.

"Heaven help me! My kitchen!" Pearl gasped. Without another word she marched over to stand before Elijah and demanded, "What have you done, you old goat?"

Elijah squeezed his eyes shut. "Charming. Now my day is complete. The tyrant's home." He opened his eyes and glared back. "As you can see, I've had nothing to do with this. I'm innocent."

"You're about as innocent as...."

"They're at it again."

Samantha jerked around as a velvet voice crooned beside her. With all the stealth of a stalking hunter he'd slipped up to her once again. She tried to edge away, only to be stopped by his next words.

"Quit treating me as if I have a communicable disease."

Samantha gazed coldly back, taking note of his lopsided grin, which seemed to slip and fade away as she continued to stare. "As far as I'm concerned you do." She stepped back and bumped into the refrigerator and was immediately cornered. "Stop it, Boston. Your fiancée's watching us."

"I don't give a damn!" he exploded, but turned and left.

When at last dinner was ready, Boston reappeared and pulled back Samantha's chair with an exaggerated flourish and waved her in. She glared at him as he sat down beside her.

Dinner turned out to be a confusing affair. Though Samantha had been raised in a large family, her father had set down rules, and meals were taken in a quiet, orderly fashion. At first Samantha thought the disorder at this table was due to the men's steady alcoholic libations, but soon realized this was a normal evening dinner for them.

Pearl served, thumping dishes and silverware before Elijah every chance she got while muttering dire threats at him. Everyone tried to talk yet still listen to the two antagonists.

Shielded by the conversation of the others, Boston leaned over and spoke in a low voice only Samantha could hear. "It won't work, Sparky. Meet me by the pool after dinner and I'll explain."

"No." She jerked her knee away from the nimble fingers walking beneath the hem of her dress and along the top of her thigh. Without thinking, she reached under the table and pinched his leg.

Boston captured her hand, holding it over the offended area. "Yes." His hand squeezed harder, then began moving up and down his thigh. She tried to tug her fingers free, but he moved them to rest in a place where heat radiated.

Samantha's face flushed; she swallowed hard and met the message in his dark eyes. The warmth under her hand was playing havoc with her self-control. "Let go, Boston," she ordered and managed to pull free.

Before he could retort, Pearl stomped back in and slapped a deck of cards beside Elijah's plate. The room immediately fell quiet.

"Cut," she barked, one bony finger tapping the cards.

"Oh, no, you don't." Elijah reared back in his chair and crossed his arms over his chest. "I'm on to your tricks."

Fascinated, Samantha forgot her anger and leaned closer to Boston. "What's going on?"

"She's going to high card him to see who washes the dishes tonight." Boston grinned, his black eyes twinkling with mischief. "Pearl always uses her own deck and it's been driving Elijah crazy that he always loses. What she doesn't know is he searched her room while she was gone and found her marked deck. The old devil remarked them for his benefit and put them back. He's been waiting for the chance to catch her red-handed.''

They watched as Elijah acted reluctant for a minute, then reached out and quickly cut the cards—queen of hearts. His Cheshire-cat smile brought a deeper frown to the old woman's creased brow.

Thin lips puckered, glasses perched on the tip of her nose, Pearl fingered the cards almost lovingly before turning over the top card—ace of spades. There was a breathless second before Elijah erupted.

"You cheated!''

"'Course I did, same as you.'' She wiped the cards from the table, shoved them into the pocket of her apron and stared at Elijah's red face. "Think I don't know when a man's been in my bedroom?'' Her cheeks deepened to caverns, camouflaging a smile as she made a precise military turn and marched out.

The room erupted with laughter and Samantha saw her chance to escape. She pleaded a headache, slipped out of her chair and hurried to the door before Boston could stop her.

CURLED UP ON HER BED, Samantha listened to the house settling down for the night. Ken and Lana had passed her door sometime before, laughing and talking softly. Her alert ears had yet to hear Boston's steps.

Out of habit she rubbed at her temple, then stopped, realizing her headache was gone—thankful she had been able to take a milder prescription instead of the debilitating one. She only got these migraines when she was exhausted and under emotional strain. She'd certainly been through that today. It was a wonder she wasn't totally incoherent with pain.

She picked up the novel she'd been attempting to read for the past two hours and knew she'd read the same page at least five times. She snapped the book shut with disgust.

"I'm glad you decided to wait up for me."

Boston leaned back against the closed door. A thigh-length white terry shaving robe was tied loosely at the waist, and his raven hair was still damp from a recent shower. He settled down on the end of the bed, taking one of her slim feet in his hand.

"What do you think you're doing coming in here in the middle of the night?"

"Wouldn't call twelve o'clock the middle of the night." He smiled, his black eyes twinkling as she pulled a corner of the covers higher to hide the low-cut sheer nightgown she wore. One dainty strap slipped off her shoulder invitingly, and he reached out to replace it, only to have his hand slapped away.

"Get out of here, Boston."

"No. You've been dodging me all evening. It's time we had our talk." His thumb caressed her ankle and she tried unsuccessfully to jerk free.

"Such pretty feet," he murmured, lifting her foot to his mouth to run his tongue across her high instep.

"This is no place to hold a serious conversation."

"I can't think of a better place. This way you won't be able to escape so easily."

"Stop that!" she demanded, her voice a little

husky as he nibbled her toes. His mouth stopped its teasing torment, but he now placed her foot between the long V-opening of his robe to rest on his smooth warm chest.

"Go to your fiancée. I'm sure she's wondering where you are."

"Jealous?"

"Jealous?" she sputtered. "Jealous!" She pulled back her foot a little and shoved hard against his chest, toppling him off the side of the bed. Scrambling to her knees, she grinned down at his surprised expression as he lay sprawled on the carpeted floor. "Jealous! Of all the numskull, harebrained, totally ridiculous things to say," she hissed above him.

"Enough!" he roared, climbing to his feet. "You'll listen to me now or I'll tie you to the bed until you do."

Samantha settled back, a militant sparkle in her eyes. She watched warily as he straightened his robe and sat beside her. Her father hadn't raised a fool, she thought grimly. She knew when she'd pushed just a tad too hard and too far.

"First of all, let's get something clear between us. I'm not...I repeat, *not* in love with Lana. And though we're engaged, I'm really not engaged."

Samantha gave an unladylike snort. "You're not engaged to Lana, but she's engaged to you?"

He raked a hand through his hair, a grimace of exasperation twisting his mouth. "Yes...I mean no. Ah, hell! What I'm trying to say is it's not a real engagement as far as I'm concerned."

"It is to Lana, isn't it?" she interrupted.

"Well. . . yes." His eyes flashed at her. "Will you hush and let me explain how it happened?" She opened her mouth to retort, then snapped it shut as he shook a pointed finger at her. "Not another word," he threatened.

"Lana and I met a little over three years ago. Ken had just hired her as his private secretary. It didn't take me long to see his interest in her, but he's got a hang-up about mixing business and romance." Boston leaned back against the footboard and crossed his arms, a smile playing at the corner of his mouth. "I asked her out. At first it was just to needle Ken's pompous attitude. But she turned out to be enjoyable company—always ready to listen to my problems, never making any demands. With her featherhead personality, she made me laugh. There was never any mad passion between us. I guess you could say we were close friends rather than lovers." His eyes met hers directly, honestly, and she nodded for him to continue.

"After the bombing at my last concert, I was laid up in the hospital with a broken arm and ribs, and unable to talk. She was there every day, running errands, keeping away the press and fans, acting as a voice for my written messages. It took me a couple of days to realize something was really wrong. Then the doctors finally told me the chances of regaining my voice enough to sing again were less than fifty percent. My life did a dramatic turnaround then. I was forced to do a lot of soul-searching and reevaluation of what I wanted for the rest of my life. I lay in that sterile hospital room, after being told I wasn't going to sing again, and nearly lost my mind. Never to enjoy the incredible high of hearing the hush of thousands of people hypnotized by my songs or the indescribable feeling when they awarded me a standing ovation and screamed for more.''

Boston reached over and took hold of her hand, his eyes reflecting his remembered pain. ''I took a good look at my future, and it scared the hell out of me. My priorities needed to be rearranged, and suddenly a wife, children and a home sounded perfect. Can you ever begin to understand a little of how I felt? In pain, depressed, scared, I grabbed for a lifeline, something stable and secure to hold on to— Lana. I bought this place and moved out here determined to leave the singer half of myself behind and start a new life.''

Samantha swallowed the lump in her throat and gave his hand a squeeze. ''It doesn't alter the fact that you're an engaged man.'' She slipped her hand from his and pulled her knees to her chest, wrapping her arms around them. ''How could you do this to me, Boston? You knew I didn't remember your telling me you were engaged. Even when I specifically asked who lived here, not once did you mention Lana. Why?''

''Lana doesn't live here; she only comes on the weekends with Ken.''

''That does not answer my question.''

He raked both hands through his hair in frustration and closed his eyes, a grimace of self-condemnation twisting his lips. ''I didn't want to take the chance of losing you.'' His eyes flew open and he glared at her.

"I *wanted* you. So I kept my mouth shut and hoped you wouldn't remember. Listen to me, honey. When I made the deal with your father and uncle to take you away, it was like the gods dropping a golden plum in my waiting hands. I decided I'd give myself some time alone with you and sort out my feelings—that's why the horseback excursion. How could I ruin it? And I knew I would if I so much as murmured Lana's name." He shrugged his shoulders and smiled uneasily, not sure if his explanation could ease the hurt.

Samantha drew in a ragged breath. All she could truly understand was that Boston had used her for his own needs. He was attracted to her and wanted her, and like a spoiled boy denied a new toy, he had pulled every trick in the book to achieve his goal, no matter whom he hurt along the way. Her eyes deepened with pain. "You wanted me and you had me. But do you have any idea of my feelings now, knowing that you were successful and all the while you love Lana? Damn! I thought we had something special."

Boston's hands wrapped around her shoulders and hauled her onto his lap. "I'm not in love with Lana."

"I don't believe you." She shook her head miserably. "Lana's beautiful and sweet and lovable and ...tiny!"

"But I like my women tall." Boston pressed her close, his words stirring her hair above her ear and sending little shock waves of awareness with each breath. "I've wanted you from the first moment I saw you standing in my room, dressed in those lacy scraps of underwear. You looked so fresh and alive. All color and sparkle and temper, even though you were sick." She tried to push away but he wrapped his arms tighter around her body. "While you're here I want you to watch Lana and Ken carefully."

Samantha looked up at his request, wondering if he had suddenly lost his mind. She was confused enough without his quick change of topics.

"No, Sparky. I'm not crazy. They're so much in love I don't think they realize the extent, or else they're masters at deception."

"Then why are you still engaged?" None of this made sense to her and a frown furrowed her smooth brow. "I don't understand. If they're in love you should do something...*you*."

"What?" he demanded, his voice becoming suddenly harsh. "Tell them I know they've been deceiving me? Ken's supposedly my friend. Why hasn't he come to me openly, honestly?"

"That's not being rational, Boston." She tried again to get up, only to be roughly pulled back.

"Not rational, no. But what you don't understand is that I lost more than my voice—I lost my ability to trust. One moment I had friends, people I'd known for years. The next thing I knew they were gone." Boston studied her confused expression and went on. "Trusted friends, Sparky. The second they learned I wouldn't be a star, a news item, a man to be seen with, they ran for the nearest exit."

Shifting her weight so she could see his face better, Samantha searched the dark eyes filled with hurt before they quickly went blank. "Ken's still here."

"Yes." Boston nodded slowly. "But why? Because of his fifteen-percent investment or Lana?"

"Oh, Boston, surely not either. He's here because of you." His cynicism had struck every nerve. "You're testing him, his friendship, his honor and his love for Lana. That's wrong."

"Maybe, Sparky, but it's the only way I'll know for sure."

"And Lana, Boston. What happens to her in all this?" she demanded.

Boston closed his eyes and sighed. "I love Lana like a sister. She'll get the man she loves. An honorable man, Sparky."

"What about me? Are you planning to keep me here as your mistress for the weekdays and hide me on the weekends?" She managed to get up this time and slip back under the covers, pulling them high as a shield.

"Hell, no! Dammit, woman, what sort of man do you think I am?" He reached for her, but she backed away from his touch. "Earlier, in the barn, you said you loved me. All I'm asking you is to wait a while longer and give Ken and Lana a chance to come to me on their own. Give me time to learn to trust again."

"Why should I?"

"Because I want you."

"Not good enough, Boston."

"All right, I love you," he said.

"Well! Don't strain yourself with that enthusiastic declaration of undying love and devotion, to say nothing of passion." She tried to wiggle free of his hands.

He grinned into her angry face. "Be still. This hasn't exactly been easy on me, either." He pushed her backward and stretched out beside her. "Let's forget our problems and enjoy ourselves. I don't like sleeping without you in my arms." Boston smiled down into her widened eyes, his hands cupping her face as his lips lowered to hers. When he didn't receive the response he expected he lifted his head, frowning. "What's wrong?"

"You want to stay here—make love to me?" He nodded his head like an eager little boy, a suggestive smile pulling at the corners of his mouth. "You'd do that with Ken and Lana just down the hall?" She placed both hands against his chest and began pushing.

"Get out of my room!" she said, her voice low and cold.

"What on earth's the matter with you? They won't know."

"No, but I will," she answered quickly. "How do you think this makes me feel? You're playing games with Ken and Lana at my expense. You'll acknowledge me only in the privacy of the bedroom—it's cheap and shoddy." Her expression went blank as she met his murderous look.

"You're the one playing games and I've warned you before, Sparky, don't do it with me." His hands tightened in her hair. "I want you—now, and I know damn well you want me." His mouth covered hers in a bruising kiss.

Samantha twisted her head, breaking away from him. "Stop it, Boston."

He yanked her face back, covering her mouth with his again, but this time there was a tenderness in the thrust of his tongue. A muscular thigh captured her legs as he eased his body over to hold hers down. She felt his fingers trail toward her hips then across her stomach, pulling her gown higher.

"Don't," she gulped, her eyes clashing with his as his hand slipped between her thighs.

"Now tell me you don't want me." His rough laugh punctuated each word, grating against every nerve.

"Not like this, please." Frantically, she searched for something to say, anything to make him stop. Because of her sudden rejection and his anger she realized he'd soon be out of control. He'd take her regardless of her protest, and to let him would shatter the precious feelings they shared. Her head swam with words to make him stop, but she knew with sudden insight that only the truth would reach him. She willed her body to go limp. "I love you, Boston," she whispered. "Don't treat me like a whore." Holding her breath, she felt his stillness, and then as her words penetrated, she felt the shock of them tremble through his body.

In a torment of muffled oaths he sat up, swung his long legs over the edge of the bed, retied his robe and stood.

"Boston, listen to me."

"Not another word." The low menacing voice roared with injured pride. "Do you hear me, Samantha?"

She stared openmouthed at his uncontrolled fury, almost quaking at the taut control of his voice.

"We'll play it your way," he ground out softly between clenched teeth. "But when you get tired of sleeping alone, come see me." His hand on the doorknob, he looked over his shoulder. "I just might be in the mood to take you up on your offer."

"Don't you dare walk out!" she cried, shaking her head in disbelief that he had the nerve even to make such a suggestion. She picked up a pillow and threw it at him.

"Missed!" He smiled. "Someone should have broken you of that habit years ago." He took a menacing step toward her. "I've a good mind to give it a first try."

"You wouldn't dare," she taunted him, but she was smiling.

"Don't push your luck, honey." Boston turned to leave, then stopped. "Sparky, don't wait too long to come to me. I need you."

Samantha lay back after he left, smiling smugly. She'd succeeded. The going had been rough for a few minutes, but she knew he understood no matter how angry he was at first. How could she explain her attraction for him? He was handsome, wickedly so. Humor? Yes. His teasing nature was appealing even at the times he brought out the worst in her. He always made her laugh—at him and herself. Sex appeal? Most definitely. The sudden longing for his touch no longer shocked her senses. Never blatant or vulgar, he was a man totally comfortable with his masculinity. She'd always thought sex was a serious matter, but Boston had taught her differently. He was fun! Maybe it was his ability to raise her usually cool temper that attracted her. No, that was crazy. She couldn't fall in love with a man because he could make her lose her temper. But, didn't he usually have her laughing afterward?

What was happening between them was very confusing, she admitted to herself, and realized one important thing. She didn't intend to let him go. When it came right down to winning or losing him, she knew she'd do anything to keep him.

CHAPTER EIGHT

HOURS MELTED INTO DAYS, days flowed smoothly into weeks, and Samantha was thoroughly enjoying herself. Ranch life here was almost like being home with her family. Until now she hadn't realized just how cleanly she'd cut herself off from her previous life. She felt the old Samantha emerge from the serious businesswoman she'd forced herself to become. She didn't have to impress anyone, only be herself. With an almost giddy sense of freedom, she'd called her boss and taken an indefinite leave of absence, even though her vacation time wasn't yet over, overriding his vehement protests and threats with a shocking lack of concern.

Standing at the library window, Samantha watched the erratic movements of a fluffy brown squirrel as a feisty robin scolded loudly above his head. She smiled. In some ways they were reminiscent of her and Boston, who'd fallen into an easy relationship over the weeks. Samantha's smile widened as she thought back over the teasing and fights they'd had. Neither wanting to give an inch, they'd back off, eyeing each other warily, then approach their disagreements from a different angle and usually end up laughing over some silly remark.

Samantha tore her eyes from the empty spot where the two antagonists had been and raised them to the craggy peaks of Sangre de Cristo. Where once the mere sight of the majestic formations of rock and snow-covered caps had given a soothing solace they now seemed a menacing encroachment. She frowned and blew at an errant strand of hair falling over one eye, her smile slowly fading away to a taut line. Every weekend when Ken and Lana arrived a black cloud seemed to hang over the household, an undefinable tension spreading through everyone. At first she thought it radiated from the strain of having to hide the emotions between her and Boston, but she soon realized Ken and Lana were generating their own share of tension. Whatever was happening made for short tempers and frazzled nerves. She remembered her snapping words to Boston only a few moments earlier and winced.

"I'm supposed to be on vacation and all I've seen of New Mexico are the paintings hanging on the walls, a glance or two out the windows and an occasional stroll to the barn to talk to the horses."

She flinched again as she murmured the words over out loud. She had tried to keep her voice pleasant, but it had come out sharp and petulant. Ashamed of her childishness she'd quickly left the house and headed for the cool shade of the tall trees and cleansing scent of fragrant pines. Instead she'd been blasted with summer's throat-searing heat. Without further thought she'd circled to the back of the house and taken refuge in the library.

She swung around from the window and flopped

down into an overstuffed chair, closed her eyes and sighed in relief as the cool air began to circulate around her overheated body. Suddenly she had the prickling feeling she was being watched. She peeked cautiously through long lashes, then opened her eyes fully to meet the stoic stare of Elijah. He was seated beside her in a matching chair, and his sphinxlike gaze seemed to be placidly probing, seeking out some corner of her mind he knew she was hiding behind. She hadn't even noticed him, and wondered how long he'd been there.

"Had another fight with Boston, have you, missie?" Without waiting for an answer he laid down his book and eased his aged body out of the chair, leaving her to watch his slow steps as he left the room.

Well! Things were definitely looking up. For weeks he'd been addressing her as "girlie," and that was only if she pressed for an answer to a question. Now "missie." She kicked off her sandals and thrust her long legs out, propping them up on the low coffee table.

The door opened and Elijah came back in. Her eyes widened at the tray he was carrying. A slight smile twitching at his mouth, he handed her a cold bottle of beer and a glass stein, took his own and began to pour carefully.

Straightening up in her chair, she gave him a level look. "You don't like me much, do you, Elijah?"

The lengthened pause became an echo as the big grandfather clock chimed the half hour. Elijah finished pouring his beer and took a small sip.

"I think you're bad tempered, sharp-tongued and...."

"Now see here!" she protested.

". . . and just right for Boston." He grinned.

Samantha let out her pent-up breath in a long sigh as if someone had punched her in the middle, then threw back her head and laughed. His chuckles joined hers and she saw his first real smile, a smile that for a fleeting second reminded her of Boston's. Then it was gone and she wondered if she'd imagined the resemblance. He reverted to his expressionless stare, and Samantha, suddenly self-conscious under his close scrutiny, pulled at her shorts, curling her legs under her protectively.

"Have you and Boston considered what your shenanigans are going to do to Lana?"

"They're not *my* deceptions," she retorted roughly. "And it's not just Lana I'm concerned about. You forget, Elijah, I'm stuck in the middle, too. Boston's determined to play his mind games with Ken, and right now he seems content to let things ride as they are. I don't like it any better than you do. But what can I do?" That question had plagued her every waking hour. Deep down there was a feeling that no matter what happened someone was going to end up getting hurt. She just prayed it wasn't herself.

Samantha lifted her eyes to meet his. "We're in a terrible fix, aren't we?" He nodded in agreement and she closed her eyes, tilting her head to rest on the high-back chair. "I've thought about leaving—going home—until Boston can work things out for himself."

"No." The soft voice cracked in the quiet room.

"Boston needs you, now more than ever." He took another sip of his beer. "Did you know that Father Brian, director of the orphanage where Boston grew up, is holding a fund-raising benefit and asked Boston to perform? Boston turned him down."

"But, Elijah, his voice?"

Elijah shrugged. "The doctors say there's nothing physically wrong with his vocal cords."

"You mean he *can* sing?"

"No, I mean he won't even try. Talk to him, convince him he owes it to Father Brian."

"He won't talk to me about his voice. When I tried, he told me the subject was off limits."

"Try," he demanded, and their eyes locked.

The door opened and Lana stuck her head around. "There you are! Boston and Ken have made our lunch and packed it. They're taking us on a picnic down by the river. Come on."

"Try, Samantha, please."

She trailed after Lana, Elijah's plea echoing in her thoughts, sending a sudden chill up and down her spine. Her finely tuned sense of danger and trouble warned her that the subject of Boston's voice would only cause them more problems. If his vocal cords were healed, why did he refuse to make the test and sing? Maybe he was afraid of more disappointments, but to ignore the chance altogether left her mystified.

She propped herself against the kitchen-door frame, unnoticed, and watched as Boston gave directions to Ken and Lana about where to find the stored fishing equipment in the barn. He followed them to the door, smiling at their bantering, then turned and saw Samantha.

"Come here."

His arms were warm and gentle and she snuggled close. "I'm sorry about earlier."

"I know." Boston kissed the top of her head and tightened his arms. She tilted her head back, her eyes focused on his grinning mouth, then lifted them to meet his gaze. He clasped his hands around her arms and firmly pushed her away. "Don't look at me like that, woman." The huskiness of his voice made her smile. "Here," he shoved a can in her hand, "help me finish packing the basket."

Another push, gentle this time, turned her toward the table, which was stacked with an assortment of wrapped food. She began to place the packages in the wicker basket, asking what each one was as she packed them away. Receiving only silence in response to her questions, she glanced over her shoulder and caught him thoughtfully inspecting her body. From her bare feet, his eyes traveled up the long legs to the white shorts and skimpy red-and-white striped halter top. The half-formed smile froze on her lips when she met the desire flaring in his dark eyes. She quickly turned her head, breaking his hypnotic stare, her breath fluttering between clenched teeth.

"Sparky?"

"Don't say it, Boston."

"Why?"

"You know how I feel. Lana...."

"To hell with Lana," he burst out savagely and jerked her around, his mouth capturing hers.

Moaning deep in her throat, she pushed him away. "Stop it!" she lashed out. Boston recognized her frustration and smiled down into her flushed, freckled face. She wondered who he took his tension out on, then remembered Elijah's arguing with him to go easier on the ranch hands. "Let's go. Ken and Lana are coming."

Samantha laughed when Lana walked in. An old fishing hat with hooks and lures stuck in the wide band was propped atop her honey-blond curls. She wielded a fiberglass fishing rod dangerously close to Ken's backside while he cursed and sidestepped out of the way.

"Boston!" Ken yelped as one of Lana's thrusts caught him across the legs. "Take the rod away from her before she strips the hide off me."

Lana snapped the rod at him again. "He promised to bait my hook. Now, just because of a little accident, he says he won't do it."

"Little accident!" he roared. "Look at that." He turned for them to see the hook still hanging from the back of his jeans. "And this." He held out his hand and showed two bloody punctures in the palm. "That's only for starters. She dropped a heavy tackle box on my foot." He limped farther away, out of Lana's reach. "The woman's a menace to anyone within a mile."

"Well, if you wouldn't be such a know-it-all," Lana bristled, her hat quivering with indignation.

"Children, children," Boston scolded; then they were all laughing. Amid teasing and bantering they managed to collect everything and start out. Samantha and Lana, fishing rods draped over their shoulders, led the group. Boston and Ken were farther behind carrying the picnic basket, which was topped with two heavy quilts, and in their free hands each carried a tackle box.

"Boston, I don't believe Samantha and Lana believe in equal rights for women," Ken said loudly. "You've noticed they're not carrying an *equal* share of the load?"

"I think you're right, but they're sure worth watching. Just look at those wiggles." Boston paused to get a firmer grip on the basket handles. "Sure beats going on our own. Your backside doesn't affect me in the least."

"I should hope not!" Ken grinned at the women as they began a series of exaggerated hip movements.

"Now you take Lana," Boston commented, "she has something that moves." His voice rose louder. "Poor Sparky, she's a little on the skinny side."

Samantha shot him a dirty look over her shoulder. "Don't pay any attention to them, Lana," she said to the sputtering woman at her side, "our time will come, just wait." More bawdy remarks drifted around them, and Lana squealed with a mixture of anger and laughter.

"I wish I could think of a way to pay them back." Lana said wistfully.

"Oh, I'll figure out something." Samantha lengthened her stride, putting more distance between herself and the two men. She slowed down when she noticed Lana puffing to keep up with her.

"How do you do it, Sammy? The way you talk to

Boston and the things you get away with. You never back down and always speak your mind. I'd be scared to death to try. Ken would never stand... uh...I mean Boston."

Samantha bit back a grin at the sudden rush of color in Lana's cheeks at her mistake, but knew she'd have to play along. "Boston would never hurt you."

"Oh, no. No, not physically. But you've never seen him when he really loses his temper—" she shivered "—or never been on the receiving end of his sarcastic tongue. I've seen him reduce strong men to weaklings when they didn't follow his orders."

"Does Ken have a temper?" Samantha asked, tongue in cheek.

"What? Oh, yes. About the same as Boston's." She answered mournfully.

They walked on and Samantha thought about Lana's remarks. She'd witnessed Boston's foul temper a few times and felt the bite of his tongue. It wasn't an experience she wished to repeat with any frequency. He was usually easygoing and teasing, but when he did lose control it was devastating to watch. "Lana, I was raised with six older brothers. To survive I had to learn to speak up for myself because no one else would. If Boston or *anyone* else does something you don't like or agree with, tell him."

"Maybe you're right," she said thoughtfully, "but I hate to argue and fight. That's all I heard all my life from my parents."

Boston halted their conversation, issuing orders to stop and spread out the quilts under the shade of the long branches of a cluster of willow trees. Ken, an avid fisherman, picked up his gear and wandered downstream with Lana at his heels, her small can of worms held at arm's length.

Samantha scanned Boston's thoughtful expression as he looked after the two receding figures. "You're giving them plenty of rope to hang themselves, aren't you?" she needled, envious of the tender smile he bestowed on Lana's disappearing form. Boston smiled smugly at her tirade and she snapped, "By all means, let's keep the tension going. Why don't you just go after her and offer her some help? I'm sure she'd love the company."

"My, my. You're in a fine mood. But Ken's the expert angler, so we'll let him take care of Lana."

He lifted two bottles of wine—one white, one red—from the basket and tied a length of rope around their necks. Walking to the edge of the stream he lowered the bottles to chill. "I'm the expert on lunch." He grinned and stretched out on the quilt, closing his eyes.

"Are you going to sleep?"

"Hmmm. I haven't had much lately." He opened one lazy lid and stared at her in a suggestive manner, then closed his eye with a long sigh.

"Why not?" she grinned.

"Need you ask? I've heard you moving around during the middle of the night, so you can stop the innocent act." His hand searched for hers, and finding it, he lifted it to his mouth. "How do you like taking cold showers?"

"I haven't...."

Boston gave a short bark of laughter. "Well, I

damn well don't like it! I used to be six foot three.
When I measured this morning I'd lost an inch." His
face twisted with mock disgust. "My body's shrivel-
ing up from all that cold water." Samantha tried to
keep a straight face. "It's no laughing matter,
Sparky. If this keeps up, I'll need a stepladder to
reach your mouth."

"That's all right, I have nothing against shorter
men. I've even dated a few."

Boston reached up and pulled her down beside
him. "I don't want to hear about them—ever."

All her good intentions to keep their relationship
platonic until their problems were resolved evaporated. She studied his face and saw it filled with love,
hunger and desire, then she leaned over and tenderly
kissed his warm mouth. Her mind issued a warning
to stop, but her body turned traitor to the advice.

Boston's arms tightened, the aphrodisiac of her
mouth igniting the dampened fire into a frenzy of
flames. He pulled her closer and flipped her over
onto her back. "Oh, woman, woman, what are you
trying to do to me?"

"I didn't mean for that to happen," she said con-
tritely, then felt his body go rigid. "Boston...?"

"Be quiet a minute." He cursed beneath his
breath.

"What?" Puzzled, she frowned as he sat up,
paused, then moved away from her side.

He cocked his head, listening. "If I'm not mis-
taken, Lana and Ken are coming back. I don't
believe it! They're having a fight, and sweet, unflap-
pable Lana seems to be doing all the yelling." He

shot her an unreadable look. "I wonder who put her up to talking up for herself?"

Samantha gulped, remembering her earlier advice to the other woman. She watched Lana round the bend in the river, her face flushed but triumphant. Ken slowly followed, and as he neared Samantha he gave her a look of pure fury. He knew who was setting the example.

"Let's eat." Boston tried to break the strained atmosphere.

Later, feeling indolent and satiated with food and wine, Samantha lay back with a contented sigh and closed her eyes. Though Boston might not have mastered the art of cooking a meal, he certainly could put together a culinary delight for a picnic lunch. Wine, three selections of cheese—creamy Camembert, Brie and cheddar. Rye and wheat crackers for the *pâté de foie gras* and smoked oysters. Fresh slices of apple and pear to munch with pecan and black-walnut halves. They ignored Ken and Lana's sulky silence and had their own private party.

"Wake up, sleepyhead." Boston tickled her nose with a long blade of grass.

She scowled and brushed the irritating prickle away with a lazy swipe of her hand. "Go away."

"Come on, get up. I promised to show you where to find arrowheads and now is a good time to go." Her eyes flew open at the blatant lie and he shot a telling glance toward Ken and Lana, seated at opposite ends of the quilt from each other, their hostility still evident in the glaring looks that periodically bounced between them. Samantha nodded and Boston clasped her extended hand and pulled her to her feet.

Away from the others, he draped a casual arm around her shoulders and guided her through a maze of tall trees. When they reached a wall of tangled vines, he parted one end and motioned her through. "I found this place about a week after I bought the property. It's my special hideaway."

Samantha bent over and stepped through the opening he'd made. Her breath caught at the back of her throat at the beauty of the lush, grassy enclosure before her, sheltered by trees. The babble of water drew her attention to a large rocky formation at one side. Brilliant colors sparkled as the sun's rays caught the water's droplets and reflected a shower of colors across the small glade.

Boston's hands encircled her waist, pulling her back. She rested against him, eyes closed. When she felt the touch of his lips on her neck, she didn't protest, only moved her head sideways to allow his seeking mouth easier access to the sensitive area.

"I want you, Sparky. You're not going to say no, are you?" His hands moved up from her waist to her breasts. He felt them swell at his light touch, and he groaned into the curve of her neck.

Her eyes fluttered open and she looked around and realized she couldn't deny him or herself any longer. "No," she whispered. "No, I'm not going to turn you away."

Boston led her to the cool shaded center of the tiny glade and lay down beside her, his fingers busy with the tie of her halter top. When the stubborn knot finally gave way and the material slipped to her waist, exposing the small firmly rounded breasts, he raised his head. "You're beautiful, Sparky," he said in a husky voice, "so beautiful." Strong fingers caressed and cupped one breast as his mouth lowered to the already hardened rosy nipple of the other.

Samantha reached out to place a trembling hand against his smooth cheek. His lips left her breast and kissed the palm, his tongue circling the center. Their eyes met and she felt as though she would drown in their dark depths. Her fingers tangled in the springy waves of his hair and she pulled his mouth up to hers. "Do you love me, Boston?" Her lips moved softly against his. "You've never really told me, not with any feeling." He was silent for a second, and in that space of time she felt something die then come alive again with his next words.

"I'm not very good at saying words of love, Sparky. I'm much better at writing and singing them."

"Then sing them to me now!"

"I can't. You know that."

She tightened her fingers in his hair and forced his head back when he tried to turn away. "Do I? Elijah said there's nothing wrong with your vocal cords. You just won't try. Why?"

"Damn it," he exploded, "I didn't bring you here to talk about my voice."

"Now's as good a time as any. And what about the fund-raising benefit Father Brian's giving? He needs your help."

"How did you find out about Father Brian's

troubles?'' He sat up. "No, don't tell me. Elijah, right?''

She nodded her head and lay back, watching his face turn hard and forbidding. "He only wants to help you.''

"Interfering old man.''

"Boston!''

"Listen to me.'' He jerked her up into a sitting position, his fingers biting into the tender flesh of her shoulders. "I will not sing for Father Brian's benefit, or anyone else's.''

"Have you even tried?'' she demanded.

He gave her a sharp shake. "You're missing the point. I can't do it.'' His mouth descended on hers, cutting off her next question.

Samantha suffered the almost harsh kiss, telling herself he wasn't punishing her but himself for the total loss of his voice. She hugged him closer, harder, and the storm within him lessened and died. His mouth softened, becoming tender and persuasive, and she returned the erotic movements of his tongue. The sudden stillness of his movements puzzled her for a second until she heard the ranch bell toll three times, its muted clanging echoing across the mile distance, the message clear. Boston was needed at the ranch house.

"Hell and damnation,'' he ground out, resting his hot forehead against hers. "I believe you plan these intrusions. What do you do, send out mental messages? Witch,'' he snorted, "let's go. Elijah will keep ringing the bell every fifteen minutes until he sees us coming.'' Reluctantly he retied her halter top and helped her to stand.

She followed him out of the enchanting glade, walking behind him, her knees still shaky from the passion of his kisses, her lips reddened from desire. When he had almost reached the picnic site he gave a loud shout and orders to pack up. As they rounded a tree barrier they were in time to catch Ken and Lana's broken embrace and guilty start of surprise. Samantha shook her head in renewed frustration. Would Boston ever put an end to this charade? What she needed, she decided, was to get away from everyone and think things over.

WHEN THEY RETURNED to the ranch, Elijah met them at the back door. Samantha caught the old man's inquiring glance and shook her head. His shoulders slumped, and when she would have passed him, he held her back.

With a hasty jerk of his head, Elijah turned to Boston. "Father Brian's here." The others filed past, but she stayed beside Elijah. "Did you talk to Boston about the benefit?"

"I tried, Elijah, but he's extremely hostile about his voice. I think it's best just to let the subject drop for a while. Maybe later he'll be ready to give his voice a try." She flinched at the coldness lingering in his black eyes.

"It's too late now, missie. Father Brian's here to discuss the show with him."

Samantha shifted her weight uneasily from one foot to the other in agitation. "How can that be?" she whispered fiercely. "You said yourself nobody knows the extent of damage, so...." Her voice trailed off as she studied the leathery face. "Oh, no. Elijah, you didn't?"

"Yep. Figured if you couldn't get a rise out of him, maybe Father Brian could persuade Boston to at least try."

"He's going to be furious."

"Yep," he sighed. "Guess I'll have to hide out for a couple of hours."

"More like a couple of days," she murmured, and couldn't help smiling at his soft raspy chuckle. There came a long, low, hissing sound from behind and Samantha jumped and spun around. Pearl glared at them, her faded green eyes wide and even more owlish with anger, but her anger was directed at Elijah.

"You interfering old coot. Why can't you leave the boy alone?"

Elijah growled back and Samantha began to step away. She was stopped by a gnarled, dry, callused hand on her arm. "No, you don't, missie. You're not running out on me. I want you at this meeting with Father Brian."

"Elijah, I don't think...."

"You don't have to think. Come along." Still muttering under his breath about Pearl, he led Samantha, her steps lagging to the living room.

CHAPTER NINE

SOFT, MUTED EARTH TONES and subtle nut shades of leather didn't radiate any warmth to the frosty atmosphere of the room. Four people sat in a frozen tableau as if waiting for a catalyst. Samantha felt the different degrees of coolness as all eyes turned upon her entrance. Her glance flickered over Ken and Lana and landed on Boston. Her heart contracted at the whiteness of his face and the controlled fury burning in his jet eyes. She gulped, knowing if she didn't do something immediately to stall the eruption, she'd be sucked into the fire of accusation and retaliation. Breaking Elijah's hold on her arm, she hurried across the room and introduced herself to Father Brian.

"Quickly, Father, bless me before Boston takes it into his head to strangle me. It's not in my nature to wear sackcloth and ashes for something I didn't do."

She heard the laughter behind her and relaxed her stiff shoulders. Meeting the priest's twinkling blue eyes, rosy cheeks and cherub face, she forced a smile to her strained lips.

"Thank you, Miss Griffin," he whispered, "that was magnificently done."

"Samantha, please, Father." She stepped back

and sat down next to Lana, determined to keep her mouth shut.

There was a long uncomfortable lull before Father Brian spoke. "Boston, you remember Hal Storm from the orphanage, don't you? Well...." He paused, coughed, shifted in his chair before going on. "Well, my boy, he handles the entertainment bookings for the Summit in Houston." He sat back and folded his hands in his lap, relieved there'd been no hasty outburst yet. "It seems one of his one-night bookings has canceled and he's offering me the use of the facilities for our charity benefit—on one condition." Father Brian cleared his throat loudly and sent Elijah a pleading glance, which was met with bland innocence.

"I take it, Father, that the condition is that I do a one-man show for him. Right?"

The steady building of tensions as Father Brian spoke seemed to crackle in Samantha's ears. Her heart pounded then skipped a beat at the agony that twisted Boston's face, an agony that shut off her own breath. She wanted to run to him, hold him close and scream at them to stop. Couldn't they see what the loss of his voice had done to him?

Father Brian sighed and visibly sagged with relief. "That's exactly what Hal wants. I tried to explain that you still didn't have the full use of your voice, but for some reason he was adamant. No Boston, no Summit for the benefit. I don't know what he could be thinking of," he choked out nervously.

"Don't you?" Boston's hard eyes focused on Elijah, then back to Father Brian's guilty flush before they once again came to rest on Elijah. "I think I know why he's so insistent." Black eyes met and clashed. "Someone's been spying and sticking his nose in where it doesn't belong."

Spying. The one word jolted Samantha out of her self-imposed silence. "Spying on whom, Boston?"

"Stay out of this, Sparky." His voice cut across the room, its tone bringing her upright. But like a bloodhound sniffing out danger who turns tail and runs, she clamped her lips shut on the questions that threatened to tumble out.

Boston inhaled deeply. "I'm sorry, Father, but I can't do it. As much as I'd like to, I just can't." He stood up and without another word stormed out of the room.

Samantha slipped out of the room and ran toward the kitchen, but before she reached the open doorway she heard the back door slam shut. She met Pearl's sympathetic gaze across the table. "Where did he go?" she demanded huskily.

"Let him be, girl. He needs some time alone."

Samantha agreed without comment, even though she knew she couldn't wait. She rushed to her room, took a quick shower and slipped into jeans and a blue blouse, not bothering with a bra in her hurried attempt to escape before anyone noticed her absence. She tiptoed down the stairs and out the front door, rounded the side of the house, and headed for the outbuildings and the trees beyond. Elijah would just have to face the fact that Boston would never sing again. Slowing her steps, she wondered if the best thing for everyone all around was for her to go home? She passed the barn door and stopped in mid-step, a frown gathering across her brow at the faint sounds of music issuing forth. The ranch hands were off today, the last of them having left early that morning for a day in town. Reaching out, she pulled the partially closed door open a few inches and listened. When no further sounds filtered out, she shook her head, rejecting the thought that the voice she'd heard was Boston's. She was about to turn away, then stopped again as the light strumming of a guitar reached her ears. Radios did not stop and start in the middle of a song! She eased the door open enough to squeeze through, and stood in the gloomy interior, straining to determine the location of the music.

The horses snorted and shifted nervously at her intrusion and she passed them without her usual friendly pat, following the music coming from the far corner. When she reached the spot she found it vacant, but still the music persisted. Looking up, her eyes narrowed at the loft above, and the words of the song became clearer. Her hands and feet found the slats of the ladder on their own accord and she began to climb, entranced by the deep, mellow voice pulling her upward, mesmerizing her with its perfect tone and control.

Samantha stepped from the ladder onto the straw-covered floor and glanced over the bales of hay, her eyes drawn to Boston. He was sitting cross-legged on a quilt, guitar in hands, head bowed, as he picked the chords to another song and began to sing.

"These are the eyes that never knew how to smile...
till you came into my life."

He raised his head and their gazes locked. His jet eyes were bewitching and the words penetrated her spinning mind, compelling her closer, step by step.

"And these are the arms that long to lock you
inside...
every day and every night."

Spellbound, she moved toward him, captive to the magic he conjured.

"Here is the soul of which you've taken control...
can't you see I'm trying to show love is right."

She stood in front of him and he rose smoothly to his feet, still luring her nearer with his spell.

"These are the hands that can't help reaching
for you...
if you're anywhere in sight."

She wondered if he could hear the wild beating of her heart as his words danced through her veins, leaving her weak with a throbbing need to have those hands caress her.

"And these are the lips that can't help calling
your name...
in the middle of the night."

Boston eased the guitar to the floor, then gathered her into his arms. No preliminaries were needed for the storm that raged in both of them. Samantha looked up at him and felt herself devoured in the loving depths of his eyes, their ebony luminescence flashing with expectancy.

With deft, experienced fingers he unbuttoned her blouse, pushed the silk from her shoulders, then slipped it off completely. Irritation played across her flushed face as she worked frantically at the buttons of his shirt, but her fingers trembled so much that she gave up the fight and caught both sides of the opening and wrenched them apart, severing the row of buttons from the material. A deep growl of pleasure brought a satisfied smile to her lips. Within seconds jeans and underclothes were added to the pile of discarded articles.

Boston drew her to him and she stroked his back, savoring the rigid muscles and sleek skin. His arms tightened convulsively, crushing her to him, and she felt the heat of his skin and the heavy hammering of his heart. Her breath came in tiny gasps as his mouth slid from her neck to her breast, then back to the sensitive base of her throat. He lowered her to the quilt and his kiss drew her downward into a dark abyss of sensations, blocking out all sound but their rapid breathing. She felt as if she'd been thrown on a turbulent sea. The touch of warm smooth flesh under her grasping fingers, the taste of his mouth on hers, sweet and erotic, and the smell of his skin made her urge him on.

Like an ocean's currents his body engulfed hers, lifting her upward. Then he sent her crashing downward into a fathomless chasm. His movements heaved her high on a rising swell, but before she reached the top, he snatched her back to a calmer course, only to catch her and send her spiraling upward again. And when she thought she could bear no more, her body joined his in the pulsating rhythm and they crested the wave together.

Boston was a pirate, a marauder of the high seas. He plundered her soul and left her body a sedated wreckage, lulled by the ebbing tides of their passion.

She drifted to sleep. When she woke, it took her several seconds to comprehend where she was and what had happened. Curled into Boston's body, his arm resting heavily across her waist, she squeezed her eyes shut in agony.

Liar! The word blossomed in her head then spread its poisonous petals through her system. She carefully picked up Boston's arm and eased her body from his embrace. Standing up, she retrieved her clothes and began to dress with jerky movements, all the time staring down at Boston's sleeping face. She wondered how she could have been such a fool. If he had decieved her about his voice, what else did his duplicity encompass?

"What are you doing?"

"What does it look like?" Her voice trembled in an effort to suppress the anger and hurt she felt.

"Don't go. Lie down and talk to me." He stretched lazily, folding his hands behind his head, a contented smile tugging at the corners of his mouth.

"Talk! Why? To hear more lies?" she whispered and raised her head to catch his blank expression. "How could you, Boston?" Her aquamarine eyes deepened with a controlled rage she'd never felt before. She ran for the ladder, grasped its rough edges and began to climb down. Her last glimpse of Boston as her head descended through the opening was his hurried efforts to pull on his jeans as he shouted her name.

She sprinted between stalls and out the barn door, thinking of the haven of her bedroom with its sturdy lock. The sound of booted footsteps urged her on. Halfway to the back door of the ranch house, she turned her head and saw Boston gaining on her. Finally, as she clasped the knob and shoved the door open, a heavy hand grabbed her shoulder and stopped her forward movement.

"Hold it right there!"

"Take your hand off me!" Samantha lashed out at him and he let go, his arm dropping limply to his side.

She looked ahead and glared at the four people gathered around the table, each frozen in shock at her outburst. Ken stood red faced, his mouth hanging open. Father Brian was frowning with distress. Lana, her big brown eyes wide with surprise, jammed a fist to her mouth. Elijah's cold, flat black eyes sparkled with renewed life, and the unexpected smile that lit his solemn face almost caused Samantha to recoil.

"Did you know Boston has regained his voice? And from what I've heard, he's been practicing for some time." Samantha gave a harsh laugh. She was shaking badly now, her face white and pinched, the freckles standing out starkly against her pale skin. "He's lied to all of us."

"No," Boston shouted. "I told you I wouldn't sing, not that I couldn't. There's a big difference."

"Why you word-twisting Machiavellian, you...."

"I also told you I would never sing before a live audience."

"Don't play your word games with me. It all boils down to the same thing. If you'd lie about something as important as your voice, what else have you lied to me about?"

She wanted to scream, shout and cry, but the pain weighing her down held her back.

Boston shook his head wearily, chilled by her cool manner. All trace of the hot-tempered, vibrant woman he loved to tease was gone. In her place stood a stranger with a wall erected around her for defense against the pain he'd inflicted. He shot her a probing glance and then smiled crookedly in self-contempt. "The thought of performing before a live audience scares me to death."

"Coward," she shouted. The word slipped out before she had time to think. "You've put me through hell because you're a coward?"

Boston flinched and grabbed her shoulders. "Do you have any idea what it's like to see a fan—a woman—place a rose on stage, then be blown fifteen feet in the air?" He lowered his voice to a painful whisper that ricocheted around the silent room. "Do you know how it feels to be knocked off your feet, lie there hurt and helpless while people almost trample you to death?" He dropped his hands from her in disgust.

Samantha had never before watched the blood drain from a man's face. His skin became chalky white and his eyes turned blank. She stared at him as he walked the perimeters of the kitchen like a wounded panther. Those dark eyes came to rest on Samantha, not seeing her but seeing, she thought, the destruction of his concert and the screaming, stampeding people. The anguish in his words melted her own icy anger into puddles of shame.

"Coward, you say. Maybe I am." He had returned to stand in front of her, his eyes flashing hotly. "What you don't realize is the police never caught whoever planted the bomb. They don't know if it was some nut that did it for kicks, or someone who had a grudge against me."

Samantha turned her head away from his tormented expression, but biting fingers captured her face and forced her to look into his tortured soul.

"I will not endanger the people who made me rich and famous. And to ensure that it won't have the chance to be repeated, I'll never sing again."

"But, Boston," she whispered.

"Woman," he snarled, "you've torn my insides out enough for one day." He stormed out of the kitchen, Ken and Elijah following his retreating steps.

Standing in the center of the room, numbed, Samantha thought she now understood the term shell shock. Boston had dropped his own kind of bomb and she was his target. A sobbing feminine voice brought her back to earth.

"You love him, don't you?"

Samantha nodded her head. "Lana...I..." She couldn't go on. The pity and understanding in the other woman's face sent her flying from the room.

SAMANTHA SAT ON THE EDGE of the bed, her face buried in trembling hands. What had she done? The anger she felt was overshadowed by her shame. Why hadn't she seen his fear? It was there, staring at her the whole time, but she'd been too blind to see. Elijah knew Boston had regained his voice and was practicing. Yet, hesitant to rake up old pain, he'd used her to discover the truth for herself—used her to push Boston into admitting his fears—used her in the final showdown.

Samantha groaned aloud, remembering Boston's last words and the look on his face when he walked out of the kitchen. He would never forgive her! She'd forced him to face his fear, and for a man with his pride to admit before his family and friends he was a coward was unforgivable. She shivered and prayed he wouldn't hate her for what she'd done. Samantha groaned again, realizing she'd ruined everything. She tried to push aside the thought of the hurt she'd caused, but it lay like a stone on her heart. Had she destroyed Boston's love, or did he really love her? Her mind grabbed hold of that thought, pushing all others aside.

Thinking back, she couldn't remember his actually saying he loved her. No, that was wrong. He did say it once, but the words held no tenderness and were like a forced admission. Not even at their most intimate moments did he say I love you, just that he loved her ways of exciting him. Samantha wrapped her arms around her chest and rocked back and forth, all her doubts resurfacing. She desperately needed someone to talk to, and with that thought she reached out and snatched up the telephone, carried it to her lap and began to dial her father's private line at home. As the hollow ringing began, she squeezed her eyes shut. *Please be there, dad.*

"Dad."

"Sis?"

"Mark. What are you doing answering dad's phone?"

"Where the hell are you?" came the gruff emotional voice. "Are you all right? Do you realize everyone's nearly crazy with worry?" There was a hardy sigh, then his voice changed to a puzzled tone. "Except dad. He doesn't seem in the least concerned."

Samantha couldn't suppress a chuckle. Of all six of her brothers, she loved Mark the best. She forced a smile in her voice. "I'm fine, Mark."

"Where are you?" Reassured by her tone, his anger surfaced again. "You're sure you're okay?"

"Yes."

"Sure?"

"Mark, have I ever lied to you?" she demanded, exasperation clouding her voice. "Now do me a favor, brother mine. Don't tell the family where I am."

Mark gave a loud snort. "How can I? You haven't told me yet." There came a string of muffled oaths and Samantha grinned. "Wait a minute. Wait just one minute! Dad's known all along where you are, hasn't he? The old man must be getting senile to let you go off with that...."

Samantha tried to interrupt, but the sudden shouting of two male voices brought a halt to her explanations. She recognized the lion's quality of the other voice. Her father was berating Mark for answering his private phone, then wringing promise after promise out of him to keep quiet about her call.

"Sammy."

"Dad, can you talk?"

"'Course I can! Is something wrong, baby? You sound strange."

"No," she whispered, instantly regretting the call. What could she tell her father? That she was in love with Boston and having an affair? That she was a fool and had believed he was in love with her? Could she tell him of the mess she'd made?

"Sammy, you still there?"

"Yes." Her mind suddenly clear, she went on. "I wanted to let you know I'll be home in a couple of days."

"Oh." His voice hesitated a moment. "Boston didn't mention your coming home when I talked to him early this morning."

"You called him?"

"No, he called me. Sammy, didn't you know he telephones me about every other day?"

"No. No, I didn't, dad." Her father laughed and the warm familiar sound brought a misty blur to her eyes. She choked down a sob and cleared her throat.

"Sammy, about coming home...."

"Yes?"

There was another distinct pause. Then her father continued. "I don't think it's a good idea. Not right now."

"Why?"

"Listen to me, baby. Your brothers are suffering from your disappearance, but not enough. You wouldn't believe the changes going on around here." He chuckled with pure glee. "Your sisters-in-law have had the law laid down and are walking a very fine line."

Samantha gave a watery laugh in return, "Okay, so I go to Houston and stay with Aunt Sally."

"No, that's not a good idea either. Why can't you stay put for a while?"

"I can't, dad. Please." All the hurt surfaced in that one word. "I want to come home."

"Did you have a fight with Boston?"

"Yes." Samantha clutched at the ready-made excuse. "Yes, we did, and I don't want to stay any longer."

"That's not like you, Samantha, to back down. Why?"

Samantha shifted the phone to her other ear and frowned. Her father never denied her anything within reason. Why was he being so insistent now? "I'm coming home."

"No, you're *not*." The harsh ring of his voice caused Samantha to jerk upright. "Things are just beginning to cool down here. We barely missed a scandal and if you return without Boston, it will only add fuel to the fire as far as my opponent is concerned."

Samantha sat staring at the phone, its dial tone buzzing from the broken connection. "Then I'll go to New York," she said, slamming the receiver down.

Resentment flared at her father's treatment, and her anger and courage returned. She'd leave today—right now! Samantha jumped off the bed, sprinted across the room and yanked open the closet door. She pulled out her luggage and dropped the cases on the crumpled bed. After a few minutes she had cleaned out the chest of her lingerie and had it neatly packed in one case. Hands on hips she nodded and turned back to the closet for the rest of her clothes.

"What the hell are you doing?" Boston kicked the door shut with an angry shove of his booted foot.

"Packing."

"I can see that! But where do you think you're going?"

"Home." She added the slacks she'd been folding into the case, ignoring his presence. He walked to the side of the bed and she backed away.

Boston picked up a handful of lingerie and dropped it back in the open drawer. Samantha followed, retrieved her things and threw them back into the case.

"Stop it." She grabbed his wrist as he picked up another handful.

"You're not leaving, Sparky," he growled. Breaking her hold, he tipped the full case onto the carpeted floor, spilling its contents.

Samantha looked down and shrugged. She'd just repack them. "I'm going home, Boston, and this time you can't stop me."

"I wouldn't bet on that, Sparky," he said dryly. "Tell me something. How did you plan to get to town?"

Samantha frowned at his question. "I'll borrow your car." He shook his head and her frown deepened. "Ken can drive me." He shook his head again. "One of the ranch hands?"

"They won't be back till Monday." He shook his head a third time and clucked his tongue.

"Then I'll walk!" she declared, her eyes flashing her irritation.

"It's a long, long walk, city girl," Boston taunted, struggling to contain his amusement. He watched her angrily pace the length of the room, breaking her stride to kick articles of clothing out of her path. "You're going to stay right here."

"No, I'm not."

When she passed in front of him, Boston grabbed hold of her arm and swung her around. "You're staying, even if I have to lock you in this room. You've torn my quiet existence apart, hurled accusations at me and fought me at every turn, but no more!" He pulled her closer and snarled down into her upturned face. "What's the matter, Sparky? The going gets a little rocky and you want to run home to daddy? Or is it you think because I show fear that I'm weak?" She shook her head in mute denial, but he didn't seem to see. "I'm as human as the next man. I laugh, cry, hurt, am afraid sometimes, and love." He pushed her away from him. "Understand this clearly. I might be an image and a voice without depths to some people—they're not important. But I'll be damned if I'll allow you to put me above others then watch you fall apart the minute you realize I have weaknesses and imperfections like the rest of the human race.'' He strolled to the door and, holding it open, turned and surveyed the room. "Clean this mess up. You're not going anywhere."

"We'll see," she grumbled. A plan had begun to take shape, and as the door closed she bent down and started to retrieve the scattered clothing.

A SUBDUED GROUP met for predinner drinks. Samantha deliberately tried to make her entrance late in the hope everyone would be there and she could avoid Boston and his knowing eyes. Dressed in pale peach silk pants and blouse, she glided across the room to where Ken, Lana and Father Brian sat sipping their drinks. Her eyes searching the room for Boston and Elijah.

"Where's Boston?" she asked Lana as she sat down beside her on the long tufted couch.

"He's in the kitchen trying to persuade Pearl to join us for a drink."

There was no joy in the room, she observed, and knew everyone's thoughts were still reliving what had happened hours earlier. Ken fixed her a drink and they made small talk until Boston entered, pushing a reluctant Pearl before him.

"My dinner," she protested with every step.

"One drink won't take that long. Besides, I bought your favorite peach brandy. See, Father Brian has already poured you a glass."

Before anyone could reiterate Boston's urgings for her to stay, there came a long wailing cry from the depths of the house. A chill inched its way up Samantha's spine. Her eyes traveled from one person to the next, puzzled by their calm acceptance of the blood-curdling scream. Then, as if in unison, all heads turned toward Pearl. Samantha followed their gazes and bit her lip at the old woman's owlish expression as she innocently sipped her brandy.

The library door rattled open. It flew against the wall, then bounced back, only to be shoved open again.

Elijah charged into the room at a fast shuffle. His pewter eyebrows slashed upward in a forbidding line and his braids flew out behind him. He was waving a handful of white underwear before him, which seemed to pop and crackle like thin paper.

"Woman," he bellowed at Pearl. "This is the last straw! You starch my unmentionables one more time and I promise you you'll lose that ridiculous knot of frog hair atop your head."

Pearl surveyed the rampaging Elijah over the rim of her glasses, her lips pursed in a familiar pucker. "Busybodies who interfere in other people's business usually find the going a little *stiff*. Don't get too used to the soft life, old man." She set the crystal brandy snifter down gently and left the room, all eyes following her triumphant retreat. "Dinner's ready if anyone's hungry," she called back from the safety of the hall.

The room erupted with laughter and Elijah threw down his crumpled, starched underwear and stomped off to the dining room with everyone trailing behind.

Throughout the meal, Samantha tried to act as normal as possible. She kept her head down, hiding the sparkle in her eyes from Boston's searching looks. All she needed was for him to catch her excitement and figure out that she was up to something. When Lana offered to help Pearl with the dishes, she excused herself from the table and headed for her room.

CHAPTER TEN

BEHIND LOCKED DOORS, Samantha began to carry out her plan. She rummaged around in her drawer and pulled out a pair of clean jeans, socks and a plaid flannel shirt. From the chest she snatched a heavy black cable-knit sweater. Nights in New Mexico could become a bone-chilling cold even at this time of year. She lay her clothes across the foot of the bed and folded the bedspread back over them, concealing their presence if for some reason she had to leave her room. From the closet she took out the sheepskin coat Boston had bought for her and lovingly ran her fingers over the fleece lining. She stuffed a pair of gloves and a knit cap into the coat pockets before hanging it up again. She checked the contents of her shoulder-strap purse and emptied out everything but credit cards, drivers licence, money, a tube of lipstick and a comb. She was anticipating a long walk to the main highway and didn't want to carry any additional weight.

Samantha switched off the lights and stumbled toward the bed. Now all she had to do was wait till the house quieted down for the night and everyone was asleep. She stared into the darkness. Boston wouldn't allow her to leave, but she was going anyway.

The sudden thought of never seeing him, never being held in his arms, was almost unbearable. Her anger over his deception was unreasonable. It wasn't the issue of his voice that had enraged her so, but the lies. She didn't care if he ever sang again. She wasn't a fan and it wasn't his voice she'd fallen in love with.

Samantha kept a close vigil on the clock and made several trips to the bathroom to splash cold water over her face in an effort to stay awake. At one o'clock she switched on the bedside lamp and began to dress. At the door she ran a mental check to be sure she hadn't forgotten anything. Through the room's gloomy darkness she could distinguish the lumpy bed where she'd stuffed pillows under the covers to make it appear as if she were still there.

The knob turned easily under her fingers, and the door glided smoothly open and closed again. A pale ray from a night-light at the end of the hall cast the wood floor in amber shadows, a guide for her stockinged feet. She stopped at the head of the stairs, reminding herself to hug the wall. From her youth she remembered hearing squeaking steps in the middle of the night. She'd been the one to inform a red-faced Mark one morning that the center of a stair would always give you away because it was weakened from constant use.

Like a dark, clothed ghost she slipped down the steps. Standing perfectly still at the bottom, she listened for any sound of life. She rubbed her sweaty palms on her jeaned thighs. "So far so good," she mumbled out loud, then clamped her lips tightly shut. All she needed, she thought grimly, was to get caught there talking to herself, fully dressed, boots dangling from one hand and the other hand on the doorknob. She didn't think she could convince Boston she was just going out for a very early morning stroll.

Samantha smothered a chuckle and turned the knob. Inch by painful inch she eased the door open, her breath coming in short gasps. She was halfway out, between the door and the frame, when she stopped. Stupid—stupid! With each silent word she butted her forehead against the edge of the door. She'd forgotten a flashlight! Angry with herself, she dropped her boots on the front porch and hissed at the hollow echo they made. Whirling around on tiptoe, she ran to the kitchen, and by touch, feel and bumped toes, she pulled open the drawer that contained candles and flashlights for emergency use. She tested the flashlight to make sure it worked, then hurried back to the front door. A nervous giggle escaped her lips as she pulled the door shut. She sat down on the cold stone porch and hurriedly put on her boots.

The thin beam of light wafted in a small radius before her as she traversed the graveled surface of the drive. The muffled crunching beneath her feet sent a shiver up her spine. It was the only sound and seemed sinister. Suddenly she realized how alone she was. She stopped and listened, straining her ears, trying to catch the imagined footfalls from behind. Her eyes searched the murky depths of the trees a few feet away. She shuddered and pulled the knit cap down further on her head. All those old horror movies she'd avidly watched in her youth began to play out in her mind with startling clarity. Wind rustled through trees and felt like a ghoul's cold breath rushing down her neck. She increased the speed of her steps, refusing to look over her shoulder. Small insects that glowed in the night masqueraded as menacing, watching eyes.

Her heart began to pound, and even in the cool night air a fine film of perspiration beaded her forehead. Her hands trembled, shaking the beam of light eerily from side to side. What about all those wild animals—wolves, bears, mountain lions—lurking in the gossamer shadows, waiting with drooling jaws to tear her apart? She recoiled as her booted foot snapped a small twig. What a fool she'd been to attempt her flight at night. She tried to whistle, but her lips refused to cooperate. "Get hold of yourself," she grumbled, a faint edge of hysteria in her voice.

A glowing red eye in the distant trees snapped her head around. Samantha froze in terror and watched as the luminous glow arched high in the darkness. Her horrified gaze followed its skyward path until it faltered in the breeze, then dropped to the ground. She looked down dumbly at the half-smoked cigarette lying at her feet.

"I was beginning to wonder when you'd show up." The phantom voice drifted out of the brooding shadows.

Samantha had let out a bloodcurdling scream and dropped her flashlight before she realized it was Boston's voice that had taken ten years off her life. "Damn you, Boston Grey!" she yelled, grinding out his cigarette with the heel of her boot and wishing it

was him under her foot. She struggled to catch her
breath, her hand covering her pounding heart protectively.

"What are you doing out here in the middle of the
night?" she demanded, searching the shadows.

"I should ask you the same question, but I already
know the answer—don't I?"

She ignored his remark. "Where are you?"

"Scared?"

"Of course not!" Her breathless voice rose higher.

"But you were, weren't you?"

"No! I've never been afraid of the dark." Samantha winced as a deep unearthly chuckle floated
around her. She spun around to where she thought
the voice came from. "Stop playing games with me,
Boston, and come help me find my flashlight. I can't
see my hand in front of my face."

"Games, Sparky? You seem to be a master."

A low moan hovered overhead and she yanked the
knit cap down further on her forehead.

"Stop it, this minute." When nothing but the rus-
tling of leaves answered her demand she twirled
around in the opposite direction. "I'm sorry I ran
away," she whispered into the night. Surely he
hadn't gone, she thought frantically, and left her
there alone with her flashlight lying somewhere along
the side of the drive. "I'm *very* cold, Boston," she
said, her teeth chattering, but not from the night's
chilling temperature.

"Are you?"

"Yes, yes, I am." She silently sighed with relief.
"I'd like to go back to the house now."

"Would you?"

"Dammit, show yourself!" Samantha snapped. She took a deep breath to calm her rising temper. "I want to go home...I mean back. I'm cold and hungry."

Samantha threw up her hand as a blinding shaft of light beamed brightly from the trees, bathing her in its brilliant rays. What kind of light could put out such a strong beam, she wondered.

"You don't look cold to me. From the way you're dressed, I'd say you planned this escape pretty thoroughly, wouldn't you?"

She shaded her eyes and watched as the light moved closer. "Well, yes, I did actually. But I'm sorry I ever started it." She could make out his face now and sighed again, relieved at his flashing smile.

"Why's that?" he asked.

Samantha straightened, her voice prim. "I've decided I don't like the dark."

Boston threw back his head and erupted in a full roaring laugh.

Samantha stood there frowning till she realized what she'd said and how foolish she'd been. A half smile twitched the corners of her lips. "It wasn't that funny."

"Oh," Boston gasped, desperately trying to sober his expression. "I wish," he stopped then started again, "I wish I had a mirror so you could see yourself. Better still, I wish I had a camera."

His laughter was becoming contagious and Samantha bit her lip to keep from joining in. "Why?"

"That hat."

"What's wrong with my cap?" She proudly patted the bright orange-and-green-tasseled pom-pom on top. "I'll have you know Chris bought this for my birthday."

"Who's Chris?" he demanded, his expression changing with lightning speed.

"Ah, Chris...." Samantha dreamily gazed up toward the starless sky.

"Sparky!"

She looked up into his glittering eyes and her pulse began to race. "Jealous?" she taunted and skipped out of his reaching hands. "He has the most beautiful gray eyes you've ever seen. And when he looks at you, you just want to melt and hug him to death. He's so lovable."

"Sparky," Boston growled threateningly, "do you want me to leave you?"

Samantha stepped out of his reach again. Before she could goad him further, her heel contacted a round object. Her arms windmilled and she squealed as her feet flew out from under her and she landed hard on her bottom.

Boston quickly knelt beside her. "Are you all right?"

She pushed the knit cap from her eyes and looked at his concerned face. A small giggle escaped her lips, and then she lay back and laughed up at the sky. "What a night of errors!"

She told him of the mishaps she'd had trying to get out of the house and the wild workings of her imagination as she walked down the lonely drive. When she was finished he was lying beside her, joining in her laughter.

Then they fell quiet for a moment, and Boston asked, "Who's Chris?"

Samantha turned her head and smiled into his eyes. "My five-year-old nephew."

"Come on." He helped her up. "Let's go back to the house. I'm cold." Boston picked up the spotlight he'd been carrying and flung his arm around her shoulders.

They made the half-mile journey in silence and when they reached her bedroom, she turned. "Good night, Boston."

"Oh, no. We're not through yet." He shut the door and shrugged out of his coat as she stood there watching him. "Better shed some of those clothes," he advised.

Samantha did as he said, loath to start an argument. She was tired and realized he was waiting for an explanation.

"Well!" he demanded. "Why did you try to run away? Do you have any idea how dangerous your little escapade could have been?"

"No."

"No!" he snorted. "If that's not just like you, go off half-cocked without thinking of the consequences or the worry you cause others. Why, Sparky?" He moved closer and she could smell the scent of fresh pine that clung to his clothes. "I know you were angry with me for not telling you the truth about my voice, but that wasn't enough to make you take off."

Samantha's eyes were glued to his face. "You're going to hate me."

Boston reached out and tenderly pushed a long, bright strand of red hair behind her ear. "I could never hate you, Sparky. No matter what you did or said."

"You will when you hear what happened." She took a deep breath and went on. "I've been wrestling with my conscience all evening."

"Get to the point."

Her breath trembled in exasperation and she rushed on. "I've done exactly what you were so determined not to let happen."

Boston smiled at her hedging. "Go on," he urged. "It can't be that bad."

"Yes, it is! After the scene in the kitchen, Lana knows I'm in love with you," she blurted out. "And...and...oh, Boston, I saw the hurt and pity in her face and couldn't stand it. We've both deceived her and now she must feel like an absolute fool. You do realize she's been so wrapped up in Ken and their problems that she's never noticed what was happening with us." A sob rose to her lips and she choked it back. "I didn't do it deliberately, you must believe me! Lana just stood there, frozen with surprise and shock and said, 'You love him, don't you?' All I could do was nod." She felt an eternity slip by as she watched him close his eyes tightly, his body rigid.

"Oh, Sparky, what have I done?" he muttered vehemently and reached out for her, pulling her cold shaking body next to his in a fierce but tender embrace.

"I didn't mean...."

"Hush. I know." Boston buried his face in the rich thickness of her hair and moaned. "How could I have been so insensitive?" His hand gently tugged her head from his shoulder, forcing her face up. "I've been so tied up in knots over my own problems. I never realized how all this would hurt you," he said hoarsely. "God knows I didn't mean this to happen. Can *you* forgive me?"

Samantha wrapped her arms around his slim waist and hugged him close, then leaned back in the strong circle of his arms.

Boston watched the emotions playing across her face, and they pulled at his heart. "I owe Lana a lot for what she's done for me, but not at your expense. I'm telling her and Ken about us in the morning."

"Do you mean that?" She touched his face with shaky fingers. "I love you."

He looked down, a smile in his heavy-lidded eyes, and nothing mattered any longer but the warmth of her body pressing close to him. "Do you?" he purred. "You'll have to show me."

Samantha's eyes were afire with the same flame she saw burning deep within his. She breathed his name softly, and coming up on tiptoe, placed her mouth against his and traced the shape of his lips with the tip of her tongue. When she felt his arms tighten, she moved back, allowing her breasts to rub sensuously against his chest. "Aren't you forgetting something?" she said, managing a weak smile. Moving away from his warmth and the male scent of his body was an enormous effort, but she pushed him back when he tried to draw her to him again. She dropped her gaze from his frowning face to the strong column of his neck, then to the partially opened shirt and the smooth tan skin beneath. How she yearned to feel his lean muscular body beneath her hands.

"What are you talking about?"

With supreme willpower she forced her attention away from his body and her thoughts. "You're supposed to say I love you, too."

Boston's frown deepened. "You know I'm not any good at this sort of thing." He thought a moment and smiled. "But I'll sing it to you!"

"No," she shook her head, enjoying his discomfort. "That won't do at all."

He jerked her to him, crushing her body against his, and his mouth captured her lips in a kiss that commanded response. Under the onslaught of his passion a sensuous spiral began to spread its burning languor through her body. A little awed, she remembered it had always been like this. From the first kiss they shared he had lighted the fuse to her desires.

"Does that say it for you?" he asked, his voice husky with his own need.

"No! I don't understand you at all, Boston. You write beautiful songs of love and loving. And you sing them with such honesty and emotion that every woman who hears them believes you are saying those words just for her." Samantha placed a pointed finger in the opening of his shirt, then trailed it downward as he watched, trancelike. She paused at the large silver belt buckle and smiled at his shallow breathing. Her hand dropped to enclose the warmth of the firm bulge. "Why can't you say three simple words to me?"

Boston sucked in a hard breath and groaned. "I love you."

Samantha stepped away from him, smiling. "Now that wasn't so hard, was it?"

His answering smile twisted his mouth in a wolfish grin. "Come back here, you little devil. You're damn well going to finish what you started."

Samantha laughed and slipped further out of his reach. "Say it again," she teased.

"Sparky!" he barked.

"One more time and I'll do anything you want." Under her slightly drooping eyelids her eyes sparkled.

He stood still a moment, watching her. "I love you," he said clearly this time, and his heart began to hammer in his chest as she glided into his arms.

"You're not just saying that in the heat of the moment, are you?" She smiled up at him, but there was an edge of uncertainty to her soft words.

"No, my love." He cupped her freckled face in his hands and kissed each eye shut. "I dream about seeing that exquisite look of rapture on your face and hearing your moaning voice speak my name." He gave a short laugh. "Those thoughts have placed me in a few embarrassing positions and I've taken some strong ribbing from my men."

Samantha opened her eyes and searched his face. "That's lust, not love."

"Yes and no." He gazed into her eyes, his expression thoughtful. "Who's to say that just because you love someone you can no longer lust for that person. Desire, lust, love—they're all mixed into one. And when you really think about it, if one of those ingredients is missing, how long will a healthy relationship last?" Boston began to undo her shirt, his fingers working impatiently down the row of sturdy buttons. "I love you, but right this second—" he bent down and kissed her lips "—I lust after your delicious body."

"Do you think Lana will understand?" Her shirt hanging open, Samantha made a halfhearted effort to stop him, and he pushed aside her hands and kissed the rounded top of one breast.

His searching lips traveled downward to the rosy nipple. "I think she will," he murmured against her warm flesh.

They both jumped apart as the door crashed open and slammed against the wall. Samantha clutched her shirt together, her eyes widening. Ken stood framed in the doorway, naked to the waist, his pajama bottoms hanging precariously on his hips. But it was his wild eyes that stopped her angry words.

Ken's mouth worked spasmodically for a second until the rush of words erupted. "Boston, come quick. It's Elijah."

Before anyone could move, Boston had shoved Ken out of his way, bumping into Lana in an effort to get out of the room. "Where?"

"Library."

Samantha sprinted after Boston's retreating frame, but she was unable to catch up with his long running strides. "What happened?" She shot her question back at Lana, who was valiantly trying to keep pace.

"I was hungry and went down to the kitchen to make us...uh...me a sandwich," she puffed. "Oh the way back I heard a choking noise from the library, then a loud thud. When I looked in Elijah was slumped across his chair, his book on the floor." She shivered and began to sob. "I didn't know what to do. I ran back upstairs to get Ken."

Samantha didn't pursue the question that rose in her mind—why didn't Lana try to find Boston first? She took the stairs two at a time, leaving Lana behind.

As she entered the library she stopped, her hand covering her mouth to stifle a gasp. Elijah was stretched out on the floor with Boston over him breathing his life breath into the still form.

Boston raised his head, tears filling his eyes. "He's alive." He frantically searched Elijah's pockets, mumbling, "Old fool, where are your pills? Lana," he roared, "run to his room and get his medicine from the first drawer of the night table. Ken, call Doc Lang and tell him to get out here with an ambulance."

Helplessly, Samantha watched as Boston picked Elijah up and tenderly cradled him in his arms like a baby, carrying him from the room and up the stairs. As he passed she heard his plea, and tears spilled down her cheeks.

"Don't die on me now, old man. I need you." Boston whispered the words into Elijah's deathly pale face.

It seemed hours before the doctor arrived. All they could do was wait. Ken paced, prowling the four corners of the library, until Samantha felt her nerves would snap with the tension. When she was about to scream for him to stop, Lana's soft voice halted his steps.

"Come here, Ken." She patted the cushion next to hers and he obediently followed her request.

They sat in a raw unyielding silence, refusing to voice their fears, afraid someone would say something that would force them to abandon a small ray of hope. Samantha could barely breathe as grief for Boston gripped her. What would he do if Elijah died? Though not of blood kin, Elijah was the only family Boston had. She sensed the deep love and respect between the two men. They were so close they even thought alike, and sometimes for a fleeting second they even looked alike. She tried not to let her mind drift back to the moments she and Elijah had shared. They were few, but she'd come to appreciate his strength and down-to-earth intelligence, and even his cunning. Elijah was one of those rare people with the ability to read others, finding their weakest points and then playing on their emotions. He maneuvered them around at will without their being the wiser. Wily old fox.

When Boston entered they rose in unison, watching, waiting for the miracle they'd all prayed for. There was a painful pause, then he slowly shook his head in defeat. The gaunt paleness of his face told them the bad news.

Samantha's whole body began to shake violently

as she tried to empathize with his pain. How would she feel if her father or one of her brothers died? What kind of comfort would she need? Swallowing hard, she tried to dislodge the lump in her throat. She watched Boston's lagging steps and hunched shoulders turn toward the window, facing the night-darkened land beyond. She felt an unbearable ache for his pain and loss and wanted desperately to go to him—hold him. Her mind wrestled with inadequate words of sympathy and her first tentative step toward him faltered. A hollow sob broke the frozen silence and she turned in time to see Lana catapult herself into Ken's arms.

"No, no, no," she sobbed wildly, clutching Ken's arms. Her blond head was thrown back and tears poured down her pale cheeks. "I can't stand any more. Tell him."

"Hush, sweetheart." Ken's cracking voice rustled over the still room.

"Please, Ken!"

"Lana, hush," Ken implored her.

"No!" she yelled, her voice high with hysteria. "No more lies, no more deceit. *Tell him*."

"Not now! Can't you see he's had enough?"

"Please, please, tell him," she begged between broken breaths.

Ken bowed his head to hide the tears that snaked a silvery path down his roughened cheeks. "I can't, Lana. How much pain do you expect a man to stand in one day?"

Lana wrenched herself from Ken's arms and whirled around to face Samantha, her hands held out before her. "Help me, Sammy," she begged, and stumbled into Samantha's open arms. "You know how it feels to love someone. You know what it's like to have to hide that love till you think you may go crazy. Tell them it can destroy love—the hiding, the cheating. You know. Please, make Ken tell him."

For a long moment Samantha couldn't speak. She stared at Boston and blinked back her own tears, then looked at Lana. Yes, she knew. There was more here than she and Boston realized. The whispered conversations; the moments of shared laughter; the few times she'd caught Ken and Lana in each other's arms; the private scowls and not-so-private fights. How had she been such a fool? Lana and Ken were more than in love. When had it happened? It wasn't her place to say the words. Lana or Ken must tell Boston. She looked at him again and realized from his blank eyes that he'd heard, but in his numbed state he had yet to put the words together into any semblance of meaning.

Samantha bent her head toward the whimpering woman so only she could hear her words. "Lana, go tell Boston. He'll understand."

Lana's eyes were wide with uncertainty. "You really think he'll understand? He won't hate us? Oh, Sammy," she wailed softly, "I couldn't bear it if he hated us."

"He won't," Samantha reassured her. "Boston will be very happy for you."

Lana turned and made her way slowly toward Boston, twisting her hands together. She stopped before him, head bent. "Boston, I'm so sorry," she said choking, then went on, "Ken and I...."

"Lana, no!" Ken's agonized appeal carried across the room.

Lana glanced over her shoulder and squeezed her eyes shut, blocking out his tormented face. She stiffened her back and threw back her head, gazing straight into Boston's eyes. "Ken and I are...married," she said slowly, then went on very quickly. "We were married a month ago. I tried to tell you— Ken tried. But...we're such cowards." Lana buried her face in her hands, her shoulders shaking. "I'm so sorry," she mumbled.

Boston shook his head, his dazed mind finally fitting the puzzled pieces of the conversation together. "Lana, Lana, don't cry any more." He reached out and stroked her blond curls. "You'll make yourself sick." He gave Ken a strained smile and nodded his head. "I knew you two were in love long before you even realized it yourselves." He gathered Lana into his arms and hugged her close. "Ken, come get your wife before she completely waterlogs me. We'll talk later and I'll explain." He relinquished his hold and stared after their retreating backs.

Even through her sadness Samantha felt a great weight lifted from her shoulders as she watched and listened. Boston was free; they were free to show their love openly.

"Come here, Sparky." She flew across the room and into his arms. "Hold me," he said, and the hoarseness in his voice brought a sob to her lips. "No, don't cry. It's better this way. Elijah would never have tolerated living as an invalid. But, oh, God! I'm going to miss him." His arms tightened, crushing her to him.

"I'll be there, Boston." She turned her tear-filled eyes up to his grief-ravaged face. "I'll never leave you."

A weary smile touched his lips and the tenderness eased some of the harsh lines from his face. "It's dawn and you've been awake all night. You must be tired. Why don't you try to get some sleep." He absently picked up a bright red curl and rubbed it between his fingers. "There's nothing you can do now and I need to make some calls."

"I. . . ."

"Go to bed, Sparky."

His voice sounded incredibly tired and she felt him prop his chin on the top of her head, his body weary with the weight of what was to come.

"Please, let me stay with you." It was a whispered plea and his answer was only a nod of his head. When he dropped his arms from around her, she shivered at the loss of his warmth.

"Make some coffee and bring me a cup—no, make it a pot."

He'd already forgotten her, and she walked to the door, turning back to watch as he picked up the phone and began to punch out the numbers. She stepped into the kitchen and faced Ken and Lana. Wordlessly, she opened the cabinet for the canister of coffee and began to prepare the electric percolator.

"Samantha." Ken cleared his throat and started over. "Samantha, I'm sorry."

"What's Boston doing?" Lana questioned, her face puffy and red from her tears.

"Making some phone calls." She plugged in the pot and leaned against the counter. "Where's Father Brian and Pearl?"

"He's...he's staying with Elijah till the ambulance arrives. Pearl wanted to stay with them." Ken pulled Lana to him when another sob broke from her lips.

"I meant it when I said I was sorry, Samantha. In the past weeks I haven't treated you very fairly." He looked down at the curly blond head nestled against his shoulder and smiled. "Lana's scolded me for being a cold, insensitive bastard. Boston's been my friend for years and I've always tried to protect him from the leeches of this world. He's famous, handsome and rich. Those assets leave him wide open for all types. Being a cynic myself from the things I've been exposed to, I felt you were like all those women who throw themselves at him. But you're not."

"No, Ken, I'm not. I love him very much."

"He needs you, now more than ever." Lana twisted her head from the warmth of Ken's shoulder. "He loves you, Sammy. I can see it every tim~ he looks at you. Believe me, he never looked at me or anyone else with that hungry longing in his eyes. Besides, you two get along so well." She gave a watery smile. "You're always fighting."

Watching them, Samantha wondered again how she could have been such a fool and not seen. Ken had the same hungry look that Lana said Boston wore. The coffee finished its cycle with a loud gurgle.

She explained to them the mix-up of the hotel room and the disastrous effects it had had on her family. By the time she'd told them about her brothers and the ride to the farm she had them chuckling over her adventures. The coffee tray fixed, she excused herself and returned to the library.

She sat curled in a large leather wing-back chair, listening to the rumble of Boston's voice, her eyelids growing heavier. When strong arms lifted her up, her eyes popped open. "What's the matter?"

"Come on, honey. To bed with you."

"I can walk," she stated groggily.

In reply, he bent his head and kissed her lingeringly on the lips. "Sure you can, but I'd rather have you in my arms." He carried her to her room and eased her down on the bed.

"Are you going to get some rest, too?" He nodded, and she turned back the blanket, patting the space beside her. "Please, let me hold you." She sensed his need not to talk and settled herself in the curve of his body, her arms wrapped across his chest. He gave an exhausted mumble and fell instantly and deeply asleep.

Samantha listened to the even cadence of his breathing and watched the shallow rise and fall of his chest. She reached over and unbuttoned his shirt, sliding her hand across the silky skin. She nudged her body closer. How peaceful he looked, the strain melting away with slumber. He'd suffered too much in the past hours. She longed to help ease the pain but knew sleep was the best medicine nature could offer. She closed her eyes and thought about all the things she wanted to talk about, the plans they needed to make. How many children did he want? They'd never talked about children—did he even like them? A contented sigh escaped her lips as she thought of a little boy with Boston's ink-black hair and midnight eyes. And the wedding. It would have to be at her home, of course, to accommodate all her family and relatives. Boston would be gaining a large family, one she hoped he would not regret marrying into.

Her thoughts squealed to a halt and her eyes opened wide in surprise. He did want to marry her, didn't he? But never was a word mentioned of marriage. Of course he did, she told herself sternly. She paused in her thinking. Hadn't she always been the one who pushed to tell Lana? No, no, Boston wanted it too. There was nothing to worry about. Still that nagging little imp in the back of her mind warned her to find out. Samantha's eyes grew heavier and she contented herself with the thought that there was tomorrow to think about and the rest of their lives— together.

CHAPTER ELEVEN

"HAVE YOU SEEN Boston?" Samantha lounged against the kitchen-door frame, a frown marring her smooth forehead. Lana and Pearl turned at her question, and her lips twitched at the sight of them standing side by side. Mutt and Jeff, she thought.

A smile touched her lips as she studied Pearl. Two weeks had passed since Elijah's death and the woman seemed to have come to terms with the loss of her old antagonist and friend. Samantha thought back to a week before when she'd found Pearl in the pantry with her glasses pushed up on her forehead, her face buried in a damp dish towel, and her shoulders shaking with grief. She'd tried to comfort Pearl but was waved away, and had left her to cry her heart out in privacy.

Samantha picked out a shiny red apple from a bowl in the center of the kitchen table and took a generous bite. "Where's Boston?"

Pearl's dour frown deepened. "I don't keep tabs on that young man. He's old enough to play outside without my supervision."

It hadn't taken long for Samantha to figure out Pearl's pattern of speech. She'd deny knowledge, then give the answer in the next sentence or with a gésture. Outside was the key word here. "Did he go toward the barn?" Samantha asked, taking another bite of apple to keep from smiling at Pearl's gruffness.

"How would I know? He just walked out." She waved her thin bony hand toward the river. "Get out of my kitchen, both of you. Always underfoot. A person can't even finish dinner," she grumbled, then ruined the effect of her cranky words by thanking Lana for her help peeling the potatoes and dicing onions.

Samantha grinned at Lana's pained grimace and slipped out the back door before she was put to work, too. She took the trail toward the river, munching thoughtfully as she skirted bushes and large rocks in her path. There was something wrong with Boston. Ever since Elijah's death he'd been acting strange. It was more, she sensed, than losing Elijah. He spent long periods of time away from the ranch.

At first she thought he'd been out working with the ranch hands, but when one of them came to the house that morning with a problem only Boston could solve, she'd learned they hadn't seen him in days. He'd been exceptionally quiet around the house, and at night she would lie awake for hours waiting for him to come to her room, but he never did. His moodiness was out of character, and his rare smiles were strained. If he had a problem, why didn't he talk about it with her? Boston had locked her out and the loss left her empty inside.

She came to the forked path leading to the river

and stopped, instinct telling her he wasn't going to be there. Her steps carried her in the opposite direction—toward the glade. Pushing aside the tangle of vines, she crouched down and stepped through. Her gaze lingered on the cool beauty of her surroundings before she shifted position and studied Boston.

He was seated on a small moss-covered boulder, his head bent, elbows resting on his knees. His restless fingers were plucking at the ragged petals of a wild flower. He presented the pose of a man with the burdens of the world on his shoulders, and she felt the weight of his troubles.

"Boston?" She watched his body jerk with surprise as he looked up. For a second she thought he was about to speak, but he only shook his head and looked down again, studying the mangled flower between his fingers. She knelt before him and reached out a hesitant hand, wanting to brush back the lock of raven hair that had fallen across his forehead. She dropped her hand slowly, suddenly unsure and a little frightened of this new side of the man she loved. He seemed unreachable and distant, and she wondered if she had ever really known him at all. His lack of communication these past few days had left her with a bitterness, and the thought struck her that maybe they were destined to love with only the shallowness of a strong physical attraction. "Boston!" she tried again.

He began to speak, his eyes on the rocky ground between his feet. "I should have known or suspected." His voice was harsh with emotion. "Everything's so clear now. All the things he did for me. At the time I never questioned them, just accepted. It was as natural as the sun rising every morning to have him beside me, guiding, advising, teaching. Dammit! I never questioned his reasons for doing those things.''

Boston raked both hands through his hair and looked up, his black eyes dulled with distant thoughts. "He taught me, disciplined me, and loved me, and I always accepted it as his right." His eyes sharpened and focused on Samantha's pale freckled face. "You don't understand what I'm rambling on about, do you?" She shook her head and he reached out, his hand caressing the silky mass of her bright hair. "Elijah was my grandfather." Samantha's shock was audible as she gasped. "He told me—everything—before he died.''

"Why, Boston? Why didn't he tell you earlier?'' Her knees took the trembling weight of her body as she knelt before him. Her arms encircled his waist and she laid her head against his chest, listening to the heavy pounding of his heart. She should have seen it. There were so many clues. "I don't understand why he waited so long to tell you.''

"Shame,'' Boston whispered into the curly mass of her hair.

"Oh, no! You can't mean that? Elijah was never ashamed of you." She pulled back and met the sadness in his eyes. "He loved you and was so *proud* of you. Why do you think he pushed me into needling you about your voice and the benefit? Because he loved you so much he couldn't stand to sit by and see you suffer. But he knew he was too close to your problem to think straight and convince you to go on, so he maneuvered me into doing it for him. His pride...."

"Sparky, Elijah's shame was for himself...for what he did years ago." Boston grasped her arms and held her away from him, studying the puzzled expression on her face. He sighed and dropped his hands, and she settled herself on the ground and waited. "Elijah and his wife—my grandmother—and my mother worked for many years for a wealthy rancher. Elijah was proud of his beautiful daughter, but realized there were going to be problems with the rancher's son, a spoiled, rich playboy. He warned her to stay away from the scoundrel, but it seems his warning was too late—she was already in love with him."

He fell silent for a moment, then went on grimly. "I'm sure you can guess what happened. She was pregnant. When Elijah confronted the rancher and his son, the son tried to make Elijah believe the child my mother was carrying could have been the responsibility of any number of ranch hands. You can imagine Elijah's humiliation and my mother's hurt. But what was worse, he turned on his daughter, even though he knew deep down in his heart that the young man lied. Still, he had his pride and ordered her to leave."

Boston's hands clenched his knees and Samantha grasped them both firmly till his fists loosened and his fingers wrapped around hers. "My mother ran away that night and it was ten years before he saw her again. What's so ironic is the next morning the rancher came to Elijah and confessed his son had lied about everything. Oh, he was very contrite, even offered to allow my mother and his son to marry. It seems he wanted a grandson and at that point he didn't care that it—I—was a half-breed. Elijah quit, but before they left he nearly beat my father to death.''

"What happened to your mother, Boston?"

His eyes were bright with suppressed tears as he studied the perfection of Samantha's face, and a sad smile lifted one corner of his mouth. "That's something we'll never know. She left at sixteen, returned at twenty-six and looked forty. Elijah said she was sick when she arrived. Later they found out she had cancer. From the little she said about her life, Elijah believed she was a nightclub singer. I guess I inherited my musical talent from her.''

Boston plucked another flower from the ground and twirled it between his fingers, then went on. "My grandmother died a few weeks after she arrived. When mother realized she was dying, she told Elijah where she'd left me. He waited until she was buried before he came to the orphanage. He said he knew me the minute he saw me and felt God had forgiven him because I wasn't adopted or fostered out.''

Samantha rested her head against his leg, tears streaming down her face. She hurt for them all.

"You want to hear something funny?" She winced at the hardness in his voice. "Now that I know who my father was, I remember meeting him in Monte Carlo a few years before my accident. Believe me, my mother was better off without him.''

"How do you feel now that you know about Elijah and your mother?"

"Relieved." He was pensive for a long moment. "Isn't that strange? When I was young, before Elijah came into my life, I used to wonder who my parents were. Later it really didn't make any difference. I'm just thankful I had Elijah all these years. He was much more to me than just my grandfather."

Yes, she thought, Elijah was more. He was your friend, father, brother and confessor. Now she recognized the extent of Boston's pain. He'd lost more than just one man. "Why couldn't you have told me sooner? Did you think I wouldn't understand, or that confirmation of your illegitimacy would somehow make a difference in the way I feel about you?" She sat up straighter, her tears still trailing one another down her flushed cheeks. "I don't care who your parents were or where you came from. I love you."

"You're beautiful, did you know that?" He smiled. "Freckles and all."

"You like them, do you?"

Boston pulled her close and kissed away the tears from her cheeks. "Every one, from the tip of your nose to the tip of your toes."

She flashed him a dazzling smile and leaned back. "You still haven't answered my question. Why didn't you come to me?"

"You don't give up, do you?" He slid off the boulder and settled down beside her, his arm around her shoulder. "Sparky, before Elijah died he made one request of me, that I do the benefit for Father Brian. You know how I feel about going back on stage? It was something I needed to work out for myself. I'm sorry if I hurt you, but there are problems and decisions a man must work out for himself.''

She nestled into the warmth of his body and asked, "Boston, as callous as it may sound, you can't let the bombing of a concert and the death of one fan rule your life."

"I know, and I've decided to do the benefit."

Samantha flung her arms around his neck, her lips inches away from his. "I'm so glad. It will all work out, you'll see." Her lips met his and his hold on her tightened. She pushed him backward and rested the length of her body on his, feeling his instant response to her nearness.

"Hussy," he murmured against her mouth, and chuckled as she wiggled closer. "Stop that. I want to talk and you're too distracting."

. "I don't want to talk anymore. I've missed you." Her hand trailed down his chest, but he grabbed her fingers before they made contact with her target.

Boston rolled away from her. "Listen to me—no, no, stay where you are." He inched back, out of reach of her teasing fingers. "I'm serious, Sparky. There are certain things we must discuss."

"Oh, all right," she pouted, "but do you know what I'd like to do to you right this minute. I . . . .''

Boston shook his head. "I don't want to hear." He cleared his throat and she gave him a wicked smile, noting his discomfort. "If I do the concert, do you have any idea what that means?" She nodded.

"I don't think you do. It means hard work for all of us. I'll have to get in touch with my orchestra and they'll have to come here. It will mean endless hours of rehearsal. There will be twelve extra people to take care of. They'll have to be fed, housed, and catered to, and at times you'll have to soothe their artistic temperaments. Are you willing to be my lover, hostess and psychiatrist? Lana and Pearl will help, but the main responsibility will fall on you. Can you take the long lonely hours and my temper? Because, Sparky, I'm a perfectionist about my work and it won't be easy for you. I warn you now, I'll take all my troubles to you and out on you, so before you answer, think very carefully. Do you want to stay and be a part of this madness? If you say yes and the going gets rough—" he leaned over, his face serious "—remember one thing—I won't let you go. You'll have to trust me."

"I'll stay."

"You're sure? And no matter what happens you'll remember I love you?" Boston picked up her hand and kissed the open palm. "Don't ever forget that, Sparky."

She reached for him and this time he didn't pull away, but crushed her to him, his mouth lingering on the velvet softness of her lips. She closed her eyes at the heady excitement of his kiss. It amazed her how naturally his words of love came now. She'd sensed by talking about his feelings he'd come to terms with himself and his newfound knowledge of his past. Lying quietly in his arms, she mentally went over his warnings. She felt strong and capable of handling everything he'd outlined. There would be a few problems adjusting, but she'd dealt with worse situations before. The main thing was that he wanted her totally involved in his life and work. Their love was so intense and solid now, nothing could come between them.

"You're very quiet. Having second thoughts?" He looked at her gently, but there was apprehension in his expression.

"No," she said firmly and kissed him hard on the lips. She laughed as he reached for her and she slipped away. "Come on, let's go tell Lana." Jumping up, she offered him a helping hand.

BOSTON LET THE SCREEN DOOR slam behind him, his lips twitching at the scowl Pearl sent him.

"How many times do I have to tell you, boy, close the door gently. Sounds like a herd of elephants." Pearl pursed her thin lips and narrowed her eyes at his smile. "What are you up to?" she demanded. "No, don't shake your head at me. I know that sweet-faced look of yours from experience. You want something."

Samantha laughed as Boston grabbed Pearl and swung her around the kitchen, Pearl protesting with every step.

"Have you gone crazy? Put me down this instant," she ordered breathlessly. Her bony hands began to straighten the once crisply starched apron. "Fool," she snapped at him, but Samantha saw her suck in her cheeks to keep the smile from spreading.

"Tell me something, Miss Pearl. Do your culinary

talents run to cooking three meals a day for sixteen to twenty people?'' Boston asked seriously, then frowned. "No, that's too much for you to handle. I'll have to hire another cook.''

Pearl stiffened all six feet of her skeletal frame and stated loudly, "You'll do no such thing. I'll have you know there's nothing I can't handle, you included, young man. Bring 'em on.''

Boston kissed her warmly on the cheek and explained what was about to descend on the ranch. He grabbed Samantha and doing a tango step danced her around the kitchen and out the door. They stopped and turned. "Ice down the champagne, Pearl, we're going to celebrate tonight. By the way, where's Lana?''

"How would I know? She received a telephone call and rushed out of here like the hounds of hell were on her heels. Nobody tells me anything,'' she grumbled and whirled around, turning her back on them. "You wouldn't catch me on an airplane, though.''

Boston and Samantha grinned at each other, both speaking the same words aloud. "Lana's gone to pick Ken up at the airport!''

They were like two children, giggling their way to the library, where they flung themselves on the long pecan-colored leather sofa. There was a fierce sparkle of mischief in Boston's eyes and he looked so pleased with himself that Samantha burst out laughing all over again.

"Where," she gasped for breath, "did you find Pearl?''

Boston's grin broadened. "She came with the

house. The previous owner asked me to keep her on."
He shrugged his shoulders. "It took a couple of weeks
for us to come to the understanding that I wasn't ten
years old, but we made it—I think." A bright flame
shone in his eyes. "She's the only person I know who
could make Elijah lose his temper and raise his voice."

"I know."

"Come here." Boston pulled her onto his lap and
settled comfortably in the corner of the sofa.

Samantha looked up at him and his black eyes
flashed. She stared, hypnotized, as his mouth moved
slowly toward hers. Her heart increased its tempo
with each second he hesitated. "You're teasing me,
Boston Grey!"

"I know," he whispered.

"Are you going to kiss me or not?" she asked
breathlessly, their lips almost touching.

"I'm thinking about it. There's only one problem."

"Oh." His strong arms pulled her close and she
melted against him. "What?" She couldn't resist him
if she wanted to.

"If I start now, I don't think I'll ever be able to
stop."

"So? We're alone."

"No, listen."

Samantha cocked her head and heard the voices of
Ken and Lana coming closer. She mumbled a few
choice obscenities under her breath, bringing a reluctant chuckle from Boston.

"Sparky!" he chastised, giving her a mocking look
of reproach. "Shame on you!"

Before she could retort, the library door swung open and the couple stood there grinning.

"Sorry," Ken said offhandedly. "Are we interrupting something?"

"Nothing important," Boston replied, and dodged Samantha's fist.

"Boston!"

He laughed and lifted Samantha from his lap. When she started to move farther away he hauled her back, his arm imprisoning her to his side. "Be still. You know I was only joking." He turned his attention back to Ken and Lana. "Sparky and I have something to tell you."

"Oh," Lana interrupted, "you've decided to get married."

"Lana!" Ken choked.

"No." Boston smiled at Lana's embarrassment. "Not yet."

Samantha watched Boston as he explained his decision to do the benefit for Father Brian. She half listened to Ken's and Lana's excited congratulations, but her mind was filled with the one question Lana had inadvertently asked. Was Boston going to marry her? All his talk of staying together, working side by side, was all fine and good. She observed him shrewdly and he sent her a quizzical smile at the change in her attitude. There was no way she'd be his live-in bed partner with no commitments, she thought grimly.

A cold glass of champagne appeared in her hand and she glanced up at Boston. He was standing above her now, watching the emotions play across her face.

"I wish I knew what was going on inside that pretty head of yours."

"Do you?" she asked more harshly than intended. Softening her voice, she added, "I don't think you'd appreciate it."

He put a hand under her chin and lifted her face to his. "Why don't you try me?"

She caught Ken observing their actions and mumbled, "Later." Lifting her glass to her lips she took a large swallow, then began to cough and choke as champagne bubbled from the back of her throat to her nose.

"Careful." Boston tapped her several times on the back and released her hold on her glass of the sparkling pale-amber liquid. "That, dear lady, is Piper-Heidsieck 1975, and it's not to be guzzled like beer."

"I'm well aware of what it is," she snapped back crossly.

"So I see!"

She grinned at his look of outrage. "May I have some more, please?"

In the worst exaggerated French accent she'd ever heard, he answered, "Only if madame will promise not to chugalug like a savage American."

Dinner that evening was a festive occasion. Everyone was high on excitement and champagne. Even Pearl unbent long enough to smile briefly at all their nonsense.

After dinner, Boston and Ken retired to the library for a long session on the telephone locating members of Boston's disbanded orchestra. After many jaw-cracking yawns, Samantha and Lana decided to give up the fight of staying awake and waiting for the men's return. As they passed the closed library door the sound of loud male laughter caused Samantha to raise her eyebrows inquiringly at Lana.

"There's no telling how long those calls will last. Good night, Sammy."

"Good night, Lana."

SAMANTHA LAY SUBMERGED in the huge claw-foot tub. Fragrant bubbles reached her chin and she closed her eyes in the ecstasy of warmth and the silky feel of the water caressing her body. Reaching for the sponge, she lazily opened her eyes and jerked bolt upright, sending a scented wave precariously close to spilling over the tub's rim. It was pitch black. "Hell and damnation," she muttered out loud.

"Don't get in a dither, Sparky, I'm coming," Boston's disembodied voice called from the darkened hole of his bedroom. Their rooms were separated by the bathroom, and as long as she'd been at the ranch his connecting door had remained shut, affording her total privacy while he used another bathroom down the hall.

"What happened to the lights?"

"I turned them off."

"What on earth for?"

"Just wait and see."

She was about to call out again when she heard the scratch of a match; then the blackness gave way to a weak, wavering glow. Shadows ghosted across the far wall of the bedroom. They flickered, then took on the form of a man. Curiously she watched the moving shadow recede and transform itself into flesh and blood as Boston stood in the bathroom doorway, a burning candle held out before him.

Samantha frowned up at him, suspiciously eyeing the short, thigh-length terry shaving robe, open to the waist. "Would you mind telling me what's going on?"

"Not at all. Just give me another second." He set the candle down on the edge of the washbasin and disappeared into the darkness of his room once more.

Again she heard the striking of several matches. He returned carrying two filled champagne glasses. Grinning, he handed one to her.

Samantha's eyes traveled the length of his body slowly. She stopped her inspection abruptly as she caught his eyes gleaming wickedly in the weaving candlelight. "What is this all about?"

Samantha watched Boston set his glass down beside the tub, his eyes never leaving hers as he slowly untied the robe and shrugged it off. Her heart began to pound and her breath caught painfully in the back of her throat. The sight of him standing before her in such a virile display caused her hand to tremble, spilling icy champagne on her naked breast.

Boston smiled at her sputtering. "Careful, sweetheart, that's to drink not bathe in." He stepped over the high sides of the tub and settled down at the opposite end. Reaching out, he picked up his fluted crystal glass and brought it to his lips, eyeing her over the rim. "I almost feel guilty sitting here with you."

"Why?"

"Because you look about twelve years old with your hair pinned up like that and your face clean and shiny." He took another sip of champagne. "But I thought you might need some help," he murmured. "I'm a very good back scrubber."

Returning his smile, Samantha drained what was left in her glass. "I bet you are," she countered, making room to accommodate his long length. Flesh caressed flesh as his legs slid along the outside of hers. Lifting one foam-covered foot, she planted it in the center of his chest, walking her toes up as far as she could go without sinking backward. Her eyelids drooped down, hiding the bright flame in the depths of her eyes. "This is a nice surprise. What did you have in mind?" She kept her voice as innocent as her expression.

Boston chucked. "What did I have in mind? Why, the very same thing you've had on yours all day." Strong fingers wrapped around the high arch of her foot and pulled it toward his mouth. Black eyes blazed into gleaming life as he watched her intently, and Samantha felt a flush run up her neck and face.

She grabbed the side of the tub to keep from slipping under as he gently drew her foot to his lips and tongue. Fire scorched a lightning path from her toes, spreading its hot fingers through the rest of her body, and she shivered violently from its force. She yanked her foot free from his hold, braced her arms on the edge of the tub and slid forward. Balancing her weight above him, she floated down to rest on the length of his body and felt his desire surge beneath her. She smiled down into his eyes. Now was the perfect time to get some answers. "Boston," she breathed against his lips, "are you going to marry me?" The last words were spoken firmly and she grinned at the puzzlement on his face.

Expecting a totally different question, Boston was momentarily stunned. Then he threw back his head and laughed. Losing his supporting hold on the tub, he plunged beneath the bubbly surface.

Impervious to his coughing and sputtering, and the comical picture he presented with a white cloud of foam clinging to his hair, she glared at him. Her hands clutched his wet shoulders and she demanded, "Well! Are you?"

Boston wiped the sudsy water from his eyes and grinned. He traced the natural arch of her eyebrow with a wet fingertip, then outlined her flushed freckled cheekbone, moving on slowly to the delicate curve of her ear and finally the sculptured softness of her lips. "My impetuous darling. What a treasure you are. Of *course* I'm going to marry you."

"When?"

He ignored her demand and said teasingly, "This is the most romantic marriage proposal I've ever had. Do you think we'll be able to tell our children the circumstances of your proposal?"

"If you don't answer me, Boston Grey, there won't be any children to tell. Due, I might add, to your early demise." She inhaled a quick breath and opened her mouth to repeat her question, but the words were cut off in a muffled groan as Boston's lips captured hers. He held her head firmly between his hands and the kiss deepened and became filled with desire.

"Let's get out." His ragged warm breath caressed her cheek. "The water's cold and we're beginning to resemble prunes." Boston stood, showering her in a spray of water and bubbles before he helped her out.

Still slightly modest about her nudity, she made a grab for the large bath sheet. Boston snatched it from her fingers before she could wrap it protectively around her body.

"I'll dry."

She presented him her back.

"Shy?" He peeked around her shoulder, kissed an averted flushed cheek and chuckled. With one hand holding her by the arm, he began briskly to rub her back. Second by second the rubbing slowed to short brushing strokes as he moved farther down. How he loved every inch of this woman, every freckle, every small imperfection. He dropped his hold on her arm and his fingers followed the towel's movements.

Her leg muscles began to weaken then tremble as he turned her around to face him. Intense concentration sharpened his features and hardened the fiery black eyes. Lightly the towel blotted her breasts dry then she saw Boston's head dip. The heady dizziness was back, and a warmth spread through her body. His lips teased the rosy tips of her breasts and she clutched his shoulders in a frantic effort to stand. Her head thrown back, she sighed and emitted a small groan of pure pleasure. He was driving her crazy, and she wondered how long she could stand the torture of his hands and lips. She wanted to wrap him in her love and hold him to her for the rest of their days.

"To hell with being dry," Boston grumbled. Throwing down the towel, he smoothly scooped her up into his arms and marched out of the bathroom.

As she swayed in his arms, a smile hovered around the corners of her mouth; then her eyes widened as she took in the sight of his transformed bedroom. Two cylinder candles had been placed on the ornately carved bedside tables. Their translucent light delicately wrapped the room in a shimmering mantle, and shadowy images danced across the wall. The bed was invitingly turned back. The radiant glow cast a delicate luster on the sheets and bedspread and transformed the stark masculine room into a cavern of softness. An iced bottle of champagne stood in its elegant silver stand beside the bed and a long covered tray rested at the foot of the bed. The mysterious tray intrigued her and she asked, "What's that?"

"Forget it." He glowered at her as he eased her body down till her feet touched the carpeted floor. "We have better things to do than eat."

"Food!" She ducked under his arm, but before she could reach the tray strong hands caught her around the waist and hauled her back.

"We'll do it the way I planned." Boston turned one side of the bedcovers further back, bowed and waved her to slide in.

Samantha smiled at the absurdity of his formal gesture as he stood there totally naked, but she did as he requested. Covers tucked securely over her breast, plump pillows behind her back, she looked up questioningly as he stood there watching her settle down.

"Must you?" He nodded his head at her covered chest, his expression pained.

"Yes." Her eyes sparkled with love and curiosity. What, she asked herself, was this elaborate setting for?

Boston popped the cork of the champagne and filled two glasses, handing her one. He slid in beside her, reached down for the tray and placed it over their laps. With a flourish he whipped off the white linen covering and smiled at her expression of disbelief. "Tempting, isn't it?"

"Did you plan and put this together?" she whispered, impressed by the tray's contents.

"Of course."

Plump red strawberries, their dark-green stems still attached, crowded one another in a pale beige, bone-china bowl. Smaller matching bowls encircled the larger one, and Samantha dipped her finger in each to taste its contents. The first contained white powdered sugar, the second brown sugar, and the third melted rich chocolate. Licking the heavenly chocolate from her finger, she pointed with the other hand.

"What's in those two bowls?"

Boston tapped the rim of each. "Grand Marnier and Amaretto." He picked up a strawberry by its stem and dipped it in the Grand Marnier, rolled it in brown sugar, then held it to her lips.

Samantha closed her eyes in ecstasy as the blend of orange-flavored liqueur, sugar and strawberry melted in her mouth. "Oh, that's good." She sipped her champagne, then reciprocated by placing a strawberry in the almond-flavored liqueur, then dipping it into thick dark chocolate. She cupped her hand under the dripping mass, moving it quickly to Boston's waiting mouth, and watched as he savored its delight.

They mixed different concoctions and fed each other, breaking their feast only for sips of champagne.

"Enough." He groaned and removed the tray from their laps.

Samantha rested back on the pillows and sighed aloud with contentment. "I can't find the right words to describe this little snack of yours."

"How about romantic, sensual, sexy or erotic?"

"Definitely all those. And more!" She turned her head and their eyes met and held. "But why, I'm wondering, did you go to all this trouble? Surely not to seduce me?"

"No," he grinned. "Actually, I did have something in mind, but you beat me to it."

"Me?" she asked, puzzled.

"Yes, you." Boston leaned over and kissed the tip of her nose. "I was going to surprise you and ask you to marry me."

"Oh." Sudden tears filled her eyes. "And I ruined it," she sniffed.

"Don't you dare start crying!" He looked into her aquamarine eyes, swimming with crystal tears, and then pulled her into his arms. "Please don't, Sparky. I can't bear to see you cry." He wiped away one glistening tear with the edge of the sheet. "Come on," he coaxed, "smile."

She hugged him fiercely, filled with so much love and happiness she was unable to express her feelings. "Make love to me *now*."

Boston gazed into her darkening eyes. "With pleasure," he sighed against her lips.

She pulled away suddenly from his hungry persistent mouth. "Did you get in touch with the members of your orchestra?"

Boston cast his eyes heavenward. "I don't believe this. You demand I make love to you, then decide you want to talk!" Rolling over, he pinned her down. "Now! Let's get all your questions answered in one clean swoop. I can't take many more interruptions." He shook his head and scowled into her innocent, smiling face. "Yes. I contacted them all, except my pianist." She opened her mouth, but he went on as if anticipating her next question. "They'll start arriving tomorrow. Yes. We've made arrangements to pick them up." He went on with his mind reading. "Yes. I realize we'll need to restock the groceries. I'm taking Pearl with me when I leave early in the morning. She can shop while I take care of some business. No, I don't know when we'll be back. You and Lana will have to hold the fort." She was openly laughing at his pistol-shot answers. "Now, not another word." And he lowered his mouth to hers.

The lambent light changed their skin from pink and tan to satin and gold. Boston's lips and tongue began a leisurely journey over her body that left her shaking with a need only he could fulfill. His fingers stroked and caressed, and she reached out for him and returned the same movements till his harsh breathing thundered in the quiet room. When he finally moved above her and entered her she gasped, not in pain, but with the long-awaited sensation of becoming complete, and knowing that he too felt whole.

CHAPTER TWELVE

SAMANTHA AWOKE THE NEXT MORNING with her arms wrapped around a pillow. She wanted to lie there in the warm bed remembering the feel of Boston next to her, but her conscience continued to nag that it was well past time to be up.

The silent house attested to its emptiness and she mentally berated herself for leaving Lana to start the work she knew must be done. She flung the covers back, and bounded out of bed, goose bumps on her skin as the cold morning air rushed over her naked flesh. She hurried to the bathroom and quickly bathed, brushed her teeth, applied the bare essentials of makeup and ran a comb through her tangled hair. She pulled on a pair of jeans and a white western shirt, flopped down on the edge of the bed and began to tie the laces of her once-white sneakers. Her wandering gaze spotted the tray from last night's feast and she smiled, propped her chin in her hand and recalled the fun they'd shared. No matter how hard Boston tried to hide it, he was a romantic at heart. Jolted out of her reverie by the slamming of a door, she leaned down and retrieved the tray. The evidence needed to be cleared away before anyone saw the remains of their food orgy and drew their own conclusions.

Balancing the long awkward tray against her body, she backed through the kitchen door and abruptly halted. Lana was coming through the opposite door with an identical tray held in the same position. They stared at each other, their cheeks suffused with a shared flush.

Samantha dropped her gaze to Lana's tray and noted the same number and size of bowls. "I wonder," she gasped, "just whose idea it was?"

Lana set her trembling tray with its rattling dishes on the table and leaned against the edge. "Certainly not Ken's. There's not an original or adventurous bone in his body." She followed Samantha and flopped down in a straight-back chair. "I wish I could have been a fly on the wall and seen them preparing this." She laughed and waved her hand across the dirty bowls and empty champagne bottle.

Samantha could imagine the smug remarks and leering looks the two men must have traded. "And here I was trying to sneak down and clear the mess away before anyone could catch me."

"Me too," said Lana. "We'll have to think of something equally exciting for them."

"Yes indeed!" Samantha's eyes sparkled wickedly. "We can't be outdone by mere men!"

They set to work, side by side at the kitchen sink. When they had each finished, Samantha untaped Pearl's long list of instructions from the oven door and moaned. "Lana, will you look at this! The woman's mad. I haven't done this much housework since I left home." She scanned the sheet of paper once more to make sure she'd read it correctly. "Do you think she's serious about dusting under the beds in the guest rooms, or is it just her sadistic sense of humor?''

''No, she means it.'' Lana nodded, then turned her big brown eyes worriedly up at Samantha, ''Sammy, I think you should know...I'm not very good at housework. You see....'' She hesitated. ''I never liked it, so I always found excuses to have something *very* important to do.''

''What does Ken have to say about your lack of enthusiasm?''

''Oh, he does the housework. No, really he does.'' She grinned proudly. ''I just let it pile up and he gets disgusted, then goes to work. He's very thorough— says it was his orphanage upbringing.''

''That's right, train 'em early and you're set for life. Come on.'' Samantha grabbed Lana's arm and hauled her out of the kitchen. ''Just remember, I'm not Ken. We divide the work.''

The amount of work to be done wasn't as appalling as Samantha let on. With six brothers who couldn't do a thing for themselves, she was used to hard work. She'd just gotten out of the routine. Besides, she thought, she had plenty to occupy her mind; only her body was required for the work ahead. She secretly admired Lana for her sly handling of Ken when it came to mundane jobs. But she didn't want that type of relationship with Boston, and he had made it clear last night that he wanted her totally involved in his life. Theirs would be a shared loving, each shouldering an equal weight and fulfilling each other's dreams. Nothing could go

wrong to ruin their happiness and their future together.

SHE WAS EXHAUSTED: too tired to think, too bone
weary to move from the kitchen chair she was
slumped in. She couldn't even escape the house to relax and breathe in the fresh pine-scented air. A
savage wind hurled torrents of rain against the win-
dowpanes, and thunder intermittently boomed overhead with a violence that shook the glass. On top of
the noise Mother Nature was forcing on them, the
nerve-jarring stopping and starting of guitars, violins
and piano had left her with a permanent headache.
From early morning till late at night, music assaulted
her ears. Eleven musicians as highly strung as their
instruments had invaded and sent the once-peaceful
ranch into a turmoil. Eight men and three women ate
and rehearsed, rehearsed and ate, breaking only long
enough to scream insults at one another. What
amazed Samantha was their complete change at dinner. It was as if their harsh words had never been
spoken. They behaved like intelligent human beings,
cordial, polite and soft-spoken. She shook her head,
baffled by their seesaw temperaments.

The most significant and horrifying surprise was
the change in Boston. In the previous three days
his personality had taken on a marked resemblance
to Jekyll and Hyde's—more Hyde's than Jekyll's,
she acknowledged grimly. But she'd managed by
sheer willpower to keep a tight hold on her hot
temper. Lifting tired eyes from the now-cold coffee
cup clasped in both hands, she gazed across the

table at Lana. "Has Ken found Boston's pianist yet?"

"He hasn't called today." Lana's words came out in a whisper. She looked up and caught Samantha's strained expression. "Sammy, for what good it will do, I've never seen Boston so...savage before. Please bear with him. I think he's excited and frightened at the same time."

"I know his faults, Lana—or at least I thought I did." She gave a choked laugh. "But it's encouraging to know he's not like this before every show he does." Lana quickly averted her eyes. "He's not, is he?"

"Well—not so brutal. But, yes, he's a slave driver. Maybe he'll calm down when Ken finds Thomas."

Samantha rested her head against the high-backed chair and closed her eyes. "I hope so. I think I'd fall over in a dead faint if Boston uttered *one* civil word to me." She remembered her run-in with him that morning and cringed. After days of never being alone to talk and lonely nights without him by her side, she'd been delighted to catch him in the library, his ruffled head bent over his music.

"Hi, can I help?"

His head jerked up, eyes snapping with irritation. "What the hell's going on around here? Can't I have a little peace and quiet?" he demanded. "And just what could you possibly know about a musical score?"

"Now look here—" She had clamped her lips firmly together and she and Boston had glared at each other. Spinning around on her heels, she had marched out, slamming the door behind her as she left.

His words and sarcastic tone still stung. "You'd think they would be sick of all that rehearsing," she sighed.

"They're not rehearsing, Sammy."

"What!" Samantha's eyes snapped open and she frowned at Lana's sympathetic expression.

"Boston's feeling them out and organizing the songs he's going to use. You'll have to remember it's been three years since they've played together. He's assessing their response and their ability to comply with his directions and leadership. Boston is their maestro, their general. They must follow his demands unquestioningly."

"You mean unlike leading a horse to water, Boston *makes* them drink whether they want to or not?"

Lana grinned at her choice of words. "Something like that," she laughed.

"What are you girls doing just sitting there?" Pearl demanded, her lips thinning with reproach. "Dinner's about ready and here you two are gossiping." She shook her head disgustedly, her sharp eyes scrutinizing Lana. "You look terrible. Why aren't you getting yourself gussied up?"

"Why should I?" Lana asked, shooting a now-smiling Samantha a puzzled glance.

"Suit yourself." Pearl shrugged a bony shoulder indifferently. "No business of mine if you want to look like yesterday's leftovers. But if I were your man I'd turn and run after one good look at you."

"My man?" Lana's doe-brown eyes widened then narrowed. "Ken's not here."

"'Course he's not. Do you think I'm senile? But he will be here in about thirty minutes."

Samantha laughed at Lana's squeal of pleasure as she jumped up and ran from the room.

"What's so funny, young lady?" Pearl scowled at Samantha, taking in her pale features and dull eyes. "You don't look much better. Go on, get out of here. No, don't argue with me. I'll handle what needs to be done. You fix up for Boston tonight. Show him what he's been missing for the past three days—and nights."

Samantha felt a surge of blood rush to her cheeks. She leaned over and kissed Pearl on the cheek. "Thank you."

"Get out of here—go on, get. I don't need you slobbering all over me." She wiped the kiss away impatiently, but her eyes grew misty as she watched the slim retreating figure.

Head bent, Samantha pushed through the swinging kitchen door, only to be pulled up short by strong male hands clasping her shoulders.

"Hold on, Sparky. Where are you off to in such a hurry?" Boston scanned the pale, unsmiling face and his dark eyes hardened.

"It's time to dress for dinner," she told him.

Her shoulders moved impatiently beneath his grasp and he dropped his hands, kissed her absently on the forehead and began to walk away. "Rest a while. You look bushed," he said offhandedly, his attention already returning to the young man following at his heels.

"Insensitive...." She broke off and muttered curses at the back of his head. Of all the nerve, she thought. He was acting as if they'd never had a cross word between them today. Did he care so little? One moment he could be as loving as they were a few days before. Then in the blinking of an eyelid he would change to a snarling, unfeeling jackass. She wanted to stamp her feet in a childish tantrum. It wasn't fair! She'd tried to reason with herself that he was under pressure, but all his reassuring words of involvement and togetherness seemed to be fading farther and farther into meaningless platitudes. Did his grim hostility reflect her own doubts that she didn't fit into his life?

SAMANTHA CIRCULATED among Boston's orchestra members, a false smile curving her mouth. *Act like a hostess,* she reminded herself for the tenth time as she lifted her second gin and tonic to her lips. Predinner drinks had become a ritual in the past few days, and she'd come to hate this hour. It used to be a leisurely time when she and Boston would have a quiet interlude, talking or just enjoying each other's company. She resented the intrusion as much as she resented the others' presence. On a few occasions she'd made an effort to converse with the three women, but all they were interested in was music. They talked scores and notes and other gibberish. To Samantha's ears they might have been talking in Swahili. How could she possibly be a part of his life if she couldn't understand the language? She could tell by Boston's dark frowning looks that he was disappointed in her attitude.

Her fingers trembled slightly as she straightened the already perfectly pleated front of the ivory silk Victorian blouse, its high collar reaching just beneath her chin. Head bent, she grimaced at the full-length black velvet skirt. Another scheme ruined, she thought wryly. The extra care taken with her appearance was a waste of time and effort. Boston hadn't even noticed. She turned her back on the buzzing room, lifted her gaze to the night-blackened window and caught the bewilderment of her expression in the reflection of the glass. Would their life ever return to normal? Or was this an example of what to expect in their future? She shivered with a feeling of doom.

The slamming of a door filtered through her thoughts, jerking her back to reality. An excitement permeated the room as the others waited for Ken and the long-sought-after pianist.

Before she could turn around, the library erupted with laughing voices greeting the newcomer. The other musicians surrounded him, blocking her view. Taking a deep breath, Samantha forced a welcoming smile to her lips. The crowd parted and forest-green eyes met hers. Her smile froze, then flashed into dazzling brightness.

"Tom," she whispered, her eyes devouring the six-foot, bronze-skinned, sun-bleached blonde from California. It was obvious from his incredulous expression that he was as surprised to see her as she was to see him. They had met in Los Angeles over a year before and become fast friends. Tom Cole's talent for writing commercial jingles had made his newly formed company the most sought after in the advertising industry. But what amazed her now was to learn he was Boston's pianist.

"Samantha?" Tom roared. Pushing Boston aside, he reached her in four long-legged strides, wrapped her bodily into his arms and swung her around in a wide circle.

"You're. . . ?" She broke off breathlessly.

"What in heaven's name are you doing here?" he demanded, his eyes intent on the pale freckled face turned up to his.

Samantha watched as understanding sharpened his features and those brilliant eyes turned toward Boston.

"Oh, no—not him, Samantha? Please tell me you're not involved with Grey?"

"'Fraid so," she grinned. "We're engaged, Tom."

"That's a new one," he snorted. "What did he do, trade Lana in for a prettier model? The man's a. . . ." He broke off what he was about to say as Boston reached them.

"I take it you two know each other?" Boston asked. His voice was bland, but his glittering eyes rested pointedly on Tom's arm, slung intimately around Samantha's shoulders.

Tom grinned and hugged her closer. "We sure do."

Tom's words implied more than their close friendship and Samantha stared at him. She shifted her gaze to Boston and bit her lip. "Tom wrote and produced the Captain Puff cereal jingles for my agency."

Boston's next question was cut off by a request for his attention from across the room. For once, Samantha was relieved at the interruption. "Just what are you trying to pull, Tom? You definitely led Boston to believe there was something more to our friendship."

"Did I?"

"Yes, you did. And what did you mean about 'that's a new one'? We are engaged."

"Funny," he mused, "this is the first I've heard about an engagement. Boston usually doesn't have to go that far to get a woman into his bed."

She winced at his cruel insult and jerked free of his hold. "Damn you, Tom Cole. I thought we were friends."

He pulled her back into his arms and kissed the top of her flaming red head. "We are. Make no mistake about that. It's just going to take some adjusting on my part to understand all this," he murmured. "I'll tell you one thing, though. If I find out he's playing one of his games with you...." He stopped when her fingers touched his lips.

"No games, Tom. He loves me."

"We'll see about that." He clasped her elbow. "I believe we're being signaled for dinner."

Boston suddenly appeared at her side and took hold of her other elbow. "Thank you, Thomas, but I'll escort Sparky to dinner."

"No trouble, old chap. I'm sure you're busy. I'll do it." He gave a gentle tug to urge her forward.

"Hey, you two. My arms, please." She disentangled herself from their grip. "I really need them."

Smiling, she left the two men glaring at each other and hurried to the dining room.

Two extra tables were set up to accommodate their guests. Because of the quantity of food, Pearl had deemed it wise to erect a long buffet table along one wall, allowing everyone to serve themselves. Samantha snatched up a plate and began to help herself. She wanted to be seated before Boston and Tom arrived.

For once the meal was surprisingly quiet. Boston, at he head of the main table with her and Tom on either side of him, kept the conversation on the subject of music.

Bored, Samantha interrupted and asked, "Tom, why didn't you tell me you used to work for Boston?" She glanced up from her plate and looked across the table, waiting for an answer. She was shocked to see the seductive expression on Tom's face.

"We never seemed to get around to discussing my past," he murmured huskily.

Her fork suspended in midair, she shot a quick, apprehensive look at Boston, wondering if he'd caught the nuance of Tom's tone. She watched, fascinated, as Boston's glass clattered to the table, and stifled a groan. What was Tom up to? Didn't he realize how angry Boston was becoming with each sly smile and the implications of his words? Then she understood—Tom had deliberately set out to make Boston jealous. She ducked her head to hide the gleam in her eyes. It might be fun to see just how jealous they could make him. But on second thought she decided it wouldn't be beneficial to her or Tom's health. Boston wasn't in the mood for their brand of teasing. She raised her eyes and caught Tom's exaggerated wink. She frowned. This had to stop.

"Samantha, did you finally get over your sunburn?" Tom asked, turning his attention to Boston before she could reply. "We went to Laguna Beach one weekend and you wouldn't believe where this young lady got a most unique sunburn."

She watched Boston's hand tighten on the heavy cut glass as he swung his head from one to the other like an angry bull. "Tom," she warned, and gave a weak laugh, "you'd better clarify that statement. We did *not* spend the weekend together." She turned to Boston to explain. "The whole production crew was there to film a segment on the beach and—and Tom tagged along."

"Yeah," Tom laughed. "I couldn't get a room, either. It's a good thing Samantha had a nice large one, 'cause as it was she needed me."

Samantha couldn't believe her ears. She drew back her foot and delivered a hard kick to Tom's shin.

"Ouch!" he yelped. "Did I say something wrong?"

She suddenly realized the room was silent and everyone was avidly listening. Switching her gaze back to Boston, she forced a laugh. "It's not what you're thinking," she whispered.

"No?"

"No!"

Black glittering eyes bore into hers. "Just where did you get this terrible sunburn?" he asked between clenched teeth.

"My toes! No, really," she insisted, seeing his skeptical expression. "I'd been so careful to keep covered all day. I wore jeans, a long-sleeved shirt and a big floppy hat, and went barefoot. My toes and the tops of my feet were burned to a crisp. By evening I thought I was going to die, they hurt so bad. Tom called the doctor for some medicine, then sat up with me all night. That was very considerate of him, don't you think?"

"To say nothing of having to carry her around for the next couple of days." He turned to Boston. "She's no lightweight."

She relaxed into her chair as she saw some of the tension melt from Boston's face.

After dinner, Samantha made a determined effort to corner Tom, but he seemed as elusive as a sleek alley cat, stalking from one person to another, renewing old friendships and sniffing out the latest show-business gossip. She finally spotted him standing behind the bar, refilling his glass.

"How could you, Tom?" she hissed at his broad back. He whirled around, spilling the sticky liqueur over his hand. "What are you trying to do, get us both killed?"

"Oh, come on, Samantha! Boston might punch my face in or break my fingers." He waggled a dripping appendage at her then licked it clean. "But kill?" He shook his head, his bright green eyes twinkling. "I don't think so."

"I don't give a damn what you think, Tom Cole. It's me I'm worried about. Boston hasn't been the easiest person to live with the past few days, and

Succumb to
temptation...

Get this romance novel FREE
as your introduction to new

See exciting details inside.

now you've gone and deliberately made things worse.''

His indulgent smile vanished. ''Let me tell you something, friend. I've known Boston a lot longer than you have. I've seen how he operates around women. I've also picked up the pieces of a few when he was through with them. That's not what I want to happen to you. You forget I know you, too, and under that brave, feisty exterior you put on for all the world to see, you're as vulnerable as his past ladies, if not more so. Before this night is over I intend to find out what he's up to.''

''Find out what who's up to, Tom?'' Boston spoke softly behind them, his voice controlled, but there was anger in every line of his taut body.

''You, old buddy.'' Tom frowned. ''I want to know what she's doing here with you of all people.''

''You mean you want to know if my intentions are honorable? My, my,'' he drawled sarcastically, ''when did you appoint yourself Sparky's guardian? She does have a father, you know, and six bruisers for brothers.'' Tom looked a little startled at Boston's knowledge of Samantha's family. ''I've had the pleasure of meeting them all, *old buddy*. I'll thank you kindly to stay out of my affairs. Do me another favor. Stay away from Sparky. Whatever you two had in the past is just that, the past. She's mine now and I don't want her upset.''

''I'm not upset,'' interjected Samantha.

''Of course you are,'' Boston corrected her. ''It's not every day you run into an ex-lover and find he's trying to worm his way back into your affections.''

"Now you listen to me, Boston Grey. Tom is not my lover nor has he ever been." She glared at him, then turned her angry gaze on Tom. "Now see what you've done."

"She's right, Boston. We've never been anything more than friends."

Samantha held her breath and watched both men as they stared at each other. Something passed between them and Boston nodded.

"Then why the charade, Tom?"

Tom shrugged. "I have a long and vivid memory from working with you. The thought of Samantha ending up like so many of your women sickened me. I guess I just wanted to make sure you're serious."

Boston smiled with genuine warmth. "More serious than I've ever been in my life." His arm slipped around Samantha's shoulder. "This is the woman I'm going to marry, Tom." Boston shook hands with him formally and guided Samantha off to the corner of the room. "You look tired." He cupped her cheek with a warm hand, his thumb gently tracing the outline of her lips. The flame in the depths of his eyes made her knees tremble with remembered passion. "Why don't you go on up and I'll be there as soon as I get these people settled down?"

As casually as possible she crossed the room and walked out the door, excitement urging her steps upward. Once in her room, she flew through the routine of preparing for bed. Her breath caught in her throat at each sound, but there was no sign of Boston. When her eyelids finally began to droop she crawled into bed to wait.

Samantha snuggled down under the covers, her cold feet searching for a warm body. Finding an empty bed, she propped herself up and peeped at the clock. Three o'clock in the morning and still Boston hadn't come to bed. She rolled over on her back and closed her eyes. All his fine words, she thought angrily. If he loved her, why did he persist in staying away from her side at night? Didn't he realize how much she needed him? But, what was more crucial, did he need her? It didn't look that way. Her eyes closed again in sleep and she drifted off, only to wake again as Boston pulled her into his arms. She murmured his name but received no answer and slipped back into sleep.

CHAPTER THIRTEEN

BRIGHT SUNLIGHT GLARED through the window and across her closed eyelids. She buried her face in the pillow to blot out the inevitable, then groaned and forced open one eye. No, she hadn't dreamed of being held in Boston's arms in the early hours of the morning. The dented pillow next to hers was evidence of his presence. With a muffled curse she swung her legs out from under the covers and hopped out of bed. She'd had it. Today was hers. No more bed making, cooking, washing dishes or running errands for Boston. She'd put up with his neglect long enough. She'd just see if a day without her to order around would bring any changes in his attitude.

Samantha found Lana sitting at the kitchen table nursing a cup of coffee. Her face looked gray and Samantha's mouth twisted into a wry smile. "What's the matter, Lana?"

"I should know better than to drink tequila. You should have stayed and partied with us last night, Sammy."

Samantha produced a heavy mug, and filled it with strong black coffee. "Is that where Boston was till the wee hours?"

"Yes." Lana glanced up and her eyes focused on

Samantha's angry face. "He tried to get away several times, really he did, but they just wouldn't let him."

"You mean they tied him to a chair and poured drinks down his throat?" she hissed.

"Well...no. Please, Sammy, don't yell, my head is killing me."

"What you need, my girl, is some fresh air." She got up and retrieved two pairs of rubber boots from the doorway. "Here," she said, thrusting a pair at Lana, "put these on and come with me." Grabbing hold of Lana's arm, she hauled the groaning woman up.

"I don't want fresh air," Lana wailed. "I want to go back to bed."

They trudged down the muddy trail toward the swollen river in silence, sidestepping fallen tree limbs in their path. Finally they reached the banks of the swirling water. Lana flopped down on a large boulder, her head bowed and her breath coming in short gasps.

"You do whatever it is you want to. I can't move. Just give me a holler when you're ready to go back."

"That bad, is it?"

"I think I died about twenty yards back." She shaded her red-rimmed eyes with a shaky hand. "But don't worry about me, breathe as much fresh air as you want. I'll just be sick on the other side of this rock."

"I won't be long, Lana. I just want to check on something." Grinning, Samantha pulled up one booted foot, then the other, from the soft muddy ground. Her steps carried her to the vine-tangled barrier, and pushing the wet leaves back she crouched down and slipped through.

Crystal tears filled her eyes as she glanced around the glade. The storm had destroyed its beauty and left it an ugly bog. The lush green carpet of grass had been washed away by the overflowing stream, and the fragrant scent of honeysuckle and wild flowers had been replaced with an unpleasant swampy odor of decay and rot.

Samantha sank down on the large rock Boston had sat on, buried her face in her hands and sobbed. It was almost prophetic that the very place where she and Boston had made so many promises to each other was now demolished. Ever since he'd made his decision to return to the stage she'd watched their love slip further away, taking second place to his career. She wiped the tears away with the cuff of her shirt. She'd tried everything she could think of to keep his waning attention, but nothing worked.

His absorption with organizing his comeback had totally locked her out. A half sob escaped her lips. She supposed she ought to be grateful for the small bits of attention she did receive. An absentminded kiss on the forehead or a patronizing pat on the shoulder was better than being completely ignored. Things couldn't get much worse, she thought grimly.

Or could they? She remembered waiting for him through the long hours of the night and into the early hours of the morning, longing for him to hold her in his arms and reassure her that he still wanted and needed her. And what had happened? He had sent her to bed like a four-year-old with a promise to

come kiss her good-night, then stayed with the adults
and thrown a party. She felt useless and unwanted.
Why hadn't he come and invited her to join the fun?
Because, she told herself, *you don't fit in with his
life-style anymore and he knows it.*

She clenched her fist. What was she going to do?
What could she do?

She looked down at her wristwatch and realized
she'd been sitting, wallowing in self-pity, for over an
hour. Lana must be wondering where she was. Without a backward glance she'd left the glade and headed for the spot where she'd left Lana coddling her
hangover. Her head jerked up at the sound of her
name being called. She was just about to answer
when she saw Lana only a few yards from where she
stood. She froze in her tracks.

"There you are!" Lana was walking toward her, a
tiny black-and-white bundle nestled cozily in her
arms. "Look what I found, Sammy. Poor baby,"
she crooned, "did your mama run off and leave
you?"

Samantha slowly backed away. Her mouth worked
spasmodically for a second before she found her
voice. Her words come out low and urgent, with an
edge of panic. "Lana," she whispered, "put him
down and step away very carefully."

"Why?" Lana looked up from the precious ball of
fur, a puzzled frown gathering across her brow. She
stroked the little head, murmuring soft baby sounds
into the sad dark eyes.

"It's a *skunk*! Please do as I say." She backed up
another couple of steps. The heel of her oversize rub-

ber boots landed on the sharp edge of a protruding tree root, twisting her ankles sideways. A high-pitched scream escaped her stiff lips as she tumbled backward onto the muddy ground. As if in slow motion, she watched the startled skunk leap from Lana's arms. He landed on all fours in front of the now-petrified woman. Indignant at being disturbed from its warm loving nest, the little animal stopped, raised its fluffy tail and retaliated by spraying its unmistakable scent in a wide arc before it pranced proudly away.

Samantha shot to her feet. She ran toward Lana and dragged the screaming woman to the edge of the river, where she gave her a push, tumbling her back into the icy water. Pity and laughter warred inwardly, but pity won out. She remembered her run-in with a skunk about ten years earlier. What few people realized was that a direct spray could make its victim deathly sick. The obnoxious odor could irritate delicate eye membranes and cause a constant stinging and deluge of tears; sensitive skin burned and itched. But worst of all was the overwhelming nausea.

Lana came up sputtering and howled, "What happened?"

Squatting down, Samantha offered a helpful hand and pulled. She had to struggle hard to keep a straight face at her friend's drowned-rat look. "You, my girl, were thoroughly sprayed by a skunk."

"Oh no! Help me. I'm going to be sick."

Close proximity to Lana's overwhelming fragrance brought a flood of tears to her own eyes and Samantha stepped away. "Lana—Lana, listen to me. Strip."

"Wha... what?" she stuttered, looking at Samantha as if she'd lost her mind. "I'm freezing and you want me to *strip*?" A violent shiver racked her petite frame and she sagged against the nearest tree, crying and sick at the same time.

Samantha looked down at her smelly hands and shrugged. The idea of getting any closer turned her stomach, but she realized Lana was totally ignorant of what needed to be done. She inhaled a deep breath and bent down, working quickly at the buttons of Lana's blouse. "Lana, your clothes are soaked with skunk scent. They have to come off." She managed to get the blouse off, then unzipped Lana's jeans and pulled them down. Stepping away, she gulped in huge quantities of fresh air, "Now kick them away."

Lana followed her instructions, and inhaling deeply once more, Samantha stepped forward, her hands filled with mud.

"What are you doing?" Lana wailed as Samantha began to spread the cold slimy mess rapidly over her body.

"Don't argue, just help."

"But...."

"Lana, I know what I'm doing."

They worked as quickly as possible, only stopping when the sobbing woman was hit by a new bout of nausea. Samantha covered her own arms and hands with mud and helped Lana to her feet. "Come on, we need to get you back to the ranch."

Lana looked down at herself and began to cry all over again. "Will I ever be clean again?"

Samantha bit her lip, forcing back the laughter

that threatened to erupt as she surveyed her handi-work. Two round tear-filled eyes shone against the brown face and pleaded mournfully for help. "Let's go," she said, and slung her arm around Lana's slumped shoulders and urged her limp body forward. "What ever possessed you to pick up a baby skunk?"

Lana sniffed and stumbled. "I thought it was an abandoned kitten."

"Oh, Lana! Surely you could tell the difference. Didn't you notice the marking on its tail?"

"No!" She started crying again. "I'm from Chica-go," she blubbered. "I've never seen a real live skunk before. Please don't laugh, Sammy. It's not funny."

"Sorry." Samantha gave Lana's shoulder a quick squeeze.

When they reached the ranch house she held Lana back, uncertain for a moment as to her next move. They couldn't enter the house, but Lana needed im-mediate attention. "Stay right here," she said, and receiving a nod of agreement she hurried off.

Music floated out an open window, and as she drew closer she could hear Boston's deep velvet voice. The words of love he sang brought a shaft of pain. There was such feeling in each caressing lyric. She shook her mind free of the hypnotic effect of his voice, shaded her eyes and pressed her nose against the screen. Her eyes skimmed the crowded room and stopped as she spotted Ken sitting to one side.

"Pssst, pssst, Ken." When she failed to draw his attention she called a little more sharply. "Ken!"

Everything seemed to happen at once. Ken's head

jerked up, nostrils flaring, his eyes widening in horror. The music faded into off-key notes and Boston's voice trailed into silence. Samantha spun around to find Lana standing behind her. "I told you to stay back," she ordered as another gust of wind whirled around them and blew into the room.

An indignant roar and a collective spate of curses swung her back to the open window. Looking up, she met Boston's furious black eyes. "Hi...uh...we had a small accident, I'm sor...." She broke off lamely and wiped her suddenly perspiring forehead, leaving a trail of mud across her brow. They stood staring at each other in silence, till Boston turned sharply and stomped away. The little devil that seemed to be riding her shoulder lately whispered in her ear, *You've done it now, my girl. I don't believe I've ever seen him so angry before.* "Not my fault," she muttered back, turning around in time to see Ken gingerly drape Lana with his coat. Her feet took root where she stood as she watched Boston burst through the back door, barking out orders to the now-crowded yard. Incredibly weary, she closed her eyes and slumped against the side of the house.

"Well!"

Her eyes popped open. "Well, what?" she demanded.

"Dammit, Samantha, don't play games with me. How did this happen?"

"Look, I'm tired, dirty and smelly. Do you mind if I clean up first before this inquisition starts?" His lips tightened into a grim line, but he nodded. "Thank you, that's very considerate."

"Sparky," he warned, following her into the kitchen. He reached up, pulled down a bottle of ketchup and slammed it down on the counter. "Here, this will cut some of the odor."

Samantha meticulously washed her hands and arms and dried them slowly.

"That's enough," he muttered between clenched teeth, his foot tapping impatiently on the tiled floor. "I want to talk to you, privately."

Boston led the way into the library and slammed the door behind them. Samantha realized he was in a flaming temper and decided to let it run its course before she tried to reason with him. She seated herself on the sofa.

"Now! You want to tell me how you let Lana get close to a skunk?"

"I wasn't there."

"What do you mean you weren't there? Where did you go?" he demanded sharply.

Samantha shrugged indifferently. She didn't want to tell him about the destroyed glade. He'd think her foolish and sentimental. "For a walk."

Boston raked a hand wildly through his hair. He looked at her, his eyes flaring anew with a sudden thought. "Do you do these things on purpose, Sparky? Has my neglect turned you to more petty actions to get my attention?"

"Wait a minute," she began tersely. She'd taken enough and was determined to stand up for herself. "What do you mean, *more* petty actions?"

"The interruptions, the constant disruptions of my rehearsals." He watched her frown deepen in perplexity. "Come on, don't play dumb. How many times a day do you barge in? You flirt with Ken, you stand around and sing or hum—off key I might add—and the flow of coffee and sandwiches never seems to stop."

She recoiled against the sofa as if he had slapped her. "I thought...."

"No, that's the problem. You don't think. Any imbecile knows a singer never eats for at least an hour before he sings."

Samantha jumped up and stormed at him. Her voice was raised with hurt and anger at his unfair accusations. "Well this imbecile didn't know!" She punctuated each word by poking his chest with her finger. "Do you want to know why? Because no one bothered to tell me, that's why."

He moved away from her to pace before the fireplace, his hands jammed into his jeans pocket, his face gaunt and weary. "All right, I'll take some of the blame."

"Oh, how magnanimous of you."

"But don't think I haven't noticed your complete lack of interest in getting to know my friends. You're jealous of the time I spend with them." He spun around, his voice harsh and grating. "You don't even make an effort."

"Now you wait just one minute," she snapped. "I'm not jealous."

"Oh, for heaven's sake, grow up. You've been walking around in a dream world for the past twenty-five years. It amazes me how you've managed to survive as long as you have with your head in the clouds.

Quit deluding yourself. Life can't be all sweetness and laughter.'' He grabbed her by the shoulders. ''I'm a man with a demanding career. I won't always be there to reassure you of how I feel or to teach you. Take some initiative on your own and ask questions.''

''And have my head bitten off? No, thank you,'' she retorted angrily.

''I warned you, Sparky.'' She pulled away from him. ''Didn't I tell you you'd have to take a lot on trust?'' He raked both hands through his hair, his eyes bleak. ''I don't need this aggravation, Sparky—not now.''

''There seems to be a lot you don't need or want anymore,'' she said faintly with a slight sneer in her voice. ''What happened to all your fine words of sharing and me becoming involved in your life? They were just words, weren't they—meaningless words?''

''No,'' he exploded, and reached for her again, but she backed away.

''I think they were. When you decided to return to your career you were still unsure enough to want someone to hang on to. I've become your prop, your errand boy, your whipping post and a warm body to take your frustrations out on.'' She gave a choked laugh. ''No, I take that back. You don't seem to need me. I'm there, but I'm not there. I've tried to involve myself in your profession. A profession, I might add, that I know absolutely nothing about. I cook, wash, made beds, cater to you and your friends, and act as your hostess. I've tried the best way I know to fit in.''

She came closer and stood in front of his glowering

figure. "How dare you stand there and criticize me, pointing out my faults. If you'd been a little more considerate you would have seen I was floundering like a fish out of water. But oh, no. You've been so selfishly wrapped up in your own world you couldn't or wouldn't see how desperately I needed your help to cope with a situation totally alien to me." She held up her hand to stop whatever he was about to say. "You just didn't want to spare me the time."

"Sparky, I've tried to spend as much time with you as I could."

"Ha," she retorted, "the only time you spend with me is at night, or should I say the early hours of the morning when you crawl into my bed, either too tired to wake me or too drunk from your little private parties."

"I can explain that."

"I just bet you can," she retorted. "Well I'm sick and tired of being alone and left out."

"Hell." His patience was wearing thin, and frustrated he struck back. "Then find something to occupy your spare time—paint. That's something you at least have some knowledge of. But stop interrupting my rehearsals." He regretted his sneering reference to her art the minute the words left his mouth.

It happened before she could stop. Her hand connected with the side of his face in a loud crack. Appalled at what she'd done, Samantha watched the blood drain from his face, leaving the red imprint of her hand in startling clarity. They stared at each other, both stunned by the intensity of her violence.

When the color rushed back to his pale cheeks, making the imprint leap out starkly white against his flushed face, she backed away. Coward that she was, she turned around and made for the closed door, only to be brought up short by a bruising grip on her shoulder. The apology died on her lips as Boston spun her around and pushed her bodily against the oak door.

Wide-eyed and gasping for air, she felt the solid thrust of his weight as he crushed her into the hard surface, his thigh insinuating itself between her legs. His hands filled with bright red tresses and trembled with rage as he forced her face up to his. Shivering inwardly, Samantha rapidly blinked the numbness from her dazed mind and focused on the narrow, uncompromising black eyes glittering above her. The taut, cold expression promised only retribution and she waited for the biting sting of his hand across her cheek. Her lips moved to speak, but his features blurred as his mouth claimed hers in a kiss so uncharacteristically ruthless it took her breath away.

Pinned to the door, she didn't struggled but endured his counterattack as a just punishment. When his kiss deepened in a callous attempt to draw a response, she flinched. After endless seconds of his calculated reprisal she sensed a change in him from rage to passion. She drew her mouth away from his and rested her fevered brow against his chest.

"What's happening to us?" Her voice was scarcely audible as tears chased a path down her pale freckled cheeks. She raised her eyes to his and saw the agony mirrored there. "I don't understand," she whispered, her voice that of a lost child. "You've changed—I've changed. Has the whole world gone mad?"

Boston lowered his knee and stepped back, pulling her away from the door and into his arms, his hands gently massaging the muscles of her back. "We haven't changed, Sparky. Everything's just moving too fast. It's as if we've been caught up in a whirlwind." His hand pressed her face to his chest and she listened to the hammering of his heart. "Most people only have to deal with basic emotions in small quantities. But we've had them all thrown at us in an incredibly short space of time."

The steady rumbling of his words calmed her and she sighed and nodded for him to go on.

"Our love came too quickly, too effortlessly. We weren't given time to search out each other's depths and faults, or time to grow, before we were hit with a maelstrom of problems to deal with. The trouble of Ken and Lana, the pressure of doing the benefit, my fears, Elijah's death. They piled up like a house of cards, just waiting for a breath of wind to topple them from their shaky foundations." Cupping her chin with gentle fingers, he lifted up her face. His eyes were as troubled as hers. "The only difference between the cards and us is that our supports are sound. Our love is too deep to cave in under faulty construction. We've gathered some minor cracks along the way that need to be patched—that's all." He smiled and bent down to kiss her lips. "I've hurt you. I'm sorry."

"I never meant to hit you. I'm sorry, too," she said.

"Hush, love," he soothed.

"Boston, what's going to happen now? How do we go back to what we had?"

"We can't go back, Sparky—not now."

She felt a deep sinking sensation in the pit of her stomach. Did he mean they would never return to their high-spirited loving? Would there always be problems to interfere?

"I know one thing," he went on, "we can't continue like this."

Her heart took a plunge, only to be jolted upward at his next words.

"This house isn't big enough to hold us all. I've been seriously thinking of moving everyone to Houston till after the benefit."

Nestled in the secure warmth of his embrace, she mulled over everything he'd said. Boston was right. There seemed to be a mysterious conspiracy afoot to destroy the natural order of their relationship. The strain of the past weeks had taken its toll on both of them. A sudden thought struck with lightning clarity, and she tried to push it away. To be separated from Boston was unthinkable. But she knew it was the only sensible answer.

"Boston." She lifted her eyes to his, the shadow of a smile twisting her mouth. "We need some time and distance between us for a while. No, listen." Her fingers touched his lips briefly to stop the denial she saw flaring in his eyes. "It's a good time—the best, really. You knew I'd have to leave at some point. I have to return to New York and pack my belongings, close my apartment and hand in my resignation."

"But I planned to come with you, Sparky."

"I know, but don't you see, it's better if I go alone." She reached up and brushed back the ruffled hair from his frowning brow. "It won't take more than two weeks and by the time I get to Houston you'll have everything set up."

"Two weeks?" he bellowed. "One week."

"Come on, Boston. Be realistic."

"I am. One week."

"A week and a half," she wheedled.

"No!"

Samantha frowned and sighed. "One week."

"I still don't like it," he growled, but she could see she was winning. He was silent for a long moment and then said, "Okay." He frowned at her again. "I warned you some time ago I would never let you go. I meant it, Sparky. If you don't come back I'll come find you and drag you home. Remember, you have one week—seven days and no more."

CHAPTER FOURTEEN

NEW YORK HAD SOMEHOW LOST its sparkle for Samantha. She stood before the window in her apartment, on the twenty-fifth floor of a high rise, looking out over the lights of Manhattan. She sighed sadly. Seven hours away from Boston and the emptiness was beginning to set in with a vengeance. He'd given her one week to complete her business obligations and tie up the loose ends of her life. Now she realized the deadline was unacceptable to *her*. She knew she'd work herself into total exhaustion to shorten her stay.

Sighing again, she turned her back on the city she'd come to love and glanced around her apartment. There was so much to do. She was bursting with nervous energy and excitement and couldn't decide where to start the monstrous task of packing and preparing to move. From the looks of things, she'd acquired entirely too many possessions for one person. Resigned, she shrugged and carefully twisted the doorknob of the hall closet, her body wedged in the opening to stop the avalanche she knew was coming.

THE NEXT MORNING Samantha breezed into the office, leaving behind gaping mouths as her long-legged stride carried her past stunned co-workers. She kept up the steady pace toward Ben's office before anyone could recover from shock and swamp her with questions.

"Hello, Ben."

"Sam! What are you doing here?" Ben's blue eyes widened in surprise as he unfolded his rake-thin, six-foot two-inch body from behind the enormous desk and vaulted across the room.

Caught up in his exuberant embrace, Samantha struggled for breath. "How's Barbara and the baby?"

"You're back." He held her away from him and studied her flushed face. "I'm sorry things didn't work out, but you know we're glad to have you back."

"What are you talking about?" He was still speaking, and she knew from long experience she'd never get a word in until he ran down.

"We'll start you to work right away. Keep busy—that's the solution to your problems."

"Ben!" Puzzled, she attempted to stop the flow of sympathy and concern. "Ben!"

"I want you to come spend a few days with us. Barbara and the baby will take your mind off your troubles."

"What troubles?" Samantha squirmed out of his hold and frowned up at him. Had fatherhood deranged his mind? "Stop!" She clamped her hand over his mouth. "What are you babbling on about?"

He mumbled behind her hand and she jerked it away.

"...broken engagement."

"What broken engagement?" she demanded.

"I know it's hard for you to accept this, Samantha...."

She covered his mouth again to cut him off, but this time he swatted her arm away. "Stop that."

"No, you stop," insisted Samantha. "Ben, what's wrong with you? You're acting crazy."

She watched his gaunt face screw up in perplexity as his frown deepened. Ben Johnson was so ugly and endearing he was handsome. He was slim to the point of emaciation, and his features were all angles and sharp bones; his hazel eyes were deep set and as sad as a puppy's, and his mouth as mobile as a rubber band. He sported a mop of unruly toast-brown hair, which covered large elflike ears. Samantha bit her lip as she remembered how many times she'd been in meetings and looked over to see Ben deliberately turn his head and wiggle one ear at her. He was totally outrageous.

"You poor baby," he crooned and patted her shoulder.

"Ben," she yelled. "If you don't tell me what's happening I'll strangle you right here and now." She planted her fists on her hips and thrust out her chin.

Ben's wide mouth hung open for a second. "Do you mean that bastard is still engaged to you and carrying on in Houston?"

"Are you talking about Boston?" Ben nodded his shaggy head and handed her the morning society column of the *New York Post*. Samantha scanned the article and its accounts of Boston's arrival in

Houston and the hints and innuendos of a certain Hollywood starlet who had met him at the airport. She laid the paper down on Ben's desk. "I don't see what you're so upset about. You of all people ought to know his comeback would generate all types of publicity."

"You're not the least bit concerned?"

"No, I trust him." Smiling, she gazed back down at the article then pushed it off the edge of the desk and into the wastepaper basket.

"Well, if nothing's wrong, what are you doing here? I'd have thought you'd want to be at his side." Ben rounded the corner of his desk, flopped down in the big leather executive chair and propped his size-fourteen shoes on the hard surface.

Catching the calculating look in his eyes, Samantha suppressed a grin. "I'm not coming back to work, Ben, so you can just take that eager look off your face. How's Barbara and the baby? What did you name him?"

"You mean I didn't tell you?" Ben dropped his clodhoppers to the carpeted floor with a solid thud and jumped to his feet. He yanked open the top drawer of the desk and pulled out a handful of eight-by-ten color photos. "Samantha, meet Benedict Eric Johnson." He proudly handed her one picture after another, pointing out the extraordinary qualities of his son.

"He's beautiful, Ben." The baby had a rosy cherub face with none of Ben's characteristics.

"Yeah," he beamed and sighed contentedly. "He looks like Barbara. You don't know what a *relief* that is."

Samantha laughed as he twisted his face into a horrible grimace. "How's Barbara?"

"Fine." He answered absently, still engrossed in gazing at his son. "She'll be happy you're back." He looked up. "You will have dinner with us tonight, won't you?"

"You couldn't keep me away. I'm dying to see Benedict."

"Good." Reluctantly he replaced the pictures and eased his long lanky frame into his chair once more. "So, tell me why you're here?"

Samantha explained her plans, and a heated argument ensued. Ben didn't want her to quit, and though she was flattered by his high praise of her work, she remained adamant.

"Just what are you going to do with all that idle time you'll have on your hands while Boston's off on one of his concert tours?"

"Paint," she replied, and grinned as his eyebrows wiggled their way upward. "Ben, ever since I realized I had talent, I've wanted to really take the time to learn just how much I do have and what I could achieve." She leaned back and watched the warring emotions race across his expressive face. He'd always praised and encouraged her work, telling her she was wasting a god-given gift. "You needn't frown. How many times have you told me I was crazy not to pursue it further and try for a showing?"

"Okay, okay. You don't have to remind me. But, dammit, Sam, we're going to miss you." His face flushed crimson at the unusual show of sentiment. Clearing his throat, he shuffled the papers on his desk, then raised his sad eyes. "You're like a sister to Barbara and me," he burst out.

They talked of all the things she'd have to do before she could leave on schedule. Ben made an organized list of priorities for her to follow, adding that he didn't think she'd have any problems subleasing her apartment. He knew a couple of people within the agency who would jump at the chance to live within walking distance of the office.

"You might consider selling your furniture to them, too. It would certainly be an added inducement." He picked up the buzzing intercom and she leaned back, feeling better having Ben's support.

"Right, Alice. I forgot." Ben gathered up his briefcase and stood up. "We'll talk tonight, Sam. I have to run."

Samantha followed Ben's loose-jointed frame out the door, and slipped into her own office. She thought she would be able to spend the rest of the day catching up on her files and reassigning jobs, but the entire staff floated in and out at intervals till she finally gave up and decided it was time to leave.

By the time she reached her apartment, she was hot, tired and out of sorts at not having accomplished as much as she'd planned. If every day followed the same pace it would be a month before she'd see Boston again. Then she remembered his threat to come and drag her home and she smiled.

Her apartment looked as if a cyclone had hit it. She stepped over stacks of books and skirted half-opened trunks, their contents spilling over the sides. One corner was strewn with never-used kitchen gadgets she'd thought she couldn't live without but had never used because she'd lost the directions. The night before she'd spent two hours trying to figure out exactly how they worked.

Shaking her head at the incredible task confronting her, she managed to ignore the mess and head for the bathroom for a quick shower and a hurried change of clothes.

STANDING BEFORE BEN AND BARBARA'S apartment door, Samantha juggled a bottle of expensive champagne and a cloth-wrapped canvas from one position to the next, trying in vain to free a hand to ring the buzzer. She realized the impossibility of her task, looked both ways down the long hallway then pressed her nose to the small button and waited. There was no immediate answer so she was leaning down to perform the same feat again when the door was suddenly yanked open.

"Why do you have your nose on my doorbell?" Barbara Johnson asked, looking down her long delicate nose in mock disdain.

"Would you believe I have a fetish for doorbells?" Samantha suggested innocently.

"No."

"Would you believe the tip of my nose itched?"

"No!"

"Then would you believe I'd picked up your husband's bad habit of doing anything for a laugh."

"Oh, yes, that I'd believe." Barbara laughed and embraced Samantha, ignoring the sharp corners of the awkward package. She held Samantha at arm's

length and studied the sparkling aquamarine eyes.
"Love agrees with you."

Samantha handed Barbara the bottle of Dom
Pérignon and followed her into the living room.
"For a lady who just had a baby a few weeks ago,
you look pretty good yourself." There was finally
some flesh on her friend's bones and Samantha admired the new look of maturity. Before Barbara married Ben, she'd worked as a model and was forced to
stay willow thin. With her striking appearance, the
combination of creamy-white skin, jet-black hair and
apple-green eyes, she'd managed to obtain and sus-
tain the uncertain position of top high-fashion model
till she gave it up to be a wife and mother. Samantha
knew Ben never fully understood what this gorgeous
woman saw in him and he had nicknamed them
Beauty and the Beast.

"Disgusting, isn't it? I thought I'd be able to play
the tragic lady of leisure for at least a month." She
motioned Samantha to the kitchen. "Ben swears
there's a strong peasant line in the woodpile of my
upper-crust Boston ancestry."

"Where is the proud papa?"

Barbara shook her head in disgust. "Watching his
son sleep. Why don't you go see if you can pull him
away?"

It took her nearly thirty minutes to pry Ben from
the child's crib. That feat was only accomplished because her stomach was growling so loudly Ben was
afraid the noise would wake the boy.

Dinner turned out to be a hilarious event with Ben
spouting long-winded toasts and Barbara playing

straight man to his jokes. But Samantha outdid them, giving a blow-by-blow account of how she and Boston met and their stormy courtship.

"Do you mean to tell me he led you to believe he'd made love to you—just as a joke?" Barbara started to laugh at Samantha's rapid nodding. "What a devil. Do me a favor, Samantha—don't ever let Boston and Ben meet."

"Hey! I resent that," Ben protested.

"Hush, dear, and go get the champagne." With loving eyes she watched her husband lumber off, then turned back to Samantha. "When do you plan to marry?"

"I don't know for sure. No, don't look like that, Barbara." She cast her eyes heavenward. "Why is everyone suspicious of Boston?"

"You'll have to admit he has quite a track record with the ladies." She folded her napkin, placed it beside her plate, and motioned for Samantha to follow her into the living room. "I'm not going to voice all the possible problems of marrying someone as famous as Boston. But, Sammy, have you considered the times you'll be apart? What will you do? Are you going to work? Where will you live?"

Samantha made herself comfortable on the long white linen sofa. "We haven't had time to discuss those things. Honestly, Barbara, everything happened so fast. Sometimes I have to pinch myself to make sure I'm not dreaming. All I know, or care about, is I love Boston and he loves me. So what could go wrong?"

"You're very sure?"

"Yes."

"Ben briefly filled me in on what you plan to do. I just can't believe you're ready to give up your career, not after you've worked so hard to get where you are now."

"I can always go back to work if my painting doesn't progress the way I hope it will." She leaned forward, her face earnest. "I owe it to myself to find out if I have a sellable talent. Now's my chance."

"Hey, you two," Ben yelled from the kitchen, "don't say another word till I get there."

"He's worse than an old woman," Barbara snickered. "Always scared he'll miss some juicy tidbit of gossip. Look at him!"

Samantha followed Barbara's eyes and her lips began to twitch. Ben entered the room carrying a heavy tray held high in one hand and in the other the wrapped package she'd brought. With one smooth movement he lowered the tray of filled champagne glasses to the low chrome-and-glass coffee table, then straightened, the large square canvas held to his chest. Samantha and Barbara deliberately ignored his eager expression and reached for their crystal-filled glasses.

Ben coughed to regain their attention. "Ladies, before the both of you get soused I'd like Samantha to explain this." His fingers plucked at the cloth covering and his elastic mouth stretched into a wide grin that threatened to split his face. "Is it what I think it is?"

"Yes." Samantha watched with twinkling eyes as he flopped down in a nearby chair and with fumbling hands began to pull roughly at the cloth wrapper, disregarding his wife's dire warnings to be careful. Both her friends fell silent as they gazed in awe at the painting she'd done. Samantha eyed the canvas critically and realized it was one of her better works. In her early efforts she had started out doing western scenes and in the process of research had become fascinated with the lives of the mountain men and their relationships with the Indians. The painting she'd finished for Ben and Barbara depicted a ragged, gaunt young novice trapper. Knee-deep in an icy stream edged with snowbanks, he was trying determinedly to catch his dinner bare-handed while an Indian on horseback looked on scornfully at his efforts.

Ben tore his eyes from the colorful scene. "I don't know what to say." He glanced at his wife, then back at the painting. "Would you look at the proud expression on the Indian's face? It shows so clearly his disdain for the invader of his lands. Thank you, Samantha, we'll treasure this always." He leaned back and sipped his champagne thoughtfully. "I see now why you want to give your new career an honest chance. You're too good to waste your talent being a part-time artist."

His eyes kept darting back to the painting and they all fell silent again until the persistent ringing of the telephone intruded on their private thoughts.

"It's for you." Barbara handed a startled Samantha the receiver and sat back grinning at her husband.

Samantha frowned, wondering who could possibly be calling her there. "Hello."

"Good evening, sweetheart."

"Boston!"

"Who else?"

She listened to the distant mellow chuckle and gripped the phone tighter. "How did you know to call me here?"

"I have my ways," he intoned mysteriously. "I just wanted to call and let you know you have exactly six days, one hundred and forty-four hours, eight thousand six hundred and forty minutes left."

Samantha laughed. "You figured that out all by yourself, did you?"

"Oh, yes. I've always been good with figures."

"I know," she whispered. The sudden longing to be with him washed over her in a wave of loneliness that brought a lump to her throat. He must have felt the same because she heard the hoarse gruffness in his next words.

"I miss you, Sparky. Come home as soon as you can."

Samantha listened to the broken connection, and fat, glistening tears welled up in her eyes.

"What's wrong, Sammy? What's happened?" Barbara put her arm around the younger woman's shoulders and hugged her close.

"Oh," Samantha sniffed, "I'm being so foolish, but I don't think I can stand to be away from him a whole week." She smiled shakily, accepted the offered tissues from Ben and wiped her eyes. "I'm ready to just walk away from everything right now and go home. He needs me, Barbara. I could hear it in his voice."

Barbara glanced at Ben and when he smiled and nodded, she gave Samantha's shoulder another hard squeeze. "If you want to leave sooner than planned, we'll help you in every way possible. I'm sure Ben can browbeat everyone at the office to pitch in."

In the next few days, Ben did more. He cajoled his staff, screamed and pleaded with moving and packing people, charmed their long list of loyal clients who had any pull in the city and could help in any way. Ben became the tyrant everyone knew had secretly been hiding beneath his lazy exterior, and drove them crazy.

Each night Samantha returned to the disaster zone of her apartment in numbed exhaustion. She'd forgotten New York's hectic pace, the racing from place to place, the readjusting to a faster speech pattern, one that left her ears ringing. Her head ached, her muscles were sore, her brain whirled from questions and answers as she tried to train two new employees to take over her job. And through it all she had to listen to the whispered conversations of her co-workers as gossip article after article about Boston began to appear in all the papers.

She tried to camouflage her irritation and her inner turmoil at having Boston's activities flashed before her eyes. The crux of the matter was she was jealous and a little embarrassed that the people she worked with every day were beginning to doubt the truth of her engagement and her sanity.

The only brightness in her gloomy existence was Boston's calls. During the day he mysteriously managed to find her no matter where she was and briefly give her the new numbers of his countdown. Then he telephoned at night for a longer, more intimate, conversation. But never once did he comment on the scandalous articles appearing in the papers and neither did she.

After they hung up, she'd put on one of his albums and let his words of love fill her apartment and her heart. She listened to his songs, feeling only half alive, as if her body were hanging in limbo. His deep, beautiful voice leaped in and out of her head and she sensed his nearness even though he was thousands of miles away.

As his voice and the soothing lyrics of his songs renewed her strength she'd pull a stool before the standing easel and work on her surprise for him. Thumbtacked to the top of the easel was an old snapshot Pearl had unearthed among Elijah's sparse possessions. The faded and creased photo showed Elijah, his wife and Boston's mother standing before their small frame house. Samantha transferred her gaze from the photo to the big canvas propped in front of her. She'd painted Boston's portrait in the foreground. In the background directly behind him was Elijah's lined proud face, then to either side of Elijah were Boston's grandmother and mother.

When she had finished it Samantha leaned back to study her efforts. Admittedly the two women were younger in the painting's time reference, but the effect she had prayed for had come through. She slashed her signature in the bottom left-hand corner. Her endless hours and late nights had paid off. Her surprise was more than a loving gift.

She had painted a visual past for Boston to hold on to.

Her days began to wind down and suddenly she found herself with time on her hands. Arriving at the office early on her last morning there, she cornered Ben. "There's nothing left for me to do."

He grinned and ran a hand through his unruly mop of hair. "Well, don't hang around here getting under my feet. Enjoy yourself. Personally, I'd like to go home and crawl back into bed. How do you manage to be so bright eyed after last night's farewell party?"

She laughed as he winced and held his head. "I didn't try to drink the bar dry, my friend."

"Yes, well. Go away. You're through as of right now." He began to walk away and she followed. "I don't want to see your face until Barbara and I pick you up in the morning to take you to the airport." Stopping in midstride, Ben turned around too quickly and grabbed the wall for support. "Have you told Boston of your early arrival?"

"No. I want it to be a surprise. And don't you dare tell anyone in the office." She smiled at his arched look. "Someone in this group has been Boston's spy. He knows where I am every minute of the day."

Ben nodded, then rested his aching head against the nearest wall. "I think I might die," he groaned. "Oh, do go away, Samantha."

She kissed his hot cheek and slipped out of the office, having made her goodbyes the previous night. She stood on the street before her office building. There were hours to fill and she was suddenly at a loss as to what to do. Then she grinned and set out at a long-legged stride.

"WHERE THE HELL HAVE YOU BEEN all day?"

The growling voice on the other end of the phone brought a smile to her lips and a sparkle to her eyes. "Good evening, Boston. I've missed you too." She propped her tired, aching feet up and sighed loudly.

"Do you realize it's ten o'clock there and I've been trying to find you all day?"

"Oh, what's the matter, my love? You sound out of sorts. Did your spy network break down?"

"Sparky," he groaned, then chuckled. "Yes, as a matter of fact it did. Where were you, honey? I was getting worried."

Samantha shifted the receiver to a more comfortable position and lay back on the soft pillows of her sofa. "I played tourist today."

"What?"

"I went sight-seeing." She wiggled a sore foot. "Boston, do you realize in all the time I've lived here I never really took the time to see this city? It's a shame you can allow yourself to become so wrapped up in your job you forget to take a look around you. So I went on one of those bus tours. After that I walked Fifth Avenue, and toured St. Patrick's Cathedral and the United Nations Building. I even hired a taxi to take me to Chinatown and Greenwich Village, and through Little Italy."

"You're totally insane," he yelled. She held the receiver away from her ear. "Do you have any idea what could. . . ."

"And—hush, Boston—and I went to the top of the Empire State Building. Then this evening I rode the Staten Island Ferry. Did you know that you can see the Statue of Liberty from the deck?" Complete silence met this last bit of news and she frowned. "Boston, you still there?"

"Sparky, I want you to come home right now. Have you lost your mind?"

"No, but my feet are killing me. Besides," she said innocently, "I still have three more days before I can leave."

There was another long pause, then he said, "Okay, Sparky. Just let me know what your flight time is and I'll meet you at the airport."

She felt a little guilty at having upset him, but then she thought of her surprise and smiled. After all, he'd given her seven days to tie up her life in New York.

CHAPTER FIFTEEN

SHE'D MADE IT in five!

"Fasten your seat belts, please."

Samantha's head jerked up and she flashed a dazzling smile at the male steward, her fingers fumbling with the clasp.

"Here, allow me." He leaned over and efficiently buckled her in. "Your first flight?"

"No, no. I'm just excited about going home." She smiled again, a little self-consciously this time.

"To some lucky man, I guess?" the steward sighed mournfully, but his walnut-brown eyes twinkled merrily.

"Yes!" she laughed, "he is lucky." *Lucky if I don't kill him,* she thought grimly, forcing the smile to remain intact as she glanced again at the morning paper lying in her lap. The press was having a field day with coverage of Boston's return. His telephone calls were a waste of time and money. All she had to do was pick up any paper and have a minute-by-minute account of his daily—and nightly—actions.

Her fingers crinkled the edges of the folded newspaper and she gazed into Boston's gleaming eyes, mocking her from the print. The famous smile she knew so well was turned on the voluptuous blonde hanging on his arm. Felicia Carrington, a sexy actress from Texas who had made her fame with a wild mane of honey-colored hair, the body of a goddess and just enough intelligence to stuff a pea pod.

Samantha threw the paper onto the vacant seat beside her, where it slid to the floor. Reaching down, she picked it up and slapped it face down on the seat. She gritted her teeth and flipped it back over, her eyes riveted on Boston's sensuous smile. Felicia was something he'd conveniently neglected to mention when he'd called, and a perverse stubbornness had kept her from inquiring.

Trust, she reminded herself, was Boston's favorite word lately, so she would trust him. But her jaws ached from clenching her teeth together in determination, and she fought hard to squelch that nagging voice at the back of her mind.

SAMANTHA GAVE THE TAXI DRIVER the address again as they turned off the bumper-to-bumper traffic of Westheimer to River Oaks Boulevard. One of Houston's most impressive streets, it was divided into two categories—palatial and country estate. Their owners were more than merely rich. The massive and imposing homes of brick and stone lined an elegantly manicured boulevard, ending in a cul-de-sac with a towering brick building—River Oaks Country Club, a haven for the wealthy.

Samantha closed her eyes and shook her head in amazement. She didn't want to see the house Boston had borrowed. When he informed her his friend Kane Stone had insisted on their using his little Houston home for the duration of their stay, she had envisioned a small country cottage on a tiny plot of ground. She should have known, she reminded herself, that Boston moved in high circles.

"We're here, lady."

She climbed out of the taxi, trying to ignore the sprawling two-story rose-brick colonial house. While the cab driver unloaded her luggage, she concentrated on searching the massive polished oak door for a bell or knocker. Why, she wondered, did architects find it necessary to cleverly hide such simple items as door bells?

"That's thirty-four dollars," the driver said as he dropped the last of her bags and a large, narrow crate on the front porch. "You want me to wait till you see if anyone's home?"

"No, thanks." She dismissed him and returned to the problem of locating the bell, only to give a startled jerk as the door flew open and she was confronted with a tall, broad male back.

"Just remember, Pearl, you're the only true love of my life," came the slightly accented voice as the man began backing out the door.

Samantha tried to step out of the way but was knocked aside as he turned. Her shoulders were caught in a firm grip to help her regain her balance.

"Well, hello there, sweetheart. Look here, Pearl, two beauties in one day." With that, he bounded down the steps.

Samantha gave a low whistle as she watched him leave. Whoever he was he was absolutely gorgeous.

The brief glimpse of black hair and the silver flash of eyes left her with her mouth hanging open.

"It's about time you got here!" Pearl remarked, her fingers busy pushing at a few strands of hair that had worked loose from her tight bun. "You can close your mouth and stop drooling over that scoundrel." Her faded eyes managed to sparkle and her thin lips fought to keep back a smile. "He had the nerve to pinch me on the rump."

"Who is he?" Samantha asked, still a little awe-struck.

"Kane Stone."

She turned at the name and caught the blush still on Pearl's lined cheeks. She smiled. "I didn't know you were coming."

"Where else would I be?" Pearl sniffed. "Do you think I'd let some fancy-pants foreign chef cook for Boston?"

Samantha bit her lip to hide her amusement, wondering how Pearl had talked Boston into allowing her to accompany them to Houston. He probably hadn't had a choice in the matter at all. "Is he here?"

"That man's been like the devil with his tail in a vise ever since you left." She grabbed Samantha's arm and pulled her through the doorway. "Come on, you're just in time to see what's been going on."

Samantha wrestled the rough wooden crate through the door and propped it against the hall wall.

"What's that?" Pearl eyed the mysterious package with Boston's name stenciled on the outside in big black letters.

"A painting I did for Boston. Could you hide it, Pearl? I'm not ready to give it to him yet."

Pearl nodded, reluctantly dragging her gaze from the crate. "Come on, girl." She grabbed Samantha's arm again.

Samantha tried to pull back, but Pearl's strength won out and she was quick-marched to the back of the house with only brief glances at, and vague impressions of, open doors, rich warm woods, pastel walls and deep pile carpeting. As laughing female voices reached her ears, she realized suddenly she didn't want to see what was happening.

All the way to Houston her doubts and uncertainties over Boston had warred with her love and she had felt pulled in two different directions. She and Pearl came to a halt and Pearl pushed open the swinging double doors.

Soft classical music mingled with voices in the glassed in-patio. Samantha quickly took in the lush hanging ferns and white wicker furniture. Her eyes stopped their search as they landed on Boston. She stood unnoticed in the entrance. All thoughts of jealousy fled from her mind at the sight of his dazzling smile and twinkling black eyes—even if they were turned on Felicia Carrington. She watched, her heart beating an erratic tempo in her breast, as he lifted his head and his eyes widened at the sight of her.

Boston half rose from his place at the end of a love seat. "Sparky!" His voice boomed in the now-still room and he started toward her, then stopped as if unsure of his reception. "What are you doing here?"

he asked incredulously, his eyes devouring every inch of her body.

She wanted to rush into his arms and hug him fiercely, but held back, deciding to play the game out. "Things got a little *hot* in New York." She looked pointedly at Felicia, then turned a mock scowl on Boston. "To say nothing of the questions I was forced to endure."

"Oh," he smiled, walking slowly toward her again. "Such as?"

They forgot their audience and it was as if no one existed in the world but the two of them.

"Those newspaper articles, you wretch. The first thing my boss—ex-boss," she corrected herself, seeing his questioning look. "The first thing he wanted to know was if I was coming back to work, since our engagement hadn't worked out. He then proceeded to wave the first of many gossip articles about you before my eyes...." Boston was almost within touching distance and her nose twitched with the unmistakable male scent that was uniquely his own. "Really, Boston! Your escapades have to stop!" She tried desperately to keep a straight face, but he saw the glittering laughter in her eyes.

"Yes, my love," he said so meekly that she almost choked. "Were you madly jealous?"

"Spitting nails all the way here." She closed the distance between them and stood looking up into his solemn face.

"Oh, dear, that must have hurt?"

"It did."

"Maybe I can kiss it and make it better?"

He smiled and she sighed. It seemed an eternity since she'd been on the receiving end of one of his sensuous smiles.

"I missed you," she whispered for his ears only. Her next words were smothered as his mouth descended on hers in a kiss so tender and loving it shook her to her toes.

The polite applause from the bystanders broke them apart. Boston slowly lifted his head, and a wide flashing grin spread across the face.

"Come now, Boston, let's have a good look at your young lady."

A raspy female voice spoke from behind Boston's back and Samantha, still held within the circle of his arms, peeked around his shoulders; her eyes collided with a pair of shrewd cold blue ones.

"Boston, unhand the girl," the woman demanded.

Boston shot Samantha a grimace of distaste, dropped his arms and stepped aside. "Sparky, I'd like you to meet Margret Tanner." He executed a gentlemanly bow to the older woman and murmured, "Maggie, my fiancée, Samantha Fay Griffin."

Samantha had time to collect her shattered composure during the introduction and mentally kicked herself. There she was, standing before the most fashionable and feared woman of the social, political and international set, dressed for comfort, like the seasoned traveler she was, while all the others in the room were at their most elegant. Margret Tanner's long career of making or breaking individuals in her famous society column was renowned. Now those piercing blue eyes were fixed on her like a snake charmer hypnotizing its prey, assessing and judging its next move. Samantha thrust out her chin as she watched the cold eyes settle on her hair.

"Shame on you, Boston!" Margret scolded throatily. "When you said she was unique, you neglected to say how." She blinked rapidly several times and went on. "I don't believe I've ever seen that particular shade of hair before. My dear, is it yours? Of course it is," she quickly answered her own question. "No beautician could possibly achieve that color no matter how hard they tried."

"Ms. Tanner..." Samantha began through gritted teeth.

"Sparky!" Boston's fingers increased their pressure on her arm. "Maggie's been kind enough to devote her entire column to the coverage of the benefit." He began to urge her toward the door. "If you'll excuse us, Maggie?" He nodded to Ken to take over and turned Samantha toward the door.

"Oh, no you don't, Boston Grey," Margret called after them. "I want an interview with your Sparky. Your fans will want to know *everything* about her and her family—how you met and when you fell in love. And I'm just dying to find out how she acquired that interesting nickname."

Samantha felt the muscles tighten along Boston's arm at the columnist's questions. Before he had time to answer or stop her, she spun around and faced the newspaperwoman.

"I'm sorry, Ms. Tanner, but a cozy interview with me will be impossible." She smiled sweetly to take some of the sting out of her words. "I'm a very private person you see, and I intend for my life to stay that way. How Boston and I met is immaterial. The only important item is we love each other and plan to marry. As for my family—'' she shrugged ''—I would prefer if they were left out of your column completely. They're simple people, Ms. Tanner, and the notoriety wouldn't sit well with them.''

She allowed Boston to propel her from the room. When the door was closed behind them she looked up, her eyes widening as she watched his shoulders shake and his black eyes sparkle with an effort to restrain his laughter.

''Sparky!'' he chuckled. ''Did you see her face? I don't believe anyone has dared to talk to Maggie like that since she first started as a cub reporter.'' He crushed her against his chest. ''Oh, my delight. How I've missed you.'' His lips touched hers, but the kiss she expected erupted into laughter. ''They're simple people,'' he mimicked. ''There's nothing simple, common or ordinary about your family. Just pray Maggie never takes it into her head to do a little research.''

Samantha grinned. ''Well, what else could I do? I won't have that woman digging into my background. Where are we going, Boston?'' He gave her a suggestive look and her pulse accelerated.

He ushered her up a wide winding staircase and down an endless hallway carpeted in pale yellow. She was laughing and panting for breath as he swung open double wooden doors. The laughter died in her throat at the sight that met her eyes.

She couldn't say a word as she took in the

monstrous bed with its high carved headboard, reaching at least six feet above the mattress. A lush dark-brown mink coverlet was spread neatly over the gigantic bed. She turned disbelieving eyes to Boston as he flopped down on a red-velvet chaise longue. He draped his long body along its length and laughed at her expression.

"My—my." As she looked around she was met with multiple reflections of her wide-eyed expression. One whole wall was covered in floor-to-ceiling mirrors. "Oh!" she choked out, then frowned as a sudden suspicion hit her. She walked to the side of the bed and looked up. "More mirrors." She pivoted to face him. "Please tell me you've been giving me a guided tour of the house and this is not my room."

She waited impatiently for him to get control of himself. Visions filtered through her mind of Boston's naked body reflected across the room as he sprawled across the satin sheets she instinctively knew must lie beneath the mink spread. It was a deliciously wicked thought and she shivered with anticipation.

"This is our room." Boston broke up again as he caught her half-excited, half-frightened look. "Sparky, Sparky, if you could see your face."

"I can. Believe me, about ten times more than I care to." She pushed his long legs aside and sat down beside him, propping her chin on folded hands. "What sort of friends do you have? This...this room is...indecent."

"Yes, it is," he chuckled, and pulled her to lie

down beside him. "But think of all the fun we'll have."

"I don't know." She wavered, then smiled as tantalizing images began to take shape in her mind.

"You see," he whispered, "all it takes is a little imagination."

"Hmmm," she purred and nuzzled his ear. "Boston, what's Felicia doing here?"

"I don't believe you, woman. You jump from one subject to another without any warning." He lifted his lips from the pulsing vein of her neck. "You're jealous!"

Samantha scowled and met his surprised look. "Of course I am! For the past five days all I've seen or heard about is you and Felicia. Why didn't you mention she was here when you called?"

"I don't know. I guess I didn't think it was important." Tender fingers brushed the bright red tendrils of hair from her flushed freckled cheeks.

She shot him a wry grin and mumbled under her breath. "I don't like her, Boston."

"Sparky, Felicia's an old friend. That's all she's ever been. I promise you, nothing more."

"Well!" Samantha huffed, only halfway convinced. "Why does she always look so hungry, as if any minute she's going to—to bite you?"

Boston fell backward against the chaise longue and roared. "She looks at every male that way, love. It's a very artful and practiced expression—took her months before the mirror to perfect it." He raised himself up on one elbow and gazed down at her still-worried face. "There's no need for you ever to be jealous."

Firm warm lips descended on hers and she savored the cool sweetness of his mouth. A loud growl from the regions of her stomach caused him to pull back.

"What on earth!"

She gave him a sheepish smile. "I'm hungry."

"By the sound of it you'll be taking bites out of me if I don't feed you." A slow smile curved his mouth. "Come to think of it, that might not be a bad idea."

Samantha made quick snapping noises with her teeth, but before she could make a mock lunge for him there was a knock at the door.

"Who is it?" he ground out, then cursed under his breath before he called for the person to come in.

At the tone of his voice, Samantha wondered who would dare to brave the animal in his den. She began straightening her crumpled blouse, her eyes on the door as it swung open and a serving cart was shoved in, followed by a stern-faced Pearl.

"Thought Sammy might be hungry." She pushed the cart a little farther into the room, her eyes averted from the bed and mirrors. "When are the two of you going to get married?" she demanded, making a precise military turn as she marched toward the door. She stopped. "Better do it quick before a little consequence makes its presence known," she shot over her shoulder, then continued her march, closing the door behind her with a sharp snap.

"Consequence?" They said in unison, then fell into each other's arms.

"You're not expecting a consequence, are you, Sparky?"

"No." She sat up and lifted the covers from the

warm plates, missing the look of disappointment that slid fleetingly across Boston's features.

"Hmmm, this looks good." She sniffed appreciatively at the hot open-faced roast beef sandwich, drowning in rich brown gravy.

With leisurely movements Samantha ate, enjoying Boston's frustration as she nibbled at her food. When his hands became too familiar, she playfully slapped them away, laughing at his growling threats of extracting payment for her cruel torture.

"Are you through?" His patience was clearly at an end.

Samantha glanced down and shook her head. Her blouse had fallen open, one button missing because of his too-eager fingers. She lifted innocent eyes and asked, "What time is it?"

"What difference does it make?"

"I think I'll take a bath—alone."

Boston flopped backward on the chaise longue and groaned loudly. He turned his eyes heavenward and asked, "What have I done to deserve such shabby treatment? Five days I wait and she wants to take a bath." He rolled over on his side, his eyes soulful as he watched her struggle to keep a straight face. "Next you'll want to have a nice long chat."

"Well, yes, as a matter of fact I would," she teased, and jumped up, stepping away from his lunging body. She sprinted across the room and stumbled for safety behind a wing-back chair, looking down in astonishment as her slacks slid around her ankles. She'd neglected to notice just how busy his fingers had been. "Lecher, sex maniac." She stepped out of the beige gaberdine shackles and kicked them out of her way.

"Come here, Sparky!"

"No!" Her bottom lip protruded in a teasing pout. "I *do* want to talk, Boston. You haven't told me a thing. What's been happening around here?"

"Later." He faked a move to the right, then made a running dash to the left, only to be left holding a brown-and-beige stripe silk blouse in his hand. The soft material dangled from his fingers as he whirled around with a baffled expression at her eellike movements.

"Where are Tom and the rest of the orchestra members staying?" Clad now in only her lacy bikini panties she crouched behind another chair, her chin resting on its high back. Bright eyes watched his every move, waiting for the flicker of an eyelid or the tensing of hard muscles. When his eyes narrowed to gleaming slits, Samantha made a mad dash for the bed. She felt his grasping fingers on the band of her panties, heard the sound of ripping fabric as she struggled for a second to be free, then dove across the mink spread and bounded to the other side of the room. Her tinkling laughter echoed off the walls, mixing with his snarling curses. She was cornered, backed against the wall of mirrors.

Boston's mouth twitched in a smile of masculine victory as his eyes wandered over her long slim white body. Small breasts heaved with every breath; her glorious mane of shocking red hair tumbled in wild disarray around her flushed face.

Mesmerized by the stern set of his features, she

watched as he began to unbutton his shirt, his movements slow and unhurried as he walked toward her.
The pounding in her ears, the hot rush of blood
through her veins and the cold surface of the mirror
against her back added to her excitement. Eagerness
emanated from her as she realized the time for games
was at an end.

Boston stood before her, his eyes reflecting her
own thoughts. She reached out for him, running her
hands along the warm flesh of his shoulders, pulling
him to her and lifting her mouth to his. Slim arms
tightened around his neck and her tongue sought the
dark cavern of his mouth. She felt him bend and was
suddenly cradled against his chest, swaying with the
motion of his steps.

How she'd missed him. His velvet voice seduced
her as much as his hands. All during their separation
she'd envisioned their first time back together. She
knew now that all the things she'd planned to entice
him with were useless. There was no holding back for
games. She could only be herself and as naturally giving as she'd always been.

When the silky fur of the mink spread touched her
cool skin, she opened her eyes to gaze up into his loving face. "Boston," she began, but strong fingers
gently touched her lips.

"Hush. Just let me love you, Sparky. There'll be
time later to talk." He gathered her close, his hand
playing along the curve of her spine.

"Ouch!" She jerked away from him, her eyes re-
proachful. "You pinched me!" she wailed, hurt and
mystified. Rubbing the offended area, she inched

farther away, only to be stopped by the pressure of his arm.

"Sorry," he choked, "but your skin's so soft. Sometimes when I'm touching you I don't feel you at all. I just wanted to be sure I wasn't dreaming again. The past five days have been hell, Sparky. I wasn't one-hundred percent sure you were coming back to me."

She wanted him to know beyond the shadow of a doubt how much she loved him; how much she'd missed being held in his arms; how she'd suffered the long lonely hours at night, wishing he were there beside her making love to her. She searched for the right words to express her feelings, but none strong or loving enough came to mind. Her hands gently touched his shoulders and pushed him over onto his back.

"What?" he questioned, puzzled.

"Be still." She grinned and came up onto her knees beside him, her fingers trailing small circles over the smooth skin of his chest and down over the flat planes of his stomach.

"What are you up to?" His voice wavered under the tantalizing strokes.

"I'm going to make love to you." She flashed him a seductive smile, picked up his hand and began nibbling, her tongue slipping between each finger. Slowly, she worked the tip of her tongue upward, tracing the prominent veins on his arm to his shoulder till she reached his ear. There she paused to outline the bold curving lines before moving on to his strong jaw. She lingered over his mouth, and when he moved to meet her lips she pulled back, shaking her head.

Her eyes searched his, seeking an unspoken permission, and when he sighed and half closed his passion-heavy lids, she lowered her head. He was velvet warm and she caressed him tentatively at first. He tasted good—male and strong—yet the different textures of his skin from soft to faintly rough excited her more than she thought possible. She listened to the deep moan rumbling in his chest, the sound pushing her to greater daring, till she felt his muscles tense. Hard fingers bit into her arms and pulled her upward to lie full length along his body.

She lay motionless across him while his hands moved slowly up and down her back, stopping only long enough to knead the firm flesh of her buttocks. Samantha opened her eyes and lifted her head; their ragged breaths mingled with the sweet murmurs only lovers could decipher.

Boston quickly flipped her over onto her back, his body half covering hers as his lips played along the vein throbbing erratically in her back.

"Oh, my love," he groaned, "what you've done to me." His eyes captured hers. "You take my breath away," he whispered against her mouth. "Shall I return the pleasure?" And before she could answer, his lips moved to the ripe roundness of her swollen breasts, lingering over each rosy tip. Then his mouth moved downward.

She relaxed in his hold, the strength of her muscles melting away under the heated expertise of his mouth as he touched the center of her pleasure. Her breath caught and held in the back of her throat till the agonizing ecstasy faded and the shaking in her limbs subsided.

Opening drowsy eyes, she gazed up, and there in the black depths she saw every word of love she'd longed to hear. He might not say them as often as she wished, but his love for her was as visibly stamped on his face as if he'd just spoken them aloud in the hushed room.

With trembling fingers she smoothed back the crisp locks of hair from his damp brow, watching the sharp tautness of his face as he slid smoothly into her and began to move above her. She closed her eyes, giving herself up once more to the demands of his body, answering his thrust with her own need.

Time and space spun out into nothingness as everything telescoped, sending her upward to peaks she'd never ventured before. Her husky voice mixed with his hoarse cry as they called to each other. And as the waning glow ebbed and the radiance paled, still they held each other tightly in their spent passion.

"Little firecracker," Boston whispered, and kissed each sleepy eyelid closed. "You never cease to amaze and delight me."

Curved into Boston's body, held protectively in his arms, Samantha sighed with pure joy. Everything, she told herself, was going to work out. The five-day separation had worked its own special brand of magic, the past friction between them now vanquished forever. It felt wonderful to be back on an even keel: no more seesawing emotions, no more angry words or hurt feelings. The time apart had given her a better perspective on their relationship and now she could use her intelligence to grasp what had happened.

Boston's drastic change had been only a reflex to the fear of performing again, the pressure everyone was applying because of the benefit, and finally the anguish over Elijah's death and the shock of learning of his past. The overcrowded conditions at the ranch and the constant interruptions had only added to the strain he was under. He needed an outlet—her. And she'd been too wrapped up in her own hurt pride over his neglect to see clearly. From the moment they'd met, she reminded herself, they had been in each other's company virtually twenty-four hours a day. She'd become accustomed to having his undivided attention, and when she was forced to share him with others, she resented it bitterly. In her self-absorption she'd ignored Boston's need to be his own man and return to his work.

Samantha sighed softly again, secure in the knowledge that she understood him now, and there was nothing he could do or say to shake her resolve to stay.

CHAPTER SIXTEEN

SAMANTHA STOMPED down the winding stairs, grumbling under her breath. Boston was an unfeeling fiend, she thought. Her blurry vision caused her to miss a step and she muttered dire threats against him. To be rudely awakened at the ungodly hour of five o'clock was bad enough, but to have your warm body suddenly subjected to the cold air and your bottom heartily slapped was too much. Then he had added insult to injury by pulling the heavy curtains back, allowing the sun's rays to reflect off the mirrored wall and into her face. Samantha gritted her teeth as she pushed open the kitchen door, her ears still ringing with Boston's laughter.

The sight of a flaming red head, identical in color to hers, jolted Samantha from thoughts of revenge.

"Mark! What on earth are you doing here?" Before he had time to answer, Samantha flew at her grinning brother and shouted, "If you touch one hair on Boston's head I'll...I'll...."

"Hey!" Mark drew Samantha into his arms, nearly smothering her against the massive expanse of his chest. "I didn't come to slay Caesar, but to join him."

"What?"

"Here, Sammy." He released her and placed a hot mug of coffee in her hand, then led her to a wrought-iron table tucked in the corner of the huge kitchen. When she made to speak again, Mark waved his hand. "Drink," he commanded. "I know ten o'clock is the middle of the night to you." He gave her a lopsided grin. "The coffee will help—some."

Samantha did as ordered. The color rushed to her cheeks as she wondered if Mark realized she and Boston were lovers. The flush deepened as she thought about the previous night and the wild abandon they had shared. She ducked her head and sipped more of the hot, fragrant brew.

"You awake?"

She nodded and studied his smug expression. "I take it you're not going to kill Boston on sight?"

"Me! Now why would you think I'd want to do that, little sister?" Mark's eyes twinkled at her frown. He puffed out his broad chest and crossed his arms proudly. "I'm Boston's personal bodyguard!" Samantha choked on her coffee, but he paid her no attention and continued. "Boston drove out to the farm with Father Brian a few days ago to talk to dad. He offered me a job."

Mark tried to shrug off the explanation with a careless nonchalance, but Samantha could see the telltale red staining his cheeks with excitement. She stared at her brother, stunned not only by his change in attitude, but by the knowledge that Boston had taken the time to visit her father. This was another item he'd neglected to tell her, she mused, undecided whether she should be angry or happy.

"What surprised me is how Boston got away from the farm in one piece."

"To tell the truth, Sammy, it was touch and go there for a few minutes. But Adam, Luke and Matthew felt it wouldn't be very sporting with a priest watching. Besides, dad and Uncle George quickly ushered the two visitors into the house."

"How's everyone?" she asked, smiling at the picture Mark painted.

"Fine. Boston gave the entire family tickets to the concert and some of them are already in town. Adam and Luke won't be here till later. They have the quarter-horse sale to contend with." Mark took a big gulp of his coffee, a frown furrowing his brow. "You are going to marry him, aren't you, sis?"

Mark's soft-spoken question caused her head to snap up. "Of course I am. By the way, where is he?"

"He's closed up in the living room with his manager and his piano player, Thomas."

Samantha started to get up, then flopped back down. "How long have you been here, Mark?"

"Two days. Why?"

"And you've been with Boston every moment?"

"Yeah." Mark studied her innocent expression. "Ho, ho," he grinned. "You want to know about that Felicia woman."

"No! I do not," she retorted, then calmed down. "I know all about that woman. What I do want to know is where everyone is staying and what's been going on."

"Well. . . ." Mark thoughtfully rubbed his chin.

"Mark!" she warned.

"Okay, okay. Boston's band—excuse me, orchestra—are all housed in the cottages by the pool." He pointed out the window and Samantha followed his finger.

Miniature cottages curved around an Olympic-size swimming pool, their placement artfully arranged between trees and flowering shrubs. She swung her attention back to Mark as he continued.

"There's a big open playroom off the side of the pool and Boston uses it as a rehearsal hall when they're not at the Summit practicing. I don't see too much of them. They keep pretty much to themselves except for that Thomas fellow. He's around all the time." Mark leaned forward, his face serious. "I met Ken and his wife, Lana, for the first time yesterday. He's a nice guy, but I don't understand why he doesn't do something about his wife."

"What do you mean? There's nothing wrong with Lana." Samantha bristled at her brother's criticism of her friend.

Mark gave her an odd look. "Sammy, the woman smells like she bathes in her husband's cologne."

Samantha tried to swallow, but almost choked on her coffee. She grabbed a napkin and pressed it to her mouth to keep from inelegantly spraying her brother's baffled face. Poor Lana, she thought, she still carried the lingering effects of her run-in with the skunk. Trying valiantly to keep a straight face, she related Lana's disastrous indoctrination into the hazards of the wild. When she had finished she got up and gathered a tray, additional mugs and the coffee pot. Mark's laughter followed her across the hall, she had to bite her lip hard to keep from joining in.

Before she had reached the living room the front doorbell chimed. Samantha glanced around, and when no one appeared she shrugged, struggling with her heavy burden. Balancing the tray on one hip, she swung open the door and stared at the scowling platinum blonde.

"Where is he?" the woman demanded, her overly glossed lips pulled in a faint sneer as her eyes scanned Samantha's casual attire.

Samantha quickly took in the expensive designer suit, alligator shoes and bag with matching attaché case.

"I asked you a question?" She prodded, then pushed her way through the entrance, came to a halt in the center of the hall, and stood there, her foot tapping impatiently.

"In the living room, but...." It was too late to ask questions. The blonde was already through the door. Samantha lifted one shoulder, dismissing the woman's rudeness as par for Boston's odd friends. Coffee would have to wait. She pulled a face at the closed door and started back to the kitchen.

When a bellow of pure rage and frustration issued from behind the oak barrier, Samantha whirled around, sending mugs and coffee pot crashing to the floor. She threw down the tray, stepped gingerly over the spreading hot liquid—now generously sprinkled with melting sugar—and made a mad dash for the door. She pushed it open and faltered, then stopped, her mouth agape at the scene before her.

Like a coiling snake the blonde had her body wrapped around Boston. Samantha watched Boston's futile attempts to release the clinging woman.

"Lady!" Boston roared, but still she clung, whispering words for his now-red ears only. He looked frantically from Ken to Tom. "Don't just stand there. Do something!"

His pleas brought them all from their frozen state and sent them into action. Before she could take a step, Tom and Ken had jumped forward, grabbed hold of the woman's arms, pried them loose from their death grip and ushered her out of the room.

An unpleasant silence followed. Samantha guiltily drew her eyes from Boston's icy stare. As the silence stretched endlessly, she peeked at him cautiously through lowered lashes.

"Who. . .who was she?" she ventured.

Boston pulled out a handkerchief and began to wipe the smear of shiny lipstick from his lips and cheek. "How the hell should I know!" he growled, his black eyes chips of polished jet. "Who's the imbecile who allowed her to waltz in here?"

Samantha shifted her weight from one foot to the other, her cheeks flushed as she dimly realized Ken and Tom returned to stand beside Boston. Their eyes were just as accusing as his.

"Me," she squeaked.

"Why?" Boston shouted, and she flinched as the word cracked in the quiet room like a pistol shot.

Samantha straightened her shoulders, her chin thrust out mutinously. "Because she demanded to see you."

"Demanded," he shouted again, then took a deep breath to calm himself. "*No one* demands to see me, Sparky." He shook his head. "Didn't you have enough sense to guess what she was?"

"No! How could I tell? She looked like a business-woman with a purpose."

"Oh, she had purpose all right." Ken gave a disgusted snort.

"Stay out of this, Ken," Boston ordered. "Why don't you and Thomas go get some coffee."

Her eyes followed the two retreating figures till the door closed behind them. Slowly she turned, angry at Boston's unfair treatment.

"How was I to know she was an overzealous fan?"

"How indeed?" he sighed. "Sparky, you're going to have to learn the difference. As egotistical as it may sound, I can't give the general public free rein to come and go in my life. Do you have any idea of the trouble it would cause?" She shook her head. "There would be visits from irate husbands, lawsuits from women filing paternity suits, to say nothing of the rape charges brought against me. Sparky, the combination of money and power has an odd effect on people. It's like a strong aphrodisiac to most, and they're drawn to the source like a magnet. It brings the weirdos of the world out of the woodwork." He raked a shaky hand through his hair. "You really don't comprehend what it's like, do you?" He sighed in exasperation. "Where have you been? Haven't you ever seen what happens to rock stars in a crowd?"

"Yes. But, Boston, you're a romantic balladeer,

not a rock star. Those fans are young, immature girls. Yours are an older group.''

"It doesn't matter," he ground out. "They might be more mature, but they still react the same way.'' He watched her expression of disbelief and went on. "There may be none of the screaming or hair pulling—my fans are a little too sophisticated for that." His cynicism scared her, but he went on relentlessly.

"They send scorching love letters, explicit enough to make a hardened pervert blush. Hotel room keys find their way into my possession in the most mysterious ways. They throw me their underwear and other personal articles of clothing. And worst of all, they have sexual fantasies about me and tell their husbands to drive them wild.'' Boston grabbed her arms and pulled her closer, his breath warm on her burning cheeks. "When the unpredictable happens and I find myself in a crowd, they want to touch me—anywhere—it doesn't matter." His arms tightened around her, his voice deep and husky with distress. "I've tried to keep the worst from you. But I think you'll have to experience it firsthand to really understand." He knew she couldn't comprehend what he was trying to convey to her. She had it set in her head that only rock fans were capable of such wild behavior. He sighed, kissed her forehead and was about to turn away when he caught the peculiar expression on her face. "What else have you done?''

"Well...." She drew the word out as long as her breath held.

"Come on, out with it.''

"Actually it's not that bad.''

"Sparky!"

"Some of the people at the office—friends—wondered if you would send them personally autographed pictures. I told them you'd be happy to." She reached into the pocket of her pants, drew out some folded papers and handed them to him.

"Is that all?" Boston began to unfold the sheets, his eyes widening, then narrowing. "There must be fifty names here! And they all want a little personal message—right? Do you have any idea how long this will take?"

Samantha tried to smile. "It did get a little out of hand. Becky has a daughter who's a fan, and Bob...." Her voice trailed off.

"Sparky, I don't do this sort of thing. Oh, never mind." He clasped her elbow and escorted her to the door. "If you're coming with me you'd better change." He watched her retreating figure bound up the stairs and shook his head. "How can I make you understand, sweetheart, the limelight is not what it's cracked up to be?"

SAMANTHA HURRIEDLY CHANGED her clothes, abandoning her casual pants for a more sophisticated pinstripe silk dress, the varying shades of blue to violet highlighting the color of her eyes. With Boston's threats to leave her behind if she took more than twenty minutes to change, she snatched up a pair of beige leather sling-back pumps, slipping one shoe on at a time as she hopped her way to the bedroom door.

Once encased in the gray suede back seat of the long silver limousine, she shot a breathless smile at

Boston, then leaned over and kissed him hard on the mouth.

"Didn't think I could do it, did you?" She caught the eyes of the grinning chauffeur and winked. Her happiness was overflowing at the prospect of spending all day with Boston despite his warnings of the hours she'd have to spend sitting quietly while he worked. She settled back for the short ride to the Summit, remembering the controversy when Houston's city fathers had decided it was time their rough-diamond town could use some needed polish. Dallas, their sister city and rival, had already developed a sophistication that set the spurs deeper into the sides of every Houstonian, so they began their plans of a cultural rejuvenation to dazzle the world. Within a remarkably short period of time Houston had a new theater for the performing arts; a concert hall to house the ultimate in ballet and opera; and the Astrodome, which hosted indoor sports, the annual world-famous rodeo and conventions. Then came the Summit—an architectural delight with its soaring walls of glass. Set only a short distance from the magic-circle area of the Galleria and surrounded by the towering office complex of Greenway Plaza, the Summit's jeweled night-lights rebounded and reflected like a glittering crown. On many occasions Samantha had been one of the 18,000 seated on the plush upholstered seats, entranced by such performers as Neil Diamond, John Denver, Paul McCartney and Tom Jones.

Samantha caught a glimpse of the big marquee—
Boston Grey in Concert—before the limousine

turned up the curved horseshoe-shaped driveway to the entrance. She spotted a small crowd of fans idly standing around the door and smiled.

The group waited quietly as the car came to a halt, then to Samantha's horror they seemed to multiply tenfold and surge around the car. Boston shot her an I-told-you-so look and swung open the door. He turned his back on the noise and helped her out, tightening his hold on her arm as she recoiled slightly from the sudden flashing of lights. Encircled, they slowly made their way toward the entrance. When Boston stopped to sign autographs he relinquished his hold on her, and an overly enthusiastic woman elbowed her from her position at Boston's side.

Suddenly she found herself on the outskirts of the crowd looking on. She heard Boston's shout over the clamoring fans and reporters and had to jump up, waving frantically, to catch his attention. When a hand clamped around her arm she flinched and tried to jerk away, then sighed with relief to find Mark standing beside her. He bent down and still had to shout over the roar of voices.

"Boston sent me to take you in. He'll follow in a few minutes."

She turned to walk away, then stopped. A short, overweight man with small mean eyes was staring at her intently.

"You're Boston Grey's newest girlfriend?" the reporter asked, his notebook held at ready.

Samantha tried to step aside and with her brother's help had almost made it when a burst of blinding light from a nearby television camera beamed in her face, disorienting her.

"Tell me," the reporter demanded, "do you think your relationship will last? Isn't Boston notorious for his short love affairs?"

Mark gently picked the offensive little man up and set him aside with a mumbled threat.

Finally within the hushed hall, Samantha flopped down in the nearest seat to catch her breath, her limbs shaking from an overpowering feeling of claustrophobia.

"You all right, Sparky?" She opened her eyes to find Boston squatting beside her seat, his eyes narrowed with concern. "They didn't hurt you, did they?"

Still numb, she shook her head and with his help rose to her feet, her hands trembling as she began to straighten her dress and set the twisted belt back into place.

"Say something!" he commanded, his voice low and urgent.

"I'm fine, Boston. I guess I really wasn't prepared, that's all." She kept her head down, hiding the tears that threatened to spill down her cheeks. Through her blurred vision she caught a glimpse of her beige shoes, now scuffed with black marks from being stomped on. She looked up, the tears now sliding down her pale cheeks. "They've ruined my shoes," she whispered, puzzled because she couldn't remember feeling the pain when it happened.

Boston waved everyone away and gathered her in his arms. "I warned you," he said grimly, then dropped his arms and stepped back. "That was a very orderly crowd compared to some." His mouth tightened when what little color remained in her face drained away. "Come on. You can sit down in the front while we rehearse."

Samantha didn't think things could get much worse, but they did. Boston's coldness toward her the rest of the day hurt her more than she was willing to admit. She felt she'd let him down and the feeling of doom remained, no matter how hard she tried to fight it.

When rehearsals broke for lunch, she thought they would return to the house. Instead, Boston took her to an exclusive restaurant. There she nibbled at her food, watching in appalled silence as seemingly intelligent people turned rude and callous. They stared and whispered, and when the shock of recognition wore off there began a never-ending stream of well-wishers and autograph seekers. Boston's plate of food lay untouched and cold before him as he calmly and politely answered their questions. He scrawled his name across menus and linen napkins, his smile intact. She thought at one point the owner was going to ask them to leave for ruining his property. On the way out she saw Boston slip the harassed owner a very large tip to cover the damages.

Settled once again in the luxurious back seat of the limousine, she stayed on the far side, huddled against the door, her eyes sightless to the world outside.

"I have to do some local television interviews. Do you want to go or return to the house?"

The gruffly spoken question brought her out of her

thoughts and she turned to study the back of Boston's head. Obviously he found the scenery as absorbing as she had. "The house, please. Boston?"

"Don't say it, Sparky."

They rode on in strained silence. When they reached the house Boston remained seated, his head still turned from her. She watched the long car pull away, a sadness growing in her heart that she hadn't lived up to his expectations.

A SHOWER OF MULTICOLORED SUNSPOTS danced in dazzling rainbow patterns over the glassy surface of the clear blue water in the swimming pool. Lounging on a redwood chair, her shoes kicked off, feet propped up on the edge of a matching table, she wiggled her bruised and sore toes. Under the onslaught of the ninety-degree temperature she watched the waves of shimmering heat waft over the brick walkway, and closed her eyes, stifling a sharp sigh. She wondered if the day would ever end. She still had the second rehearsal to attend that evening.

Four hours of being pushed, elbowed, stepped on and generally ignored had taken its toll. Never had she dreamed that Boston's warning about his public life was anything but exaggeration. Now she had firsthand knowledge, and she was totally appalled at the thought of spending the rest of her life fighting strangers for the privilege of standing by his side. Samantha leaned her aching head back against the padded chair and shivered despite the heat. There was a sudden coldness surging through her veins, building a wall of icy dread around her heart.

"What's the matter, Samantha?"

She opened her eyes and blinked rapidly to clear her vision as Tom sat down in a chair beside her.

"From that sour expression of yours, I'd say you've just found a rotten apple in your little garden of Eden."

"Go away, Tom. I'm in no mood for your particular brand of witticism right now." His humorless chuckle set her teeth on edge and she closed her eyes again.

Tom leaned forward to examine the darkening area on the top of her foot. "That's going to be a nasty bruise."

She tried to ignore his presence, hoping he'd go away. But she'd forgotten Tom's bulldog determination once he had a bone to chew on.

"Why don't you leave him, Sammy? He's not for you." Tom reached over and picked up her limp hand. "You're only going to end up in more pain than you are now."

She tried to pull her hand free, but he tightened his grip. "Boston has not hurt me, Tom."

"No?"

"No!"

"Oh, Sammy," he said sadly. "I saw your face when you walked into rehearsals this morning. You'll never be able to cope with his life-style."

"The reaction of the fans just took me by surprise, that's all." She tugged her hand free and sat up sharply. "You really don't like Boston, do you?"

"That surprises you?"

"Yes, it does." She wondered if it was professional jealousy or something deeper. "Why are you here if you hate him so much?" She watched as he bent down and picked a small twig off the ground, his thoughts far away.

"I don't hate him." Tom sighed. "I admire his talent and enjoy working with him—he's a genius. As a man—no—I can't respect him. You forget, I've seen Boston in action and been there to pick up some of the women he's used."

Samantha shook her head, surprised at Tom's lack of perception. "Did you ever think that most of those women got exactly what they deserved? I saw it all today, Tom. They threw themselves at him. Why shouldn't he have taken advantage of what was so freely offered? He's only human, after all."

"You're defending him?" Tom asked, shocked.

"Yes! Yes, I am," she said vehemently. "And I don't appreciate your comparing what Boston and I have with his past relationships."

"You're a fool, Sammy." Tom stood up and began to pace the ground in front of her. "Is this the way you want to live? Like a beautiful bird in a cage." He waved a hand at the surrounding richness. "A few minutes here and there with hours of neglect in between. Should a wife have to compete for her husband's time?" He gave a harsh laugh. "Don't lie to yourself about thinking Boston will change. It's you who will change and grow old before you should."

He grabbed the wooden arms of her chair and leaned down, his face close to hers. "What happens when you reach forty and Boston's still performing?

Don't kid yourself that women will stop throwing themselves at him just because he's married. If anything, it will only add to the challenge. Boston has the type of looks that improve with maturity. And don't fool yourself that he'll quit. As long as his voice holds out he'll be center stage. Don't you see? He loves the adoration. It's in his blood like a drug— his own personal prescription for a never-ending incredible high.''

''You do hate him,'' she breathed, backing away from the sickening expression on Tom's face. ''What happened? Did a girl you love drop you for Boston?'' She watched the pain of the truth flicker across his face.

''What's happened between me and Boston is no concern of yours. Can't you see I'm trying to help you from making the biggest mistake of your life?''

''Stop it, Tom.''

''No!'' He pulled her hands away from her ears and held them tightly. ''By the time you reach middle age, a whole new generation of girls will follow their mothers to his concerts. There'll always be younger and prettier women than you. And where will you be? Home with your children, crazy with jealousies and uncertainties. Afraid to show your feelings for fear of losing him to a younger woman.''

Samantha pushed him back and jumped up, a sob rising in her throat. ''You don't know what you're talking about.''

But he did know, and it scared her more than anything she'd ever had to face. Spinning around, she sprinted for the house, the torture of Tom's questions echoing with piercing clarity in her head. She passed a startled Lana and Pearl in the kitchen but didn't stop even when she heard Lana's shout and Pearl's angry voice directed at Tom.

She rushed up the stairs, her long-legged stride taking the steps two at a time, the specter of her thoughts snapping at her heels. Once closed off from the rest of the household, she stumbled across the room and threw herself onto the big bed. There she lay, stiff and tense, fighting the agony of Tom's words, her hands bunched into tight fists, her breathing quick and shallow. Tom was right—so damn right.

Her mind projected breath-stopping images of what a life with Boston would be like. How could she possibly explain her doubts to him? He'd just laugh and call her a worrier, but it was no laughing matter. Boston was a free spirit, living from day to day, while she, her feet firmly planted, always worked and planned toward the future. What was even more frightening, she realized, was that she'd have to work out her problems herself. Boston would never understand her anguish over something that hadn't happened yet. His male ego would make him vehemently deny any thoughts of unfaithfulness, now or in the future.

"Sammy, may I come in?"

Lana's softly spoken question brought her out of her inner turmoil. "Sure." Samantha got up from the bed and walked over to the window.

"Tom told us what happened. He had no right to say those things, Sammy."

"Didn't he?" Samantha turned around, grasped the windowsill and leaned against it for support. The bright sunlight fell across her pale features. "Are you telling me Boston's past affairs were only fantasies of sick reporters?" She saw Lana's cheeks slowly stain red, and a humorless smile twisted her lips.

"But you're different."

"Am I? What about the way he's treated women in the past? From what I've heard and what Tom's told me, the newness can wear thin very quickly." She pushed a shaky hand through her disheveled mass of hair. Why was she even trying to explain to Lana? Lana was safe and secure with Ken. She would never have to stand back and watch helplessly while other women circled her husband like a school of hungry piranhas, excited into a feeding frenzy.

Lana grabbed Samantha's arm and led her to a nearby chair. "The news media have always exaggerated and exploited Boston's affairs. As for Tom, he has his own devils he must live with. But he should never have added to your problems." She smiled warmly at Samantha's surprised expression. "Oh, yes. I know what's been going on in that head of yours. I've been there myself."

"You mean when you were engaged to Boston you had the same doubts as I have now?" Samantha sat up, the unbearable weight around her heart brightening temporarily. Maybe Lana did have the answers to the questions that had haunted her all day.

"Yes. I mean, no!" Lana gave a strangled little laugh and hurried on. "Oh, dear. I'm not doing this very well . . . and I had it all planned." She leaned forward on the edge of her chair, her expression earnest. "Sammy, my doubts were about Ken." She saw the disappointment in Samantha's face and continued, stressing each word. "Listen to me. You might not believe this, but when the fans couldn't get to Boston they tried a new route—Ken. He always had women hanging around him, clamoring for an introduction. And he enjoyed their attention, even though he knew their motives were to get to Boston. You forget, Sammy. Ken is not exclusively Boston's agent. His agency handles all types of entertainers—actors, singers and musicians. So on top of Boston's hangers-on there are the female hopefuls, the aspiring young girls with no scruples who are willing to sell their souls, their integrity—and sleep their way to the stage lights."

"How did you come to terms with it, Lana?"

"I'm sorry, Sammy." Lana shook her head, her eyes filled with understanding and sadness. "There aren't any clear-cut answers I can give you." She reached out and lightly touched Samantha's clenched fist. "Like you, I've always looked ahead. Finally, to keep my sanity, I made the decision to change and only look as far as tomorrow." She gave Samantha's hand another reassuring pat and stood up. "Trust Boston's love for you, because no matter what you think, he loves you deeply. Does the future really matter? In today's world do we have any guarantee of a future? Whether your life together lasts two years or a lifetime, it's not something to be thrown away now just because you have a few doubts of what lies ahead."

She walked toward the door then turned. "Oh, I forgot. Boston called a while ago. He said he won't be through with the television interviews in time to pick us up and we're to go on to the rehearsal."

CHAPTER SEVENTEEN

Samantha and Lana slipped unnoticed into the Summit. They slowly felt their way down an aisle in the darkened cavern, groping for guidance along row after row of plush seats till they reached the front and slid silently into place.

Samantha looked around, her eyes adjusting to the gloominess, and marveled at the versatility of the Summit's structure. Depending on the time of year and the lack of concert bookings, the ground floor could be set up for a championship tennis match, a hockey game, indoor soccer, a boxing arena, the Ice Capades or a Big Top Circus. And even though the Astrodome was Houston's claim to fame for indoor entertainment, she preferred the Summit's more intimate size. It's oval design and two levels lent a cozy atmosphere.

She tried to picture the vast expanse of seats now locked into place on the ground floor. An additional 2,000 had been set up to accommodate a select group of charity-going patrons, those people who would never blink an eyelid at the one-hundred to five-hundred-dollar price for the elite section. She thought it was a good thing the remainder of the 16,000 seats were in a lower price range. Still, it was a staggering shock to learn the concert had been a complete sellout only eight hours after the public announcement.

The nerve-grating sound of wood scraping wood brought her wandering thoughts back to the present—in time to see Boston fling a folding chair halfway across the stage.

"No! No, no, no!" he roared at the top of his powerful lungs. He threw down a handful of musical scores and kicked them away, sending the sheets flying across the floor in a shower of fluttering white paper. Music died away in varying notes of discord. "What the hell do you people think you're doing? Must I come up there and play each of your parts for you?" He glared up at the men and women seated on the split-level dais in front of him and waited.

"What's happening, Lana?" Samantha watched as Boston began to walk the perimeter of the stage.

"I don't know and I don't want to get close enough to find out, either. He looks about ready to pitch a fit." She shuddered, then made a grab for Samantha. "Come back here, Sammy," she hissed, but it was too late to stop her friend. She closed her eyes tightly and prayed.

Drawn by the stranger pacing the stage like a sleek caged cat, Samantha mounted the side stairs, stopping only long enough to snatch up a discarded towel. Her gaze ran the length of him, from the tight faded jeans, which accented every line and sinewy muscle of his long frame, to the snowy white shirt, unbuttoned and pulled free of the waistband of his pants. A glistening sheen of sweat rolled down his chest.

"I take it you can read music?" He continued his tirade, and Samantha winced at the sarcasm in his voice. "Though right now, I doubt whether any of you have the brains to know your...."

"Boston!"

His pacing stopped at the outside edge of the glaring lights, his eyes like dark stones in the shadows. Samantha knew he was watching her approach, watching each carefully placed step. There was a tension in the air, a strange quiet pressure, as the calm before a storm. Ridiculous, she chided herself, and gave a mental shake to bring her out of her fanciful thoughts.

"Why don't you take a break, Boston?" There was a shuffling of feet, a muffled cough and a murmur of hushed whispers. From somewhere down in the vast room came a loud groan. A sudden nervous laugh escaped her lips. "Ease up a little. Everyone knows you're a perfectionist and they've beat their brains out to please you. You're tired, they're exhausted. Why not back off for a while and let it rest. Maybe when you come back to it, it will work itself out."

"Heaven help me." Boston threw up his hands. "Not only am I surrounded by incompetence, but now I have an unwanted musical advisor and a self-appointed public-relations arbitrator." He stepped out of the shadows and began to walk toward her, his look filled with open hostility. "What do you know about putting together a show of this magnitude? You produce trivial crap for thirty seconds of television time." His lips twisted into a sneer. "What could you possibly know of what it takes to entertain a live audience for two full hours? I won't have my name connected with a slipshod show." He continued his slow journey toward her. "I'm going to give them something they've never seen before, something to be remembered. You know absolutely nothing of what I'm trying to accomplish, so butt out."

Samantha's cheeks flushed bright red under the harshness of his attack. This was no lover coming at her, but a violent angry enemy. His belittling of her work stung and she struck back. "I know people and respect their feelings. It's obvious you don't."

"Feelings, feelings," he barked out. "I don't pay these people to feel. I pay them to play my music. What do you think I'm doing, providing welfare to help solve the nation's unemployment problems?"

"Okay, okay. Just calm down."

"Don't you patronize me, Samantha."

She squeezed her eyes shut and groaned. He was steaming mad and she felt totally helpless as to what to do.

"Half my musicians skip notes like a novice. The other half have decided on their own—" he turned and glared upward "—to suddenly become composers and rescore *my*—" he pounded his chest "—*my* arrangements. I won't have it." He took a deep breath and went on. "The piano's out of tune. The sound system stinks. The technicians can't find out what's wrong and those damn workmen keep pounding out that infernal racket. Now—" he yelled and came to stop a few feet away from her "—now you have the nerve to stand there and tell. . . ."

"I haven't tried...."

"...tell me how to run my rehearsals. Give me strength," he bellowed and she flinched at the loudness. They had both forgotten the hand-held microphone tucked under his arm, picking up every word and amplifying it with mortifying clarity around the huge room.

What did all this have to do with her? She couldn't read his music, fix the sound system, tune the piano or stop the workmen. So why was he shouting like some madman, blaming her for everything that was going wrong today? She realized Boston was in the midst of an artistic tantrum. Still, it was no excuse to humiliate her like this. She politely offered him the towel she held, only to have it snatched out of her hand and thrown on the floor.

She forced a smile. "Don't take your frustrations out on me, Boston Grey."

"You think this is funny?" he growled.

"No," she shouted back.

"And don't you talk to me about frustrations. My life's been in a constant state of turmoil since the first day I met you. You've been like a nagging sore tooth." She paled and choked back a sob. "This is *all* your doing. You wouldn't let well enough alone, would you?" He brought his face close to hers. "Would you? No. You pushed and shoved and prodded, till you had me backed against the wall."

His voice dropped to a normal volume, but the tone held an extraordinary harshness, sounding as if it weren't coming from a human body but from a mechanical device. "Well, baby, I got news for you—this is how it is. This is the glamorous life you were so determined I go back to. You wanted to share the glory and the limelight. Here's your chance.'' Her eyes filled with tears and she blinked furiously to hold them in check. ''Tears won't change a damn thing, so stop it.''

Samantha recoiled a few steps from his brutality. ''I wouldn't waste my tears on you.'' She tried to sound sarcastic, but the lump in her throat made the words come out weak and feeble. Why was it, she thought frantically, at any other time she could have stood up to him and fought back. Now she could only stand there like a store dummy, frozen by the hurt he was inflicting on her.

''Look here, Boston.'' Mark gingerly stepped between the miles of electrical cords snaking their way across the floor. ''You can't talk to my sister like she's some hired hand. Listen, man, she's the woman you're supposed to love.''

''Heaven forbid. Another Griffin to interfere.'' Boston turned his glittering eyes on Mark. ''She may be your sister but she's my future wife, and she has to learn her place. Which is backstage.'' There was a collective gasp from around the stage. ''You just might remember something, Mark. You *are* a hired hand, my friend, and expendable at any time. Right now you're pushing your luck.''

Samantha closed her eyes, her face growing rapidly more transparent at each word. ''Don't, Mark, don't say anything more.'' She motioned him away before he could take a swing at Boston. She was embarrassed for herself, Mark and everyone else who was witness to Boston's anger. "Please, Mark. I can handle this."

"Handle!" Boston bellowed, and his voice seemed to echo around the huge room, taking on the vibrations of a brass drum.

An eerie silence settled over the room. Samantha stood straighter as she faced the blazing contempt on Boston's face. In the depths of those stone hard eyes she saw something shimmering like a reflection on black water.

"You think you can handle me, do you? Then maybe you think you can take over this show?"

"Look, Boston, I didn't mean...."

"You think the song sounded right? I don't. But since you know so much, you sing it. Here!" He shoved the hand-held microphone under her chin.

"This is ridiculous."

"That's enough." Tom yelled from his place behind one of the Steinways. "You've gone too far."

Boston whipped around, forcing Samantha with him. "I've had about all I can take from you, Thomas. One more word and, concert or no concert, you're fired."

"Boston," Samantha whispered on a broken sob, gazing blankly past his shoulder into a sea of pity-filled faces. Her eyes returned to Boston's, filled with the raw pain of humiliation, and he dropped her arm. She felt as though he had just torn out her heart and thrown it on the stage floor.

"Stop this before you destroy everything." She looked around blindly, all the important things they'd done together flashing before her sightless eyes in a whirling frenzy. This couldn't be happening. Only people facing death could see their past, but the pictures continued to spin out in her mind. Numbly she tried to reach out and snatch one clear memory and hold it close, but they kept slipping by with a frightening speed. Their first disastrous meeting; the days spent on horseback; the first time they made love by firelight; the time she made him admit his love for her. She saw the flower-and-velvet greenness of his special glade, and the smell of hay filled her senses. She thought of the first time he'd sung to her and the hours they had spent holding each other, just talking, the secrets they had shared of their past and their plans for the future. She saw the loving sparkle of his black eyes, teasing, laughing, dark with passion. And the most shattering memory of all, the way she felt after they made love, the peace and security she savored from his embrace.

Samantha reached out for him, her expression soft and luminous. But once her eyes focused again on his face and the furious expression registered on her confused mind, any hope of rebuilding what he'd so ruthlessly torn apart died. Their eyes locked, and something deep inside her began to crack and crumble. She stepped back, wiping away fresh tears with the back of her hand, and she turned to leave.

"That's it, run. Just don't expect me to come after you. I warned you and warned you what it would be like. But you wouldn't listen. If you walk out that door now, don't come back till you grow up." She kept walking and he threw down the microphone. "Where do you think you're going?"

he shouted after her. "I'm not through with you yet."

His last words brought her to a stop and she turned very slowly to face him again. "That's just too damn bad, Boston," she said, "because I'm sure through with you."

She whirled around and walked away, concentrating only on the precise placement of one foot in front of the other. Her numbed senses carried her across the endless stage and down the side stairs. With each slow step the tears dried and the soft sobbing stopped as a stony mask shuttered her ravaged features. Surely this was all some wild dream and she'd wake to find the black eyes she loved so looking down at her. She'd open her eyes to find Boston leaning over her and shaking her out of her nightmare. She walked up the aisle to the door, ignoring the scandalized expressions of the workmen as she passed.

How had their confrontation gotten out of hand, she wondered. At first, the more she'd tried to soothe, the angrier Boston had become. He had started out using her as an outlet for his frustrations and disappointments. She could have accepted that if he hadn't turned to a personal level. Why had he? There was more here than met the eye, but she realized in her befuddled state she'd never figure it out. Then she remembered the rest of their disastrous day together and knew. He'd finally realized they could never be happy together. She didn't fit into his lifestyle.

Nor will I ever be able to, she thought. With this last bit of insight she felt the crushing weight of her loss and stumbled against the door, closed her eyes and waited for her body to shatter into a thousand little pieces. Instead, a coldness surrounded her like an icy fog, penetrating every bone.

"Sammy, you okay?"

"Go away, Mark." The glacial tone of her voice shocked them both. Mark clasped her elbow and she allowed him to escort her outside.

"I'm taking you home." Mark urged her down the stone steps.

"Sammy! Samantha, wait a minute."

She and Mark turned and waited for Tom to catch up with them.

"I don't know what to say to you, Sammy," Tom began nervously.

"Then say nothing at all," she answered coldly, her brilliant eyes as icy as her words.

"May I talk to you?" He shot an apologetic glance at Mark. "Alone, please."

"No, Tom," she said stiffly, her gaze wandering to the darkened blotch along his high cheekbone.

He touched the puffy area self-consciously, then gave a harsh laugh. "That crazy cook, house-keeper—whatever she is—called Boston earlier and told him what I'd said to you."

"Too bad."

"Look, Sammy. I know now's not the time to bring this up, but . . . ."

"Then don't." She turned to leave.

"Wait." Tom grabbed her arm and took a deep breath. "Come away with me. We'll leave right after the concert and go to California, back to Los

Angeles. I'll take care of you, Sammy." His green eyes pleaded and he hurried on in spite of her unresponsiveness. "You'll get over Boston and in time you'll come to love me. I'll make you happy. I'll. . . ."

"I might get over Boston in time, Tom, but will you?" she interrupted him. "I thought you were my friend," she accused him, her voice stinging with sarcasm, "but ever since you found out I was in love with Boston, you've done everything in your power to place doubts and suspicions in my mind." Sharp nails dug into her palms. "You deliberately set out to break us up. Didn't you? Do you call that friendship?" She took a stop closer. "Now you have the nerve to ask me to go off with you. Why? You don't love me." She looked him up and down rudely. "What's the matter, Tom, aren't you man enough to find a woman on your own? Must you always be on hand to pick up Boston's castoffs?" She watched a shocked expression spread over his features. "Come on, Mark, let's go." Stiffly she reached for her brother's arm and walked away.

"That wasn't like you, sis."

"I know. I don't feel like myself right now, but he had it coming."

"Yeah," Mark mumbled, and opened the car door for her.

Samantha stared blindly up at the glass-fronted Summit and sighed. It was all over and all she could feel was empty, barren. She closed her eyes wearily and leaned back as a lethargy seemed to settle over her body. How was she going to exist, feeling only half alive?

"You should have let me hit him."

"What?" Opening her eyes, she watched Mark's big hands tighten around the steering wheel until his knuckles turned white under the fierce pressure.

"Boston. You should have let me hit him."

"It wouldn't have helped any, Mark."

"Maybe, maybe not, but it sure would have felt good." He flicked the ignition on and eased the big Cadillac down the drive. "When I took this job, I thought it would be a nice change from slaving all day around horses. But you know something? Entertainers are no different than the temperamental thoroughbreds I work with every day. They're ornery, bad tempered and just plain mean. They don't even talk the same language we do. I think I'll go home. At least my horses can't yell at me."

Mark's disenchantment registered on her exhausted conscience, but her present state made it impossible to respond with any sympathy. "Mark, would you do something for me?"

"Sure, sis. Name it."

"Don't tell dad or the rest of the family what happened here tonight. Let me do it in my own time." She knew her father would want a detailed account, and the thought of disillusioning him about Boston only added to her pain.

"Okay," Mark growled. "Where to, Sammy? I won't allow you to stay in the same house with that crazy man."

"I need to pick up my clothes." There was a long, thoughtful silence as Mark maneuvered the car onto River Oaks Boulevard. "I'll go to Aunt Sally's for a while."

"Oh, no," Mark groaned pitifully. "Will I have to go in?"

They came to a stop before the rose-brick house and Mark asked, "You want me to go get your things?"

"No, I'll do it myself. Don't worry, Mark, Boston won't be here." She opened the car door and slid out, her feet leaden weights as she walked to the front door. She reached out for the bell and jumped back as the door was yanked open.

"Oh, Sammy," Lana wailed, her hands twisting a much-used handkerchief, her eyes red and swollen from crying. "I'm sorry," she babbled, "I ran out on you. I couldn't stand what Boston was doing."

"It's all right, Lana," she soothed, but when Lana started to put her arms around her, she stepped back, away from any human contact.

"No, no, it's not all right. You were there when I needed you. Oh, Sammy, what got into him? I've never seen Boston act that way before. As soon as I got here I called Ken and told him everything. He's on his way to the Summit right now. Where are you going?" She followed Samantha up the stairs to her room.

"I'm leaving."

"No, you mustn't do that. Boston will come to his senses."

"Really?" Samantha said over her shoulder. "Right now I couldn't care less what he does or doesn't do."

"You don't mean that?"

Samantha stopped at the landing, her eyes dull and almost colorless. "Yes, I do, Lana. What you don't understand is Boston and I are through. He knows it. I know it now. We're like two pieces of a jigsaw puzzle someone has tried to make fit, and it just didn't work." She pushed open her bedroom door and stopped.

Pearl snapped the locks on the last of Samantha's luggage, set it on the floor, and looked up. "Young man." Pearl directed her suspiciously bright eyes toward Mark and pointed to the mound of bags. She turned to Samantha and studied her for a few silent seconds before she nodded her head in complete understanding. Taking the rigid young woman into her bony arms, she whispered, "It will work out." Then she dropped her arms and stomped out of the room.

"Sammy, please." Lana followed her back down the stairs. "Don't leave like this. Give Ken some time to find out what's wrong. Sammy, please, where are you going? How can I reach you?"

Samantha gave Lana her aunt's telephone number and slid into the waiting car. "Goodbye, Lana." At the end of the drive she turned for one last look, a chill working its way slowly up her spine as she silently said goodbye one more time. *Why can't I feel? Why don't I cry,* she asked herself, then shrugged lifelessly.

"I called Aunt Sally, sis. She's waiting for us."

"Good." Samantha sat back, her mind blank as she watched the city lights rush by. Maybe the hurt would come sometime but right now she welcomed the coldness that kept the pain at bay.

When Mark turned the big car down the familiar

street, Samantha felt a lessening of the tension that had held her so rigidly. Her dull eyes quickly scanned the houses ahead, searching for the first glimpse of the two-story yellow-brick Victorian house with its white-trim shutters and bay windows. For years this old-fashioned house and its clutter of antiques had been her haven, a sanctuary to escape to when the overpowering personalities of six brothers would wear her to the breaking point. Sally Morgan, Samantha's maternal aunt, would take her in, wipe the tears away and listen to her troubles. But it was the gentle and steady love she showered on her niece that kept Samantha returning time and time again with her heartbreaks and victories. It was at her aunt's urging that she finally decided to take the job offer in New York. Miserable at leaving her beloved yet interfering family, she later saw the wisdom in her aunt's insistence.

"You should have let me hit the bastard." Mark bit the words out between clenched teeth as he punched repeatedly at the doorbell.

Jolted out of her lethargic state, Samantha shrugged lifelessly. "It wouldn't do any good."

"Still...." He broke off as the door swung open and he met his aunt's steely blue gaze, level with his own. "Good evening, Aunt Sally." He coughed self-consciously and fingered the tight collar of his shirt. "I've brought Sammy."

"So I see," she drawled. She offered a lined cheek for the ritual—and reluctant—kiss. "Bring Samantha's bags in and put them in her room."

"Yes, ma'am."

"And don't forget to wipe your feet."

At any other time, Samantha would have laughed at Mark's red-faced discomfort. Her aunt's philosophy for controlling six overactive boys was by intimidation. And though they loved her and would fight anyone who spoke against her, they still held her in respectful awe.

Without further conversation she led Samantha into the cool living room. "Sit," she ordered, intently studying her niece's desolate young face. She poured a cup of hot spice tea, generously laced with brandy and honey, and placed the dainty china cup carefully in Samantha's hands. "Drink." The two women sat staring at each other in a silence broken only by the mellow chimes of the ornate grandfather clock.

"I finished, so I'll be leaving now." Mark stood in the doorway, unnerved by the speechless communication between the two women.

"Thank you, Mark. Please lock the door behind you."

"Yes, ma'am. Bye, Sammy." When his sister continued to sit mutely, he shrugged helplessly and sent a pleading look to his aunt.

She favored him with a rare smile and nodded her head in dismissal. Sally leaned back in the wing-back chair till she heard the familiar click of the lock. "Now, Samantha, do you want to tell me what's happening?"

Calmly setting her teacup on the table, Samantha began to tell her aunt everything. Her voice a bleak monotone, she began with her first meeting with Boston and brought her story to an apathetic end by relating the scene a few hours earlier.

"You've left something out, something very important. I might be sixty-five years old, but I do keep up with what's happening nowadays." At Samantha's continued silence she went on. "You are lovers, aren't you?" Still Samantha sat noncommittal. "Answer me," she commanded. "I have to know everything to understand."

"Yes," Samantha uttered between stiff lips.

"I see. You were such a loving, giving little girl— old beyond your years in understanding human nature. What's happened?" She shook her silver head. "I don't think I particularly like what you've become."

Samantha's hands began to tremble slightly and she clenched her fingers together. Never had her aunt used that tone of voice with her. She knew Sally wasn't speaking of her sex life with Boston, but of the lack of emotion she was showing. Didn't she understand she couldn't feel, that if she did she would fall apart?

"Do you think Boston truly loves you?"

Did Boston love her? Samantha studied the striped arm of her chair, running the tips of her fingers over the smooth surface. "Yes, he loves me in his way. But now he's back singing, he's changed."

"Of course he's changed from the man you first knew." Sally snorted in disgust and leaned forward, her icy blue eyes snapping with irritation. "You're selfish, Samantha Griffin. Yes, you are, so don't shake your head at me. You want Boston to yourself.

My dear, it's not possible to hold a man with those types of shackles. People have to have room to grow—even married couples. We all need a certain amount of freedom. You of all people should be cognizant of the fact. You want to change him, strangle him with your love." She stopped and drew in a deep breath. "For heaven's sake, let go."

"I *have* let go," Samantha replied flatly.

"You silly girl, that's not at all what I meant and you know it. I'm talking about trust. You're so wrapped up in your own insecurities you can't see the forest for the trees. Trust and love, they go together. You don't or won't trust the strength of Boston's love. Why?" She stood and walked over to the bookshelves, pulled out a thick dictionary and slammed it down on the coffee table. "There's a difference between involvement and commitment. I suggest you look up the definition of both so you don't forget. You...."

"I'm well aware of the difference," Samantha snapped hotly, then the controlled chilliness returned. "I don't want to live in Boston's shadow for the rest of my life." She rested her head back and closed her eyes tightly, only to have them pop open at her aunt's next words.

"You're afraid!" Sally laughed harshly. "Now we get to the real core of the matter. You're afraid to totally surrender your love into Boston's hands. Afraid you'll have to fight the rest of your life for your own individuality." She gave a great sigh of relief. "My darling girl, don't you see! It's not Boston or his life-style you're fighting, but the struggle you've had all your life." She was quiet for a few seconds. "I blame myself for this," she murmured thoughtfully. "I should have insisted you come live with me when you reached your teens."

"Aunt Sally, what are you mumbling about?"

Sally reached over and grabbed Samantha's hand. "You're scared of becoming a nonentity in his life. Samantha—" she squeezed the slender hand she held "—listen to me. You're wrong. All your life you've lived in your brothers' shadows and fought a battle to be yourself. Now you feel because of Boston's overpowering career you have to go your ten rounds with him, too. But it's different this time. A husband is not like a brother. When the fighting is over the two of you will have the intimacy of your loving to work out your problems." Eyes bright with memories, she chuckled. "Believe me, more misunderstandings have been worked out in bed than any other place!"

Samantha began to feel her barren soul fill with warmth, but pushed it frantically away. She was too petrified to hope her aunt was right. Had it all been her fault? Was she still a little girl and not the woman she pretended to be? She was so confused.

"Do you still love him?" Sally held up a hand to stop Samantha. "Think very carefully before you answer."

Hopelessly, Samantha shook her head, her feelings of love and pain warring with each other. "I still love him, but . . . ."

"There's no room for buts in love."

The frosty brilliance of her aquamarine eyes settled

steadily on the warmth of her aunt's face. Suddenly she gave a loud groan and catapulted into her aunt's open arms, resting her head against the ample bosom as she'd done so many times when she was young. The faint scent of gardenias filled her senses and she felt the soft brush of thick silver hair against her cheek. Eyes that had remained dry till now filled with bitter scalding tears. Great choking sobs racked her body as all that had happened came flooding back, rushing at her on a mammoth wave of grief for what was and what might have been.

"Yes, yes, I love him," she sobbed incoherently over and over again. Then she wailed, "I didn't even get to give him the painting I did."

Her aunt crooned against the bright red head. "It's not good to hold back. You need to let it out or live the rest of your life in bitterness."

"Ally, Ally, what am I going to do?"

Sally Morgan smiled on hearing Samantha's childhood name for her. It had been years since she'd heard the pitiful childish plea for help.

Samantha raised her tear-drowned eyes, simmering like jewels, to her aunt's face. She struggled for air to speak. "I love him so much, but how can I forget the things he did to me today? How could he humiliate me in front of all those people?"

"I don't know." Sally patted the shaking shoulders. "There's an old cliché, and as trite as it sounds, it's true—you only hurt the ones you love. You're going to have to learn when you love somebody you must not listen to what they say. In the heat of the moment lovers say things to cause pain. But don't

you understand, Samantha? They're afraid of being
hurt themselves. You must look in their eyes and feel
their hearts.''

Samantha sighed and went limp in her aunt's arms,
then stiffened as the phone beside them rang. Sally
hurriedly picked it up and Samantha listened to the
one-sided conversation, frantically shaking her head.

''Yes, Mr. Grey, she's here.''

Quiet fell as her aunt only stared at her and
listened to what Boston had to say.

''Then I take it you have nothing to say to Samantha, Mr. Grey?'' She hung up and gathered a newly
sobbing Samantha into her arms.

''How could he deliberately do what he did, then
have the nerve to call? What's he trying to do to
me?'' She buried her head in her aunt's shoulder.

''I think 'deliberate' is the key word. It sounds to
me as though there's more to this than a temper tantrum. But I can't give you the answers you need.
Those can only come from within you.'' She helped
an exhausted Samantha to her feet and led her to the
bedroom. ''Sleep, Samantha. Maybe tomorrow
you'll find the answers.''

CHAPTER EIGHTEEN

SAMANTHA SCARCELY SLEPT that night or the next. Tossing and turning, her mind was torn between wondering how Boston could have been so cruel and waiting for him to call again and apologize. When she did finally manage to drop off, it was only to awaken minutes later, her heart thumping wildly in her chest with a sense of unexplainable panic.

She moped around the house, never wandering far from the telephone, till her aunt's temper snapped.

"You'll have to make up your mind, Samantha." She glared at her niece. "Either accept Boston for what he is, and his work, or you lose him forever. It's as simple as that." She mentally dusted her hands and stomped out of the room, only to return immediately. "Are you going to the concert tonight?"

"No—yes—I don't know," Samantha cried. "Why doesn't he call back?"

"Why haven't you called him?" her aunt shot back. "Pride, my girl, will not keep your bed warm. And if you don't plan to go to the concert, why have you shampooed your hair and painted your nails?" Sally chuckled as Samantha whirled around and marched out of the kitchen. She raised her eyes to

heaven. "Oh, Lord, was there ever a more hardhead-
ed girl?"

"I heard that, Ally." Samantha called back over
her shoulder and laughed, her first real laughter in
days.

She roamed restlessly through the house, touching
familiar objects, and these brought back happier
thoughts. When her drifting steps ended her in her
bedroom, she sat down before the triple-mirror vani-
ty and stared hard at her face. Determination lined
her forehead as she searched for a change in the pale
freckled face gazing back at her. Two days—a hundred years. The time stretched endlessly. She had
counted every second and it showed. Shadowed eyes,
wide and vulnerable, pleaded with their reflection for
answers. Colorless lips, which in the past always
bowed up at their corners, now seemed permanently
frozen in a downward curve. How dare he do this to
her! She looked old. With a snort of disgust, she
gathered bottles and tubes together and began expert-
ly to hide the evidence of the sleepless nights.

The arduous task completed, she sat back and
squeezed her eyes tightly shut, fighting to block out
the images that danced in her head. She'd go to that
concert!

Samantha opened her eyes and nodded to her mirrored image. In a flash she turned away, breaking eye
contact with her other self. The thought of swallowing her pride and admitting she'd been wrong stung
as sharply as a bee sting. With a soft groan she
dropped her face in her hands.

The firm grip on Samantha's shoulder jerked her

head up. Confusion and indecisions clouded her eyes.

"You're breaking my heart, Samantha." Sally stroked her niece's head. "I don't think I've ever seen you so distraught before." She cupped Samantha's face with slim gentle fingers and raised her chin. "You know as well as I there will never be another man in your life to take Boston's place. We Morgan women have always been notorious for being one-man women. Surely you realize in your own heart you and Boston have been married for weeks. You might be impetuous and hot tempered, but your ingrained sense of morality would never have allowed you to become as involved as you have if there wasn't a deep love there. Don't throw it all away simply because at this point difficulties have arisen. As insurmountable as they seem now, they can be worked out if you give them a chance."

Samantha cocked her head to one side and smiled. "You're right. I've been a fool." She jumped up and hugged her aunt, whirled around and sprinted out of the room, only to return at a run to hug her aunt once more. "You're wonderful. What if he won't talk to me?" she wailed, promptly losing her newfound confidence.

"Samantha!" Sally grabbed her niece's arm and guided her from the room. Both women halted as the telephone rang. "I bet that's Boston." She shoved hard at a suddenly lead-footed Samantha. "Go on, answer it." She laughed at the dazzling smile shot in her direction and the flash of long legs as Samantha rushed into the kitchen.

Samantha skidded across the highly polished wood floor, snatched up the telephone in her headlong slide and banged into the refrigerator before coming to a stop. "Boston!" she panted, and laughed into the receiver.

"Samantha?"

Disappointment slumped her shoulders on hearing the female voice at the other end. She straightened and frowned as she heard the quaver in Lana's voice.

"Sammy."

"What's wrong, Lana? What's happened?" The cool air-conditioned house suddenly became suffocatingly hot as she listened to Lana take a deep breath.

"Sammy, Boston's received a bomb threat."

For what seemed like hours a suspended silence held. Lana was joking, she thought, a mean cruel joke, but it couldn't be true. "Repeat that, please." Her hand tightened on the phone, waiting for the other woman to laugh.

"Boston's received a bomb threat!"

Dazed, Samantha listened to the soft whimper. Realizing it was coming from her own throat, she gave in to her weak limbs and slid down the refrigerator door to the floor. "When? Damn it, Lana, calm down and tell me—when?"

"Last night at rehearsal. Sammy, this isn't the first one. It's been happening for days. Initially he didn't tell anyone, thinking it was a prank. But when the calls continued, he had to inform the management of the Summit."

Samantha let out a great sigh of relief. "So they're

going to call off the concert?'' She knew the answer as soon as she spoke. With only three hours left till the start, it was far too late to cancel. Besides, Boston would never agree. ''What are the people at the Summit doing?'' She was calmer now and wanted answers—fast.

''They called the police, of course. Right now the Houston bomb squad have dogs checking out the entire building. The stage, every room, every seat, anywhere they think a bomb could be hidden. I can't believe this is happening,'' Lana wailed in anguish. ''Boston's so calm it frightens me.''

''Get hold of yourself, Lana,'' Samantha commanded, struggling to conceal her own rising hysteria. ''Where are you?''

''At a telephone booth across from the Summit. They wouldn't let me in, even to use the phone.'' Her indignant sniff carried across the line and brought a strained grin to Samantha's lips.

''Where's Boston?''

''He's in his dressing room with Father Brian, Ken and Mark.'' She lowered her voice as if the four men might still hear her. ''They made me swear I wouldn't call you.''

So Mark was still working for Boston, Samantha realized with relief.

''Thank you, Lana. I'll be there as soon as I can.''

''Wait! Sammy.'' There was a long hesitation before she went on. ''Boston's left word that if you find out and show up you're not to be admitted.''

Samantha closed her eyes tightly for a brief second. ''Oh, he has, has he? We'll just see whose orders are followed. Bye." She stood up on rubbery legs and slammed down the receiver. So he didn't want her there, did he? The lovable fool.

There wasn't time to consider how she was going to gain entrance to the Summit or what Boston would do when she did. As the full impact of what might happen struck, she shivered. All she could think about was reaching Boston and ending their differences once and for all. She had to be there, had to see him. Because if anything happened, she couldn't live knowing their fight would lie between them for an eternity. What if Boston was seriously injured again, or worse, killed? The slight tremble in her hands worked its way up her arms with such devastating speed that her entire body started to shake and she grabbed the countertop for support. The thought of losing Boston was more than she could bear. Aunt Sally was right. Life would be a barren waste without him.

"Samantha? What's the matter?"

Her aunt rushed to her side, but Samantha waved her away, inhaling deeply for some semblance of control. "I'm all right," she whispered and straightened, meeting her aunt's concerned expression with a false smile. "I'm all right." She tried again to reassure her aunt.

"No, you're not. You're as pale as a ghost." She followed Samantha out of the kitchen and into the bedroom. "What on earth is going on?"

Samantha began pulling clothes from her closet, explaining everything that was happening and all Lana had been able to tell her as she moved around the room.

"Surely you're not thinking of going down there?" Sally asked incredulously, the horror of Samantha's explanation registering with shock.

"Damn, damn." Samantha ripped off the panty hose she'd ruined in her rush and snatched up another pair.

"Samantha, you can't!"

"But I am."

"Do you have any idea what your father would do to me if he found out I let you go?"

"Then don't tell him." She gently pushed her aunt out of the way and reached for the sleek, cream satin blouse, its capelet collar outlined in antique lace.

"Be reasonable." In growing frustration, Sally followed her across the room, watching helplessly as her niece stepped hurriedly into the black crepe tuxedo pants and slipped into low-heeled black pumps. "What if something happens?"

"Don't say that, Ally," Samantha groaned. "Don't even think it."

"Your father would never forgive me." Without thinking, she picked up the wide, intricately woven gold-and-black silk cummerbund and handed it to Samantha.

"The bomb squad's there," Samantha said calmly. "If there's anything to be found, they'll find it. May I borrow your gold-mesh bag?"

Sally moaned. "No, you can't. And you're not going anywhere."

Samantha cast her aunt a killing glance and rummaged through her own things, scattering items of clothing till she spotted her black evening bag.

"Samantha, stop this. You're not thinking rationally."

"You're wrong, Ally. For the first time in two days I'm completely clearheaded. I intend to be with Boston tonight and for the rest of my life."

"Hah," Sally pounced. "But Boston doesn't want you. You said Lana told you he left strict orders not to allow you admittance. So there's no need to go. You'll just end up being humiliated all over again."

Samantha ignored her aunt's sound reasoning and marched out of the room with Sally at her heels. "Where are your car keys, Ally?"

"Oh, no." The thought of her new fire-engine-red Corvette being destroyed, either by a bomb or by Samantha's reckless driving, left her breathless with dismay. "You're not taking my car," she shouted. Then a satisfied smirk turned up the corners of her lips. "I'm going to call your father this minute. Maybe *he* can talk some sense into that stubborn head of yours." But Samantha beat her to the telephone and Sally demanded, "Who are you calling?"

"A taxi. Let go, Ally," Samantha demanded as her aunt grabbed the receiver. "Listen to me. Please!" She took the receiver from her aunt's limp hand and replaced it in its cradle. "You're the very one who told me to take Boston for who he is and his career for what it is. Well, I've accepted it totally, and that means everything that goes with it—women, fans, temper tantrums, and yes, bombs too, if that's what it takes." She brushed back a few loose strands of her aunt's hair. "I'm going. If you won't allow me to use your car or to call a taxi, I'll hitchhike. But make no mistake—I'm going to be there tonight if it kills me.'' A bad choice of words, she thought, as tears filled Sally's eyes.

"You're just like your father," Sally sniffed, giving in and handing Samantha her car keys. "Be careful, darling." She watched her niece sprint toward the back door. "Samantha—" Samantha stopped and looked back, and she called out "—I love you. Good luck."

"Thanks, Ally. I love you, too."

Engulfed in the tantalizing smell of new leather, she jammed the key into the ignition and heard the high-powered engine turn over with an ear-splitting roar. Shifting into reverse, she backed down the driveway, tires squealing as she hit the street at a high speed and threw the small sports car forward. She gave a quick glance in the rearview mirror and waved before racing away, leaving Sally standing in the front yard, her hands covering her eyes.

Dusk was descending slowly over the city. The bright orange globe of the sun made its westerly plunge, streaking the sky with an artist's palette of colors. Although the temperature usually decreased with the sunset, it still remained a sweltering, humid ninety degrees outside.

The car's cramped interior seemed freezing to Samantha and she reached out blindly to turn the air conditioner off, then realized she'd never turned it on. The chill penetrating her bones came from her own fears. She shuddered, appalled at the thought of some maniac roaming the grounds of the Summit, waiting, watching for his ungodly act to occur. Who

could do something so monstrous? It was an unspeakable, vile act, ugly with implications. Could
there be someone out there who hated Boston enough
to endanger others just for revenge? Even though she
worried about the thousands of people who could be
hurt or maimed, her main concern was for only one
six-foot three-inch, black-eyed man.

From force of habit and without conscious
thought, Samantha drove onto the ramp of the freeway then instantly realized her mistake. Though well
after Houston's peak traffic hour, cars were lined
bumper-to-bumper on the endless concrete track.
With a growing sense of panic, she knew she could be
held prisoner by irate drivers for hours.

Gritting her teeth, she began a dangerous maneu-
ver of weaving in and out of traffic, heading for the
first exit. Once off the congested freeway, she executed a series of intricate turns and twists, crisscross-
ing through side streets and residential areas. In her
frantic effort to reach her destination in the shortest
possible time, she ran stop signs and red lights, slowing down only long enough to check for oncoming
cars. In one sharp breath she prayed for the sight of a
police car and in the next second she prayed she
wouldn't be caught. Finally forced to come to a complete stop at a busy intersection, she clenched her
already aching jaws at the delay. Her eyes darted hotly as she followed every passing car, cursing her luck.
Clammy fingers drummed the steering wheel impatiently; then she sighed deeply and relaxed against the
seat. Over to the right she spied the line of tall
flagpoles that fronted the Summit, the majestic red,

white and blue Lone Star emblem of Texas undulat-
ing in the light evening breeze. Her eyes kept straying
from the light to the colorful flags when she suddenly
realized she was in the wrong lane to make a right
turn.

She cursed under her breath and beat her fists
against the unyielding wheel. She'd have to go at
least two blocks down and double back through
heavy traffic. With a determined thrust of her chin, a
narrowing of her overbright eyes, she glared at the
admiring man in the silver-blue Ferrari next to her.
The look she sent was condemning, damning the
helpless recipient for being her only obstacle to
reaching Boston.

Samantha shot him a stunning smile and gunned
the powerful motor in a challenge. She knew the male
ego well enough to hope he wouldn't be able to resist.
When he in turn revved his purring engine to a lion's
roar, her daring smile altered to a cunning twitch of
her lips. Eyes forward, Samantha stared at the red
light, waiting for the first flicker of change. She
gunned the engine one more time to ensure the
challenge was understood, and received her answer.
The light blinked from red to green and her
challenger shot forward, leaving her behind but
allowing her the room to quickly switch lanes. She
jerked the gearshift into low, spun the wheel and
surged into the space the duped man and his car had
just vacated. With a cringing screech of rubber and
blasting of horns, she made the turn.

There was so much horsepower behind the Corvette's little engine that she was at the entrance of the

Summit before she knew it. She turned sharply to the left and sent the car plunging up the horseshoe-shaped driveway, braking hard only when she reached the glassed front. Head bowed, her breath coming in short gasps, she fought the momentary madness and hysteria that had been building since the call from Lana. The only thought pounding in her head was to see Boston. Her hand trembled violently as she fumbled with the door release.

Once on the firm ground, she inhaled deeply and looked around before heading for the doors at a run. Out of the corner of her eye she caught sight of two uniformed policemen hurrying toward her.

"Hey, lady!" one called. "You can't go in there."

She ignored their warning and kept moving. They were almost upon her when she swerved to the left, only to put herself in close proximity to another policeman she'd neglected to spot.

"Whoa there, honey. Didn't you hear Officer Davidson? He said you couldn't go in."

"I heard," Samantha ground out. "But I'm going through." She pointed a shaking finger toward the entrance. "I'm going through that door." She yanked her arm free from his hold and took two steps before her path was blocked by another grim-faced policeman.

"We got our order, lady. No admittance."

"Fine, but your orders don't apply to me." Samantha stared at the four men with steely determination. "I appreciate your position, but you'll just have to overlook *me* and believe me when I say I'm an exception." She searched her mind desperately for an

excuse, any reason that would move the blue uniformed wall. "I'm Boston Grey's fiancée and he's
waiting for me." Four pairs of eyes meshed with one
another in understanding, and she knew she'd said
the wrong thing. Hands on hips, she raised her chin
defiantly, her eyes sparkling with anger. "Step aside
please," she commanded with a bravado she was far
from feeling.

"It's for your own safety. We can't let you
through."

"I don't care what happens to me. I'm going in
there, and the only way you're going to stop me is by
physical force." She took a deep breath and forged
on. "You lay one more hand on me and I'll scream
loud enough to wake the dead," she threatened.
"I...I'll yell police brutality." The realization that
these men were going to keep her from Boston only
increased her desperation. Couldn't they see how important this was to her? Why wouldn't they understand?

"Look, ma'am, be reasonable...."

"I don't want to be reasonable."

"We're here to protect you and the rest of the people who plan on attending this concert tonight. Give
us a break and get back in your car and go home till
show time."

"Problems, officers?"

Samantha whirled around at the familiar voice of
her brother. "Mark!" She launched herself into his
arms. "Make them let me in. Please, Mark. I don't
care about the danger. I must talk to Boston."

"Calm down, sis. I'll take you in." Samantha

sagged against her brother in relief. He nodded his head toward the policemen. "It's okay, I'll take the responsibility for her." Mark guided Samantha through the double glass doors then stopped her hurried steps with a firm hand on her shoulder. He swallowed hard as she looked up at him, her eyes wide and full of pain and fear, her face pale with worry and something else he could only guess at.

"Tell me, Mark, have they found the bomb? Do they know who made the threats? Is Boston all right?"

"There wasn't an actual threat, Samantha," said a voice behind her.

She turned, still in the circle of her brother's embrace, and faced Ken and another man she'd never seen before, but knew instinctively was a policeman, despite the dark navy suit he wore. "What do you mean there was no threat? Lana. . . ." She broke off suddenly.

"Lana, huh. I might have known she couldn't keep this mess from you," Ken groaned, but there was a tiny sparkle in his eyes.

"I don't understand." Samantha looked from one man to the other. "Is this all a joke?" She felt sick inside.

"Not a joke, Miss Griffin." The man in the blue suit interjected, then introduced himself as Detective MacNabb. "The caller," he went on, "didn't say he'd planted a bomb, but only kept reminding Mr. Grey of what happened three years ago. Mr. Grey felt he couldn't take the chance that the person might psyche himself up and try something. There are all sorts of crazies in this world. Your man is a prime target for their demented frustrations." Samantha recoiled and clutched Mark's hand for strength. "We couldn't take any chances, either, so we made a thorough sweep of the place." He held his hand out, palms up. "It's clean."

"You're very sure?" Samantha asked, a slight quiver of relief in her husky voice.

"Oh, yes, ma'am. My men don't miss a thing." His piercing eyes were no longer on her but studying a lone man walking toward them.

Samantha turned and they all fell quiet. She could feel the tension build as they watched the young man make his way toward them. He was dressed in a T-shirt and faded patched jeans, his worn leather jacket zipped halfway down. Samantha realized the strangeness of wearing a jacket in ninety-degree weather. The silence stretched and she sensed the alertness of the men around her as the fellow came abreast of them. He popped his gum a few times, staring at them with equal curiosity.

"Hey, man, you know where I can find Boston Grey?"

As he talked, Samantha saw his hand slip between the opening of the jacket, and flinched. Before she knew what was happening, she was shoved aside and forced to the floor, her brother's weight knocking the air from her lungs. Confusion reined as she struggled to see what was happening. There was yelling and cursing and heavy pounding of shoes on marble floors, a pounding that matched the pumping of her own heart.

When the voices receded to an echo and Mark's harsh breathing in her ears subsided, she turned her head, meeting his scared expression. "I think they've gone and you can let me up." She couldn't help smiling at his dazed widened eyes. Mark had acted instinctively to protect her, and from his disoriented state, she realized he was just now beginning to comprehend what had taken place. He helped her up and with a flutter of her hands she brushed off her tuxedo pants, tucked in her blouse and straightened her cummerbund. If anything could have cracked her resolve, she thought, that incident should have. But, though shaken, she was still determined to be a part of Boston's life. Good or bad, they'd be together. If she could weather this, she felt she could weather any storm that broke around her in the future. Samantha grinned at her brother, a mischievous glitter he knew only too well.

"It's not funny," Mark growled. "So stop laughing. How can you face the possibility of this sort of madness recurring again and again?" He reached out, wanting to gather her in his arms and comfort the little girl he still believed her to be.

Samantha surprised him by stepping back. She no longer needed her family's solace, only the nourishment of Boston's love, and there wasn't a doubt in her mind that he loved her. "Without Boston, Mark, my life's nothing at all." Tears filled her eyes. "Just pray they've caught the maniac now." She blinked, trying to hold the tears back. "Can you imagine what Boston's been going through?"

"Hey, your mascara's going to run. How can you

face Boston looking like a raccoon?'' he teased. ''Why, he'd never take you seriously if you showed up like this.''

A weak smile turned up the corners of her mouth as she realized he understood her better than she'd thought. ''I bet I've aged ten years in the past couple of hours,'' she quipped. Samantha allowed him to dab at her tears one last time.

''Naw, you still look like a kid dressed up in Aunt Sally's old clothes. To me, anyway. You're trembling, baby.''

'''Course I am,'' she laughed. ''I've been shaking so much in the past two and a half hours, I'm not sure I don't have an advanced case of malaria.''

He laughed reluctantly at her glib remark, then sighed. ''I guess we've really lost you, haven't we? You truly love that man.''

''Yes, I do,'' she stated firmly. For the first time since Boston decided to do the benefit she realized what life would be like as an integral part of his world. She felt strong, at peace with herself, able to cope with any and all problems.

''Listen, sis,'' he began, but broke off when he saw Ken approaching.

''You two okay?''

''Was he the one, Ken?'' Samantha burst out.

''No. He works for the Summit. Seems he's an apprentice technician who happened to be in the wrong place at the wrong time and got caught. His excuse is he has an older sister who's a big fan of Boston's and he only wanted to get her an autograph as a surprise.''

Samantha looked down at her watch and ex-claimed, "The time! I have to find Boston." She glanced up at Ken's frowning face. "You're not thinking of stopping me, are you?"

"Heaven forbid! I've seen that temper of yours one time too many."

"Come on, sis. I'll take you to Boston's dressing room." Samantha grabbed his hand and took off at a run, only to be pulled to a sedate walk by her brother. "Sammy, I think there's something you should know."

She suppressed her irritation at Mark's dragging steps and looked up. He cleared his throat a few times then plunged on. "Boston was receiving those calls almost as soon as he arrived in Houston. The night he blew up at you he'd just gotten another one. When I confronted him later he finally confessed, under pressure, that he'd deliberately picked a fight with you to run you off. But I honestly don't think he meant it to go as far as it did."

"I know, Mark. It took me a while to figure it out, but when Lana phoned today and told me about the calls, all the pieces of the puzzle fell into place." They stopped outside a door with a big white star and Boston's name printed in stark black letters in the center.

"Sammy, don't let him push you away. There's always a chance something could happen tonight. So no matter what he says, just remember he thinks he's protecting you."

CHAPTER NINETEEN

SAMANTHA TOOK A DEEP BREATH, her heart pounding
in her ears, her mouth suddenly dry. She turned the
brass knob and quietly pushed open the door. Her
nose twitched appreciatively at the delicate yet pun-
gent fragrance of flowers that assaulted her senses as
she stepped inside.

"What the hell are you doing here?" Boston demanded, rising slowly to his feet. Father Brian,
seated beside him on the long leather couch, rose also
and placed a warning hand on Boston's arm.

After one brief glance at Boston's cold expressionless face, Samantha ignored him and turned her attention to the other man. "Would you mind leaving
us for a while, Father Brian?"

"Not at all, child."

Samantha played for time, allowing her eyes to follow his slow shuffling departure. Boston looked tired
and gaunt, she thought. She knew she'd have to
break through his resistance before she could make
him listen. When the door shut behind Father Brian,
she straightened her shoulders and pivoted back to
Boston. A lump formed in her throat as she gazed at
him. He looked so handsome, resplendent in his
black evening clothes and the blazing white ruffled

shirt. The silence remained unbroken as they stared at each other, and Samantha marveled at her own self-control. She wanted to run to him, hold the tall lean body close, kiss away the grim line of his beautiful lips, taste the warm, tantalizing depths of his mouth. But not now, she forcefully reminded herself.

"I asked what you're doing here?"

She locked her eyes with his, exploring the hard flat blackness for some spark of life. Finding only icy indifference, she walked toward him. "I've grown up." Her lips trembled into a wistful smile.

"That's nice." His expressionless voice momentarily shook her determination.

"It's taken time and a painful amount of soul-searching."

"So?" Boston reached and pried away the hands she had raised to his arms.

"You won't put me off with your coldness." She smiled up at him sweetly, but there was a blue flame in the depths of her eyes. "I've spent the most wretched two days of my life. I've torn myself apart, rearranged my way of thinking and put the parts back together again. In the final analysis you were partly right. I'll take the blame for most—not all— but most of our problems." She reached for him again, her body aching for the reassuring feel of his arms, but he backed away, his face unreadable.

"I don't have time for this, Spar—Samantha."

Samantha suddenly realized she was going to have to talk fast if she wanted to divert the disaster she felt coming. Boston's iron resolve to push her away and out of danger was likely to take the form of another humiliating scene. She knew if she allowed that to happen again there would be things said this time that could cause irreparable damage.

"Boston, what you did to me the other night was uncalled for." A fine sheen of perspiration collected on his brow and she snatched a tissue and forced it in his hand. "I can understand why you did what you did—well, part of it. It may take a long time for the pain of your words to fade." His black eyes burned like jet embers in his bloodless face. "But I can and do forgive you."

He opened his mouth as if to speak, but she stopped him with a wave of her hand. "No, don't interrupt. You're going to listen to me." She closed her eyes a second to collect her thoughts. "We're going to settle our problems here and now." She loosened her death grip on her evening bag and tossed it on the lighted makeup table. "It took a while for me to realize I wasn't really envious of your glamorous career. I didn't want to be just a part of your life; I wanted to be your life. I know that's unrealistic now." She gave a helpless shrug. "And the women in your life, past and present, don't bother me anymore. You see," she smiled, "I've learned to trust you totally. I'm not even scared of your fans anymore—though I think the way you threw me into that situation without any warning, then stood back and watched me flounder around helplessly was a rotten trick." She moved a step closer and Boston retreated another step backward. Taking a deep breath, she swallowed her pride once and for all. "Do you want to know what went wrong?"

"No!" Boston bellowed with the anguished roar of a wounded lion. "Stop it, Sparky." He rubbed wildly at his forehead. "Go away. Go home! Can't you see I don't want you!"

"No, damn you!" Samantha shouted angrily, his continued stubbornness pushing her beyond her bounds of reasoning. If he wanted a fight, she thought grimly, he'd get one. She could feel the fire boiling in her veins and welcomed it. "You're not going to hurt me again. So stop trying to protect me. I came to have my say and you're going to listen to me if I have to lock the door."

"Sparky, don't do this. Believe me, it's not necessary. All I want you to do is leave, now."

She watched his eyes drink in her every feature as if setting them to memory, and it frightened her. "It is necessary, Boston, to me. I have to make you understand. Don't you see that?"

"No," he answered warily. "Please. . . ."

She ignored his plea and went on. "I foolishly thought if I married you I'd never be myself again. I was scared of losing my identity, my independence, and being swallowed up by your fame and notoriety." She sensed his withdrawal and hurried on. "I don't want to be an extension of anyone. All my life, Boston, I've fought tooth and nail to keep my father and brothers from running my life. When I finally made the break from their stranglehold, I swore I'd never be put in that position again. Then you decided to return to your work and I had to vie with it for your attention. I somehow got everything mixed up in my mind and you became someone to fight. I saw myself being pushed into the background only to come forward when you needed a bed partner. That sounds so childish now, but I felt you slipping away from me and didn't know how to bring you back.''

She paused and waited for him to say something, anything, and when he just stood there white-faced, she began to grow desperate. ''I love you so much, and yet I even started doubting the strength of your love for me.''

They both jumped, startled by the sudden loud knocking at the door.

''Twenty-five minutes, Mr. Grey,'' a phantom voice called.

''Listen to me, Sparky.'' A shaky hand reached out for her. Then, as if he couldn't bear the thought of touching her, he dropped his arm to his side and turned his back on her. ''I want you to go. After the concert I'll come over to your aunt's house and we'll talk.'' Boston picked up the bottle of Kentucky bourbon from his dressing table and poured himself a stiff shot. He tossed it back without any finesse.

What was happening, she thought desperately. ''I won't accept this, Boston. If you don't love me anymore, then you tell me right now. Look me in the eye and say it.''

She walked up behind him and wrapped her arms around his waist, resting her head against his rigid back. ''Tell me you don't love me and I'll walk out that door and never see you again. But if you do, remember one thing. I'll always love you.'' She heard a low, deep rumbling groan against her ear and held her breath.

Boston freed himself from her hold and spun around, his fingers biting into her shoulders. "You idiot. Don't you understand? Anything could happen here tonight. I won't have you hurt."

"And what about you?" she demanded huskily. "Why didn't you cancel the concert when the calls started?"

His hands glided up and down her arms, restoring the circulation. His eyes glittered fiercely. "I've been living with fear for three years." His jaw hardened, the muscles clenching and unclenching. "No one is ever going to make me go through that agony again." Boston dropped his arms and moved away. "That's why I want you to leave. I'm afraid for you."

Samantha sighed softly and whispered, "What a pair of fools we are. Don't you understand? What happens to you happens to me." She moved to stand before him, her eyes caressing his stern features. "Do you honestly believe I would want to live without you?" She reached out and touched the warm wetness on his cheeks, her own vision blurred by the fat tears filling her eyes. "It doesn't matter where we are or what comes, we'll always be together."

Boston cupped her face, his thumbs flicking away the tears from her freckled cheeks. "You're sure?" She nodded. "And you forgive me for the unspeakable things I did and said the other evening." She nodded again and smiled. He pulled her into his arms, crushing her body to his, and groaned brokenly. "I don't know what I've done to deserve you."

"Ten minutes, Mr. Grey," the phantom voice called again.

Boston visibly tried to regain control of himself.
"There's so much I want to tell you." He allowed her
to wipe away the traces of his tears until his patience
evaporated at her gentle slowness and he snatched the
tissue from his hand, his mouth descending on hers,
kissing her deeply. "You're going to have to leave,"
he murmured against her lips. "I need a few minutes
to myself."

He clasped her elbow and guided her to the door.
"I love you, Sparky. As soon as the concert's over, I
want you to come straight back here. Kiss me once
again for luck."

She laughed, a bright ringing sound that sent a
hard jolt of desire through him.

"Break a leg, my love."

"You'd better pray I don't, lady. It could make
for a very uncomfortable honeymoon."

Samantha threw her arms around his neck and met
his mouth with all the love and tenderness she was
feeling. But Boston wanted no part of gentleness. He
gathered her close, his hands molding her lissome
form against his, letting her feel his desire to her re-
sponses. She returned the kiss with equal strength.

Finally Boston pushed her away, his eyes sparkling. Looking down, he shook his head in mock
despair. "Well, this is another fine mess you've gotten me into."

Puzzled, Samantha followed his gaze and burst out
laughing at the very visible bulge in his pants.
"Sorry," she apologized.

"No you're not." He flicked the tip of her nose
with a playful finger and opened the door. "Now

scoot.'' He patted her lightly on the backside. ''I'll see you in about two hours.''

Boston watched her take a few steps away from him, then reached out and pulled her back, grinning at the surprise and happiness lighting her face. ''Promise me one thing, Sparky.'' He captured her busy hands as they adjusted his bow tie one final time. ''If there's any sign of trouble, please promise me you'll leave immediately. Mark knows what to do, so don't worry about me. I'll get out.''

Ready with a flippant remark, she stopped, studying the grim seriousness of his face. ''Boston, nothing's going to happen.''

''Your promise, Sparky,'' he demanded.

She went up on tiptoe and kissed him hard and quick. ''You have my word.'' Giving his hand a firm squeeze, she whirled around, leaving him to watch until she disappeared around the corner.

SAMANTHA DIDN'T KNOW how she arrived at the back entrance of the stage, nor did she know when Mark had clamped a guiding hand on her elbow. She floated along on her happiness, wondering if her feet would ever touch the ground. Mark led her down the wide stairs and to the already full concert floor. The babble of voices and the orchestra's tuning brought her out of her daydreams. She looked up and flashed a dazzling smile at Mark.

''I take it everything's been worked out?'' He grinned at the radiant face, sparkling with love.

Samantha didn't answer. Instead she gazed out over the thousands of people seated and waiting patiently for Boston to appear. Pride and a little fear swelled in her heart as she realized the monumental attraction these people felt for Boston.

"Come on, sis." Mark grabbed her arm and led her to the front row.

Her eyes widened and her steps slowed to a complete stop. She threw back her head and laughed. Her entire family lined the first row. Seat after seat of varying shades of redheads turned at her approach. With cheeks aflame she watched, horrified, as the practical jokers of her family stood and applauded her entrance. Strangers within hearing distance fell silent and whispers rumbled through the rows as her father, a grin of unholy glee on his face, rose and escorted her to her chair.

"Daddy, how could you?" she whispered fiercely, her cheeks blending with the bright color of her hair.

"Honey, we've been holding our breath for two days. It's a relief to see you happy again and all your troubles solved. We couldn't think of anything more fitting than a standing ovation."

She opened her mouth to retort, but the house-lights began to dim and she settled back. Her heart in her throat, she reached for her father's hand on one side and her Uncle George's on the other.

The lights dimmed further, then plunged the audience into total darkness. An expectant hush filled the cavernous room, the only sounds an occasional cough, a whispered voice, a hushing hiss.

On the night-blackened stage a thin pinpoint of blue light appeared, illuminating a hard, shiny wood surface.

Out of the darkness the famous voice spoke. "Ladies and gentlemen, this benefit concert is being held for the Boys Ranch Orphanage and for my long-time friend Father Brian. But I'd also like to dedicate it to two special people—Elizabeth Jones, the young lady who died while attending my last concert, and to Elijah Lightfoot."

The soft mellow sounds of a single piano began to spill out over the room. The light expanded into a cir-cle, growing larger and larger, and the haunting tune "*Liebestraum*," Dream of Love, washed over the hushed audience. Samantha heard the collective gasp when the pale glowing light completely encircled the solitary man at the Steinway. She smiled, remember-ing Boston's promise to give this audience something they'd never seen or heard from him before.

For two short hours he hypnotized 18,000 people to the point that she could hear a pin drop. Silent, fascinated, they watched and listened and loved. His deep rich voice brought back dreams, weaving a bond among all who were there, young and old.

Boston worked the stage from side to side, singing his magic to each and every person, making them be-lieve the words were for them alone. He gave them no time to show their love and appreciation but sang nonstop, pulling them tighter into his spellbinding net, pushing them to feel emotions they'd never ex-perienced before.

A wizard, a sorcerer of love, he broke down years of emotional barriers, forcing grown men to reach for their handkerchiefs.

Samantha looked up at Boston. He stood before

her, coat and tie discarded, his ruffled shirt open to the waist and wet with sweat. He spoke directly to her, but his voice carried to everyone present. "My last song, ladies and gentlemen, is for my life, my love—Sparky."

His eyes drew hers like a magnet, sleepy lids partially closed over gleaming eyes as he sang now, only to her.

Mesmerized, Samantha listened to the words as she'd done once before.

"These are the eyes that never knew how to smile. . . till you came into my life."

She watched the corner of his mouth lift in a sensuous smile and knew he was remembering too.

"And these are the arms that long to lock you inside. . . every day and every night."

Captured once again by his magic, she felt the heat of desire flowing in her blood. Pictures flashed in her head of her lying in his arms, warm and complete.

"Here is the soul of which you've taken control. . . can't you see I'm trying to show love is right?"

He'd changed her life. He had shown her love and embraced her with the strength of his soul.

"These are the hands that can't help reaching for you. . . if you're anywhere in sight."

His hands, taking her to heaven and plunging her to hell. Strong, gentle and always loving.

"And these are the lips that can't help calling
your name...
in the middle of the night."

She closed her eyes. His love was all she ever wanted in this world; everything else faded in comparison.

A hard nudge from her father jolted her out of her dreamy memories. Her clouded vision refocused and she looked around dazed, her ears hurting from the thundering applause. Eighteen thousand people were on their feet applauding wildly and screaming encore. Goose bumps broke out over her body as she proudly watched Boston take his bows, politely shaking his head as the audience yelled and begged for more. He hushed them long enough to wave a hand toward his orchestra, now standing and applauding too.

"Please, thank these men and women. They've done a magnificent job under trying circumstances."

The minute Boston exited from the stage after his last bow, Samantha jumped to her feet, anxious to be the first to meet him in the dressing room. But the unpredictable crowd seemed to have a mind of its own and she became separated from the protective circle of her family. Pushed, shoved and caught in the crush of people trying to leave the Summit, she was halfway to the front entrance before she completely lost her temper.

"Excuse me," she said, and began elbowing her

way back down the aisle. "Pardon me." Dodging between the groups of people, she finally managed to flatten herself against the wall and inch by inch move back the way she'd come.

"What's the matter, baby, lose your man?"

Samantha glared at the persistent man in front of her who seemed to take it for granted she needed his help. When she realized she was losing ground fast and her explanations were falling on deaf ears, she gave the overly enthusiastic stranger a hard kick in the shin and slipped away, his flowery curses ringing in her ears.

"Where on earth have you been?" came a deep familiar voice in her ear.

"Mark! Get me out of here." She was frantic to reach Boston now that she figured out how much time she'd wasted.

Mark brought his fingers to his lips and before Samantha could stop him gave three short, undignified, piercing whistles. As if by magic, two more of her hulking brothers appeared. Giving herself over to the humor of the situation, she became the center of their battering ram. They moved through the masses like a monstrous wave, laughing uproariously.

CHAPTER TWENTY

WHEN THEY ARRIVED at the dressing room door the smile was wiped from Samantha's face in disappointment. Mobile walls had been pulled back, enlarging the room to three times its normal size. The party was in full swing, the popping of champagne corks barely heard over the din of guests milling around. Already high on excitement, they were congratulating anyone they thought was connected with the concert.

"Where's Boston?" she demanded, punching her sharp nails into Adam's broad back.

"Hold on, sis, here we go." Her loving human wall took off again. When they finally came to a stop she heard Boston's deep baritone and her heart began to pound.

"Well, where is she?"

Adam grinned and stepped aside and Mark and Abel melted away into the crowd, leaving her to stand before him in frozen silence. Where were all the pretty words she'd planned? They seemed to flee from her brain the instant she gazed up into his brilliant eyes and triumphant smile.

"You were...." Again her mind went blank and the words dried up in her throat. It wasn't the knowledge that she loved this man beyond belief that left her mute, but the wonder that he returned her love just as deeply.

Boston leaned down and kissed her gently. "I was beginning to think your brothers had spirited you away from me." He scowled fiercely. "I was ready to take them all on."

"You feel that cocky, do you?" She grinned and brushed back a lock of damp hair from his brow.

"Like I could take on the world." He leaned down again and kissed her.

Samantha refused to accept the gentle peck and wrapped her arms around his neck, her heart bursting with pride and happiness. His embrace tightened and she deepened the kiss. A loud embarrassed cough and chuckling voices broke them apart. Cheeks aflame, Samantha accepted the glass of champagne from her father, her eyes sparkling at his retreating back over the rim of her glass.

Boston accepted congratulations from the steady stream of well-wishers, politely shaking hands and thanking them for coming. When there was a short lull he whispered out of the corner of his mouth, "Would you mind telling me what that kiss was all about?"

A mischievous smile lifted the corners of Samantha's mouth. "I don't know what you're talking about." She batted innocent eyelashes at him, then choked on her sip of champagne as he gave a good hard pinch to her backside.

"Explain!"

"Ah, well," she sighed, "it looks like I can't have any secrets from you."

"Sparky," he warned under his breath.

"I saw Felicia headed this way and thought a little public display of our mutual affection would be a good deterrent. Speak of the devil, here she comes."

"Darling!" came a high-pitched female voice.

Samantha watched Felicia throw her arms around Boston's neck and fumed inwardly as she caught the devilish gleam in his eyes. Though Boston held the other woman off and stopped her from kissing him full on the mouth, he did allow her to press her bright glossy lips to his cheek. Samantha's eyes followed the stroking movement of Felicia's long red nails on Boston's arm. She looked up, caught his wary expression, then looked down again.

"Felicia, dear—" she flicked the possessive hand from his arm "—you may coo and drool and make eyes at Boston all you want—" her voice hardened just enough to take the teasing quality from her words "—but don't touch."

Boston smothered his laugh with a muffled cough and pulled Samantha tighter to his side as they watched Felicia flounce away.

"Getting rid of the competition, Sparky?"

"You bet," she cooed, mimicking Felicia's tone. "I can't do a thing about the fans, but that lady gives me the creeps. I don't care what excuses you make—she wants you."

"That's it, tiger. You keep those hungry females off my back."

"I don't believe that's where they want to be," she retorted evenly, and burst out laughing at Boston's raised eyebrows.

"I didn't realize you were so perceptive."

She smiled at him. "I am learning." They were interrupted again by several more people who wanted Boston's ear. Samantha started to drift away to join her family when she realized the newcomers were not mere well-wishers but businessmen in the entertainment field. Boston pulled her back to his side. He kissed her quickly on the cheek and rejoined the conversation.

Samantha marveled at his stamina. He stood there, humbly accepting praise, totally rejuvenated after two exhausting hours. Tonight she'd seen another dimension of Boston, and her respect for him was profound. To hold an audience spellbound was no easy feat. Singing always looked so effortless to her that she had never really considered it work. But she'd learned in the past weeks that a career as a professional entertainer wasn't just a matter of standing up and utilizing a natural talent. There were hours, endless hours, of preparation and hard work involved. Boston deserved the homage these people paid to his talent.

When the three men were gone she turned to him.

"Where are Lana and Ken? Come to think of it, I haven't seen Tom, either."

"Sparky, Tom left for the airport immediately after the concert," Boston answered hesitantly, waiting for her comment. When none came, he went on. "Ken took Lana back to the house to rest. She wasn't feeling well."

They were interrupted again and Samantha waited till the next well-wishers had left then asked, "What's wrong with Lana?"

Boston looked down at her, his eyes dancing, his

smile wistful. "Oh, it's nothing she won't get over in about seven months." Samantha's bright eyes widened and he nodded as comprehension dawned. "That's right, the rabbit died."

"I can't believe it. She never said a word to me." There was a note of hurt in her voice and Boston gave her a brief hug.

"Honey, Ken didn't find out till tonight. It seems Lana didn't want any of us to worry about her with everything else going on." His voice trailed off as a new group of people claimed his attention.

Lana pregnant, she thought, surprised and a little envious. Then she grinned, trying to imagine the pompous Ken a proud, bragging father.

While Boston talked, her gaze roamed the room. She spotted several members of her family, drinking and enjoying themselves. She was just beginning to turn when her eyes collided with a pair of gray ones. No, she amended, silver, as silver as a bright shiny new coin. She watched as the eyes narrowed, raking her body, stripping her of every stitch of her clothing, then one heavy lid lowered in a wicked wink.

Where had she seen him? She remembered those silver eyes, but from where? Whoever he was, he was the most beautiful, totally decadent man she'd ever seen. The tall, powerful, elegantly clad body lounged casually against the wall. His eyes were a startling contrast to the deeply tanned face, and the tumble of curly blue-black hair only added to his rakish appearance. Samantha stiffened as he straightened lazily and began walking directly toward them.

"What's wrong, Sparky?"

"Who...who's that man, Boston?" she asked quickly, frightened of the man's intensity. Then he flashed a smile and she remembered. Kane Stone.

"Who?" Boston followed the line of her gaze.

Silently, they watched as the man wove his way slowly through the crowd. When he stood before them, he nodded to Samantha and smiled at Boston. Without a single word he handed Boston a folded piece of paper, then disappeared back through the milling throng of people.

She tore her eyes from Kane's retreating back and turned, paling a little at the strange expression on Boston's face. "What's wrong?"

He didn't reply, his eyes riveted on the unfolded paper in his hand. She craned her neck and read the bold scrawling writing.

Carl Wilson arrested yesterday in L.A. for the bombing of your concert three years ago. Wilson signed confession and has been recommited by his family to Mountain View Mental Hospital.

You owe me one, buddy.

Kane

"Thank God," she whispered.

Boston seemed to change before her eyes. Lines of strain and worry melted away and with them the years of torment faded. The controlled mouth relaxed and he smiled down at her, a boyish smile that lit up his entire face.

"I can't believe it's over," he choked, and crushed

her to him for a quick strangling bear hug.

"So that's the notorious, Kane?" she asked, still intrigued.

Boston's reply was laughter, so full of innuendos Samantha wondered what wild carousing he and Kane had done together.

"Is he married?" She scanned the crowded room for the silver eyes and raven hair.

Boston chuckled. "Kane? No. I don't know of any woman who could tie him down long enough to get a ring on his finger. He's a rich wanderer, a renegade throwback to another era." He glanced down once more at the piece of paper in his hand before stuffing it in his pocket. "And he's a damn good friend."

"I have a feeling the two of you raised a few eyebrows when you were together."

"More than eyebrows," he chuckled. "Hello, Maggie."

Samantha glanced over her shoulder, meeting the cool blue eyes of Margret Tanner. "Maggie, how nice to see you again." She slipped out of Boston's arms and extended her hand. She and Margret had gotten off to a bad start and Samantha was determined to rectify the situation. Boston needed good coverage from the press. Maggie Tanner, powerful as she was, couldn't ruin his career now, but she could make public life uncomfortable for them.

Maggie visibly started at the sincerity in Samantha's voice. She gave her a stiff cold smile of acknowledgment, ignored the extended hand and turned to Boston. "You realize anything I say about tonight will be totally inadequate. The concert was

magnificent. Your voice is even better than before.
I've already called my story in, but...."

She paused, her reporter's instincts and bulldog
determination still chewing over the tidbit of news
she was now obsessed with obtaining. "I'd still like
to know how you and Miss Griffin met."

"Samantha, please, Maggie." Samantha smiled
warmly into the glacier blue eyes. "I'd love to tell
you how Boston and I met." Her eyes twinkled merrily up at Boston's stunned expression. "But you'll
have to wait till we're married. I don't know
whether Boston has told you or if you've noticed,
but those six very large redheaded men over there
are my brothers. They're still not too sure if I'm
doing the right thing marrying this man." She had
Maggie's full attention. "They'd just love an excuse
to take their frustrations out on Boston. If they
knew the whole story, they'd more than likely tear
him apart."

Maggie's eyes widened. "It's *that* sensational?"

Samantha shot an uncomfortable and fidgety Boston a wicked glance. "Well—" she hedged a second
"—I'd say a mix-up over hotel beds, a scandalous
newspaper report, dodging my brother's fists, verbal
fights with my entire family and kidnapping would
qualify." Maggie was laughing openly now and
Samantha paused to catch her breath before going
on. "A quick getaway in a stolen car, a wild ride
through the back roads of rural Texas, a borrowed
Lear jet." She stopped and touched the tip of one
finger to her lips thoughtfully. "I'm still not sure the
plane wasn't stolen too."

She shrugged and went on. "There was a five-day trek on horseback across half of New Mexico, a campfire seduction under the stars. All that could make a pretty sizzling story for your readers. On second thought—" she looped her arm through Boston's "—maybe I shouldn't tell you, and write a book instead."

"Sparky!" Boston warned, but the delight he took in her teasing made his voice waver and crack.

"Oh, well." She shook her head in mock regret. "I guess you have your story, Maggie. I don't think I could find a publisher."

"No, no." Maggie laughed. "You'd better write it yourself. My readers would never believe me. I was wondering how you were going to keep this sexy man in line. Now I can see it's Boston who has his job cut out for him." She turned to Boston. "How do you put up with this young lady?"

Boston frowned fiercely at both women, his jet eyes sparkling with laughter. "Oh, I'll whip her into shape. In about ten years," he murmured mournfully. He took a deep breath, the laughter dying in his eyes. "All joking aside, Maggie. I have an exclusive for you." He captured both women's full attention. "I'm sure you realize this benefit was solely for Father Brian and the orphanage."

He let the suspense hang between them before he went on. "I won't be back on the tour circuit again. Tonight was my swan song, so to speak. As of now you're looking at a retired man."

Retired. Samantha felt the explosion of his last words vibrating in her head. Paralyzed, she stared up at him, watching his mouth move but hearing nothing of what he was saying to Maggie.

One firm finger pressed beneath her chin and pushed her gaping lips closed. "Catching flies?" he teased. She tried to say something and he pressed the same finger across her lips. "I'll explain in a few minutes." Boston signaled to Mark, grasped her elbow and began walking them toward the door.

Retired. The words finally jerked her out of her shocked state and into a flaming temper. How dare he do this to her? Always making important decisions without the least thought for her feelings. She'd suffered enough just coming to terms with his career. Now he was retiring. All the tears, hours of soul searching and sleepless nights made her feel a fool.

They reached the limousine and Mark opened the door. Her eyes narrowed as she caught the exchange of conspiratorial grins. Yanking her hand free from Boston's grasp, she tried to move away.

He reclaimed her wrist with a quick movement. "Get in," he ordered between clenched teeth.

Samantha flopped down on the suede seat and scooted across to the opposite side of the car. She heard the slamming of doors, and while Boston stood outside, giving instructions to Mark, she turned and looked out the rear window. A frown creased her brow and she wondered what was going on. All her family were entering the long line of limousines parked behind them.

"Listen, Sparky," Boston began as he pulled the door shut.

Her head whipped around and she glared, her eyes

turning a deep turquoise as they flashed fire at him.
"How could you do this without telling me?"

Boston quickly pushed a button and a darkened
window slid smoothly up, separating them from
Mark's and the chauffeur's view. "I didn't mean to
say it this way. Believe...."

"Damn you, Boston. How can we have any sort of
life together if you won't trust me?"

He reached out and pulled her onto his lap.

"Let me go," she snarled, and tried to squirm
away.

"Please, Sparky. Listen to me."

"Why?" She became still at the regret and unhap-
piness in his voice and raised her furious eyes to his,
seeing the love he felt for her reflected there.

She sighed, the anger melting away beneath his
steady gaze. Resting her forehead against his, she
wailed softly, "Oh, Boston. What am I going to do
with you? Do you have any idea of the anguish I went
through trying to accept your life-style, and now you
spring this new decision on me right out of the blue."

"I know, love, and I'm sorry. But I didn't make
up my mind till the evening I blew up at you." He
kissed her hair and pulled her head to rest on his
shoulder. "When I lost my voice and was forced to
find another outlet or go mad, I slowly began to realize there was more to my talent than just singing."

She moved and he tightened his arms. "No, just
listen. Living in an orphanage and being just one
among many can do strange things to kids' minds. I
was lucky. I had a talent—a talent that prompted in-
dividual attention from the fathers and the teachers.

Some of the kids were envious and resentful of the special treatment I got, but most were a little in awe of me. They began to hang around, trying to share some of the limelight. I'm ashamed to say I enjoyed and used my power over them. While I practiced they did my chores and in return I fixed it so they shared some of the privileges I received. As the years went by I believed I deserved the adoration.

"You need to understand, Sparky. I had nothing— no past, no family, no name. Only Elijah and Ken. After I became a success it didn't take long to realize the friends I acquired were nothing but leeches. My fans became a substitute family. Women were my lovers. They were sisters, daughters of someone else, and I took them in for a while as my family. But it didn't work. They weren't mine."

He stroked the bright red head nestled against his shoulder and smiled. "When I first saw you, standing across the hotel room from me, wearing those ridiculous skimpy pants and bra, your lovely body as freckled as your beautiful face, and that wild mane of outlandish red hair, I was a goner. It didn't matter who you were, or what you were. I wanted you."

"You thought I was a prostitute."

"No, never that," he corrected her harshly. "I've known whores in my life and I knew instinctively you were not one. Now don't interrupt. I want you to understand about my decision to retire."

He tilted her head back to rest in the crook of his arm, his fingers stroking the soft curve of her cheek, his eyes velvet black. "When Elijah died and I learned about my past, everything began to change for me. I did have a family, a background and a grandfather who loved me. I had you and *real* friends in Ken and Lana. There was the future to consider, and all the things I'd secretly longed for were there within reach. My career as an entertainer began to fade with visions of you as my wife, visions of a home and hopefully lots of children. I can write and produce music, cut an occasional album, but no more concerts that will take me away from what I have now. Where I go, you go.''

The car moved on through the night, a caravan of ten other limousines following behind. Samantha lay cradled on his lap, quietly thinking of all he'd told her. ''Do you realize for a man without a family, you're suddenly going to have a lot of in-laws to contend with? Our gatherings and holidays are total madness. Think you can cope?''

''Yes, indeed,'' he chuckled. ''Your family and I understand each other completely.'' His hand slid from her rib cage to cover her small rounded breast. ''Sparky, I opened the painting.'' He swallowed the large lump in his throat and the velvet voice dropped to a hoarse whisper. ''I just don't know what to say. It's the most precious gift I've ever received.''

''I wanted you to have a past and your own family to look at when the bad memories began to crowd in on you.''

Boston nodded, understanding, but at a total loss for words. Swallowing hard, he nuzzled the warm fragrant valley between her breasts. ''I'd like to get started on our own family.''

''How many?''

Distracted by the warm firm mound swelling with

desire beneath his touch, he murmured. "How many what?"

"Children."

"Half a dozen would do—for a start."

"Six!" Samantha pouted up at him, her hands busy with the buttons of his shirt. "How about just—" She held up two fingers.

"No." Boston's grin widened and he pulled her tighter into his arms. "Six little Greys all in a row. I may even write a whole new set of nursery songs for them."

"You male chauvinist, I bet you want all boys. Miniature images of yourself."

"No, no. A girl or two would round things off nicely. I wouldn't even mind if they had red hair," he teased. His voice was low, seductive, and she shivered from the deep husky tones.

"Daddy." He rolled the words out slowly and nodded. "I like the sound." His lips found the warm hollow at the side of her neck and with a tantalizing flick of his tongue he traced the line to the soft lobe of her ear.

"Boston?"

"Hmmm," came his throaty whisper.

"All this planning the future is grand, but when are we getting married?" Samantha asked, her voice hoarse with the warm glowing feeling he was invoking.

"Tonight, at your home." He pulled back and grinned sheepishly into her surprised face.

"What!" Samantha sat up. "How?" What about blood tests and licences and—"

"All taken care of." He cuddled her head on his shoulder, his fingers threading themselves through the bright mass of red hair. "It's not what you know," he chuckled, "but who. Your father pulled some powerful strings in this state. We've all worked hard to bring this off."

"You mean dad's going to marry us?" She felt the tears welling up in her eyes, and blinked furiously to keep them from overflowing.

"Yes, honey. Your dad and Father Brian."

"Oh, Boston," she wailed softly.

"Don't you dare start crying," he groaned.

"I won't." But tears sparkled on her long lashes like diamonds. There was so much to ask. Where would they live? So much she didn't know, but then she realized it didn't make any difference.

"Where would you like to spend your honeymoon?"

She thought for a long moment. "At the ranch. I want to arrive the same way we did the first time."

His kiss was a promise of everything she'd dreamed of. Love and tenderness, passion and companionship and a vow for a lifetime. It wouldn't always be a smooth road, not with their volatile personalities, but with a strong foundation of love and understanding they'd make it.

"Sparky," he murmured against her lips, "I love you."

That was all she needed to believe in. For eternity and beyond she'd always hear those three words rumbling deep within his chest, coming straight from his heart.

ABOUT THE AUTHOR

For twelve years Evelyn Crowe worked as a media director for various advertising agencies. She wrote and produced radio and television commercials. But it wasn't until she switched careers and became the manager of a bookstore in Houston that she decided to write a novel. Surrounded by romance fiction, in which the bookstore specializes, Evelyn was inspired to write a Superromance.

Like the heroine of *Summer Ballad*, Evelyn is an accomplished painter. She works in oils and has sold several of her paintings. Western themes are prevalent in her art. But for total relaxation she likes nothing better than to head out to the country and her brother's home on Lake Livingston. There she can pursue her favorite pastime—fishing. And along with the bass and the catfish Evelyn reels in come ideas for new Superromances.